"ABDUL HAS OFFERED TO GIVE UP THE CHASE."

Sharp sarcasm edged Peter's words. "Damned good of him to give you up, don't you think? Not every man would make such a sacrifice out of gratitude."

Jenny was stunned. "Do you mean that because you saved Sheikh Abdul's life, he's agreed to stop seeing me?"

"Exactly. But I told him his kindness is unneccessary, since there's obviously nothing between us."

Nothing! Against her will a sudden image leaped into Jenny's mind—the image of how Peter had reached for her, his hard chest pressing against her, his mouth hungry, burning with commanding heat. She had run her fingers up his strong back and into his hair, feeling the silky softness of tousled strands. . . ,

So Peter considered that nothing! Well, then, Jenny thought, let the sheikh pursue me. . . .

FROM THIS BELOVED HOUR

WILLA LAMBERT

A SUPERROMANCE FROM

WORLDWIDE

TORONTO · LONDON · NEW YORK · SYDNEY

Published, July 1982

First printing May 1982

ISBN 0-373-70023-7

CHAPTER ONE

"THE *BENNU*," he said, referring to the hieroglyph of a heron with two long feathers growing from the back of its head. The man had quietly joined Jenny in the small alcove on the first floor of the Egyptian Museum in Cairo. She was facing a sandstone relief that had been saved from the area around Abu Simbel when the Nile had been backed up behind the multimillion-dollar *Saad al-Ali*—the Aswân High Dam.

She was surprised by his company. Though the museum was kitty-corner from the Nile Hilton, and therefore quite accessible to tourists, most of them usually kept to the more impressive Tutankhamen exhibit located on the second floor. Jenny was saving that until last, rather like saving a fine dessert to be savored after a thoroughly enjoyable and deliciously filling meal. She assumed the man was a tourist—he spoke perfect English, albeit with a thoroughly enchanting accent that was more British than American. She should have been forewarned by the fact that he was able to identify a key figure in hieroglyphic script. Jenny knew very few people, besides her colleagues in the archaeological profession, who were so thoroughly informed. "Yes," she said, turning to him, quite prepared to further define the heron character so he would know he wasn't the only one with a modicum of knowledge on Egyptology. Despite being handicapped by the warehouse dimness for which the Egyptian Museum was notorious, Jenny had recognized him immediately.

"It really isn't a heron at all, you know," he said, failing to notice in the poor lighting how the blood had drained from her face. "It represents the phoenix—that legendary bird that lived for five hundred years before converting its nest into a funeral pyre and cremating itself in the searing flames." He held up his hand as if to prevent an interruption. In truth, Jenny hadn't found her voice yet. It was caught somewhere at the base of her throat, where it had become lodged when she first realized who he was. "But there is a happy ending," he continued, "for it emerged anew from its own ashes to live for another five hundred years—give or take a hundred years, of course."

He smiled—a very attractive smile. If he'd been smiling from the beginning, she might not have recognized him, because his pictures always showed him as very somber. Oh, yes, she had his picture— several of them, in fact, culled from archaeological journals and magazines. She had faithfully filed them in an album begun in 1922. Not that *he* had been alive in 1922. No, the album's first pictures hadn't been of him but of his grandfather, followed by his father, *then* by him.

"I do believe you have a place in the United States called Phoenix, do you not?" he asked. Jenny got a strange feeling at the roots of her hair, a feeling that shivered its way down to the soles of her feet. She had assumed he had recognized her, too. However, if that *were* the case, she couldn't believe he could still be blasé about it. "It's in Arizona, isn't it?" he asked.

"Arizona?" Jenny said, sounding very much like a parrot and feeling silly because of it.

"*Phoenix*, Arizona," he elucidated. "That is the place, isn't it?"

"Oh, yes," she admitted, trying desperately to get her thoughts back into some semblance of order. If he could carry this through with such aplomb, Jenny was determined to match him. Her whole problem was that she hadn't expected this ordeal quite yet. She had arrived in Egypt early just so she would have time to get herself mentally prepared for their scheduled meeting in Hierakonpolis. Oh, she had told herself she needed the extra days so she could take the leisurely boat trip up the Nile to the excavation site, but the real reason had been her need for a little time here in Egypt to prepare.

"It symbolized the morning sun rising out of the glow of dawn," he said. For a moment Jenny didn't know what he was talking about, then she realized he was still giving her a lesson on the heron hieroglyph. She found his patronizing attitude just a little insulting. He must have known she was as well acquainted with what he was saying as he was.

"Hence it was conceived as the bird of the sacred sun-god, Re," he continued. If he sensed her growing chagrin, he certainly didn't let on. "It represented the new sun of today emerging from the body of the old sun of yesterday—a manifestation of Osiris, the symbol of resurrection and light." He finished off with a quote from Job that, some scholars argued, indicated that the phoenix legend had passed over into Judeo-Christian teachings: " 'Then I said, I shall die in my nest, and I shall multiply *my* days as the sand.' "

" 'Who forgiveth all thine iniquities, who healeth all thy diseases, who satisfieth thy mouth with good things, so that thy youth is renewed like the eagles,' " Jenny shot back, glad her voice had finally lost its confused squeak. Her quotation had come from Psalms. While neither reference probably had anything whatsoever to do with the phoenix, although that mythical bird *had* always been represented as an eagle in Greco-Roman art, she had at least proved she could match him obscurity for obscurity.

"I say, that's very good!" he complimented her, seeming genuinely appreciative. Jenny really couldn't believe he hadn't expected her to be as knowledgeable on the subject as he was. She might not have got her education at Oxford, but she had all the accreditation in their mutually shared field to match him diploma for diploma. There were some people who might even have said, after her work at the dig at Avaris on the eastern side of the Nile delta, that she was far more qualified to work on this excavation at Hierakonpolis than he was. "My name is Peter," he told her. "Peter Donas."

She automatically held out her hand. She hadn't wanted to. At least that's what she told herself. Hers had merely been a natural reflex born of introduction after introduction at lectures, college teas, or while meeting the never ending stream of academicians who moved in, out of and around Jenny's circle. She certainly wanted her hand back the moment he took it, finding he held it far longer than was prescribed by good etiquette. She would have pulled it away by force, except she found that the power in his calloused fingers had somehow drained her of all her strength.

"Yours?" he asked, making her wonder whether he was referring to her hand, which he wouldn't release. Her fingers seemed insignificant within the cupping of his powerfully larger ones.

"*Yours?*" she questioned, unsure just what he was asking. She continued to be a little muddled, this whole scenario somehow unnerving her. She didn't know why their meeting couldn't have taken place later, as scheduled, instead of now. She had so hoped to be calm, cool and collected.

"I've already told you *my* name," he said, clearing up the problem and delivering a delighted laugh. "Peter Donas, remember? What I was hoping, of course, was that you might tell me *yours*. I know you're American because I overheard you ask the guard back there a question about the present location of Ramses II's mummy and I detected your accent. So, since we both speak a common language and are both far from home, I was hoping you might not take too unkindly to some company.''

She did find the strength to pull back her hand. What's more, she managed with a force that surprised him. She had to admit, however, that he was exceedingly quick in his recovery.

''I assure you,'' he said with an accompanying laugh of apparent pleasure, ''my intentions are purely admirable. I have nothing more sinister in mind than a mutually shared wander through these murky halls and then, perhaps, a bit of tea back at the hotel. By chance are you staying at the Hilton, too?'' Jenny was furious. Whereas she had blanched stark white upon first seeing him standing beside her, she was now a dark pink. He stepped back just a bit, as if to verify that he wasn't about to leap at her. ''Really, I'm all innocence,'' he assured her. ''Cross my heart; hope to die. All I'm suggesting is walk, talk and tea.''

Apparently he thought she was concerned that he might try to make a pass at her there in the alcove of the museum, thought she was upset because he appeared to be some kind of lothario out to sweep a poor young—twenty-nine wasn't all that old— American tourist off her feet. Yet that was not what was bothering her. He hadn't recognized her; that was the trouble. She had known him right off, but he *still* hadn't recognized her. Which meant he'd thought she hadn't known the *bennu* hieroglyph from that of a ba—a depiction of the Egyptian soul by a bird's body with a human head. No wonder he'd been so surprised when she'd shot back her biblical text about youth renewing itself like an eagle. It had been bad enough when he'd confronted her, engaging in harmless small talk. To find he'd been assuming from the start that she was a Miss Everyday Tourist was frankly a blow to her ego—professional and otherwise. He *should* have known. He *should* have recognized her. She was Jenny Mowry. His grandfather had jilted her grandmother. Jenny and this man might well have been brother and sister had Geraldine Fowler and Frederic Donas got married.

"Jenny Mowry!" she wanted to scream at him. "Remember my treatise on Crete? I said that Crete was all that remained of Atlantis after it had been destroyed by the volcano on Thíra, and you came out publicly and said my theory, while not a new one, was still as much poppycock as it had always been." What audacity to call a person's work and research poppycock when he couldn't even recognize her as he stood right next to her! The lighting was bad. The lighting was *very* bad. But the lighting was definitely not *that* bad. "You'll have to excuse me; I've got to go," she said, hearing her voice sound with strained breathlessness. She wondered why she couldn't make her legs follow through with her intentions, put one foot in front of the other to move her right out of there. Possibly she thought that he would yet come to see who she was.

"Let's talk over tea, then," he said. "You're heading back to the hotel now, you say?"

"No," she answered. "I didn't say that, as a matter of fact."

"Oh," he said, seemingly chastised and a bit at a loss.

She should have moved right then and there, swept right by him out through the large vestibule and into the hot dusty Cairo street. Then, when they met again in a few days in Hierakonpolis, he would realize his faux pas. "Tea?" she said instead.

"Tea?" he echoed.

"You *did* offer to buy me tea, didn't you?" she asked, as if he were the awkward one. She had a better grasp of the situation now and felt more in control. "Or did you?"

"Yes, of course," he affirmed. "I did indeed offer you tea. I was, however, somehow under the impression that you had said no."

"You've no doubt heard it's a lady's prerogative to change her mind?" Jenny said. "Well, it might be a hackneyed and unfair truism, but I *have* changed my mind. Actually, I'd love that cup of tea." What she wanted to do was get them out into the full light of day. She wanted that bright Egyptian sun to shine down on her like a spotlight, pointing out her honey-colored hair that haloed her oval face like a lion's mane; pointing out her dark brown eyes, her pert nose with its five freckles, her sensuous but not too sensuous mouth, her dimple, her skin that unlike that of so many blondes tanned to even perfection. Then she would see that flicker of recognition sparking at last in his golden eyes. Yes, golden eyes—dark and rich gold. Jenny had seen such eyes only on certain birds of prey. No, that wasn't quite true. The eyes of the birds had been piercing, decidedly dangerous. Peter's eyes were a warm gold that pulled her toward them, seduced her into an awareness of them even more intense than her awareness of the attractive squareness of his jaw and the dimple in his chin that would have made her want to reach up and touch it, had his eyes not kept drawing her back to them.

"Great!" he said. He took her upper arm, obviously thinking she would have trouble negotiating the corridors of the museum, when in fact she had got around quite nicely before he had appeared on the scene. If there was anyone who needed help in seeing in the inadequate lighting, it was he. *She* had certainly had enough light by which to see *him*. She didn't pull away though, having successfully fought down the impulse. After all, it was gentlemanly courtesy on his part, and Jenny, though she believed in women's rights and wanted equal work opportunities, equal pay and equal recognition of her qualifications, still enjoyed having doors opened for her, hats tipped and gentlemen stand to greet her whenever she entered a room. She couldn't very well jerk away from his hold without being unduly impolite, but his hand was doing something to her it shouldn't have been doing. Not that she could really put her finger on what was bothering her, because she couldn't. He wasn't holding her too tightly. He wasn't even moving his fingers. His hand was simply there, simply sending these funny little vibrations up her arm, into her throat and breasts, down.... She found consolation in knowing he would be taking his hand away soon enough once he realized just whom he had in tow.

Thank God, daylight! There it was right up ahead, framed by the massive open doors of the museum's main entrance. It wouldn't be long now. Just a few more steps. One, two, three....

"Ohhhhhh!" she groaned, not believing she had tripped. There hadn't seemed anything on which *to* trip. Yet there she was, stumbling in the dimness of the Egyptian Museum, as if she had to give Peter Donas some valid excuse for having taken the liberty of putting his hand on her arm in the first place.

"Gotcha!" he announced triumphantly. He had her all right, like an octopus—all arms. Such big arms they were, too. Such strong arms. And how hard his chest felt beneath his shirt as her uncertain steps brought her into direct contact with him when he turned to stop her fall.

"I'm fine," she said. "Really, I *am* fine." She was trying very hard not to sound as if she had just tripped over the edge of a precipice and was still on her way down.

"They're supposed to be remodeling this place soon," he told her, his arms no longer wrapping her, his chest no longer hard against her breasts. He was back to just his hand on her arm. "They're scheduled to use some of the revenues from the recent Tut exhibit that went on world tour.''

They exited into the sunlight, and to Jenny's increased chagrin he still didn't recognize her. In any case, he didn't give any indication he did. ''The museum was dark, but at least it was cool,'' was all he said when they paused on the porch outside the large ocher-colored building. ''It must be over a hundred out here.'' She was somewhat mollified by the fact that he was obviously having trouble seeing anything at the moment. One hand shielded his golden eyes, the other still held her arm, as if he expected her to stumble down the steps leading to the courtyard. She rationalized that where the museum had been too dark, the outside was too bright. She was squinting, too, and he could hardly be expected to recognize her with her face all screwed up. So if he couldn't recognize her in the dark of the museum and he couldn't recognize her in the light of the Cairo sunshine, the next step was to go into the better lighting of the hotel. Although she continued to have no problems seeing *him*.

He was bigger than she had thought he would be. She was five foot seven, and he towered more than five inches above that, making him taller than six feet. He looked younger than his pictures revealed—probably because he always seemed so sober in the photographs. Editors of scientific journals had a penchant for somberness, thereby instigating rumors that no one in the scientific community ever had any fun. Which simply wasn't true.

Peter remained intent upon getting Jenny across a street congested with traffic that ranged from an expensive Mercedes to a cluttered donkey cart. The herd of goats that suddenly came barreling around the corner added to the mess. Jenny could never get used to seeing livestock parading through the middle of busy streets in a metropolis of close to ten million people. Peter's grip tightened on her arm, warning her that she had better stop or risk getting run over by a vintage-model American car that would have been relegated to the wrecking yard in the United States. Not only was it still running in Egypt, but it would probably continue to run for a good many years to come, held together by prayers and chicken wire.

Ahead loomed the Nile Hilton, a modern structure among a conglomeration of new buildings and old. Cairo was one more of those age-old cities trying to make the transition from past to present. What resulted was a hodgepodge of East meeting West and old meeting new, all of which left the visitor imagining he was caught up in a time flux that tossed him from medieval minarets one minute to glass-and-chrome discos the next.

Jenny glanced sideways, once again taking in Peter Donas in full sunlight. Damn, he was handsome, although that had nothing whatsoever to do with anything! He and she had been destined long before they'd been born to meet as enemies. That this meeting was progressing the way it was now was only because Peter didn't realize who she was.

And it was obvious he still didn't know her when, sensing her eyes on him, he turned in her direction and smiled. Peter Donas smiling at Jenny Mowry was certainly something she had never expected to see. It was a decidedly pleasant smile, too, one that carved faint crinkle lines at the corners of his golden eyes. If his eyes didn't relay any hint of danger, that didn't mean Jenny was feeling safe. She was feeling anything but safe, although she wasn't quite sure just why. She certainly didn't feel fear of any physical harm. His hand on her arm, its slightly increased pressure telling her when it was all right to move once again, was actually reassuring.

"Safe at last!" he announced, guiding her up onto the sidewalk and toward the entrance to their hotel. Jenny almost laughed at his choice of words, coming as they did at the same moment as her thoughts on danger. She realized that the danger she feared was a threat to her emotional, rather than her physical, well-being. In fact, she had probably seen that from the moment she had first agreed to come to Egypt knowing Peter Donas would be here. Which was why she had wanted a week on Egyptian soil to prepare herself mentally for their meeting. But he had managed to put her into the arena without allowing her time to psych herself up. She was vulnerable, made more so by the fact that she had always assumed the day would come when they would meet, recognize each other and feel the tragedy that linked them. Well, the day was here, and they had met, and she had recognized him, feeling the invisible links that bound them. But he hadn't recognized her. He had obviously felt nothing—which left Jenny questioning whether she hadn't been living an illusion all of this time. Maybe there was no such thing as predestination. Maybe the affinity she felt for her dead grandmother had nothing whatsoever to do with the here and now, only with the fanciful imaginings of a child who, once standing in front of a portrait of Geraldine Fowler, had been told that her face and the one in the painting were mirror images. Geraldine, dead at thirty-four in Egypt, dead like so many others who had been there when the Earl of Carnarvon's workmen, under the direction of Howard Carter, had unearthed at Thebes the stairway leading to the tomb of King Tutankhamen. Dead not because of the ancient curse on the tomb, but because the man she had loved—not her husband—had married another woman merely for a dowry.

Peter's grandfather hadn't looked any more dangerous than Peter looked now. Jenny knew because she had pictures of Frederic Donas. He had looked young, but he had *been* young—ten years Geraldine's junior. He had been handsome, although not as handsome as Peter. He had told Geraldine he loved her, and then he had gone off to marry Peter's grandmother in England. It was more than just a coincidence that the granddaughter of Geraldine Fowler and the grandson of Frederic Donas were now in Egypt, both heading for an archaeological dig only a few miles upstream from the scene of that tragedy long ago.

Peter stopped her at the door of the hotel. They both stepped back as a group of German tourists came sweeping by. They were probably off to visit the treasures of Tutankhamen, which, Jenny suddenly realized, she had left without taking in. Oh, she had seen the smaller pieces of the collection—those that had made the rounds of the world capitals—but not the bigger items kept on display at the Cairo Museum, among them the sarcophagi that, fitting one within the other, had held the boy-king, his mummy wrapped in wings of gold cloisonné. Twice previously Jenny had come to Egypt and not viewed the legendary treasures. There had been no time during the first trip. She had flown in to visit her father at the dig at Saïs and had flown out to Crete the very next day. There had been more time when she had helped excavate sections of Avaris, but the museum had been closed the one day she had made it to Cairo, interrupting a busy work schedule specifically to see the treasures. She had never got back until now, and now she had missed them because Peter Donas had invited her to tea. She couldn't believe it and still wasn't really sure how it had all come about.

The tour group passed; Jenny and Peter entered the hotel. Immediately she was possessed by that same feeling she experienced every time she entered a Hilton—the feeling that undoubtedly had something to do with her father once having said, "Blindfold me, sit me down in any Hilton Hotel in the world, take off my blindfold, and I'll give you odds I can't tell you what country I'm in, let alone

what city." He might have found the locale easier
to identify in this Hilton, however, since there was a
definite sense of the Middle East about the men
standing around in their long *galabias*, wearing
headdresses and sandals.

Peter guided her into a small area just off the lobby where she had a good view of the foot traffic. He
removed his hand from her arm, and surprisingly
she wished he hadn't. She sat down, and he took the
chair across from her. Separating them was a small
brass coffee table typical of Egypt's internationally
renowned brass work. He motioned to a waiter in
an off-gold jacket and ordered tea. "Now it might
be easier to carry on a conversation if I *did* know
your name," he said, turning his attention fully to
Jenny. He sat back in his chair, crossing his legs so
that his left ankle angled across his right knee. He
was wearing black riding boots, black slacks and a
short-sleeved shirt. He had black hair on his forearms and on the backs of his large hands, but Jenny
couldn't see evidence of any on the vee of tanned
chest visible at his open collar. She found herself
speculating on whether he had much hair on his
chest or whether there was only a smooth expanse
of bare skin stretched tightly over his well-defined
muscles. No doubt about there being muscles. She
could see evidence of them despite his shirt...
something about the way the material rested against
him. "Or shall I call you Miss X?" he said. "*Mrs.*
X?" He suggested the alternative playfully.

Jenny was brought up short by the teasing tone of

his voice. "*Mrs.* X?" he had asked, and she couldn't help wondering if it would have mattered to him if she *had* been a married woman. It had certainly not mattered to his grandfather that Geraldine Fowler had been married, or that she'd had two children, or that she'd left her husband and children in an effort to find happiness with him, only to discover too late that he had made plans to marry another woman for money. The sooner Jenny got this charade over, the better it would be. Peter hadn't recognized her in the museum, outside, or here. He didn't have a clue. "Jenny," she said, giving him that clue. "My name is Jenny."

"Very well, then," he said, and she could tell by the way he said it that her name wasn't ringing any bells. "What brings Jenny to Egypt? A holiday?"

She was Jenny Mowry, come to assist him in the excavation of the dig at Hierakonpolis. She was the granddaughter of *the* Geraldine Fowler, who had been jilted by his grandfather. Surely he had heard the story. Unless a young man wasn't as easily taken in as a young girl by the romanticism of unrequited love or by the pathos of a woman who, after having successfully begged her husband into taking her back for the sake of their children, simply lay down one morning at Thebes and died of a broken heart. Anyway, the doctor present hadn't been able to offer a more suitable diagnosis.

The tea arrived and Peter poured, asking if she wanted hers "white," adding milk when she nodded. She noticed that he took his "black." She also noticed that he managed the handling of the delicate tea service without appearing awkward, despite the largeness of his hands. There was, in fact, a certain magnificent grace in the way he lifted his cup to his mouth, sipped, made an expression of genuine satisfaction at the taste and eyed her over the rim of his cup. In any case, she *thought* he was eyeing her over the rim of his cup. Which was why she was so pleasantly shocked when he whispered, "Absolutely beautiful!"

"What?" she asked. It seemed a rather inadequate response, but it was all she could come up with at the moment.

It was when his eyes finally *did* focus directly on her that Jenny realized his compliment hadn't been directed at her but at something or someone directly behind her. "Will you please excuse me just a brief moment," he said, rising to his feet.

She turned to follow his retreating figure, immediately spotting what had caught his eye. Off to one side of the lobby, the object of inquisitive glances even from the members of the local population, was an Arab wearing a heavy leather glove that covered his left hand and much of his forearm. A falcon was perched firmly on the man's clenched fist. There were strips of leather attached to the bird's legs, restraining it on the glove. The falcon was hooded with a colorful leather cap that hid all of its head except for its sharp beak. The hood was bright orange, with a plume of cock's hackle feathers garnished with colored wool and bound tightly together with fine brass wire affixed to the crown. Jenny watched Peter approach the man. She was more than a little piqued he had deserted her in favor of some hunting bird. She was also a little embarrassed she had thought his "Absolutely beautiful!" had been directed at her. How silly of her! She should have known better, because she certainly *wasn't* beautiful. Oh, she had all of the right ingredients, but somehow they just didn't come together in a way she considered beautiful. Attractive, yes. Maybe even pretty. But not beautiful. She was beset by conflicting emotions: jealousy that the bird had elicited a compliment she could not; gratitude that Peter's comment hadn't been directed at her so that she was saved the embarrassment of telling him his flattery would get him nowhere.

She sipped her tea, more and more indignant at his desertion. She found it typical of a Donas man to be caught up in the fascination of a sport as cruel as falconry. Oh, Peter could no doubt provide all sorts of rationalizations for his interest *and* for the existence of such a barbaric pastime. People were always very good at justifying something they enjoyed. Jenny, who had done a good deal of field excavation in Middle Eastern countries and therefore knew of the continued popularity of the blood sport among the aristocracy, had heard all of the excuses before. None of them held water as far as she was concerned! It simply wasn't right to take a bird as free as the wind and train it to kill for man's pleasure, to tie up its legs, stick a hood over its head and carry it around on a fist in a hotel situated in downtown Cairo. The bird belonged out in the freedom of the sky, where God had intended it should be, and that was exactly what she told Peter when he finally got around to returning to a cup of tea that had gone cold in his absence.

He made her furious by simply ignoring her comment, brushing it aside with a slight wave of his hand, as if it had obviously come from a woman who couldn't possibly know anything about the matter. "Spectacular bird!" was what he did say, adding hot tea to the cold liquid in his cup. "A female peregrine that, I venture to say, cost her owner a pretty penny. Belongs to one of the sheikhs down south. A Sheikh Abdul Jerada."

Jenny couldn't have cared less, except that someone ought to have stuck Sheikh Jerada's head in a hood, bound his feet and carried him around the Nile Hilton to see how he liked it. Someone should have done the very same thing to the man sitting across from her. "It's barbaric!" she said firmly, pouring herself more tea. "It's something straight out of the Middle Ages."

"It's a very ancient sport," he replied, as if somehow to insinuate that old was good, purely by definition.

"So was burning witches," Jenny informed him. "You don't find that practice flourishing much anymore, do you?"

"No, well," he muttered, leaving it at that, as if he and she both knew one didn't really have anything to do with the other. There was a moment of pregnant silence between them.

"Do you do much hawking in England, Mr. Donas?" she asked, unable to leave the subject alone. It gave her an inner satisfaction to know that, just as she had always suspected, Peter Donas did have a slightly perverted and sadistic streak, much like the one his grandfather must have had.

"No," he said, obviously disappointed. "I've always wanted to engage in the sport, but it takes such a good deal of time, you know, and I never seem to be in England long enough to select a bird and put it through the proper paces."

"But you would if you had the time?" Jenny inquired, pressing on. She could see him now, delighting in snatching helpless baby birds from their nests, just as his grandfather had snatched a mother from hers.

"I doubt if I'd ever have the time for a peregrine like that one," he replied, nodding in the direction of the man who still stood in wait for Sheikh Jerada. Jenny had watched Peter all through their conversation; he had been shifting his gaze back and forth between her and that damned bird. Why hadn't he taken *it* to tea? He was obviously more interested in it at the moment than he was in her. To think she had missed out on the museum for this! "Few people I know can do justice to a superb bird like that one," he went on, as if he believed she was interested. "It's a matter of finding suitable quarry, for one thing. Peregrines are flown at small game like partridge and grouse." Yes, Jenny knew. "Besides," he continued, "and this is the really difficult part, in this day and age of cramped living space access to anywhere from one thousand to three thousand acres of open land is hard to come by."

Jenny thought she had had quite enough even before he added something about a dog—a pointer or a setter—being a necessity for grouse hawking. "I really must be going, Mr. Donas," she said, setting down her teacup very gently and flashing him a smile that, she hoped, had little more warmth in it than an ice cube. "It's been charming talking birds with you, but I really do have other things to do since I'm leaving the day after tomorrow on the *Osiris* for a trip up the Nile." She could have been more specific and said to Idfu and then to Hierakonpolis, but she didn't, wondering why. It would have been the perfect time to burst the bubble.

"You're planning to squeeze a few meals in there somewhere, aren't you?" he asked. Jenny couldn't see what that had to do with him. "So why don't you let me take you to supper this evening?" he suggested. She thought he was pretty bold—and sure of himself. There was no apparent rhyme or reason for his invitation. The man should have been able to see as clearly as she could that the two of them were as different as night and day. Not only that, but since he had asked *her* to tea and had spent the whole time ogling the spotted breast feathers of some bird, she could just imagine what it would be like trying to hold his attention for the duration of a whole meal. "I know a spot in town that serves simply excellent *hamama*," he said. Jenny nearly laughed despite herself. *Hamama* was pigeon. Their conversation had moved from phoenixes to hawks to pigeons. At least she could say he was consistent, even if he did have a one-track mind. "Do you know what *hamama* is, Jenny?" he asked. Yes, she knew what *hamama* was. Yes, she knew what *gambari*—shrimp—and *firakh*—chicken—and *gamoosa*—water-buffalo meat—were, too. "It's pigeon," he said, obviously having been unable to read her mental affirmation. "Very popular in Egypt. Raised all up and down the Nile Valley. Watch when you pass the houses on your Nile trip and you'll invariably see large domed pottery structures attached to them. They're put there expressly for raising the pigeons that are later usually grilled over a low fire."

"That does sound delicious," Jenny said. Actually, she had tasted *hamama* previously, and she *had* liked it. "However, I'm afraid...."

"You don't know what you'll be missing," he interrupted. Jenny got the distinct impression that, as if he thought he was God's gift to woman, his insinuation of her missing something had more to do with his company than with Egyptian cuisine. Really, the man was insufferable!

"Let me guess," she said, "you simply can't bear to see someone who isn't a convert to falconry, and you've planned a whole evening around proselytizing over *hamama* and *moz bi-laban*." She hoped he'd noticed that she could throw around an Arab

word or two of her own. *Moz bi-laban* was a local
fruit drink made by blending bananas with milk and
sugar. In fact, it often became a meal in itself.

"I won't utter a word about falconry," he promised, his golden eyes blazing like a zealot's as he
once again glanced covetously over her shoulder at
the female bird still perched on the waiting Arab's
fist.

"All right," she replied, thinking how amusing it
was going to be for Peter Donas to arrive at Hierakonpolis and discover that a supposedly simple
tourist, the one he had wined and dined in Cairo,
was none other than the granddaughter of Geraldine Fowler *and* his associate on the dig.

"Great!" he said, her acceptance bringing his attention back to her for the moment. "About eight
o'clock?"

"I'll meet you here in the lobby," she told him.
She stood. "Until then. . . ."

He came to his feet when she did, stooping slightly to put his teacup back on its saucer. "I shall be
looking forward to it," he said.

With a nod in parting she left him and headed
across the lobby for the elevators. She couldn't wait
until they met in Hierakonpolis and. . . . She had
been so caught up in her thoughts that she almost
collided with a tall dark-complected Arab in a flowing white *galabia*. "I *am* sorry," he said in a pleasantly modulated English. The fact that she was an
American must have stood out like a sore thumb.
He was obviously being polite to a foreigner, since

it was apparent to everyone, him and Jenny included, that their near collision had been entirely her fault.

"I'm the one who should apologize," she said. "I should have been paying more attention to where I was going."

He had dark velvety eyes, a mustache and a neatly trimmed beard. He was probably in his early thirties...as tall as Peter, if not a bit taller. Jenny should have been off having supper with someone exotically handsome like this! She was, after all, in Egypt—land of desert sheikhs and harem tents with floors covered by Tunisian carpets—Egypt wasn't known for its rugs—and walls hung with tapestries. No, she had to find herself attracted to an Englishman who.... Yes, she could perhaps get away with admitting that the word *attracted* was applicable here. But even so, it was simply a matter of her being drawn to him because he was who he was, she was who she was and their grandparents had been who they were.

She realized suddenly that she was still standing in the middle of the hotel lobby, face to face with the attractive Arab. She couldn't imagine what was getting into her. She certainly couldn't help wondering what the man was thinking, even if the slight upturn at the corners of his full mouth did indicate amusement. She hoped her reverie had taken mere seconds instead of the minutes it now seemed. "I really *am* sorry," she said, curious if she was blushing through her tan. He bowed slightly as she finally managed enough locomotion to get herself headed for the elevators. Naturally the elevators were busy stopping at every floor but this one, seemingly determined to leave her standing there forever. Her back to the lobby, she imagined that the Arab was probably musing on why the foreign tourists in his country didn't at least keep their eyes open. She speculated as to whether Peter had seen the near collision. If so, he probably thought it had been caused by her excitement over having been asked to supper by him. The elevator door slid open on an empty compartment. Jenny stepped inside, turned and pushed the button for the tenth floor. Just before the door closed in front of her, she chanced a hurried glance out into the lobby. She was definitely disappointed to discover that neither the Arab nor Peter seemed at all interested in her. They were together in front of the man with the peregrine falcon. It was quite obvious from their rapturous expressions that they were not discussing Jenny at all but were talking about a rather disgusting blood sport in which they obviously had a common interest.

CHAPTER TWO

IN ALL OF HER EXPERIENCES on archaeological digs, beginning with childhood visits to those sites being worked by her father, Jenny had never found the conveniences she—or probably anyone—would have liked. Having worked in Egypt previously, at Avaris, she was hardly expecting the dig at Hierakonpolis to be any exception to the general rule regarding the poor quality of accommodations. Therefore she had indulged herself by checking into one of the more expensive rooms at the Nile Hilton. She thought she deserved some comfort before setting off into the wilderness. The room was large and airy, done mostly in sandy colors, with prints on the walls depicting, for the most part, the temples at Karnak. One picture, however, the one hung over the small desk in the corner of the bedroom, was of the Step Pyramid at Saqqâra. The two-hundred-foot tall pyramid was composed of five major steps to its summit. It was of special importance to archaeologists. Having been started as a flat mastaba tomb, then passing through a series of construction stages to its final elaborate form, the Step Pyramid was considered a key example of the transition to the more classical pyramidal form recognizable at Giza. Mastabe-type tombs had been characteristic of the Old Kingdom and had been rectangular flat-topped masses of masonry with steeply sloping sides. They had evolved from the crude heaps of sand or mud piled over the first prehistoric graves in Egypt.

Jenny's room had a balcony facing Korneish al-Nil, the street that ran parallel to the famous artery of Egypt—past and present—the Nile River. The river was a wide flat expanse of gray water lined by green plants and palm trees that seemed even more vibrantly verdant in the brightness of the Egyptian sun. There was one large island visible from her balcony: Zamalik, and Roda Island was off farther to her left. In fact, it had been the presence of the islands in the river at this point, making bridging of the Nile feasible, that had caused Cairo to rise on this spot. The Nile Hilton was flanked by two of those resulting bridges: Kû al-Tahrir on the south and Kû 6-Octobre farther north.

Her bathroom had the luxury of a shower and a bath, allowing her an almost sinfully long soak in lilac-scented bubble bath, followed by a quick rinse in shower spray. She dried with a large Turkish towel that, as far as she was concerned, had to be one of the finest contributions to civilized society made by man.

Once finished, she draped the towel over the side of the bathtub and faced the full-length mirror, still faintly steamed, that covered one whole wall. She took a perhaps too-critical look at what she saw reflected. As with her facial features Jenny found the rest of her body a bit on the sunny side of merely adequate. Her skin was certainly flawless—divided into three distinctly tanned sections by two horizontal stripes of white. One white stripe circled her breasts and the other her hips, both an indication of the two-piece bathing suit she usually wore when sunbathing. The contrast between tan and creamy whiteness was certainly not unattractive, and it emphasized breasts that were clearly large enough. Her waist was slim, her legs long and shapely. The rigors of her frequent trips into the field had kept her muscles well-toned.

Not too bad, she told herself, then frowned. *Although definitely not better than a speckle-breasted peregrine falcon!* She immediately chided herself for that absurd comparison, wondering why she still remained upset about Peter's having rushed off the minute the bird had made its appearance in the lobby. It wasn't as if the bird were an attractive woman. Then again she didn't have the faintest idea of how to compete with a falcon, whereas she would have known what to do in the face of rivalry from another woman.

Compete? She caught herself immediately and wondered what she could possibly be thinking. She was making it sound as if she were out to get a man and resented the fact that her plans had been thwarted by a feathered femme fatale. Well, the last thing Jenny wanted was Peter Donas or any other man. Not that she was one of those women who didn't like men, because Jenny *did* like men. She had merely decided a very long time ago that there was little point in loving one of them. They invariably left you heartbroken. And she wasn't entirely basing that observation on the way Frederic Donas had treated poor Geraldine Fowler, although even more than half a century later that was certainly a good case in point. More than one of Jenny's friends in college had married and then divorced. Her own mother had confided, not two weeks prior to the airplane accident that had claimed the lives of both of Jenny's parents, that it was going to be only a matter of time before she would file her own divorce papers.

Not that Jenny had gone through life being a social stick-in-the-mud, because she had certainly had her share of boyfriends. But *friends* were just what they had been and just what they had remained. She had never found one of them who had sparked anything inside of her strong enough to make her seriously consider giving up aspirations of a career for the apparently overrated joys of holy matrimony. Although she had to admit that as a result she couldn't brag about a very eventful sex life. Despite her modern outlook on how a woman should be able to make it in a man's world she remained a little old-fashioned in her philosophy as to just when a woman should go to bed with a man. She certainly wasn't an advocate of the "you-have-to-be-married-before-you-do-it" school, but she simply couldn't discard the idea of love being involved in the bargain. Love and sex went together, and thus at twenty-nine, never having really loved, she was still.... She shook her head to clear it, disturbed at the direction her thoughts had been taking. She couldn't imagine what had made her go veering off on an aspect of her private life that she had relegated to the back of her mind—with no regrets—ages and ages ago.

She left the bathroom, suspecting her present relapse into useless musings had been caused by the cloyingly moist heat that remained after her bath. She was sure she would be able to think more clearly in the air-conditioned comfort of the room beyond.

She had selected a caftan of white silk with a simple gold braid border to wear to supper that evening. Not that she had had much choice. She had learned from past experience that it was best to travel as lightly as possible, since lugging all sorts of baggage onto the desolated sites of major archaeological digs was no mean feat. And while Hierakonpolis was only seventy miles north of the civilization offered by Aswân, those were seventy miles of dust and heat and bugs. The fact that the Nile would be only a short distance to the east didn't mean much, either. Her correspondence with Professor Charles Kenny of the University of Chicago, the man who would be her and Peter Donas's immediate supervisor on the dig, had alerted her that he was trying to find accommodations in the nearby village and that the dig itself was about as hospitable as a graveyard. Actually, Professor Kenny hadn't been speaking figuratively. It was the cemeteries with which the present archaeological party was mainly concerned. Through the years several teams had moved in and out of the area, a few actually thinking they might have stumbled upon the tomb of the early Egyptian ruler, the Scorpion King, who had long been suspected as having come from the vicinity and who was associated with the original irrigation of the Nile Valley. Professor Kenny was the latest to have supposedly pinpointed such a tomb, and Jenny agreed with his theory that it was the right one. Peter Donas—naturally—was of quite another opinion. Based on obscure papyrus references, Peter believed the Scorpion King had been buried farther north, nearer modern Luxor. Jenny would have liked nothing more than to be on the spot when Peter Donas was proved wrong. That, she figured, would give her at least partial repayment for his having been quoted in the press as calling her Crete-Atlantis theory poppycock. One of the main reasons she had accepted this assignment over another at Sybaris that she had been considering was that more evidence seemed apt to turn up proving Peter wrong.

Anyway, she could hardly expect much of a social life in Hierakonpolis once she got there, so the silk caftan and a pair of white sandals, both easily packed, had been her major concessions to the chance of needing a bit of dress-up.

From the bathroom she had entered the small

dressing area that gave easy access to the walk-in closets and a small vanity table on which she had lined up her cosmetics. Her need of them was limited, even under normal conditions, since her skin gave her relatively little trouble and somehow had miraculously escaped most of the dangerous damage possible under an unforgiving desert sun.

She used a hair dryer to evaporate the small amount of dampness that had managed to defy her shower cap. She then took a brush to her hair, stopping suddenly to study herself in the mirror. What she saw made her put her brush to one side and go into the bedroom for the copy of *Archaeological American* she had brought with her and had been reading the previous night. She came back to the vanity table and thumbed through the magazine until she found the picture taken at the recent meeting of the Archaeological Association of the Three Americas, held in New York City. She pinpointed herself in the photograph and held up the magazine to one side of her reflection. She recognized immediately that she was seeing two different women. In any case, they *looked* anything but one and the same. The woman in the picture had her hair pulled severely back and fixed in a bun, and she wore a rather nondescript black suit. The woman at the vanity table was something else again, converted to her present self by being quite naked at the moment and wearing a hairstyle created to suit her face by a Seattle hairstylist who had charged fifty dollars for, as he put it, the monumental chore. Jenny hadn't questioned at the time why she had suddenly chosen that moment in her life to go to a hairstylist, nor did she intend to probe the matter too deeply now. But the truth remained, she had done so directly on the heels of receiving notification that she had been signed on at Hierakonpolis and knowing full well that Peter Donas was going to be there, too.

Nonsense! Peter Donas had had absolutely nothing to do with it! She had merely decided it was time she got over any and all remaining guilt she might have had about being a woman in a man's world. She was ready to discard complexes that had caused her to dress as unbecomingly as possible for years, as if no one would take her seriously if she looked like the woman she was.

Her glance strayed downward to the caption under the photograph: "J. Mowry." *J.*, not Jenny or Jennifer. And *that* had been an early concession she had made while plugging away at making a name for herself in her male-dominated field. She had submitted her first article for publication—a discussion of the possibility of Italy's Herculaneum having been a seaport prior to the eruption of Mount Vesuvius in A.D. 79—under the by-line of J. Mowry. If her sex weren't readily identifiable, she had reasoned, her article would have a better chance of acceptance by an editor and by the scientific community who read it. She had since got over those feelings of inferiority, but certain habits, such as publishing as J. Mowry, such as retaining uncomplimentary modes of hairstyle and dress, had been harder to break.

Possibly, then, there had been a good reason why Peter hadn't recognized her in the Egyptian Museum, quite aside from bad lighting and the fact that he had never met her personally. The absence of a formal meeting was no rarity in a profession in which members were often scattered to the far corners of the world. A few years back Jenny had almost attended a seminar at which Peter was scheduled to speak, but just before flight time she had come down with a horrible attack of stomach pains and dizziness. She was sure she had got food poisoning from some fish she had eaten in a restaurant the previous night. She continued to believe that to this very day, even though her doctor had come up with nothing that could confirm her layman's diagnosis.

When she considered how different from her photograph she now looked, she felt infinitely better. It explained why she had gone unrecognized during their afternoon meeting. Peter must have seen her picture at least a few times, even if he wasn't presently able to make the connection with Jenny's new image. Humming to herself, she pulled her hair severely into place at the back of her neck and pinned it there. She got up from the vanity table and went to the closet, prepared to ignore completely the silk caftan she had laid out on the bed. What she now chose was a plain blouse and skirt. When she put them on and turned back toward the mirror, she looked a bit more like her old self again, a bit more like the J. Mowry in the magazine. Peter would surely recognize her now!

The only problem was, she preferred herself the

other way. There had been something positively cathartic about that day she had had her hair styled and had purchased that expensive low-cut cocktail dress from I. Magnin's. She could still remember how the men had stared at her with pleasurable shock at the bon voyage tea held in her honor by Dr. Winfield of the University of Washington. She had felt very much like the swan emerged from the ugly duckling or Cinderella at the ball. The sensation had been so thoroughly euphoric that she hadn't thought of returning to the old J. Mowry until now.

She checked her wristwatch. It was seven-thirty. That gave her half an hour before she was supposed to meet Peter in the lobby downstairs. She began to undress. She had taken one step forward in admitting her femininity, and she refused to take two steps back at this stage of the game. Besides, she didn't know how she would react if she appeared downstairs in the guise of J. Mowry, only to find Peter still unable to recognize her as his colleague and as the person linking him to a tragic love affair of more than half a century ago.

"There," she said, running the brush through her hair and making a last adjustment to her makeup. "With plenty of time to spare." The caftan, with its round neckline, its long wide sleeves and its simple gold trim did good things for her, emphasizing the golden highlights of her honey-colored hair and setting off her tan. A simple gold bracelet added the appropriate final touch.

She went down to meet Peter in the lobby and was pleased to find him waiting. She would have been a little upset, but hardly surprised, had he arrived late with excuses of having become so caught up in his discussion on the health, food, transport and molt of peregrine falcons that he had completely forgotten her. He looked strikingly handsome in a white long-sleeved shirt with tie, black pants and black English riding boots.

"Enchanting!" he said, taking both of her hands in his, holding her at arm's length while his eyes gave her the once-over. It was the kind of look few men had ever given J. Mowry. Jenny would have been somewhat embarrassed by it now if she hadn't had a little experience since her initial coming-out party at Dr. Winfield's a few weeks earlier. She went through a big production of looking this way and that, as if she were quite convinced he hadn't been referring to her. "Yes, I *do* mean you," he affirmed. His smile revealed teeth made whiter than white by the depth of his attractive tan. His eyes smoldered like gilt-tinged suns, drawing her in as though she were caught within the tremendous gravitational force of twin stars.

"I thought maybe you'd sighted another peregrine falcon," she said, immediately regretting having done so despite the immediate apologetic look he gave her in response. Maybe he remembered saying, "Absolutely beautiful!" before running off to that bird. Jenny had been the one who had insisted that he not mention falconry as a condition of her accepting his dinner invitation, but now she had gone rushing into the subject! Best to say no more.

"You, at the moment, are the most enchanting 'bird' in the place," he said. She recognized his play on the English slang for a good-looker of the female sex. He then became a real gentleman and skillfully diverted the conversation completely away from any aspect of ornithology. "You're going to love the place I've picked out for us this evening," he told her unabashedly, his hand on her arm once again conjuring sensations Jenny chose to ignore. "It's admittedly a bit touristy, but the place simply isn't to be missed during a visit to Cairo. Maybe you've been there, though? It's called the Filfila." She shook her head, amused to see how glad he was to be treating her to a first. It was obvious he liked the spot, and she began to feel his infectious excitement. "Unfortunately, it's very popular with the tour groups who stop off by the busload," he said. "But I've got an in with one of the waiters, who has guaranteed us the best table in the house."

The restaurant was on Hoda Sharawi, a side street of the Sharia Talaat Harb. They passed the busy kitchen on the way in—a cramped open area with a stand-up counter for those whose budgeted time forced them to eat and run. The aromas were undeniably exotic. Mouth-watering was about the only term, trite or not, that Jenny could find to describe them. The place was very busy, which, under the circumstances, Jenny preferred over a more intimate candlelight setting. The latter might have led to a strained atmosphere, considering Jenny still couldn't believe she was with a man who had early become a subject of avid fascination for a young girl caught up in the tragic romance and death of Geraldine Fowler at Thebes.

The waiter, whom Peter specifically asked for at the door and who did indeed seem happy to see them, led them into one of two back rooms packed to overflowing with people whose very number alone seemed to threaten the stability of tables made from large sections of split tree trunks. Jenny, prior to being seated at a corner table, thought she could sort out English, French and German from the general cacophony.

There were windows along both sides of the narrow room, and the walls were painted in an assortment of scenes typical of Egypt: graceful date palms, camels at an oasis, Arab musicians. The menu was printed on disposable place mats, and Jenny found herself automatically searching for *hamama*, although she had no intention whatsoever of ordering pigeon. What she finally did decide upon was *molokhia*—an exclusively Egyptian dish she had tried several times previously and liked. She had never been able to find out what name was given to the strange flat leaves that, cut up, were placed in a light meat broth to make the dish. They vaguely resembled grape leaves, but she had been told they were related to the mint family. The thick soup that resulted, however, had not a trace of mint in its strong flavor.

After making sure that it came from the sea instead of the river, Peter ordered *samak*—the fish of
the day—which turned out to be sole. Although the
restaurant had made a name for itself with the tourist trade and could be trusted, Peter, like Jenny,
had learned that fish from the Nile, especially if
caught as far downriver as Cairo, could very well be
contaminated. For side dishes Peter ordered *torshi*,
which while translating vaguely as "pickle," included a diversity of vegetables that had been soaked in
a very spicy brine; *wara einab*, which were grape
leaves stuffed with small quantities of rice; and
khalta, a rice dish made with raisins, nuts and
chunks of meat and liver. The bread, *aish baladi*,
was unleavened, made of coarse whole-wheat flour
and baked into wedges; it was like crisp crackers.
Jenny and Peter both ordered *shai bi-na'na*—a mint
tea whose deliciousness had to be tasted to be believed. Unlike the hotel that served tea in a small
pot with an accompanying selection of milk, lemon
and sugar, the Filfila offered small glasses of tea
already saturated with sugar.

Jenny decided halfway through the meal that
Peter was quite an enjoyable person to be with, although she immediately tempered her judgment
with the consideration that it might very well be the
place and the supper that were so enjoyable and *not*
Peter himself. However, it had been her experience
that fun people were the ones who usually gravitat-
ed to fun places and participated in fun activities. In
fact, more than once during the two and a half

hours they spent together, Jenny found herself wishing she were not Jenny Mowry and he were not Peter Donas and that tragedy hadn't touched both of them through an incident in their families' past. She was particularly aware of wishing that changes of identity could be made as easily as a change of hairstyle or clothing when, during the course of their conversation, she found herself looking at close range into the hypnotic depths of his sunny eyes. She found them so large, so golden, so warm and inviting, she embarrassedly pulled back quickly, not having heard a word of what he had been trying to tell her about a plate of *calamari*—squid— that had just been ordered by a tourist at one of the larger adjoining tables.

By the time Peter suggested they walk awhile and have dessert elsewhere, Jenny was back to thinking she was being silly in looking on all of this as ominously connected to things that had happened prior to either of them being born. It was ridiculous to harbor suspicions that an ill-fated romance some sixty years earlier could taint happenings in the here and now. After all, she was Jenny Mowry, not Geraldine Fowler, even if someone had once told her she resembled her grandmother. Peter, except for having black hair, didn't even look like Frederic Donas. Frederic had been a boy, whereas Peter was definitely a man. Frederic had been slim, whereas Peter was all muscle. Frederic had been. . . .

"A piaster for your thoughts," he said, bringing her back from her reverie. A piaster was a low-denomination Egyptian coin vaguely equivalent in value to an American penny. He had paid the bill and had led her through the boisterous chattering crowd to the comparative quiet of the street.

"I was thinking what a delightful meal that turned out to be," she said.

"Yes," he agreed, as if he had been confident all along that her pleasure in the meal would match his own, "it was enjoyable, wasn't it?"

Once again Jenny contemplated telling him who she was. It no longer seemed so important. She had pretty well convinced herself that her apprehension had been childish fear wrongly carried over into adulthood. She was even prepared to forgive him those nasty things he had said about her theories on Crete and what remained of the lost continent of Atlantis. In retrospect she could remember several different occasions, although in private and *never* for publication, when she had smiled at some colleague's reasoning, convinced that it didn't quite jell in the final analysis. Disagreement in her profession wasn't necessarily a matter of personal vendetta or bad feelings. Disagreement was healthy, for it made archaeologists think, sit back and reevaluate in an attempt to plug loopholes. If an expounded theory was sound, it eventually managed to weather any storm, coming through to stand on its own merits. Just as she was sure that when the excavation at Hierakonpolis was completed, there would be no doubt that the Scorpion King had been buried there, as she believed, and not at Luxor, as Peter believed. In a way she felt sorry for Peter. He was destined to be proved wrong. Her concern for him said something about the remarkable change that had come over her during the past couple of hours.

She didn't tell him who she was because she was enjoying the moment too much to risk spoiling it. There would be plenty of time later, and he would find out at Hierakonpolis anyway. It wasn't as if she had lied to him. He had asked her name, and she had told him—albeit only a first name, and a nickname at that.

They took a leisurely stroll, neither one uneasy at their mutual silence. Someone had once told Jenny that the best indicator of whether people were at ease with each other was a silence shared in comfort. Not that the absence of sound was complete; the city, despite the lateness of the hour, was bustling with activity.

Jenny was disappointed when Peter suddenly hailed a passing cab and hastily ushered her into the back seat. She wasn't really anxious to be returned to her hotel, especially since she had been looking forward to more walking, followed by a stop at some late-night sidewalk café where they could smile at each other over dishes of *mahallabiyya*—sweetened cream of rice topped with crushed pistachios.

She breathed a silent sigh of pleasure when he climbed in beside her and ordered the driver to take them to the Kû 26-Juillet, which crossed the Nile several blocks north of their hotel. A stroll along the Korneish al-Nil with the palm-lined river off to their right did seem a more fitting conclusion to the wonderful evening than walking more ordinary Cairo streets.

They found a small restaurant not far from the Egyptian Museum. Although there was no *mahalla-biyya*, Jenny was content to settle for *babousa*—a deliciously sticky pastry made of semolina soaked in honey and topped with hazelnuts.

She hated to see the evening come to an end. Under the spell of a glorious Egyptian night she rationalized away all of Peter's faults, except for the fact that a man so intelligent should be so fascinated with falconry. Not far from where they sat, the Nile showed itself to be far more beautiful in moonlight than in the sun, which made it appear dark gray. The moon, large and exceptionally beautiful, was poised in a sky black with night and alive with the sparkle of a million stars. A slight breeze, almost unfelt, stirred the fronds of nearby date palms, causing them to whisper softly to the warm night air.

She began cutting her *babousa* into smaller and smaller pieces in order to extend the moment, remembering the principle of mathematics that said a thing would never completely disappear if continually halved. However, she began to feel just a bit ridiculous when she reached the point of squashing small bits between the edge of her fork and the plate.

She and Peter must have realized simultaneously

that some moments could be destroyed merely by trying in vain to extend them, because they both came to their feet in unison without any words having been spoken between them. In that shared act of spontaneity they were successful in preserving the feeling of specialness. He put his arm around her waist, and she didn't stop him. She liked the feel of it there, liked the feel of his strong body pulled sensuously into contact with her own as they walked.

When they reached the hotel, Jenny found herself once again thinking of her grandmother, knowing very well how that woman might easily have been seduced into loving an attractive young man who came to her in nights filled with big yellow moons, with palm trees whispering as dark silhouettes, with feluccas sailing the dark waters of the Nile as their counterparts had done prior to the time of Christ, with exotic fragrances of lemon and orange blossoms suffusing the air. Such thoughts, however, confused her, warning her that the place might turn out to be even more dangerous than the man. Together Egypt and Peter might prove to be an aphrodisiac too powerful for Jenny to resist, no matter how much she had come prepared to learn from her grandmother's mistakes.

But she was not Geraldine Fowler, she told herself again. She was not married. She didn't have two children. As far as she knew, Peter Donas wasn't committed to another woman's bank account. How foolish she was becoming! One night did not a romance make! Whatever magic had spun itself like a gossamer web around them, it would be dissolved by the morning light, and Jenny would be a fool to shatter the illusion prematurely—especially since it was proving to be such a pleasant one.

Peter walked her to her room, and after unlocking the door for her, gave her back the key. Jenny considered just briefly what it would be like to invite this attractive man beyond the door and, having him there, to watch as he took off his shirt to reveal a smooth and powerful expanse of muscled chest. "I do thank you for a wonderful evening," she said, wondering if he could know she was inwardly blushing from secret thoughts concerning him. She didn't understand what was getting into her, causing her to fantasize such things about a man she had just met that afternoon.

"How about tomorrow?" he asked, standing so close to her that they were almost one in the hallway. "Maybe lunch?" he suggested, hurrying on, perhaps rightly sensing that she was beginning to get skittish. "Maybe we can have a look at the sights and ride a camel at the pyramids?"

"How boring you would find having to squire me to places you've undoubtedly seen," she said, not sure why his invitation to extend the magic was making her so nervous. Maybe it was because she had already assured herself that the magic between them would automatically be gone by morning. Besides, she had already visited the pyramids and had certainly ridden enough camels to suit her.

He stepped back to give her breathing room.

How clever he was to do so. He had sensed her fear like an experienced falconer could read the nervousness of a newly captured bird. Maybe he saw her as a falcon—a bird to be won by slow and careful seduction. Falcons never surrendered their independence easily. It took a good deal of time, gentleness and patience to tame them. In the end the bird was no longer what God had made it, having so thoroughly forgotten its freedom that it kept returning to its master's fist, even when it had the opportunity to return to the vast sky.

"Places once seen are always seen differently and certainly more completely with another person," he told her gallantly, his voice so seductive, his eyes making her want to close the distance between them again. "Usually things shared are the most memorable, don't you agree?" he asked. "You wouldn't really be so cruel as to deprive me of sharing parts of Cairo with you, would you, Jenny? After all, what will it matter—one more day out of your life—when you're soon off to the upper Nile on your cruise and I'm....'' He shrugged, as if even he didn't know where he might be next week or next month. Jenny knew where he would be. He would be at Hierakonpolis with her. Now he saw her as a woman who had come into his life for one evening, maybe one more day, a stranger passing conveniently in the night, sharing things briefly in the Egyptian heat before passing on forever. It didn't seem logical that he would be so anxious to spend these hours with someone with whom he was destined to pass the next two months. He should have been out finding someone else with whom to share memories, memories to be savored when he was dirty, exhausted and sweaty and there were few women within miles except for Jenny. But of course he hadn't given even a hint that he knew her identity.

He stepped forward, taking her in his arms, kissing the base of her neck, her cheeks, her forehead, the tip of her nose. She knew she ought to protest this sudden and unsolicited intimacy, but down deep she wanted him to do what he was doing. She felt comfortable in his arms, as if she had been there forever, feeling the excitement of his hard chest pressed tightly against her breasts, his thighs brushing enticingly against her own, his mouth hungry on her face, burning her with the heat of his demanding kisses.

She opened her mouth beneath the insistent pressure of his lips, sensing that his eagerness more than matched her own. She ran her hands along his sides, feeling muscle taut beneath his shirt, just as she had known there would be hard muscle there. She ran her fingers up his back and into his hair, feeling the silky softness of tousled strands. She worked her body shamelessly closer, feeling even more of him pressed tightly against her while his mouth moved hungrily against hers.

The feel and the taste of him, the smell of his cologne, the sound of his voice, took her breath away and left her gasping for air. Her heart was beating so fast she could hear and feel its staccato rhythm hammering in her chest, in her temples, in her brain.

"No, no!" she said weakly, finally getting her mouth free of his.

"Yes," he contradicted. His mouth resumed kissing her cheeks, her forehead, her closed eyelids. "Surely you must feel it, too, Jenny," he told her. "I know I felt it from the very beginning—that something between us...that very, very *special* something."

She knew she had to find the strength to make him let her go. She definitely knew all about that *something* to which he was referring, and she had allowed him to take advantage of it. The horrible thought struck her that he might really know who she was, might carefully have engineered this moment so that he could laugh about it later. "Her grandmother was a pushover for my granddad, just as she was a pushover for me!" she imagined him saying.

"No, Peter, no!" she insisted, untangling her fingers from his hair and forcibly pushing his face away. She put her hand on his chest, feeling the hard ridges of his muscles, and pushed again. "Please!"

He released her then, so suddenly that she fell back against the wall. She knew that the door of her hotel room was open, that she could have turned and fled into the room, finding safety by slamming the door shut behind her. Yet she didn't move. She suddenly missed the feel of him, the taste of him, the hunger of his vibrant body stirring sensuously against her own. "I'm sorry," he said, his voice low and breathless. "I really don't know...damn it, Jenny, I *am* sorry. Forgive me, please." He turned and left her standing there.

She watched him go, not calling out to him because she didn't know what she would offer if he did stay. Entering her room, she shut the door behind her, hearing the loud and final click of the lock.

She couldn't help wondering what it might have been like if they hadn't been who they were, if Jenny hadn't been caught up in the story of Geraldine and Frederic for so long. How easy it would have been to give way to temptation if she had been nothing more than a simple tourist on holiday. At the same time that admission shocked her, because she had no intention of giving in to that sort of temptation, even if she did feel an attraction so strong that it almost seemed to border on love. But love didn't happen to people that fast, no matter what she had read in books. Anyway, love didn't happen to Jenny Mowry that fast! Certainly not love for the grandson of the man who had caused Geraldine Fowler so much sadness and heartache.

CHAPTER THREE

SHE AWOKE to a silence that had been a long time in coming. Car horns, the bane of Cairo streets, had persisted long and loud into the night, carrying clearly to the tenth floor and in through the glass doors that separated her room from the balcony outside. She hadn't been asleep long before some other sound, at first indefinable, had wrenched her back into consciousness.

She had left the draperies open, anticipating awakening to a sun-drenched vista that included the distant pyramids at Giza. There was no seeing those pyramids—or anything else for that matter—in the present darkness. She stretched for the night-light, switching it on as the phone rang again. Glancing at the travel clock at her bedside, she noted that it was only four-thirty. She lifted the phone from its cradle, wondering what catastrophe could warrant her being forced to awaken at this ungodly hour. "Yes?" she said, still in a state of half sleep in which she functioned without total awareness.

"Just checking to make sure you're getting ready," the voice said. She felt a thrill come to her through the maze of wiring, even if she couldn't fathom Peter's reason for calling. He wasn't offering any explanations. "Everything is ready," he said cryptically. "Will you be coming down shortly?"

She couldn't make heads or tails out of any of it—and not just because she was still half asleep. She had thought she'd probably heard the last of Peter until their reunion at Hierakonpolis. She'd been sorry that their previous evening, with such wonderful beginnings, had ended on such a negative note. She had overreacted to a simple kiss, allowing thoughts of her grandmother's misfortune to taint a moment that had been pleasurable and harmless. Men had been kissing their dates goodnight from time immemorial. It didn't necessarily lead to anything else. It certainly didn't mean he would next profess love, seduce her, propose marriage to her and then leave her for the money in another woman's dowry. "Do you know what time it is?" she asked, glad he had called, no matter what the time, and anxious to keep him on the line.

"It's still more than an hour off," he answered, "so we should have plenty of time to make it if you get a move on."

"Plenty of time to make what?" Jenny questioned, thoroughly confused. She was at a loss to imagine what he could have scheduled for that early in the morning.

"Sunrise from the top of the Pyramid of Cheops," Peter said, unable to keep a certain sense of excitement out of his voice. "I can't imagine a better way to start our day of sightseeing, can you?"

"You're mad!" she said, although the idea of viewing sunrise from the Pyramid of Cheops wasn't without its charm. Except that she had her suspicions that it sounded far more romantic than it would turn out to be. The pyramid in question, after all, had 2,300,000 blocks, each averaging three feet in height. Walking up, *climbing* up, was nothing like managing a simple flight of stairs. Success was apt to leave her too exhausted to contemplate anything but the chore of getting back down again.

"I'll expect you in fifteen minutes," he said, hanging up before she could tell him there was no way she was getting out of a nice warm bed to play mountain goat. She replaced the receiver, scooted down beneath the covers and shut her eyes, realizing she was completely wake. "I can't believe this!" she said, throwing back the blankets, knowing she was going to get up. It wasn't every morning a woman was asked to sample an Egyptian sunrise from such an impressive vantage point. Of course, the one automatically went with the other, since climbing, except in the very early morning, was prohibited. Signs reading Unlawful to Climb Pyramid could be found on virtually every flank. The prohibition could be circumvented only by paying fees to guides and local tourist police. The early hour assured that few unauthorized tourists, if any, would see them going up and down and decide to follow suit without going through proper channels.

It would have been an impossible task to assure the safety of all the climbers who might have wished to make an attempt without paying for the services of someone who could show them the safest way up. Even then some slipped past security—such as the American marine who had tumbled to his death a few months earlier.

Peter, as handsome as ever, met her at the elevator in the lobby. He was not in the least surprised to see she had come. Whatever fluster he had exhibited upon their parting the previous night was now nowhere evident. He put his hand on her arm to guide her confidently across a completely deserted lobby to the revolving doors, beyond which an armed guard stood watch. Cairo was a city where guards, guns and soldiers were a common part of the scenery. Even if there was peace between Egypt and Israel, between Egypt and Libya, it seemed the common consensus that there was little sense in being caught unprepared for the unexpected. Sadly enough Jenny knew even she had quickly got used to functioning normally in this atmosphere that resembled that of an armed compound.

A car and driver were waiting. Peter joined Jenny in the back seat, choosing to sit directly next to her rather than on the opposite side. His leg rested squarely against hers, and the only way she could have broken contact was to open the door of the vehicle and step out. Maybe she should have considered that a viable alternative. She was still too confused about those feelings conjured by his kiss of the prior night to feel prepared to deal with even this less intimate form of physical contact.

The four-lane highway to the pyramids wasn't what one would have expected as a lead-in to one of the most spectacular vistas the world had to offer. In fact, it was only by scrunching down low in the seat that Jenny was able to catch even a fleeting glimpse of one pyramidal apex above the apartment buildings, garish signs and tacky night spots that expanding Cairo had spilled to the very edge of the desert plateau.

The four lanes funneled into two at the Mena House, the royal hunting lodge for Khedive Ismail that had been expanded into a guest house for the opening of the Suez Canal in 1869, then later converted into a hotel. Sir Winston Churchill had loved setting up his easel in the Mena House gardens under fourteenth-century *mushrabiya*—harem windows of intricately carved woodwork. Celebrities galore had signed the hotel guest book, which read like a *Who's Who* in the world of politics, entertainment and royalty. British colonists once sipped tea on the hotel verandas and admired a view that even today, marred as it was by a steady daytime parade of tourists, cars and buses, remained superb. It had been from the Mena House stables that the more hearty travelers, in the days before the existing roadway, mounted camels for the ride to the pyramids. Now, however, a car could merely keep to the blacktop and deposit passengers on the very doorstep of the Great Pyramid.

The car slowed and came to a halt prior to reaching the top of the plateau. The driver left the motor running, and Jenny glanced curiously at Peter for explanations. He only smiled as two short blasts of the horn brought an Arab from the shadows, who got into the car on the passenger side. The man turned and grinned as the car started once again up the hill. "Mohammed is our guide," Peter said, introducing Jenny to the swarthy gentleman who looked old enough to have been with the Carter excavations at Thebes. His wrinkled face became even more creased as he smiled again to show completely toothless gums. "Mohammed once almost broke the six-minute record for reaching the top, but he's decided to take it a bit slower for us today. I told him you were a little out of condition. However, now that he can see what excellent shape you're in, he probably thinks I'm quite crazy. Right, Mohammed?" The old man nodded in reply, although it was doubtful he really understood Peter's words. He smiled more widely, giving his features an irresistibly friendly cast.

Jenny now saw the pyramids—impressive silhouettes against a dark sky that was almost imperceptively paling toward morning. As always, she was a little awed to see these mighty structures that had defied almost five thousand years of wear and tear, their originating civilization in total eclipse before Rome or the city-states of Greece were even conceptions in men's minds. They were a little battered and weather-worn, their outer veneer of limestone and granite stripped away so that once smooth and highly polished surfaces no longer reflected the glory and wealth of their creators, but nevertheless, of the seven man-made structures labeled "wonders" by the peoples of the ancient world, they alone had survived.

Cheops, the tallest and most important pyramid, the one she would climb, was made of six million tons of stone blocks piled geometrically, without mortar, on twelve acres of land. It rose 451 feet into the morning sky and was believed by many to be a monument to the god Re, its slant reminiscent of sun rays spilling from heaven. The base of this monument could have simultaneously contained Christendom's St. Peter's, St. Paul's and Westminster Abbey, as well as the cathedrals in Florence and Milan. If Khephren often appeared to be the taller pyramid, it was only because its architect had cleverly taken advantage of a steeper incline as well as a spot on the plateau higher than the Cheops baseline. Mykerinos, the third pyramid, was modest only in comparison to its more massive companions.

Around this famous trinity were scattered lesser pyramids and burial vaults—mostly the final resting places of influential sycophants who had sought glory while dead in the shadow of the pharaohs' monuments, just as they had sought glory while living in the radiance of their omnipotent god-kings. Finally there was the Sphinx, with its man's head and its lion's body; its paws outstretched; its tail invisible in the darkness, curled along its rocky right haunch.

The car pulled off the roadway and came to a stop in the centuries-old sand. Only a segment of the massive pyramid was visible from one side of the car. The summit of that pyramid, when Jenny did get out to peer upward, seemed impressively out of reach; it recalled biblical accounts of attempts to build a tower reaching to heaven itself and made her wonder why this structure, too, hadn't been toppled by a jealous Hebrew God because of similar sacrilege.

"'Soldiers, from the summit of yonder pyramids, forty centuries look down upon you!'" Peter quoted, coming to stand very close behind her. She felt the power of his nearness, even though he wasn't actually touching her, and she wondered whether the thrill coursing through her was a result of the awe-inspiring monument before her or a response to the superbly handsome man behind her.

She recognized his quote as words spoken by Napoleon to his troops before they defeated the Mamelukes in the 1798 battle fought within sight of the very spot upon which they now stood. She said as much, once again finding Peter impressed by hints of her extensive knowledge. Which brought home the fact that he was still laboring under the illusion that she was someone far less expert on these surroundings than he was.

"It says a lot about you that you've taken the time to do your homework about this place," he told her. His voice was a sensuous caress, and she could feel the nearness of his lips as he spoke softly in her ear. "It's surprising how many people come here to see the pyramids and leave without having any real notion of the scope of history present before them."

Jenny turned toward him, embarrassed to find his handsomeness capable of overpowering even the grandeur of these stone structures. She wasn't really listening, too caught up in her remembrance of how it had been the last time they'd stood that close, his arms reaching out to take hold of her, his hard muscled body pressing against the yielding softness of her own, his lips.... "What?" she asked, helplessly flustered, having realized he expected a response to his statement.

He smiled at her, as if to say he knew where her mind had been wandering, had read her innermost thoughts and was well satisfied at the confirmation that she found him tremendously attractive. "Are you ready?" he asked, reaching out a hand as though he might touch it to the blush of her cheeks.

"Yes," she said, turning from him before his fingertips could make contact. Because if she was ready to climb the Pyramid of Cheops, she was not ready for whatever else his question might imply. She wasn't ready to make more of one kiss than was warranted. She wasn't ready to admit that her feelings for him went beyond those of one professional for another. She wasn't ready to admit that she had wanted him to touch her once again as he had touched her the previous night, perhaps even carry that contact further than the mere caress of two eager mouths.

Their guide was already up the first tier of stone blocks. He offered his hand, and she took hold of it for a moment, wishing it were Peter's fingers closing in over her own. Mohammed moved on, and she followed. Sometimes he traversed the face of the wall, more often than not taking giant leg-tiring steps that led her steadily upward. When she stopped, so breathless she was quite sure she was too exhausted to go on, a glance downward showed her a car that had shrunk to the size of an ant. A look upward, however, only revealed just as much distance to go as she had already covered.

"Tired?" Peter asked, leaning against the rock beside her. She was only vaguely consoled by the fact that he was also a little pressed for breath.

"I think I'll wait here," she said, putting her hand to the base of her throat, as if that would alleviate the pain caused by her ragged gasps for badly needed oxygen. How right she had been earlier when she had suspected that it would be a trial to gain access to the view afforded from the summit—despite the romance of that view! There was nothing even vaguely romantic about dying at the halfway point.

"You'll feel better after you rest a few minutes," he assured her, although she didn't believe a word of it. She was fighting down waves of nausea, nearly sick from the exertion. "I'll tell Mohammed to move a little slower," Peter said. He did not intend the comment to embarrass her into attempting to match the pace of the guide—a man twice her age. But even had he intended it that way, Jenny's condition was such that the barb wouldn't have succeeded. What finally did prod her on was Peter's gentle reminder that they wouldn't find it any easier should they decide to come back another day. "We're not getting any younger, are we?" he said, and his mocking tone let Jenny know that he, at least, had begun to breathe normally.

Jenny herself was still a little breathless, but she found a reserve somewhere. She pushed herself away from the stone on which she had collapsed and accepted the hand Mohammed was once again lending in assistance. Although consumed with the sheer effort of making it all the way to the top, she was acutely aware of Peter's strong fingers around her waist each time he offered her support.

"We're almost there," he said a little while later. But considering that it wasn't the first time he'd said it, the comment provided Jenny very little by way of encouragement.

"I must have been crazy to let myself be roped into this," she said, stopping again. The words didn't come out in a fluid sentence but were punctuated by the rasps of a woman who sounded as if she were gasping out her last. Suddenly his arm was around her shoulders, and she told herself she really didn't know it was there. As she turned her face into the muscled warmth of his shoulder, smelling a combination of cologne and his own masculine scent, feeling his chest expanding with each breath he took, she tried to see herself merely as a woman who, figuring she had reached the end, would have clung to whatever or whomever happened to be handy. She was sure that it was only the unusual circumstances that made it seem so right for her to be in his arms like this. As a matter of fact, she pulled away as soon as it became obvious that he was holding her far more closely than was warranted by a mere gesture of assistance. Fearful of any similar lapses into the temptation of finding an excuse to be embraced by him, she redoubled her efforts at climbing and, with a final exhausted step, reached the summit.

She didn't make any immediate attempts to admire the view, even if that view was a decidedly exceptional one. She moved instead to the center of an area that had resulted from the removal of the original capstone or, more doubtfully, from there never having been one in the first place. She collapsed to a sitting position and put her head on drawn-up knees, wrapping her arms securely around her legs.

"Tell me it wasn't worth it," Peter challenged finally. "Go on, I dare you."

Jenny couldn't deny that being at the top was worth the arduous trek, especially since she was surprisingly revived by the few minutes he had diplomatically given her to catch her breath. In the dim light of predawn the view down along the four giant stairways that converged at the narrow platform on the top was breathtaking. The desert on two sides, the green of farmland on another and the city and the Nile off to the east all combined into a collage of expansive grandeur. But it was the view of the ruins close by that was of most interest to Jenny as an archaeologist. There was nothing like the present vantage point to give a proper perspective on a necropolis whose state of decay often made its layout seem lacking in organization from ground level. From where she sat, distance blurred many imperfections, much as individual brush strokes merged in a painting viewed from across a room. Along a line leading north was the *sirdab*, or offering chamber, the mortuary temple and satellite pyramids, the courtiers' mastabas and the causeway leading to the Valley Temple. All were visible with a clarity missed by anyone who didn't put out the effort to make the climb.

She came to her feet. Her legs remained a little weak in the knees, but she felt that that was small enough payment for the opportunity to stand beside Peter and face east to witness the beginning blush of dawn on the far horizon.

She was momentarily distracted by a sudden realization that their guide was nowhere in sight. "Mohammed is within calling distance, I assure you," Peter said, guessing he had read her thoughts. "If that's what you're thinking."

"I wasn't thinking that at all," she said, feeling guilty about the little white lie.

Cairo was a blackness shrouded in a dusty veil.

The desert beyond the city, above which the sun hadn't yet lifted, was shadowy gray. The sky in the distance was a flux of changing colors more subtle than sunset hues but no less beautiful. Above Cheops the heavens were still fading ebony, except for the most brilliant stars flickering faintly now, destined to drown soon in that flood of more intense illumination that was rushing to claim them.

"Oh!" Jenny said in response to the sun's peeking over the horizon. It was a mere sliver of orange, growing as she watched, adding brilliance to the dawning sky that glowed pale pink and yellow. A lacy scattering of clouds became stained with the bleeding colors, then expanded into a filigree of varying shades.

"'Oh, Re, who smileth, joyfully...'" Peter said, again putting his arm around Jenny's waist. She made no effort to pull free, wanting to savor their mutual sharing of a very special moment. "'And whose heart delights in the perfect order of this day thou enterest by coming forth into Heaven from the east; the Ancients and those who have gone before salute thee!'"

Jenny didn't recognize the quote, thinking—correctly—that it must have come from the Egyptian *Book of the Dead*. No matter. The sun chose that particular moment, as if conjured by Peter's centuries-old incantation, to make its full appearance on the horizon, doing so in a blinding flash of light that caused Jenny to turn away toward Peter at the same instant gray desert unfolded golden, black sky went blue and Cairo burst forth like a glittering diadem on the landscape.

His eyes were golden suns with profound, almost brown, centers. In the light of the large sun lifting itself steadily on the horizon, he held her captive, drawing her deeper and deeper into his spell. His body moved closer still, and he held her, breathless and willing in the strong confines of his arms. He began,

"My well-being is her entrance from outside:
For when I see her, I am well.
If she opens her eyes, I find my youth again;
If she speaks, I gain my strength again;
When I embrace her, she casts out devils from
     me...."

It was a love poem from the Egyptian New Kingdom, punctuated with a gentle touching of his lips to hers that seemed to Jenny like a gentle breeze across the sweet-smelling petals of a rose. He followed with another kiss more forceful than the first, one that made her mouth open slightly beneath subtly applied pressure. He tasted of mint and of something even more delicious, making her want more of the same, as if she were a starving beggar turned loose upon a rich man's banquet.

. She ran her hands down his back, feeling contoured hardness beneath his knit pullover. She wanted the warmth of his naked skin against her fingertips, and she quickly discovered that that was possible by running both of her hands upward under his shirt. Her fingers trailed around his rib cage to discover, like a blind woman reading braille, a well-defined chest rippled with steellike muscle.

"Jenny, Jenny," he whispered, fumbling with the buttons on her blouse, peeling back material to put against her breasts his callus-hardened hands that were more sensuous than the silk that had been there before them.

There were, however, limits beyond which she was unprepared to go, especially with a man she didn't love and couldn't trust to love her. It didn't matter that at that moment not only Peter himself but also all the forces of nature seemed determined to unite them. Jenny still had her senses about her and would not be seduced. True, she was allowing herself and Peter certain liberties, but that was only because she had intuitively realized the built-in protection offered by the time, the place and Mohammed waiting close by to lead her down from such rarefied heights. If she had momentarily succumbed to temptation, it had been to prove to herself that she could handle more than a kiss without losing her head. She had proven what she wanted to prove, and she well knew the danger inherent in proceeding any further. She was, after all, only human, and she certainly couldn't have come to this point if she hadn't felt some kind of attraction for him. She certainly didn't distribute her kisses to all comers. She couldn't remember the last time she had even felt an urge to touch any man the way she had touched Peter. "Listen to me, Peter," she said, feeling his mouth nestled in the warmth of her neck and doing maddening things. "We have to get down from here before the buses begin dropping off the regular tourists."

"I want to make love with you," he said, his lips sensuous butterflies against her sensitive flesh.

She thanked God when Mohammed, apparently come out of hiding, shuffled audibly behind them, making it unnecessary for her to reply. Peter, though, did not welcome the intrusion; he released Jenny suddenly and turned to the guide smoothly requesting him to disappear for a few more minutes. Jenny was embarrassed at the disorganized state of her clothing and quickly pulled her blouse closed, clumsily refastening the mother-of-pearl buttons.

Peter had spoken in Arabic. Mohammed responded in kind—something about there possibly being problems if they weren't down on schedule. "There will be no problems," Peter insisted. "I'll see to it."

"That won't be necessary," Jenny interjected, her command of the Arab tongue bringing surprised glances from both of the men, who had obviously assumed they'd been speaking in some kind of code. "We'll go down now," she said, Arabic, like any other language, holding secrets only from those who hadn't taken the time to master it. She couldn't help smiling, though, at Peter's continued amazement. "There are some excellent language courses taught in the States, you know," she said, wondering if he thought that the only place outside the Arab world in which one might learn Arabic was within the august halls of Oxford.

"You must admit, it's not a language one would normally expect to hear from your average tourist on holiday," he replied, persisting in his mistaken notions. She wasn't an average tourist, and she certainly wasn't on holiday.

"No matter, we're going down," Jenny said, her blouse finally buttoned, even if the presence of an extra button indicated she hadn't done a very good job of it. "There's no sense in running the risk of getting any of us into trouble."

"It's surprising how much trouble can usually be dissolved by the presentation of a few Egyptian pounds," Peter said, telling Jenny something she had long ago discovered for herself.

"Nevertheless," she said, "there's little point in remaining. As romantic as making love atop a pyramid undeniably sounds, I have no intention of doing so with you. A kiss is one thing, but—"

"That was more than just a kiss," he interrupted. She felt herself blushing at a point well taken. However, whether it was more than a kiss or not, it remained a long way from what he had been proposing as a follow-up.

"You seem a bit, well, shall we say—eager?" Jenny replied, trying desperately to remain cool. "Making love is a far cry from love, and we're not talking about that, are we?"

"I'd very much appreciate your letting me express my own opinion, thank you," Peter said. She was gratified to see he was obviously more than a little flustered by events.

"Come on now, Peter, please don't try to flatter me with some kind of cockamamy line about love at first sight," she said, giving him a look that told him she wouldn't begin to believe it if he tried. At the same time a certain something inside of her made her wish he would.

"How the hell do I know what I could feel for you?" he asked, a question that surprised Jenny. "We haven't had much of a chance for courtship. One day we meet and two days later you're off up the Nile. It's a bit much to expect me to define my feelings under those circumstances. But if I've offended your sensibilities, please excuse me for having done so. I assure you I would have gone through the more acceptable formalities of showing my interest if I'd thought for one moment you'd be around a little longer than forty-eight hours."

"Did you bother to ask me whether I might consider staying on a little while longer?" Jenny asked.

He gave her a look that told her just how much credence he put in her suggesting she might have changed her travel plans to coincide with the arrival on the scene of a potential suitor. "Tell me, Jenny, would you have considered staying on in Cairo for a few more days?" he asked. His sarcasm made it obvious he already knew the answer to his question.

"Not in Cairo," she said, intending to give him

at last the information she thought would stun him. She couldn't imagine what Mohammed must have thought of all that was going on. Judging by the way the guide kept nervously glancing at his expensive wristwatch, Jenny could see he was little interested in much of anything except a schedule that was decidedly not being met. "But how about my giving you two whole months in Hierakonpolis?" she asked Peter with a smile. The look he gave her at that moment was worth all the harmless subterfuge Jenny had used up until then. He genuinely looked as if he had received the biggest surprise of his life. "Maybe it would help if we went through formal introductions one more time," Jenny said, thoroughly enjoying herself and wanting to extend the moment a bit longer. Not even the sweeping magnificence of the view could draw her attention away from Peter's handsome face at that moment. "My name is Jennifer Mowry. J. Mowry. And I believe we're presently assigned to the same archaeological dig, are we not?"

"*You're* J. Mowry?" he asked, as if that notion was so far removed from possibility that he simply couldn't grasp it. "No," he said. "You can't be!"

"Why not? You've met J. Mowry before, have you?" she asked, knowing that definitely wasn't the case.

"I've certainly seen her picture," he said, and she could just see his mind working overtime to conjure up one of those schoolmarm representations of her he had probably seen a time or two in scientific journals.

"Well, you'll know definitely in a few days' time, won't you?" she said, flashing him a smile. "That's when we're officially scheduled to rendezvous, isn't it?"

"Why the hell didn't you tell me who you were earlier?" he asked. Perhaps it had finally occurred to him that she was a little too up on her facts *not* to be J. Mowry.

"Frankly, I didn't want to ruin something I was finding enjoyable," Jenny said, at least willing to give him that much.

"Ruin what? How?" he inquired, but Jenny wasn't about to start bad-mouthing his grandfather, although Frederic Donas could certainly have very few good things said about him. She didn't want to go into details because she doubted that Peter would like the suggestion that what had happened so far in the past had a bearing on the present.

"Call it mixing business with pleasure," Jenny said. There certainly had been more than a few pleasurable moments shared between them. "I suppose I had visions of our conversations suddenly degenerating into shoptalk about whether or not Crete *really* is all that's left of Atlantis."

"Oh, yes, *that*," he said, giving perfect indication of not thinking any more favorably toward her theory now than he ever had. In the same instant he obviously got the point she had been trying to put across, because he smiled rather sheepishly. "Yes, I guess I see what you mean about mixing business and pleasure," he said, looking very appealing as the rays of the rising sun continued to lighten the sky behind him.

"Well, with that said, shall we begin our trip down?" Jenny suggested, sensing more than seeing the grateful look Mohammed cast in her direction.

"I do think I should make one thing perfectly clear," Peter said, apparently thinking Mohammed's chagrin at the continued delay would be salved sufficiently by a sizable gratuity at the finish. "I still have all intentions of making love with you."

Jenny felt a pleasurable flush of embarrassment. There could be no denying that she was pleased to find that out, he still wanted her even though he was now aware they were rivals. Considering the length of time he had known her, his sudden desire probably owed more to animal instincts than tender feelings, but that didn't entirely remove its impact. Peter, after all, was a very attractive man, certainly more attractive than any other man Jenny had had in her life. She turned from him, afraid it was obvious she was on the point of becoming as flustered as a silly schoolgirl. She felt a jolt of electricity as his hand took hold of her arm and pulled her none too gently back to face him. "I do not kiss every woman I happen to meet," he said, his eyes flashing from a face whose expression was all seriousness. "I certainly do not make overtures to invite them to my bed." He released his handhold, leaving a tingling sensation where his fingers had touched her.

They proceeded down the gargantuan stairway—

a descent more wearing on their posteriors than on anything else, since it required a series of sits and slides designed to prevent any forward tumbles that would likely have ended tragically at the bottom. It also took considerably less time than the ascent and was nowhere near as exhausting. When they got to the bottom, Jenny didn't even need a brief pause prior to beginning the short trek to the parked car. Peter remained momentarily behind to pacify not only Mohammed but a scowling member of the tourist police who had appeared out of nowhere. Jenny wasn't sure she could blame the policeman for his obvious testiness. The area, after all, was already beginning to fill with people, most of whom were probably aware of the fact that two men and a woman had been climbing a pyramid distinctly posted against such violations. She felt confident, though, that Peter would take care of it.

She was still pleasurably flushed from her encounter with Peter when she saw the man and the horses a few yards from the car. Not that a man and three horses were such an uncommon sight here. The horses and camels plus those in charge of selling rides to tourists were usually the first to arrive in the morning and the last to leave at night. What was distinctive about this group was that the horses were extremely beautiful animals, even in a country known for its purebred Arabian stock, and the man looked strangely familiar. His smile, framed by his neatly trimmed beard, silently beckoned her, unlike that of a hawker of wares, who would have been screaming at the top of his lungs his invitation to take her for the ride of her life. She automatically veered in his direction, telling herself she was drawn more to the animals than to the darkly attractive man who held them.

Jenny stopped by the first horse, a gray mare with large eyes the color of black velvet. "And there's a particularly lovely lady!" the man said, looking at her and not at the horse. She had the good grace to smile at the bold compliment. She laid her hand on the animal's muzzle, stroking the short gray hair, finding the horse of a quality beyond what might be expected, considering the equestrian skills of tourists visiting Giza. "I thought maybe you might like to ride," the man said, his voice low and striking a familiar chord somewhere in Jenny's mind although she told herself she must be imagining things. She hadn't been to Giza on this trip except today, and she certainly couldn't have remembered one person out of so many seen on her last trip through. "The horse is gentle," he assured her, "though of exceptional breeding. Her line can be traced back to the stables of the sultan of Turkey."

"Which is further than I can trace mine," Jenny said with a nervous laugh. She didn't know why, but this man was making her decidedly uneasy. Not that he was coming on with a hard sell, because he wasn't. Not that his earlier compliment had been in leering bad taste, because it hadn't. It certainly didn't matter than he was lying about the horse's pedigree. It was hardly likely that an animal whose lineage could be traced back to the stables of a Turkish sultan would be subjected to the inexpert handling of tourists whose idea of a good ride was a slow walk from parking lot to pyramids. What made Jenny ill at ease was a sense that she was seeing before her a scenario wherein everything might look perfectly in place but in which something was definitely out of kilter. "How much is it for an hour ride?" she asked, realizing the man's eyes were just as darkly enticing as those of the horse she was petting.

"Surely you'd like more than just a short hour," he said, suddenly sounding more like a salesman. "There's a place I know in the desert that I think you would enjoy going to more than you would enjoy threading your way through the crowds apt to be here in a few minutes' time."

She was saved from answering by Peter coming up behind her. She turned toward him, not just sure what she was suddenly reading on his face. He eyed her and the man, looking very much as if he were jealous. "I didn't realize the two of you had met," Peter said, his voice holding just a hint of coolness that Jenny hadn't heard there previously. Not only that, but his insinuation that she knew this man was ludicrous. While she might flatter herself that he was jealous, he surely didn't imagine she could be flirting with a man whose only connection with her was that he had probably seen her as his first customer of the day.

"Actually, the lady and I haven't met—officially," the man said, his voice again compelling Jenny to face him. He was smiling to reveal teeth that seemed startlingly white in contrast to his black beard, black mustache and dark complexion. "Perhaps, Peter, you would be so kind as to do the honors?"

"Of course," Peter said, his voice still carrying a certain edge that Jenny hadn't yet been able to define to her satisfaction. "Sheikh Abdul Jerada, may I present Jennifer Mowry."

She suddenly remembered why Sheikh Jerada was so familiar. Not only had his name been brought up by Peter as the owner of the peregrine falcon in the Hilton Hotel lobby, but he was the man she had almost run down on her way to the elevator. "I'm very pleased to meet you, Miss Mowry," he said with a slight bow. "It's always a pleasure to bump into you, if you'll excuse that very poor pun." Jenny couldn't help laughing. Which made Abdul laugh, too. The slight tension between them was dispelled, but Jenny still had to deal with tension building in another quarter. Peter wasn't laughing. He wasn't even smiling. He was eyeing them curiously, much like a scientist examining two unpredictable bugs under a microscope. "I took the liberty of bringing horses, Peter," Abdul said, "having learned from the people at the hotel that you and Miss Mowry were pyramid climbing this morning. I thought maybe you'd both do me the pleasure of joining me for a short ride, followed by lunch."

"I don't recall telling anyone at the hotel where we were going this morning," Peter said, none too friendly.

"Yes, well," Abdul replied with a shrug. "If your guide knew, your driver knew and the tourist police knew, you might safely assume a good many others knew, too."

"I see," Peter answered, but he still sounded as though he considered the sheikh's presence to be an intrusion.

"Then how about that ride and lunch?" Abdul asked. If he noticed Peter's hostile attitude, he was apparently more than willing to overlook it.

"Unfortunately we've got the car and driver here," Peter said, obviously not warming to any of Abdul's overtures.

"A small gratuity will send the one away with the other...no bad feelings, don't you agree?" Abdul said, a slight wink indicating that a little money could grease all sorts of potentially annoying gears. "Shall I save you the bother by taking care of it for you?"

"That won't be necessary," Peter replied, not giving any indication that he intended to take care of it himself, either. "Actually, I'm not sure Jenny is all that much of a horsewoman."

"No formal training," she said. "Not like most of those girls you probably know back home who belong to the horsey set and had horses in lieu of prams. But I've had enough practical experience to get from one point to another without too many saddle sores—providing, of course, the distance between points A and B isn't overly far."

"Well, I stand thereby informed!" Peter said with a laugh, but there was an undertone to his light remark that made Jenny think he had found her words to be a small betrayal.

Jenny reluctantly found herself having to agree that she had deserted him. Her little gibe about his previous girl friends had been unnecessary. And besides, her anxious hurry to assure the sheikh that she was competent to ride seemed to imply that she preferred to spend her last day in Cairo in company other than *just* that of Peter. Which simply wasn't the case. Oh, the ride did sound like fun. So did the offer of lunch, since the climb had gone full circle from making her sick to making her hungry. But there was something to the old adage about two being company and three a crowd. "Maybe, though, I'd better pass," she said. "No matter how I feel now, it would be ridiculous to overdo things. I'm not as young as I once was, after all."

"Although you look the epitome of good health to me, you certainly would know best," Abdul said magnanimously. Peter looked genuinely pleased. Jenny felt she had definitely done the right thing. She was rather sorry that she had made Peter feel that his earlier overtures were out of place, and she didn't want to deprive him—or herself—of the little time that remained to them in Cairo. Perhaps they could each make amends. This last day was special, since once on the job together, considering their conflicting opinions on the value of the dig as a potential burial site for the Scorpion King, they would be treating each other as adversaries rather than friends.

"I was rather looking forward to showing off Hatshepsût," Abdul commented. Jenny knew immediately, just by noting the sudden change that came over Peter, that Abdul's reference to a woman pharaoh of the New Kingdom had nothing whatsoever to do with that lady who had assumed male trappings, complete with ceremonial false beard, to rule Egypt in the Eighteenth Dynasty. "My trainers are flying her in the desert outside Saqqâra this morning," Abdul said, seeming all innocence. "I'd thought that since Peter was so taken by the little lady...." He shrugged, as if to indicate that even the best opportunities were sometimes passed up out of necessity.

"Yes, I'm sorry, too," Peter said, "but Jenny is definitely right. She shouldn't chance overdoing things." However, his words were too little, too late. Jenny had seen all she had needed to see when Abdul Jerada had mentioned that precious bird of his. At that precise moment Jenny had watched herself suddenly become the furthest thing from Peter's mind. He had forgotten all of his pretty words to her, all that had already happened between them, all that had a potential of happening in the future. He had surrendered it all as his mind's eye had gone soaring off into the desert sky over Saqqâra. In that instant he seemed to become as much a part of that hawk as the bells attached to her legs.

"On the other hand, how often does a lady get invited to morning rides and lunches by exotic desert sheikhs?" Jenny said, darned if she was going to pass up this opportunity and instead spend time with someone who would have been bemoaning lost visions of a hawk every single moment he looked at her. "And it's more than obvious Peter would never forgive himself or me if he missed his chance to see little Hatshepsût in action. Right, Peter?" she asked, wondering if she sounded as angry and as hurt as she felt.

He looked shamefaced and embarrassed. Which, Jenny thought, was all he could probably come up with under the circumstances.

CHAPTER FOUR

How INCONGRUOUS—that sound like ice cubes tinkling against fine crystal! For the heat would have melted an iceberg. Yet the sound remained, carried on the stillness of the desert morning.

There was a clarity to the desert air, and Jenny could gaze for miles, picking out faraway landmarks that seemed so near yet were so far. It was therefore easy for her to pinpoint the source of the sound: two tiny bells, one a semitone in pitch above the other, that together produced the audible discord. They had originally come from the Lahore region of Pakistan, made by an ancient process that gave light but good repercussion by means of the striking of an irregular clapper against the metal of the bell. They were for wear by a peregrine falcon, designed to be attached to short leather strips— bewits—one of which rode each leg. Smaller bells were used on tiercels—smaller ones yet on kestrels, merlins and sparrowhawks. The peregrine in possession of these bells soared on those air currents that were active above the ground but that left the desert sand in undisturbed stillness.

There were some people born with a hereditary

tone deafness that disallowed them clear hearing of
those sounds emitted by hawk bells—a decided disadvantage to any falconer needing to locate a hawk
whose flight had ended in deep cover. There was,
however, no need to worry about cover here, for
there was none. On all sides stretched a seemingly
endless sea of sand. It was somehow fitting that this
largest continuous wasteland on the face of the
earth, extending east and west between the Atlantic
Ocean and the Red Sea, north and south between
the Sudan and the Mediterranean, embracing an
area of over 3,500,000 square miles, should most
often be called by a redundant title: Sahara
Desert—*sahara* meaning "desert" in Arabic. It
was, however, a mistake to think of the Sahara as
only a continuous monotony of undulating sand,
for it enclosed extensive plateaus and sterile rock-
strewn plains. It was not sandy everywhere, but it
was sandy here near Saqqâra. That city of the dead,
necropolis to the ancient Egyptian capital of Memphis, wasn't immediately visible to Jenny, but the
airborne peregrine could see all fourteen pyramids
and hundreds of mastabas and tombs dating from
the First to the Thirtieth Dynasty. Picked from Saqqâra's ruins had been the oldest known mummy
and the oldest papyrus ever found. For Jenny it was
decidedly apropos that the name of the place derived from the Arabic *sakr*, meaning "hawk."

Hatshepsût, hawk named for a long-dead queen
of Egypt, was a queen in her own right, regal as she
surveyed her domain, subtly shifting on the wind,

sometimes maneuvering so smoothly that she achieved a silence without bells. Her back, wings and tail were bluish gray, the feathers barred with a darker tint. Her crown, neck and a spot below each eye were nearly black. Her throat was white with dark longitudinal lines; her breast, belly and legs white with dark bars. Her wings, now open, could fold almost to the tip of her tail. On occasion she came between those who watched her and the sun, and sparks of sunlight telegraphed through her end feathers, which she imperceptively adjusted to coast through the blue Egyptian skies.

There was a beauty and grace to her movements, a power and strength, a speed and a style, that had made her species coveted by falconers in Eastern countries long before the sport was to become ancient in central Europe or Great Britain. Even Jenny could admire the aesthetic grace and beauty, the oneness of the bird and her surroundings. Under certain conditions there would have been a tragic beauty even to the kill, for it was the nature of things that some hunted and others were hunted—a balance nature strove always to achieve in the end. But whatever beauty was present this day, it was marred by the interference of man upon the scene. For Hatshepsût, though she seemed free, was anchored to men on the ground by an invisible umbilical cord that tampered with the natural scheme of things. Even her victim, a pigeon caught midflight with a force that sent a showering of white feathers earthward, wouldn't have kept his appointment with destiny if he hadn't been frightened into flight by human hands shaking him from a wicker cage.

"You don't approve," Abdul said, not having missed the fact that Jenny had once again turned her head away. They were sitting in the shade offered by an awning outstretched from the entrance to a large Bedouin tent that had been set up to accommodate lunch preparations and to provide for the comfort of the sheikh and his guests.

"I guess I find myself empathizing with the bird," Jenny said, knowing it would be quite futile to go into her objections in much depth. She had learned from experience that hawking, like bullfighting, had its attackers and its defenders, and seldom, if ever, did the two meet on common ground.

"Then you just rejoice for her," Abdul said, his attention thoroughly on Jenny and not on the peregrine, who had grounded her prey and was crouching triumphantly on the kill, "for she has the best of care, is well fed and provided for, has few of the trials and tribulations of her counterparts in the wild."

"And all she gave up for that was her freedom?" Jenny asked, unable to keep the sarcasm out of her voice. She knew she was about to beat a dead horse, but she decided she might as well get in her two cents' worth. Maybe, just maybe, this was a man who would have the openness of mind to see another side of the subject besides his own. "When I was in college," she said, "one of my professors devoted a whole class period to building logical argument upon logical argument for the introduction of controlled cannibalism into twentieth-century society. He argued, among other things, that human flesh was an ideal source of protein and easily come by in starving Third World nations with rampant birthrates." Abdul frowned, obviously not making any connection between falconry and men boiling one another in giant cooking pots. "His point wasn't that we should go around eating our fellowmen for dinner," Jenny said, a little disappointed he hadn't immediately seen what she was getting at. "It was that there are rationalizations for any horror under the sun if we want to sit down and work hard enough to find excuses."

"Ah!" he said, as if she had indeed made a good point. However, his follow-up was such that she knew she had no more made a convert of him than she would make of Peter, who was out there in the blistering desert heat with the bird's trainer, watching Hatshepsût be recalled to the fist for another cast. "Perhaps I can amuse you some other way," he said, completely changing the subject. "You've seen Saqqâra, I suppose. Still, if you don't mind seeing it again, it's but a short ride from here, and there's time before lunch."

"Places once seen are always seen differently and certainly more completely with another person," Jenny said, remembering with a bittersweet pang how it had been Peter who had used such an argument in an attempt to claim her for a day of sight-seeing. *This* day, as a matter of fact. "Usually things shared are the most memorable," she added, just as Peter had added, stung as she did so by the realization that Peter had surrendered seeing things with her to watch a falcon hunt desert skies.

"It's settled then," Abdul said, coming to his feet. "I'll merely take a minute to see if Peter would like to come with us."

"I hardly expect he would even miss us," Jenny said, wishing her disappointment hadn't come out sounding quite so evident.

"Oh, I think you're very wrong there," Abdul replied with a charming smile. He was wearing a black *galabia* that might have seemed far too warm for the high temperatures, but Jenny knew the garment was more effective in preserving body moisture than a lighter fabric, which would have allowed the moisture to evaporate. Quickly wrapping his head with a strip of matching black cloth that concealed his short-cropped black hair from the sun, he left the protection of the awning, not bothering to elucidate further on his opinion that Peter would care about being deprived of Jenny's presence. She suspected he wouldn't have been able to back up the statement with solid facts anyway. Peter, fully engrossed with Hatshepsût, was obviously not concerned about how she and Sheikh Jerada occupied their time, and Jenny wasn't going to be convinced otherwise by a comment Abdul had voiced only out of politeness. Still, watching Abdul's firm and steady stride cross the sand toward Peter and the trainer in the near distance, Jenny couldn't quell the niggling hope that Peter would prefer her company to that of the bird, even if he would have to share their moments together with Abdul. After all, Peter had been out in the hot sun watching the falcon for well over an hour. Surely even the most avid advocate of the sport would welcome a breather at some time. Her heart skipped a beat when Peter turned to greet Abdul and then faced in Jenny's direction in apparent response to hearing what the sheikh was proposing. She experienced a sinking feeling of disappointment as Peter turned back to the falcon, and Abdul headed back across the sand. "He said to go on and he might join us in a while," Abdul explained when Jenny came to intercept him at the horses.

"Oh, I think we'll manage well enough without him," she answered, once again determined that Peter wasn't going to ruin her day. He had certainly made known his prerogatives from the moment Abdul had mentioned Hatshepsût, and those prerogatives had not changed.

They mounted their horses, Jenny noticing that a short distance away three other men were simultaneously mounting theirs. Those same men had accompanied Abdul, Jenny and Peter on the ride from the pyramids. "After a while you'll get used to them and forget they're even there," Abdul said, noting her distraction as he reined his horse in the direction of a high sand dune. Jenny, though, doubted she would ever get used to being shadowed by bodyguards. Something about them hinted of violence waiting in the wings—more so than the presence of all those armed soldiers posted on Cairo streets.

"I hope your friends never have to see action," she said, nodding toward the men falling into place behind her and Abdul.

"Unfortunately they already have," Abdul replied. She glanced in his direction, thinking he would counter with a smile that would indicate he was only joking. He wasn't smiling. "Although it would be rash to expect them to offer complete protection against all would-be assassins, I can hope they'll continue to be fast enough to make any attempted killer less accurate with his gun, his knife, or with whatever other weapon he might choose." Jenny shuddered at the implications, wondering what kind of a position Abdul held that he should have been labeled a target by anybody. She knew his business had something to do with oil only because he had mentioned that he had just returned from the United States, where he had finalized a business deal with an American petroleum conglomerate. The details had been sketchy at best, mentioned to Jenny merely in passing, and she certainly hadn't felt it prudent to press for specifics then or now. "Oh, you mustn't look so gloomy, Jenny," he said, finally giving her a smile that came a little too late to dispel the somber revelations that had preceded it. "I often find myself thanking my enemies for my scars."

"Thanking them?" Jenny asked, frankly aghast. That he had scars was in itself disturbing, let alone that he might be somehow glad to have them.

"I have a knife scar here," he said, pointing to his right side and drawing a line leftward to the center of his stomach. "I have a bullet scar here," he went on, indicating a spot on the inside of his upper left thigh very near his groin. "I'll be most happy to let you have a closer look at that one later, by the way." That was an attempt at levity, but Jenny had a hard time laughing. "You'd be surprised how many women find battle scars decidedly erotic," he said. "Which is why I should be thankful to have them." He laughed, indicating that if Jenny were taking this too seriously, she would have done better, like him, to look less on the negative side.

"We all have to die sometime," he said, that still not giving her suitable consolation. "We merely spend our lives preparing for that finality." His comment on the inevitability of death had been made with macabre timing, since their horses had chosen that particular moment to top a high dune that afforded their riders an encompassing view of the Saqqâra necropolis stretched out below. This city of the dead, constructed in counterpoint to ancient Memphis, city of the living, was known mainly for its dominating Step Pyramid, a picture of which hung in Jenny's room at the Nile Hilton. Constructed during the reign of Zozer, the first pharaoh of the Third Dynasty, the pyramid's architect was Imhotep, whose genius had transferred into reality this the world's first major building in stone, a masterpiece recognized in its own time as the greatest structure known to man. "Most of the information we have on my country's past comes from the early Egyptian's preoccupation with death, doesn't it?" Abdul said, his horse stopped on the hillside, Jenny's horse halted beside it. "But then I don't have to tell you, an archaeologist, that Egyptian temples and tombs were built to last only because they were for housing the gods and the immortals. All else was made of mud brick, which has long since crumbled to dust."

Jenny was aware this talk of death shouldn't have depressed her. She was in the business of reconstructing times past by sifting through the things found in graveyards. The ancient Egyptians had come to consider death a joyous occasion and not one to be avoided at all cost. Yet she *was* depressed, and if she thought somehow to ease it by glancing back over her shoulder to catch a glimpse of the vitally alive Peter, all she ended up seeing was another death-dealing swoop of Hatshepsût to dispatch one more of the pigeons released for her from a wicker cage. Jenny's horse began to move down the hillside, cutting off even that view, and Jenny turned back to attend to her descent into the ruins.

Sensing his lovely companion's present mental state and feeling responsible for it, Abdul attempted the telling of two jokes he'd heard recently and felt were suitable for mixed company. His ineptness in recounting the first one and his forgetting the punch line of the second finally managed to make Jenny smile. Her return to good humor had also been sparked by her sudden realization that her depression had really begun with Peter's rejection of her. She was determined not to let something like that get her down. If he preferred a bird's company to hers, then so be it! It certainly wasn't as if she had been left wanting male companionship in the face of his desertion, because Abdul offered more than adequate compensation. In his desert robes, black against the golden spread of sand, he was a man of breathtaking handsomeness. He was charming; he was considerate, and he was powerful. He didn't touch Jenny's heart the way Peter had from the first, but perhaps that would change in time, especially if Jenny gave Abdul half a chance. And if he, like Peter, was caught up in falconry, he obviously preferred her companionship to that of his birds. Which was more than Jenny could say about Peter.

She asked if they might see the Serapeum, and she experienced the same sense of pleasurable anticipation she'd had the first time she'd descended the stairway to the gloom of what was undoubtedly one of the most bizarre subterranean burial complexes to be found in all of Egypt—or anywhere else. As its name implied, the Serapeum was a temple devoted to Serapis, who was worshiped as a god of the dead. Several such temples had existed in Egypt, but this one at Saqqâra was unique as the funerary site of the sacred bull Apis, the bull being the god's incarnation on Earth. Though most of the above-ground buildings had been completely destroyed, there was evidence that there had once been a rather extensive complex on the site that had included a large temple with pylons, inner and outer courtyard and an avenue of sphinxes. In the underground tombs that Jenny and Abdul now entered, after leaving Abdul's bodyguards posted at the doorway, had been deposited the mummies of the Apis bulls from times prior to the pharaoh Amenhoptep III of the Eighteenth Dynasty down to those of the Roman era.

The gallery had been tunneled into the solid stone beneath the covering level of sand. It was dimly lighted by low-watt bulbs hanging from the ceiling, with more of those bulbs off than on. There was an unworldliness to the place that was reinforced by the echoing whispers of other visitors already lost somewhere within the shadows. Another tunnel shot off of the right of the one they were in, reminding Jenny of a maze and making her wonder whether they should tail string behind them as Theseus had done in the labyrinth on Crete that had been constructed for the half bull, half man Minotaur. However, both Abdul and Jenny had independently walked these hallways previously and knew there was little chance of actually getting lost, despite all indications to the contrary.

Intermittent chambers likewise hewn from the stone opened from the gallery. Each chamber had received a mummy of a sacred bull, many such remains having been found intact within their coffins at the time of Auguste Mariette's excavation in 1851. Most of the chambers were in darkness, but a few had been made available, via more dim lighting, for closer observation of their monolithic granite sarcophagi, each of which weighed up to sixty-five tons. It was at one such chamber, filled with its polished carved coffin, that Abdul and Jenny finally stopped, taking the six steps necessary to descend to the chamber's recessed floor. The lid of the massive sarcophagus had been conveniently slid partially to one side, allowing anyone who so wished to mount a ladder for a peek inside. Knowing the container was now empty, Jenny made do with examining the exquisite outer surface detail. She wished she or Abdul had thought to bring a flashlight to better illuminate the workmanship.

Her attention, however, was soon diverted from the coffin to Abdul when she got the distinct feeling he was staring at her. Turning to face him, she caught the gaze of his dark steady eyes. He stood between her and the exit, completely filling the small space between sarcophagus and chamber wall. "Oh, but you're beautiful!" he said, a strange tremor in his voice. "But then you know that, don't you?" His comment had come so unexpectedly that Jenny didn't know what to say. She was overcome with conflicting emotions—flattered that he thought her beautiful, yet slightly embarrassed by his having gone so far as to tell her. While this compliment had been similar to the one delivered at

Giza when he had been standing with the horses, it somehow came with far more impact now. "But maybe I'm overstepping my bounds, yes?" he asked, coming closer. There was nothing threatening about his advance, so Jenny didn't recoil reflexively. His commanding good looks were far more evident in the better lighting than they had been in the shadows from which he'd moved. His eyes were large pools of darkness, taking in all light and reflecting none of it. "Perhaps you're already spoken for?" he suggested. "By Peter?" he specified.

"By Peter?" Jenny echoed. No doubt Abdul was aware that she was attracted to Peter, though she was embarrassed to think it was so obvious. But spoken for? Of course she was not spoken for. "Peter and I just met yesterday," she said, slightly flustered. She struggled to remain calm—not only because she had been surprised by Abdul's interest in her, but also because she wanted to hide her interest in Peter. "Although we're associates scheduled to work together at Hierakonpolis, our meeting in Cairo was entirely unplanned."

"Yes, that's what he led me to suspect, too," Abdul said. "However, I thought it would be best to check. I have, after all, no desire to interfere if you and he have reached an understanding. Nor, quite frankly, do I wish to embark upon a plan for winning you if there's no chance for me from the outset."

"Abdul, I . . ." she began, not knowing where to go from there. This on top of the conflicting emotions she had been experiencing lately toward Peter was enough to confuse her completely.

"Oh, I can certainly hold my own in any battle against equal odds," Abdul said. "I'm not, after all, without my own arsenal of decided charm." His warm smile made light of his boast. "I just wanted to make sure I wouldn't be treading on any toes. Not yours. Not Peters."

"Peter certainly doesn't think about me...that way," she said, finding her mouth gone dry, wondering why it had been somehow painful to make that admission about Peter's disinterest. "We're merely business associates," she said, adding with a surge of emotion that made her voice crack noticeably, "and not even very close ones at that."

"While I doubt you're fool enough really to believe that—or think me fool enough to believe it, too—I do derive hope from its having been said," Abdul replied, reaching out and putting a hand to each of her shoulders. If Jenny had expected the same lightning-bolt sensations to accompany his touch as had always accompanied Peter's, she found none. She was simultaneously disappointed and pleased by their absence. "But I'll tell you why I shall succeed, now that I know there's an opening," Abdul said, drawing her closer to him. "Because victory goes to the fleet of foot, and Peter has been hanging back, for whatever reasons. He's too slow to express his emotions, while I will let you know mine from the start. I love you, Jenny Mowry," he said, his voice a low and caressing whisper.

"I loved you from the very first moment I set eyes on you in that hotel lobby, and I want you more than anything else in the world. Does my want frighten you?"

It should have amazed Jenny that he had conceived so strong a passion for her without even knowing her. She had spoken to Peter about love at first sight, but it was not a notion to be taken seriously. Abdul, this powerful lord of the desert, seemed used to deciding what he wanted without much thought—and used to assuming he would get what he wanted. And if Jenny had wanted him, she *would* have been frightened by the suddenness of his declaration of love. But it didn't frighten her, though she wished with all her heart that it did, because she felt there had to be something wrong with her for not experiencing some kind of dangerous thrill in living the fantasy of many a young girl to be whisked off her feet by a handsome desert sheikh.

"You mustn't be frightened," he said, having mistaken her silence for an affirmative reply to his question. "We sheikhs aren't really the impulsive and passionate men so often stereotyped in literature. Not quite, anyway," he amended with a smile. "I have a little more finesse than to carry you screaming to my camel in order to spirit you away to some isolated spot in the desert where you'd learn to love me or grow old loving no one."

Jenny wondered if she wouldn't have preferred the kidnapping, the swift desert ride, the seduction beneath stately palms at some romantic oasis. It would have simplified things tremendously by entirely removing the chore of putting her feelings for Abdul and Peter into perspective. "I really don't think I'm ready for any kind of relationship right now, Abdul," she said, wondering if that were really true. Lately she had felt a lack in her life, an emptiness that her profession no longer seemed to fill. Perhaps that was because she had finally managed, after years of struggle, to reach a significant position in the field of archaeology and now she missed the vigorous expenditure of energy that had been necessary in her striving for success. That this mysterious lack had something to do with her personal life seemed evident by the way she had recently gone back to her childhood obsession with her grandmother's tragedy. She had grabbed at the chance of joining the Hierakonpolis dig, deluding herself into believing that the fact that Peter Donas would be there was destiny. She was dangerously on the brink of letting her undefined needs and overindulged fantasies run away with her common sense. She had felt the magic of Peter's embrace atop the pyramid just a few short hours ago, and she couldn't deny that she had responded, just as Geraldine Fowler would have responded to the heated embrace of her lover. But she was not Geraldine Fowler, Peter was not Frederic Donas, and if she didn't get hold of herself soon, she was liable to find herself a prime candidate for a psychiatrist's couch. "It has nothing whatsoever to do with you personally and certainly not with my taking lightly anything you've said," she remarked to Abdul. "It's merely that I have a firm commitment to my job, and I decided a long time ago that certain private aspects of my life would have to take a back seat."

He put the fingertips of his right hand to her lips to motion her silence. Her immediate reaction was to think he had heard someone coming. Since Peter had said he might join them, she glanced furtively over Abdul's shoulder, expecting to see Peter there with a frown on his handsome face as he looked down on the scene he had obviously interrupted. She realized Peter wasn't there, but her heart continued beating with excitement at the thought that he might have been. However, he was back with Hatshepsût, hardly caring if Jenny fell under the charmed spell of Abdul—or of anyone else, for that matter. "Don't say anything now," Abdul said, "except to promise you'll take the time to think about it."

"Yes," Jenny finally granted, "I'll certainly do that." At least he had mentioned love. . . not leaped at the prospect of a physical relationship, as Peter had done. Also, Abdul seemed patient, undemanding, whereas Peter had expected Jenny's passion to match his own immediately. It was absurd to think Abdul could actually love her at first sight; it was far too romantic an idea. But still, it would be stupid not to give this whatever chance it had for development—especially since there didn't seem to be much other promise for romance. Despite Abdul's not-so-veiled insinuations that he considered Peter his competitor for her affections, Jenny knew better. Whatever there could have been between her and Peter had been forever destroyed by a peregrine falcon and by an incident that had happened between their grandparents more than half a century earlier at Thebes.

"I want to kiss you, Jenny," Abdul said, his fingertips having slipped from her lips to a point beneath her chin where he could angle her face slightly upward to match her lips to his easily. "I want to kiss you very much." She let him do so, once again missing the fireworks. But then fireworks weren't everything in a relationship. Abdul was exotic, handsome, kind, considerate, gentle and apparently very wealthy. He was everything a woman could want in a husband or in a lover, except that Jenny still couldn't be completely sure she was looking for either. "Peter's disadvantage is that it's not in his blood to be romantic," Abdul said, speaking once again of his rival. "While some men have lost the art of romance, seduction and gallantry, not all have!" Jenny had every reason to disagree with him. Oh, not about his being romantic. There was certainly no denying the romantic aspects of riding horses through the desert, lounging in the comfort of a Bedouin tent, being told she was loved by a man whose exotic good looks and charm would have bowled over almost anyone. But Peter was romantic, too. He had walked with her on a balmy night in Cairo, his arm around her waist, while palm trees shifted in silent breezes and the moon shone on the rippling surface of the Nile. He had invited her to climb the Pyramid of Cheops to view a sunrise, reciting New Kingdom love poetry and telling her he wanted to make love with her. And the location in which Peter had chosen to profess his desire for her had been a far more romantic locale than this subterranean catacomb.

Yes, Jenny definitely needed to think—and somewhere other than here with Abdul. If she let him kiss her again, it was because he rather caught her off guard this second time, and once the kiss had begun, it would have been a little inconsistent suddenly to begin fighting him off.

"I hope I'm not interrupting anything," Peter said, knowing he was and not much giving a damn. Jenny pushed away from Abdul, automatically glancing beyond him and upward to the top of the steps where Peter and one of Abdul's bodyguards were standing. There was no denying that at that moment Jenny felt very much as if she had been some farm girl whose father had just caught her behind the woodpile receiving passionate kisses from the local Don Juan. There was something undeniably condemning about the look Peter gave her—a combination of hurt and suspicion that made her feel guilty. Following closely on the tail of her guilt, however, was anger—anger not only at being spied on, but also at the fact that this scene might have been engineered by Peter in the first place. He could just as easily have come with them, instead of stealthily following behind like a common sneak.

"Actually, we were just about to head back," Abdul said. Though Jenny was disturbed, he seemed to have taken the interruption in stride, rather pleased that his intentions were now clearly out in the open and there could be no accusations later that he had hit anyone below the belt. "I hope you're both as ready for a good meal as I am."

Jenny's anger did not subside on the way back to the encampment—in fact, it increased whenever she caught one of the condemning glances Peter kept casting in her direction. She was furious that something inside her really seemed to care what he thought of her, especially since her actions were none of his damned business. If he hadn't got all hot and bothered over a peregrine falcon, they could have been in Cairo sightseeing at the Citadel and Muhammad Ali Mosque about then, and Jenny would have had no notion whatsoever of how Abdul Jerada felt about her. But oh, no, he had to come and watch Hatshepsût, then not even have the common decency to allow her the privacy of getting on with her own life. She found Peter maddeningly contradictory, and she was frustrated that she couldn't seem to read him. He fluctuated confusingly between hot and cold. Now he was acting as though he cared that she had been kissing Abdul, whereas for most of that morning he'd cared about nothing except the aerobatics of a bird. If he really objected to what she and Abdul had been doing, he shouldn't have thrown them together by refusing to come along. If his failure to accompany them had been specifically designed to trap them into doing something, then he deserved the eyeful he got. If his hurt now was merely the bruised ego of a man who had missed his chance, a man upset because he thought another man hadn't, then he was thoroughly despicable and not very confident of his manhood in the bargain.

They ate lunch while sitting on rug-covered sand in the main room of the tent, a low table covered with food before them. They reclined against large overstuffed pillows and dined on *mashi*—a selection of cold pepper, tomatoes, zucchini and miniature eggplant stuffed with a lightly spiced rice; *labon zabadi*—Egyptian yogurt that had been flavored with strawberry preserve; a salad of spicy tomatoes and soft white cheese eaten with pieces of thin Egyptian bread called *aish shami*; a kabob made of lean pieces of lamb cut into small cubes and marinated in a mixture of onion shavings, parsley, marjoram, lemon juice, salt and pepper before being skewered and grilled over hot charcoal; and *umm ali*—an exquisite bread pudding topped with pine nuts and milk and served piping hot. Jenny only wished she could have done the meal justice, since it was apparent that someone had gone to a good deal of bother in its preparation. She was little consoled that Peter seemed no more enticed by the offered delicacies than she was. At least nothing seemed to have affected Abdul's appetite—which was considerable. He went back for seconds, then thirds, all of the while attempting to carry on a conversation that continually kept drifting into long periods of silence. Jenny had long since given up as hopeless any attempt to get anything out of Peter except an occasional monosyllable that couldn't even pass for small talk.

"Well, since I suppose you two are ready to call it a day, how would you like to make the trip back to Cairo in the comfort of a car?" Abdul asked. He couldn't have come up with a better suggestion as far as Jenny was concerned. The ride there had been accompanied by Peter's unending questions regarding bewits and bells, manning and mews, haggards and halsbands, followed by Abdul's in-depth answers. Jenny had no desire to spend the next few hours on horseback with someone who suddenly seemed determined not to be drawn into conversation even about his all-consuming passion—falconry. "I've sent someone for a Land Rover to take you to the road at Saqqara, where my car is waiting," Abdul said, stretching across the table for one final juicy cube of lamb kabob. "You must let me thank you for allowing me the pleasure of your company." Perhaps his thanks had been meant to include Peter, too, but he was looking only at Jenny.

"The pleasure was all ours, I assure you," Jenny said, taking her cue to push back from the table and come to her feet.

"We must make it a point to do this again sometime," Abdul said, all smiles. "You say you're sailing on the *Osiris* tomorrow morning, Jenny?"

"Yes," she answered, rather looking forward to those days she would have to herself. "I'm not due at the dig until the twenty-seventh."

"Perhaps, then, I shall see you there," Abdul said. "I have extensive business commitments that will be taking me down to that area. May I call on you?"

Peter, who had been edging his way to the door, paused suddenly. Jenny was well aware that he had done so. "Yes, by all means, *do* stop by," Jenny said. Without a word Peter stepped outside, leaving Jenny and Abdul alone. "But you'd better bring Hatshepsût along with you if you want Peter's interest," Jenny added. Though she had meant it more as a silent afterthought, it had come out bitterly vocal.

"I have an extensive mews at my villa in Aswân," Abdul said with a knowing smile. *Mews* was the falconer's term for those accommodations constructed exclusively for the use of the owner's hawks. "I'd be most happy to put it at Peter's disposal when I'm there," he added.

"The Land Rover is coming," Peter said, sticking his head back inside. Jenny could very well imagine that he might have thought he was going to catch her and Abdul in a madly passionate embrace. Well, they had fooled him, and Jenny headed for the outside before Abdul could get any ideas of his own. She had had quite enough kisses for one day.

They moved to the outer edge of the awning, keeping to a line of shade that no longer seemed quite adequate in the face of a heat that was increasing now but that toward nightfall would undergo a sudden and almost miraculous dissipation. Land, unlike water, didn't retain warmth, and this was nowhere better illustrated than in the Sahara, where one could be sweating one minute before sunset and freezing one minute after the sun had gone down.

The Land Rover was approaching from one of the larger dunes that kept the camp isolated from Saqqâra. They all turned in its direction, watching as it approached, picked up speed and veered amid a flurry of loud cracking sounds. That someone in the Land Rover might be shooting at them was the last thought that ever would have entered Jenny's mind. Thank God there had been more than one person with faster reflexes than her own!

Peter took hold of her arm, jerking her down alongside himself. There was another volley of shots. Peter took a quick glance up, rose and scooped her up in both of his strong arms, heading back for the tent, where he lowered her unceremoniously to the floor. "Damn it, Jenny, stay down and stay put!" he commanded, and was gone before she really even knew what was happening.

One of Abdul's bodyguards had stopped the vehicle the best way he knew how—by riding his horse in front of it. The force of impact had permanently crippled the animal, later to be put out of its misery, and had tossed the rider to one side, injuring him. The Land Rover had rolled on its side, spilling its three occupants, shaken but still functioning, onto the sand.

Abdul was down, his head bloodied by a bullet. If Abdul wasn't dead, Peter had apparently figured the man soon would be if left in his presently exposed position. "Peter! Come back!" Jenny screamed as soon as she realized he had left her to return to a world suddenly very much alive with the sound and danger of gunfire. She had sense enough to realize it would be best to stay put, knowing the tent might not stop a bullet but would prevent anyone from taking accurate aim. But she was too worried about Peter's safety to refrain from endangering herself as much as was necessary to assure that he was still alive. When she moved to the entrance of the tent, the scene she witnessed made her heart lodge in her throat. Peter had gone back for Abdul, having successfully thrown the Arab's unconscious body over his shoulder by the time Jenny was kneeling in a position to see what was happening. Even as she looked on, several bullets kicked up the sand at Peter's feet. He took two steps forward and dropped to his knees. "Peter, my God, Peter!" Jenny screamed, sure he was dead and feeling a surge of grief jet through her accompanied by a determination to get at the men responsible, even if she had to attack them with her bare hands. She got up and lifted the flap of the tent just as Peter struggled to his feet.

Abdul still on his shoulder, Peter saw her. "Damn it, Jenny!" he shouted. "Get down!" Whatever else he said, and he did say more, it was lost in a spurt of gunfire. Once again Jenny thought for sure one or more of the bullets had hit him. It had certainly sounded as though there were too many for him to have possibly survived. Their origin, however, was a submachine gun fired from the camp to keep the enemy under cover long enough for Peter and Abdul to complete a successful retreat.

Peter came into the tent and collapsed with his burden. Jenny saw, with indescribable horror, that the whole front of his shirt was soaked with blood. With a swiftness born of near hysteria, she crawled over to him, taking hold of his shirt along its hem and making an attempt to pull it up far enough to expose his wound. At the same time she hadn't the foggiest notion what she would do once she found the bullet hole, except that she would somehow have to stop the flow of blood. The shifting material revealed an expanse of ridged and rippled stomach muscles punctuated by a slightly indented navel. She pushed his shirt higher, finding her mind flashing with remembrance of how her fingers had blindly explored this very same territory only that morning.

"Jenny, what the hell are you doing?" he hissed, his massive hands taking hold of her wrists and holding them tightly. She told him something about his bullet wound, blood, needing a bandage, none of it coming out in a particularly lucid manner, except that in the end she apparently did get her message across. "I'm not the one who's hurt," he told her. More gunshots sounded outside. "Abdul is!" She couldn't believe Peter wasn't wounded. She certainly could tell blood when she saw it. She'd heard how shock sometimes numbed a person to pain, at least making death merciful. But she didn't want him to die. She had waited most of her twenty-nine years to meet him, and she refused to let him leave her after one day, taken from her before she really even had a chance to know him. She couldn't stand the thought of his being killed by some bullet that probably hadn't even been meant for him. She tried desperately to get back to the business of find-ing his wound, managing very little because of his refusal to let her do what she was attempting to for him.

"You're bleeding!" she told him, her voice cracking, furious that he was fighting her efforts. "Damn it, you're bleeding!"

"I'm fine," he insisted, still clasping her wrists in his large hands. His voice was calm and soothing, even though accompanied by the high whine of a bullet passing very near. "Do you hear me, Jenny? I'm fine." He must have sensed, though, that she wasn't buying it, the blood on his shirt—leaked there from Abdul's head wound—having made all of his assurances seem like lies. "Look," he said, "I'll show you if you just give me a chance. Okay?" He shook her gently to calm her. "Jenny? Okay, Jenny? I'll show you, all right?" He released her, gripped the lower edge of his shirt and peeled the garment off over his head. His chest was a chiseled

expanse of bronze-colored flesh, almost completely
absent of hair and composed of two well-defined
muscular squares above a washboarded stomach.
The sight took Jenny's breath away, even as she
breathed a sigh of relief at seeing Peter's satiny skin
free of any wound. "It's Abdul who's hurt, Jenny," Peter repeated.

She felt a sudden rush of guilt in realizing she
hadn't given Abdul more than a passing thought.
She hurried to make amends, moving into position
beside him.

"He's alive," Peter said, having had enough
sense to check the injured man's pulse. He was telling Jenny that he hoped Abdul wouldn't have to
wait too long for medical assistance when a well-
placed barrage of machine-gun bullets set the gas
tank of the overturned Land Rover off in a ball of
yellow orange flames.

CHAPTER FIVE

A POCKET OF PITCH exploded like a rifle shot in the heat of the campfire, making Jenny jump. The wood had been brought in by whoever had set up the campsite, since there were no trees, no bushes, no type of flora within the immediate area. It would have been more in keeping with their surroundings for them to have been burning camel dung, but Jenny had seen little of that lying around, either. She stirred the flames, marveling at the inane thoughts her mind could come up with to blot out the more startling reality of a Land Rover still smoking, three men killed and two men wounded, not including Abdul, who was with a doctor in the tent.

"Here, take this," Peter said, handing her a cup of hot coffee. He was seated with her by the fire. Up until the moment he had reached for the pot to pour the steaming contents, he had been silently absorbed in his own thoughts. "You look as if you could use it," he added. He wore one of the outer garments the Arabs used for additional warmth, and it was hiding the bloody shirt he had put back on. Jenny had on one of the wraps, too. The clothing had been volunteered by Abdul's men when it had finally become apparent that circumstances made anyone's departure prior to nightfall impossible. There had been all sorts of questions asked by the police, even more asked by a major in the Egyptian Army who had arrived on the scene via helicopter and had left a few minutes earlier with the bodies of the three dead men.

"The doctor would have told us at once if Abdul were in danger of dying," Jenny said. She didn't make it a question, determined to be positive. Peter chose to answer her anyway.

"Yes, I'm sure we would have heard," he said. "Head wounds often tend to look far worse than they are." Jenny had once been ice skating with friends on a country pond outside of Spokane, Washington, when a young boy had slipped and fallen. There had been a lot of blood then, too, but the kid was back on the pond as soon as his head had been bandaged. Getting a bump on the head, though, wasn't the same as getting hit in the head with a bullet. "It looked like only a graze," Peter added, though he didn't know enough about bullet wounds to make his attempt at consolation as convincing as he would have liked.

"It's freezing out here!" Jenny said with a violent shiver, sipping coffee to warm herself, wistfully wishing Peter would put his arm around her to share a bit of his warmth. At any other time the beauty of the night would have claimed her attention more than its cold. The sky was a vast canopy of blackness punctured by brilliant stars and a moon gone golden on the horizon.

She looked up at the approach of Zeid Talal. Zeid was one of Abdul's men who had been wounded, and he now wore his arm in a sling that was angled across his chest like a row of medals. He was a tall man with angular, almost Oriental features. His high cheekbones and hollow cheeks were only emphasized by the shadows cast from the flickering fire. "Come with me, please," he said, his voice the kind Jenny imagined would be quite suitable for a conspiratorial whisper.

She had expected to enter the tent to see Abdul laid flat on his back, being hovered over by the doctor who had arrived from somewhere soon after the incident had come to its exploding conclusion. The doctor was nowhere in sight, and Abdul was up and about, exhibiting such exuberance that Jenny had to blink hard to make sure she wasn't seeing things. The bandage wrapping his head, while beginning to stain red on his left temple, was no larger than the sweatband Jenny sometimes wore while playing tennis. "Ah, there you are!" he said in greeting. His dark eyes were mostly dilated pupils. Whether this was caused by the dim lighting, the preponderance of adrenaline that had been turned loose in his system by the excitement, the drug the doctor had probably administered to alleviate his pain, or a combination of the three, Jenny couldn't tell. "I certainly don't think our simple lunch really warranted such a spectacular leave-taking, do you?" he said in obvious good humor.

"How are you?" Jenny asked, unable to believe he should be up and around.

"It did look rather nasty," Peter added.

"Head wounds often look worse than they really are," Abdul said, echoing what Peter had told Jenny earlier. "I imagine I shall come through this with merely another battle scar." As if amused by his discussion of such wounds with Jenny, he smiled at their private joke. "And this one, I'm informed, will be far less impressive and certainly less interestingly positioned than some of the others."

"You have this happen to you often, do you?" Peter asked, not having been privy to any previous insights on the subject. "I'm afraid I would find the excitement a little hard to take."

Abdul laughed, motioning them over to the table now moved to the side of the tent. Sometime during the course of the afternoon and evening the lunch dishes had been completely cleared, replaced by a coffee service. "Sit down, please," Abdul said. "Unfortunately there's going to be another delay this one only a short one—before we can get you home. I'm afraid I put your car at the disposal of one of my men who, unlike myself, needed the more extensive facilities offered by a Cairo hospital. Coffee?" He didn't wait for their reply but proceeded to pour. He then turned to address Peter's question. "Actually, no, this doesn't happen all the time," he said, lowering himself to a more comfortable position on the floor, gathering his *galabia* in close around his folded legs. "It's been almost two years since the last attempt."

"But who would want to kill you?" Peter asked. It had been a question Jenny would have put forth herself if he hadn't beat her to it.

"Oh, we all have enemies, haven't we?" he answered cryptically.

"I can't imagine a colleague, even one whose theories I might have criticized, coming after me in retribution with a loaded gun," Peter said. For a moment Jenny suspected he might be referring to his bad-mouthing of her archaeological attempts to link Crete with Atlantis, but he didn't oblige her by taking the statement any further.

"It's the nature of my business that makes my enemies a little more volatile than yours," Abdul said, sipping his coffee.

"The oil business, right?" Peter asked. If he, like Jenny, had skirted the subject earlier, willing to let Abdul volunteer whatever he figured it was their business to know, he apparently now found the circumstances suddenly giving him a right to know more. Thinking about those circumstances, Jenny shivered once again at the recollection of how Peter had risked his life to pull Abdul out of the line of fire and how she had experienced such a life-numbing reaction to thinking Peter had been fatally wounded.

"Yes, oil," Abdul admitted, ostensibly agreeing that some explanation was in order. However, it soon became just as evident that he wasn't going to volunteer it without a bit of prodding—which Peter and soon Jenny were more than willing to engage.

"I'm not really all that sure I get the connection," Peter said. "Would it be too much to hope for a few more specifics?"

"Unfortunately a good deal of it is considered classified," Abdul replied. "However, I'm sure I can come up with a few facts that won't breach national security," he added with a wave of a hand that insinuated he sometimes felt all of the rules and regulations governing his present work assignment were a royal pain in the posterior. "Egypt is, as you might or might not know, not one of the Arab world's major producers of oil at the present," he said. "Oh, I realize many people imagine that *all* Arabs are floating atop an ocean of crude, but that really hasn't been proven the case in Egypt so far. I certainly won't bore you with statistics that are classified anyway, but our neighbor to the east, Saudi Arabia, puts out many more barrels for every one that we manage to squeeze out of Egyptian soil. I'm one of those people who would like to see Egypt's piece of the pie become just a little bit bigger. There are, needless to say, those who don't."

"For that the Saudis want you killed?" Jenny asked, thinking that could certainly be one logical conclusion to be drawn from what he had just said. Abdul, however, if his smile was any indication, didn't seem to agree.

"Quite frankly we're not really sure who's behind this latest assassination attempt," he admitted. "But I really do doubt it's the Saudis. You're well aware of the complexity of social, political and economic matters in this part of the world. Suffice it to say that I very much want Egypt's production of oil to increase, while there are others who do not. I suppose you might comment that powerful men have powerful enemies. Perhaps I flatter myself, but my enemies are many—and strong.''

"And by killing you, someone keeps Egypt's oil production back of the mark?'' Peter asked.

"Oh, I'm not that powerful! You give me a far more important position in the scheme of things than I really merit,'' Abdul said modestly. "I'm merely one piling of the foundation. However, knocking me out would certainly slow down things for a bit—though not, of course, forever.''

"*How* would it slow things down?'' Peter asked, and Jenny was glad he was there to ask that question. She wanted to hear the answer but would probably not have had the nerve to ask.

"I'm a very good organizer,'' Abdul obliged. "I have connections here through politics, position, family and wealth. I have contacts elsewhere in the world that I acquired while traveling extensively and going to school abroad. I know people with money who are looking for high-paying business investments. I know people who have the technology necessary for examining a piece of barren land and saying there is such-and-such potential for oil down there. I know people who own such barren land. Finally, I know people skilled enough to drill for that oil. I merely draw on those considerable resources at my disposal to bring everyone together into one happy family—although *happy* is usually a misnomer. And there's the rub! Fearful as they are that their associates' pockets are the ones being the most fully lined with gold, few end up happy in such arrangements. Ideally, therefore, there must be at least one person every party can trust. In many such instances I'm that man. With me dead the element of trust would suddenly be removed and the feuding would begin until a replacement could be found to fill the gap. When people are busy fighting among themselves very little constructive activity results. Wouldn't you agree?''

"How horrible, though, to be a walking target!" Jenny said, wondering if she could ever get used to living continually under such a shadow.

"It's not really," he contradicted her, surprising Jenny with his reply. "I find it merely makes each minute of my living that much more vibrant and intense. You can't truly appreciate the pure wonder of life until you've skirted close to the brink of losing it."

They heard the arrival of a jeep outside. Abdul put down his glass in a gesture of dismissal. "If you don't mind, Jenny, I'd like a quick word with Peter in private before he goes. If you'd be so kind as to tell the driver that Peter will be joining you shortly?''

"Of course," she said, curious as to what was so private that it could only be said between the two men. For a minute she thought that maybe Abdul's wound was more serious than it appeared, that he had merely been putting on an act for her benefit and was now preparing to tell Peter the truth. She discounted that idea soon enough, however, realizing there was no way he could have faked being so quickly and completely on his way to recovery. "I shall be looking forward to seeing you, then, at Hierakonpolis," she said, getting to her feet, "without the accompanying fireworks, I hope!" She decided Abdul just wanted to thank Peter in private for saving his life.

"If it is the will of Allah!" Abdul replied with a wistful smile, watching until Jenny exited from the tent before he turned to Peter in whispered undertone.

She identified herself to the driver, who went off for a quick cigarette to kill the time spent waiting for Peter. Jenny sat in the jeep, suffering the cold that hadn't left her—despite all the coffee—since the ill-fated Land Rover had come barreling down the hill toward her to release its deadly charge. It all seemed like a dream, especially the part where Peter had stripped off his shirt to show her that he'd walked through the fire unscathed.

She went over all of it in her mind, trying to pinpoint her feelings at every step along the way. Each time she managed to isolate an emotion, she tried her best to analyze the contributing factors behind it. It wasn't so much the surprise, shock and the excitement of the attack that had disturbed her. More significant, it seemed, were those feelings she had experienced from the moment she first realized

Peter had gone back for Abdul to the point at which she had realized—finally—that he had come back to her alive. As often as she told herself she had experienced no more anxiety than she would have felt in the face of any man subjecting himself to danger in her presence, she couldn't quite convince herself of that fact. The anger, frustration and utter helplessness she had experienced at the mere prospect of his dying had been so intense that she realized she had never before felt anything like it—except maybe when she had received the news that her parents were dead.

She had loved her parents. If she refused to believe she loved Peter, she was at least able to recognize that something was happening inside her, something, she decided, that would be better to stop now than to allow to flower. She reminded herself that Peter might very well be the incarnation of Frederic Donas and just as apt to betray love. She reminded herself that most of the Fowler women had been unlucky in romance: her grandmother, dying of heartbreak in Thebes; her mother, on the verge of asking for a divorce at the moment of an untimely death; several cousins whose marriages had ended on the rocks. She reminded herself that she had long ago resolved to remain unfettered by intimate involvement with any man in order to devote herself to a career she found demanding, interesting, rewarding and usually all-fulfilling. Thus any feelings she presently had for Peter had to be looked upon as an unwelcome threat to the life she had decided was best for her.

"Goodbye, then," Abdul said, emerging from the tent with Peter. "Although I suppose it's more au revoir, since it's now obvious we'll be seeing each other again."

"Yes, I suppose so," Peter said without much enthusiasm. It was his last utterance for several minutes, except for the undecipherable grunt he delivered by way of greeting when he climbed into the jeep, choosing the front seat and not the place beside Jenny. The driver emerged from the shadows after having quickly ground his cigarette in the sand and drove them to the main road at Saqqâra, pretty much retracing the route taken earlier by the Land Rover. The tracks of the latter were clearly visible in the headlights. Jenny knew it was still possible to find tracks in the desert made by troop movements during World War II. In a landscape that hadn't seen rain for literally decades, such things as mummies, pyramids, temples, tombs and car tracks were often preserved. "Well, aren't you even curious?" Peter finally asked after they had made the transfer at Saqqâra to a limousine with driver.

The Mercedes was far more comfortable than the jeep, and Jenny was even getting warm from the car's heater. She noticed blood stains on the upholstery, vivid reminders that this same vehicle had played ambulance a short time earlier, but she pulled her thoughts back sharply, unwilling to dwell on such morbid recollections. She shivered slightly at the realization that there but for the grace of God could have been Peter's blood. The thoughts of

how he might well have been killed or seriously
wounded performing his feat of heroism were still
giving her deep-running chills. "Curious about
what?" she asked, all innocence, although she knew
very well exactly what he was referring to.

"About why Abdul held me back for that private
tête-à-tête," Peter said. He was smiling, but his eyes
lacked the sparkle of genuine amusement.

"Actually, I wasn't curious in the least," Jenny
said—which was certainly a lie of first-class magni-
tude. She found it in exceptionally bad taste, however, for him to have brought up the subject.

"Why? Because you just naturally assumed he
wanted to thank me personally for pulling him out
of the jaws of death?" Peter asked. Off to the right
of the eastbound car was Memphis, an ancient city
that had reigned as Egypt's capital through four
hundred years, two successive dynasties and eigh-
teen kings after its founding by the legendary Menes
around 3000 B.C. In the darkness conspicuously little evidence was visible to suggest that it was from
here that a divided Egypt had first been joined
under a formalized central government. In the daylight the place would have been no more impressive,
boasting precious little of its famous past but an
alabaster sphinx from the Eighteenth Dynasty and a
small museum that housed a recumbent figure of
Ramses II. "Well, that's exactly what he wanted to
do," Peter continued. "Thank me."

"You deserve his thanks *and* mine," Jenny said,
finding her comment gracious, considering he had

decided to toot his own horn immodestly. "It was a very brave thing that you did."

"Abdul thought so, too," Peter said. The car turned left, heading north toward Cairo. "So much so that he figured I should somehow be rewarded for a feat of derring-do that I assured him had been more gut reaction than any consciously formulated plan to come to his rescue."

"Don't downgrade what you did!" Jenny insisted. If she resented his initial tendency to boast, she also resented his pretending he'd merely done what anyone else would have done under the circumstances. There was no way he was going to tell her there wouldn't have been some men who would have thought only of themselves at such a moment, men who wouldn't have bothered pulling Abdul out of the line of fire after already having got themselves to safety.

"He wanted to offer me reimbursement for my efforts," Peter said. "I mean, you and I both know I rescued a very rich, very important man, don't we? We know that because he told us so." Jenny was about to remind him that Abdul hadn't volunteered that information without them having had to pry it out of him, but Peter apparently wasn't going to let her get a word in edgewise. "So naturally I could have expected all sorts of offers for riches and power, don't you think?" Peter asked. "Maybe even a nice big lump of British pound sterling?"

"I find this conversation in extremely bad taste," she said, verbalizing what she had up until then only been thinking. "I would have hoped you would. have been gentleman enough to keep Abdul's offer of generosity an entirely private matter, as Abdul had the good manners to do in the first place."

"As a matter of fact, he did offer me a sizable amount of money as a reward for my heroism," Peter continued, ignoring her comment. Jenny turned her face to the window, determined she wasn't going to give him the satisfaction of her attention any longer. "Had I not already had more money than I could ever need, it would certainly have been a tempting offer," he added. "But as my family has a good deal of the filthy old stuff lying around—a feat extremely difficult to pull off in Great Britain these days, let me remind you—I was able to tell him magnanimously that the pleasure of his rescue had been all mine, my reward being the inner satisfaction of having done my good deed for the day." He paused for a good long while, and Jenny thought he had finally decided to shut up. It was about time, too. He had become totally obnoxious. To their right the Nile flowed toward the sea. Jenny found it not the least romantic, marred by the outline of two ugly barges passing in the night. She was beginning to wish she and Peter were merely passing in the night. She'd been a silly fool even to subject herself to this meeting between them. "Tell me, Jenny," Peter started up to Jenny's dismay, "you were aware that my family had money, weren't you? Or were you?"

"I thought it was an unwritten rule of etiquette

that one was never so gross as to discuss one's family finances," Jenny retorted, turning to him. Damned right she knew his family had money! And she knew from whence it had come, too. Not hard won by any great feats by one or two industrious men who worked and sweated in honest labor to begin a dynasty. Oh, no! The Donases' first fortune had been derived from the slave trade—the running of human merchandise, under the most primitive, inhumane and unsanitary conditions, between Africa and the markets of the New World. Hardly savory money, that! When they had gone legitimate, moving on from slaves to eventual major investments in South American rubber, the development of synthetic rubber had put the Donases' finances into a slide. The fortunes had gone progressively downhill until Frederic Donas had performed the needed miracle that had brought the family back to solvency. Not, mind you, by the sweat of his brow, either, but merely by marrying Caroline Byner, whose father luckily had enough money from his mineral investments to support just about everybody involved in the manner to which they had all found it very easy to become accustomed.

"I mention it only so that you can better appreciate the reward Abdul finally did reckon had to be irresistible to a man who apparently had everything," Peter said. He accompanied his words with a sarcastic laugh. "Although as it turns out he was sadly mistaken. I can't begin to imagine what made him think I was vaguely interested in you in the first place."

There was a teasing tone to his voice, but nonetheless Jenny was astounded. "In me?" she questioned, her response having been shocked out of her.

"My reaction exactly!" Peter said. He then turned to gaze out the window on his side of the car, as if he were now quite prepared to let the subject drop if Jenny were. But of course he knew good and well that Jenny would not be satisfied to leave matters where they stood.

"What do you mean, he thought you were interested in me?" she demanded, finding this man frustrating in the extreme. She didn't know what game he was playing, but she had every intention of finding out.

"Well, first off, we do know that he's interested in you, don't we, Jenny?" Peter said. He turned back to her from the window and added, "And vice versa." Jenny could not tell whether his light tone was intended to tease or to irritate her.

"That's none of your damned business!" she shot back, thoroughly furious.

"Granted!" Peter replied with a sudden iciness to his voice that put the tinkling of bewit bells to shame. "Your and Abdul Jerada's romantic inclinations certainly have nothing whatsoever to do with me—which is the whole point of my beginning this little discourse in the first place."

The pyramids of Giza had become visible in the distance, flashing on and off like neon signs—an indication of a Sound and Light show in progress. Each summer evening at eight-thirty a "History

Began Here" recording overdramatically blared out facts and figures, spotlights playing on pertinent Giza monuments, while tourists sat huddled en masse on folding chairs.

"Get to the point, will you!" Jenny commanded.

"He offered to give up the chase," Peter said.

"What chase?" Jenny asked; she was no longer interested in being discreet about the men's private conversation—she wanted to know the facts now.

"His chase after you, of course," Peter said. Jenny tried to read his face there in the darkness of the car and had a good deal of difficulty doing so, her inner turmoil not helping her any.

"Let me get this straight," she said, the obviously controlled cadence of her voice showing that she was nowhere near as calm as she would have liked to appear. "As your proposed reward for saving Abdul's life he agreed to quit chasing...me?" She added the pronoun with an accompanying little laugh that she hoped relayed her opinion of the total ludicrousness of what he had been saying.

"Damned good of him, don't you think?" Peter asked, his voice edged with sharp sarcasm. "I mean, it's not every man who would willingly sacrifice his and his true love's happiness out of gratitude to another man, is it?"

"You're lying!" Jenny accused, her voice rising excitedly.

"Don't worry, though," Peter replied, his words tinged with more than a little bitterness. "I wouldn't think of interfering in the course of true romance. I told him that no matter how tremendously flattered I was by his willingness to make the ultimate sacrifice on my behalf, it was hardly necessary, since the lady in question had obviously already made her choice, and it wasn't me." He saw how that comment left her stuttering, then speechless, and he rushed right into the breach. "I'm certainly not so much of a masochist as to enjoy banging my head against a brick wall," he continued. "And after all you *do* have every right to pick whom you willingly kiss and whom you stop in midstream."

"I hardly stopped you in midstream!" Jenny reminded him loudly, unable to control her building fury any longer. It was an indication of the driver's discretion that he hadn't once turned around to investigate the verbal uproar taking place in the back seat. "All I did was stop you from taking things much further than any decent man should have expected to on a second date with someone other than a common tramp."

"And just how far, I wonder, would you have gone with Abdul Jerada on the very first date if I hadn't interrupted?" he asked. Jenny slapped his face—hard. The resounding contact of flesh against flesh was reminiscent of the recent gunfire.

"You," she said, her voice trembling, the palm of her hand stinging, "are disgusting! Abdul Jerada is a gentleman who at least has the common decency to respect the notion that love is important. He may be misguided in thinking too highly of me too soon, but at least he is not afraid of the word *love*," she hurried on, realizing it would have been just like him to misinterpret her definition and begin arguing semantics. "Which is far different from just 'making love to' somebody."

"I never told you I wanted to make love 'to' you," he declared, immediately seeing that she had all intention of contradicting him. "I said I wanted to make love 'with' you, and there is, my dear Jenny, a world of difference between the two."

Jenny found herself momentarily without anything to say, her planned retort having suddenly become invalid. She remembered the incident atop the pyramid with a crystal clarity; she had known all along which preposition he had used. She had merely—incorrectly, it seemed—assumed he had been indiscriminate in choosing his vocabulary. That he had discerned the difference to the point of now being able to call it to her attention left her feeling she might have misjudged him. She realized, at least vaguely, that she was being a bit hysterical about all this, but she did not understand why she was overreacting. Maybe it was because Peter's seeming lack of genuine interest in her filled her with hopelessness. "Abdul is not afraid of love," she stated for want of anything else to say, having grown exceedingly uncomfortable in the silence that had fallen between them.

"How do you know that?" he asked. "Because he told you he loves you?" The car had long since entered the city and was approaching the Kû al-Tahrir. The lights from the street lamps on the bridge reflected off Peter, showing the strong lines and virile planes of his face. "You think a man loves you just because he tells you so? I love you, Jenny Mowry! Does that mean it's true?"

"No," she admitted, hearing her voice crack in her throat, finding it cruel that he should be mocking her need for honest sentiment. The car was turning left on the Korneish al-Nil, the Hilton in all its lighted splendor directly ahead.

"No?" Peter asked. "No?" he repeated, inviting her to contradict herself. "I suggest, Jenny Mowry, that you somehow learn to differentiate between a lie and the genuine expression of someone's affections before you end up making one of the biggest mistakes of your life." The Mercedes had stopped at the main entrance to the hotel. Peter opened the car door on his side and got out, entering the building without a backward glance.

Jenny started to cry. She told herself she had every right to do so, considering the tensions that had been building inside her. The man was a brute for trying to cheapen her relationship with Abdul by insinuating that it was something far more than it was. She certainly wouldn't have let the kiss in the Serapeum progress any further than had the kiss atop the pyramid. In fact, she had been prepared not to let it progress nearly as far. She was not an object to be grabbed whenever some man felt like grabbing. She had always believed that physical signs of passion were valueless unless they were accompanied by true feeling. Somehow Abdul seemed incapable of acting without feeling, but about Peter she was not so sure. For him to suggest that she would merely toy with Abdul angered her. Perhaps from Peter, though, she should have expected as much, considering he was Frederic Donas's grandson. The pain she was now feeling sprang from her reluctantly admitted wish that Peter might have turned out differently from his grandfather. She was hopelessly romantic enough to have secretly wanted a Romeo to play opposite her Juliet. Well, life certainly wasn't a Shakespearean play wherein two families were finally reunited by star-crossed lovers, and Jenny could only rationalize that she was far better off because of it. Neither Romeo nor Juliet came to a very happy end.

She was thankful the driver continued to be tactful and was not in a hurry to get her out of the car. She would have looked ridiculous walking through the lobby of the hotel with tears streaming down her face. Luckily she had a couple of Kleenexes in her pocket that held her in good stead. Peter wasn't worth the shedding of one more tear, although crying had made her feel better.

The armed guard at the revolving door was a little less gracious than the driver of the car, probably because it was his job to be suspicious. It wasn't often a man and a woman quarreled in the Hilton driveway, the woman breaking into tears as a result. He searched her purse, no doubt having visions of her going after her unfaithful lover with a gun or at least blowing him up with the bomb she always carried in her handbag with her mad money—just in case.

She headed for her room, more determined than ever to get cold water on her face after the desk clerk asked if there was anything wrong. The three tourists with whom she rode up in the elevator exercised the greatest discretion and let her know that she could have cried up gale-force winds without their interfering to ask what the trouble was.

She did look a little haggard, she decided, as she faced the mirror in her bathroom. It was no longer a mystery why the guard might have mistaken her for a jilted mad bomber. However, the damage wasn't anything that couldn't be repaired by taking a warm shower and running a comb through her blond hair a few times.

She ordered supper in her room, hardly touching the two veal cutlets, the green salad, or the half bottle of the local red wine. After that she went to bed, figuring she was more than ready for a rest. She was wrong; she found herself unable to sleep, no matter how hard she tried. She blamed it on the sound of the traffic, though it was no more raucous than it had been on any other night. The real problem was Peter Donas, whom she couldn't get out of her mind. She went over and over the happenings of the day and evening: Peter when she had been thrilled at the sound of his voice on the phone; Peter when she had stopped exhausted on the pyramid to rest her head against his shoulder; Peter when they had watched the sunrise, he reciting love poetry, kissing her, requesting they make love; Peter when he was more interested in a falcon than in spending the rest of the day with her; Peter when he had walked in on her and Abdul kissing; Peter when she had been struck numb by the thought that he was dying; and finally, Peter and his unfair accusations on the ride back to the hotel. . . .

She was glad she was going to have a few days on the ship to herself. She needed that time to sort out thoughts, and emotions that certainly refused to come together for her now. She hoped that when she disembarked at that distant spot up the Nile, she would have a better idea of how all this really affected her life, if it affected it at all. She missed those days when everything had seemed more clear-cut, when she had known exactly who she was—Jenny Mowry, archaeologist—and had known what she wanted—a position of respect among her peers within the scientific community. She longed for a return to those "good old days," simultaneously fearing that nostalgia had a definite way of erasing bad aspects and reinforcing good ones. Whether it was a lie or not that she had been completely happy in her world before hearing that Peter Donas would be at the dig at Hierakonpolis, she wasn't happy now. Lying there in bed, she remembered how Peter had looked on Hatshepsût as if the bird could do no wrong, even when the falcon had let one of the pigeons outmaneuver her. Yet he had been so quick to condemn Jenny for just one simple kiss from Abdul. Like the bird's, her error, too, had been only a mistake in timing. The thought made her sick at heart. She was not the least pleased that she continued to care that Peter didn't care. He wasn't the kind of man she should have allowed into her life, and she had been a fool for having thrown caution to the wind to play with emotional fire. Peter Donas was too tied up with her childhood fantasies and too much of a flesh-and-blood man for Jenny to have thought she might brush his world and come out unsinged. He was the flickering flame, she the moth somehow drawn to him by incidents that had happened in Thebes before either of them had been born. If she weren't careful, she would circle too close and, unlike the fabled phoenix, not survive the resulting holocaust—just as Geraldine Fowler hadn't survived her meeting with Frederic Donas so many years earlier.

Even if she didn't believe in reincarnation, there was no denying she was her mother's daughter, no denying her mother was the daughter of Geraldine Fowler, no denying there had been a passing on of genes from one generation to the next. If Geraldine had begun the scrapbook on Frederic Donas, it had been Jenny's mother who had added other bits and pieces on the Donas clan. Jenny had taken up the same duty as if it had been a religious ritual. She was now in Egypt, like a swallow that had finally returned home to Capistrano—if a generation late.

"I am not Geraldine Fowler!" she said aloud, throwing back her covers and getting out of bed. She began to pack, needing something to occupy her mind. Unfortunately she had long ago got down the knack of packing, and she was soon back to lying in bed, thinking, thinking, thinking.

When she finally did sleep, she dreamed only of Peter, of his kissing her in a warm desert night, of his asking her to make love with him. And Jenny wanted more than anything to make love with him, would have made love with him, except that a hawk very much like Hatshepsût, only a thousand times bigger, swooped down to carry him away, leaving Jenny simultaneously heartsick and relieved—heartsick that Peter had been whisked off to an uncertain end, relieved that she had been saved from making love with a man who didn't really love her.

CHAPTER SIX

"Oh, of course, Miss Mowry. Welcome aboard the *Osiris*," the man said, meeting her at the head of the gangway and taking her ticket. He wasn't the captain, the suit he had on in lieu of a uniform telling her that, although she would later learn that the Egyptian crew wore nothing more indicative of rank than typical *galabias*. She correctly assumed he was under the employ of the Hilton, the ship being a floating extension of the hotel. "Your bag?" he asked, motioning toward the suitcase in possession of the porter who had trailed her on board.

"Yes," she admitted, turning to take care of the porter for his services while keeping out an additional Egyptian pound for the young man the official greeter called over to escort her to her cabin.

"If there's anything I can do to make your trip more interesting or enjoyable, Miss Mowry," the man said before turning her completely over to the steward, "please don't hesitate to let me know." Jenny found the thought nice enough but imagined the offer had been honed to its present perfection only because it had been practiced on so many tourists who had boarded this particular vessel since its maiden voyage over fourteen years earlier. German-built, the ship had none of the atmosphere of the old paddle steamers that had once plied this river and had been immortalized in the movie version of Agatha Christie's *Death on the Nile*, but it was far better equipped to handle the demands of twentieth-century tourists who considered they were roughing it if their bathroom was two doors down the hall. The 270-foot ship was streamlined on the outside, in contrast to the newer but more blockish cruise ships operated by the Sheraton Hotel chain. Painted blue and white, with three decks, the *Osiris* had conveniences that included air conditioning, dining room, bar, boutique, game room, sun deck and swimming pool.

Whether Jenny's cabin was comfortable was a little hard to tell at first glance. Less difficult to determine was that it was certainly too small for the profusion of flowers that overflowed it. They were everywhere—on the bed, on the floor, on the shelf that ran beneath the porthole. There was a bouquet propped in the open door of the bathroom and another to be seen on the closed toilet seat. Gladioli—all-white and more expensive than roses in Egypt. The steward looked lost as to where he was supposed to put her bag in a room that was already too full. Jenny moved a couple of the larger arrangements to one side, damaging more than one flower in the process, and instructed him to put the bag in the available space. When he left, shutting the door behind him, she felt as if she had somehow stumbled into a flower shop. She could not possibly leave things as they were, although she was reluctant to begin simply chucking flowers out the porthole. They were exceptionally beautiful, and they had cost someone a bundle.

She had immediately thought of Peter, figuring that he must have realized how obnoxious he had been and that he had decided to make amends. Although he had gone all out, Jenny wasn't sure it was enough. Hurt feelings couldn't always be rectified with the mere wave of a bulging pocketbook in the face of a florist only too delighted to get the business.

"I'm looking forward to our next few days together!" she read on the card she finally found stuck underneath the edge of one vase. She read the card again, and it dawned on her that the flowers weren't a peace offering being given in a wish of bon voyage. Peter was actually planning to come with her. She shivered—a sensation that wasn't altogether unpleasurable. It was the same feeling she sometimes got just prior to that first descent on a roller coaster as she savored what she was about to experience while dreading it just the same. He seemed to delight in putting her off-balance, first by showing up at the Egyptian Museum, now by showing up here. Both times she had found herself in need of time to sort out her feelings; he had stolen that needed time from her. If she had been hard pressed to avoid him in a city of millions, she had very little hope for success in a world suddenly telescoped to less than two hundred passengers on a cruise ship. She was still lost in that swirl of disturbing thoughts when she answered the knock at the door to find Peter standing there.

"Hi," he said, looking decidedly sheepish, a little embarrassed and totally handsome. "I've brought a peace offering," he said, extending the small crystal vase and its one long-stemmed orange rosebud. "I was insufferably rude," he said, "and I didn't think I should let you have the next few days to brood over how badly I acted, considering we're going to have to work together for two months. So take pity on this poor inconsiderate bastard, will you? He was merely acting like a jealous fool, and he had no right whatsoever to presume so much." He shuffled his feet uneasily and smiled a smile that would have charmed the Devil. "The rosebud reminded me of the sunrise," he said, nodding toward the flower Jenny now held in her hand. "And all sunrises must remind me of you." There was no denying his personal apology carried far more impact than a whole shipload of flowers. Nor had she missed his reference to his having acted like a jealous fool. There was an exceptional amount of pleasure to be derived from hearing that admission. "Well," he said. "What do you say?"

"Why don't you give me a minute to think about it?" she answered coquettishly, lifting the rosebud to her nose and smelling the erotic fragrance cupped within its delicately curled petals.

"Maybe I could wait out that minute in your

cabin rather than here in the hallway?" he suggested as two people passed behind him and pushed
him to the point where only the sudden placing of
his hands against the doorjamb kept him from
touching her. "Embarkations and disembarkations
always seem to find ships' passageways exceptionally busy," he commented. Jenny laughed. "I
guarantee I'll keep my hands to myself," he promised.

"Oh, I trust you!" she replied, his strange smile
seeming to ask her to please not be too trusting. He
was, after all, still a red-blooded man, and she was
a beautiful woman. "I'm afraid you've left very little room in here for me, let alone for the both of
us," she said, stepping back and opening the door
wider so he could get a better look at the flowers
amassed inside. She could tell by the expression on
his face that it had been the wrong thing to do. She
had inadvertently spoiled a very precious moment
between them. She held on to the bud vase so tightly
that she had to tell herself consciously to loosen her
grip or she would crush the crystal into a thousand
splinters. "Let me guess," she said, trying for a
levity she didn't feel. "You're not the Santa Claus
who dropped those down my chimney."

"I came to express apologies, not sink the *Titan-
ic*," he answered, the same edge creeping into his
voice that she had heard there the previous night.
Damn, how she hated hearing it!

"Well, if this isn't like homecoming week!" Abdul said, sauntering down the hallway and catching

sight of Peter standing outside Jenny's open doorway.

"Santa Claus arrives!" Peter said, turning to Jenny after having noted Abdul's unwelcome greeting. The look he gave her was made indefinable by the sudden dropping of an invisible curtain between them.

"This really is quite nice," Abdul said, joining them. His bandage, smaller than the one he'd been wearing last night, was partially concealed beneath his cloth headdress. "Has Peter decided to join the two of us on our little cruise, then?" he asked with a wide smile, taking Peter's hand, which hadn't been offered, and shaking it.

"You're heading upstream, too, are you?" Peter asked, setting his mouth in a hard line.

"My cabin is *way* down the corridor," Abdul said, obviously in a good humor despite someone's having tried to murder him a day earlier. "I figured there was no sense in setting too many tongues wagging by pitching camp right next door. I hope you were equally as discreet, Peter."

"Rather sudden, isn't it," Peter asked, "this decision of yours to see the Nile from the deck of a cruise ship?" He turned to nail Jenny with an accusatory stare. "Or is it?"

She understood what he was insinuating, and she resented his implications. She hadn't known anything about this, and his thinking that she did hurt her to the quick. If she had been looking forward to anyone joining her for the next few days, it had been Peter. It was, however, obvious that he wouldn't have bought that if she had even bothered to tell him. She certainly wasn't going to risk the humiliation of making such a statement only to have him toss it back in her face.

"I mentioned I had business in Upper Egypt, didn't I?" Abdul said. "The excellent company I knew I could find on this cruise ship made it the logical choice of transportation, yes? I mean, the three of us should get along famously."

"I know this is going to come as a big disappointment to you," Peter answered, his words dripping sarcasm, "but I'm not a passenger."

"No?" Abdul replied, sounding as if he hadn't realized that at all. "I'm afraid I merely assumed that since we were all heading in the same direction...."

"Well, you assumed wrong!" Peter injected into the pause. "I'm staying on in Cairo for a few more days and then taking a train south."

"If it's merely a case of them telling you there are no cabins available, I'm sure I could persuade them to find you something," Abdul volunteered magnanimously.

"If I wanted a cabin, I'm sure I could bribe my own way on board, thank you," Peter said with no small degree of coldness.

"Of course," Abdul answered. "I only thought—"

"I know what you thought," Peter interrupted. "And please quit being so anxious to give me a sporting chance at Jenny when I don't want or need one. I have no intentions whatsoever of making your little love-boat ride anything more complicated than the two of you might have originally expected. Bon voyage to both of you!"

"See you in a few days, then!" Abdul called after Peter, who was already yards down the hallway. He turned to Jenny, who was feeling embarrassed, furious and heartsick all at the same time. "I really do like him," Abdul said, "even if I don't think he knows it. . . like him quite aside from the fact that I owe him my life."

Peter wasn't the only one who would have questioned Abdul's sincerity in the present circumstances, and Jenny let him know as much. "You didn't really think he was booked for passage, did you?" she said, although it wasn't a question.

"Why do you say that?" he asked. If he wasn't genuinely surprised by her suggestion, he was certainly putting on a good act. "It would have been the logical thing for him to do, wouldn't it? I mean, *I* moved to book passage as soon as I found out you had. I certainly wouldn't underestimate my rival, believe me."

"I'm not a bone to be fought over by two dogs!" Jenny shot back, angry at Peter for having once again made wrong assumptions, for storming off like a spoiled child. And she was angry at Abdul for having shown up on the scene to turn sour something that had been more than just a little pleasurable. "Furthermore, I don't know where you get off calling Peter your rival when it's obvious he doesn't have the faintest interest in me."

"Oh?" Abdul said, reaching out to run a finger down the stem of the orange rosebud still in her hand. "All I heard was a very confident man saying he didn't need me to give him a sporting chance at you." His finger came delicately to rest atop the flower. "A rather nice touch, this one rose, wouldn't you agree? One that I rather wish I'd thought of myself, instead of going in for overkill," he added, stretching to get a better view of the clutter of white gladioli behind her. "I'd forgotten just how cramped these ship cabins can be. Peter obviously hadn't. You see how it wouldn't pay for me to underestimate him?" If he'd given her a minute, she would have explained how the rose had been intended as a peace offering to make up for Peter's nastiness the previous night, nastiness pretty much repeated but minutes after the rose had been delivered into her hands. "Besides, when I asked him, it seemed very clear to me that he wanted you," Abdul said, "even if there does appear to be a communication problem between the two of you."

"You asked him?" Jenny said, not believing Abdul for a minute.

"You mean, you haven't?" Abdul queried. "It's always seemed to me that asking a direct question and getting a direct answer is a lot better than wasting time guessing. That guessing has obviously got the two of you a bit confused in your signals, hasn't it?"

A steward tried to pass Abdul in the corridor, and Abdul grabbed him by the arm and gently directed him toward Jenny's cabin, simultaneously pulling out a couple of crumpled Egyptian bills. "Here, young man, do us all a big favor and take enough of these flowers out of the lady's cabin so that she can at least use the powder room. Meanwhile," Abdul said, turning back to Jenny, "why don't you let go of Peter's lovely rose long enough for us to have a little talk in the lounge? I really think it might be wise to clear the air between us at the beginning of the trip so we can start our next few days without any bad feelings. What do you think?"

She did as he asked, following him down the corridor, up the stairs and into the lounge area. Other passengers, mostly middle-aged tourists, were sitting at the windows nearest the shore. Abdul preferred the comparative privacy offered by the chairs on the opposite side of the room. He motioned for Jenny to sit and followed suit. Their arrival immediately brought a waiter, who asked if they wanted anything to drink. Abdul ordered tea. "I'm hoping to make my pilgrimage to Mecca one day soon," he told Jenny when she said she would have tea, too. "For that I've decided to abstain from all alcohol, as prescribed by Islam. That doesn't mean that you have to do likewise."

"Tea is fine," she assured him, finding it too early for liquor, even though most of her fellow passengers didn't seem to think so.

"I'm actually quite fond of alcohol," Abdul said, settling back in his chair, pyramiding his fingertips beneath his chin. "I have Muslim friends who are fond of it, yet they, also, want to boast of having made the pilgrimage to Mecca. They give up drinking for maybe a month before going and start up as soon as they get back. I think the pilgrimage should mean far more than just being able to say you've been, don't you?"

"Yes," Jenny said, meaning it. She'd known a few hypocrites in her time, too.

"It's never wise to fool yourself," Abdul said. "You do agree with that, don't you?"

"Of course I do," Jenny replied, thinking he must have known her answer before asking.

" 'To thine own self be true,' " he said. "Very perceptive man, that Shakespeare."

"Which is bringing us just where?" Jenny asked suspiciously. She had to wait for his answer because of the arrival of the waiter and the pouring of their tea.

"Peter told you about the conversation he and I had in my tent last night," Abdul said, sipping from his cup. It was a statement of assumed fact. "You do see, however, I couldn't have refrained from making the offer to give you up, don't you?"

"I can't say as I do," she said, wondering how Abdul could have offered to give up something that, whether he knew it or not, he'd never had in the first place.

"He saved my life," Abdul said, as if surely Jenny could see the point he was trying to make. "If it was in my power to repay him, it was my duty to do so. He didn't want a monetary reward, so I felt obligated to offer him something he did want."

"It's my understanding that Peter wanted it so much he refused your gracious offer point-blank," Jenny reminded him.

"Of course he refused," Abdul said, surprising her. "I always suspected he would. In fact, I would have misjudged him as a man and as an opponent if he had accepted. No real man likes to be handed something on a silver platter," Abdul continued after another swallow of tea. "If something is worthwhile, its value is enhanced by the intensity of the struggle to get it."

Jenny put down her cup and folded her arms, eyeing Abdul over the small table that separated them. "Why is it that so many of our conversations make me feel that you see me merely as some prize, or worse, some kind of spoil of war?"

"Life *is* a game," Abdul said without hesitation. "Life *is* war. It is man's nature to compete. It doesn't deplete your worth that you should suddenly find yourself the object of such competition. Actually, you should see it as the highest form of flattery."

"What I see," she said, "is that I would prefer being less flattered and out of the competition completely. That is, of course, if there actually is one."

"I'm afraid your getting out is quite impossible, Jenny," he told her. "I really wish you could. So, I imagine, does Peter. It is, after all, not all that pleasant for a man to realize that something inside him—his attraction for a woman, for instance— makes him less the master of himself than he would wish to be. Your stating over and over until dooms- day that you don't—or won't—love either of us in return isn't going to change the way we feel. How much easier for all of us if it could."

"There's no possibility of Peter's falling in love with me!" Jenny said, lowering her voice so there was no chance of her being overheard.

"Jenny, Jenny," Abdul said, his voice chiding, his head shaking in disbelief. "It is your determina- tion not to face all of the facts to the contrary that has me wondering if I haven't lost the battle for you already. It would not be a fair fight if Peter's inten- tions were not as clear as my own."

"There are *no* facts to the contrary, and Peter *has* no intentions regarding me!" she said, wonder- ing if she were going to have to draw him a picture to get the point across.

"There's no need whatsoever for you to run from any of this," he said with a consoling smile.

"I'm not running from anything," Jenny insist- ed, giving a short laugh that she hoped further emphasized just how ridiculous she thought that notion was.

"'Then fly betimes, for only they conquer love that run away.' Thomas Carew, wasn't it?"

"I really do think that's my cue for an exit," she said, placing her cup carefully back on its saucer to make sure her trembling hand wouldn't cause the china to clatter.

"And aren't you the same young lady who just told me you weren't running from anything?" Abdul asked with a knowing smile. Determined to prove that statement valid, she picked up her cup and took another swallow of tea. "When I say Peter is halfway in love with you, I'm not just saying that out of personal insight born of having had enough experience in love to recognize the symptoms in another man," Abdul said. "Although I certainly *have* had much experience with love." He saw the faint smile playing on Jenny's lips and recognized it for what it was. "I never once claimed to be a virgin, did I?" he said, matching her smile with one of his own. "I wouldn't have insulted your intelligence by even attempting to deliver up that absurdity. It has, in fact, been my rather extensive experience with women from both our cultures that has allowed me to sort the quality from the quantity, recognizing excellence when I do come across it." Jenny was in no way immune to the pointed flattery of this attractive man, and she nodded her head in acknowledgment of his compliment. "I, too, was able to recognize a certain something between you and Peter from the beginning," Abdul added.

"That's absurd!" Jenny said. Her cup was empty, but she knew she was much too nervous to trust herself to pour a refill. Abdul, with a sixth sense, reached for the pot and did the honors for her.

"I mentioned the possibility of your mutual attraction to Peter when he came over at the Hilton to talk about Hatshepsût," Abdul said. He took a sip of tea, and there was a lengthy pause. "What he did," Abdul continued, "was surprise me by laughing, telling me the two of you had just met in the museum. He then asked me if I were silly enough to believe him capable of love at first sight." Jenny was acutely disappointed. She had been a fool to sit there breathlessly, waiting for Abdul to reveal how Peter had professed undying love. She had been especially foolish, considering the falcon had been present at the time in question. Peter's infatuation with that bird would have been to the exclusion of any affection he could have felt for a mere woman. "I see immediately that you don't get the point," Abdul said, as if he couldn't believe she was being so shortsighted.

"Unfortunately I do get the point," Jenny said, deciding that no revelations were forthcoming that were going to verify Peter's interest, as much as she might very much have liked to hear them. "If he were as interested in me as you profess, I doubt there would be a need for you to make explanations for him. If you were as interested as you profess, you'd forget about Peter Donas and get on with your own business."

"Games, especially those of love, can often be hopelessly confusing, even when those involved know the guidelines," he said.

"We are not playing damned games!" Jenny said angrily. His continued insistence that they were aggravated her no end. That she had spoken loudly enough to cause several people to look in their direction didn't much concern her at the moment. "So if you'll excuse me . . ." she said, getting up.

"Let's get this all said now, shall we?" Abdul suggested, his velvety eyes sincerely pleading with her to be reasonable. "Despite what you think, it really should be discussed."

"I've got to unpack," she said, remembering to thank him for the flowers before she hurried back to her cabin.

Once seated on her bed, gazing at several bouquets of white gladioli left in the room, she was momentarily struck with a sudden fear that the steward had taken the lone orange rosebud out with the other flowers. She breathed an audible sigh of relief when she spotted it on the shelf below the porthole. She moved the flower to a more prominent place, wondering how she would have reacted if Peter had undeniably confessed love for her there in the Hilton lobby, instead of just making some mocking comment to Abdul about the rarity of love at first sight. If there was no point in dwelling on something that had never happened, it still disturbed her that Abdul continued to be so insistent about Peter's emotional involvement. It made her wonder whether the Arab wasn't fantasizing the whole thing as a kind of booster to his ego. Maybe he actually needed the sense of triumphing over another man before he could really find himself capable of getting caught up in one of his little love games. If that were the case, she would be better off simply to tell him to look elsewhere. Jenny did not now, nor would she ever, look upon love as a game. It was something much, much more than just that.

She sat until the ship began to sail, feeling a definite sense of being locked in a prison with a man she would just as soon have left in Cairo. It was only with the realization that she couldn't spend the whole time in her small cabin without going stir crazy that she slipped on her swimming suit and robe, picked up the copy of the *Archaeological American*, which she still hadn't finished reading, and proceeded to the sun deck. She should have known better than to think she was going to hide successfully in plain sight.

"May I join you?" Abdul asked, having been to his cabin to change into bathing suit and robe. The bandage on his head wound was now no more than a simple flesh-colored Band-Aid. He actually waited for her consent before pulling up the nearest deck chair. She mumbled something about it being a free world and went back to reading her magazine. Actually, she wasn't reading it, merely going over the same paragraph about six more times before she looked up, knowing as she did so that he would be staring at her. He smiled. She sighed, closed her magazine, lay back and shut her eyes.

"You're quite determined to say whatever you have to say, aren't you?" she remarked.

"It's only that I think there are matters that need discussing," he affirmed.

"And you will persist if I tell you once again that I don't want to hear about them?" He didn't answer, making her open her eyes and face him. "Well?" she challenged.

"It need only be said this once," he assured her, the avuncular expression on his face making him appear as if he were merely out to give a rebellious child a dose of foul-tasting medicine that was for her own good.

"I don't intend to spend the next few days running around looking for little nooks and crannies in which to hide," Jenny said, shutting her eyes again. "But don't expect me to thank you after you're through."

"Don't you think it would be easy enough for him to give a straight denial?" Abdul asked, jumping right in. Jenny gave a low groan, actually finding this quite painful. "Instead he prefers making comments about how he just met you or answering with another question, such as whether I really believe he could love at first sight. The real question is whether *he* believes it possible. Do you know what he said when I told him I would give up my pursuit of you if that's what he wanted?" Jenny refused to give him the satisfaction of hearing her say she was dying to know. Which didn't keep him from answering his own question in the end. "He told me he could take care of his own love life without my assistance."

"I know someone else who has tried telling you that very same thing," Jenny said, turning her face completely from him. "You'd do a lot better if you learned to take simple hints, instead of waiting to be bonked over the head."

"He gave me a bunch of diversionary claptrap about how you preferred me to him," Abdul continued, "and how that said it all. I told him it didn't say anything, but he *still* wouldn't be pinned down."

"Which all proves nothing," Jenny said, lifting herself to face him again. "Maybe he rightfully figured it was none of your business and decided to play games of his own in order to pay you back for butting in where you shouldn't have had your nose in the first place." She was anxious to hear what retort he had to that.

"Would you say he was very pleased to see me when I showed up at the pyramids to invite you both to lunch?" was Abdul's counter thrust.

"The minute you mentioned your falcon his eyes just lighted up like a Christmas tree," Jenny reminded him, finding that memory especially painful.

"I mean, before I mentioned the falcon," Abdul said. "How about when he came over to find the two of us talking? Would you say he was overjoyed to see me?" He didn't wait for a reply. "I'd say he was anything but that. He churlishly insinuated I must have gone to a good deal of bother to find you." He smiled. "Which, by the way, I had."

"He changed his tune fast enough when you mentioned Hatshepsût would be out there in the desert waiting for him!'' Jenny said, unable to keep the annoyance out of her voice.

"As I remember it, he did no such thing," Abdul contradicted. "*You* changed *your* mind. He was saying something about how you probably shouldn't overdo things, and you popped up with how seldom it was a woman got asked for a ride and lunch by an attractive desert sheikh.''

"Are you telling me he wasn't extremely eager to see your falcon being flown?'' she asked in challenge, swinging her legs to one side so she could face him in a fully sitting position. She was just waiting for him to try feeding her that lie.

"I'm merely noting that, when put to the test of making the actual decision, he chose you and not the bird," he recalled for the both of them. "You reversed his decision, after which, assuming as he and I both did that you were pleased at the idea of sharing my company, he proceeded to sulk most of the afternoon, growing *really* despondent when he found us kissing in the Sarapeum. Hardly the response of someone completely pleased with having suddenly found himself in the company of me and the falcon, wouldn't you agree?''

"That doesn't mean anything," Jenny replied, wanting to believe each and every word he had said. "It's nothing but pure conjecture.''

"And finding him here with his rose could certainly give rise to even more interesting conjecture," Abdul went on. "Don't even begin trying to tell me he was pleased at my intrusion this time around, let alone overjoyed that I would soon be off on a cruise with you." Jenny laughed nervously. She knew she was hearing what she desperately wanted to hear, and she was scared that if she took him too seriously she would be giving herself an excuse for eventually trying something horribly foolish.

"Look, Jenny," Abdul said, his voice having very little effect at damping a heat building inside of her that had nothing whatsoever to do with the intense Egyptian sun, "I don't mind competition—in love or in anything else. In fact, I'm admittedly better in the face of it." Once again Jenny wondered whether Abdul might have been trying to make Peter seem a more formidable rival for her love than he really was. "What I don't want is a victory wherein you'll someday look back and question how it might have been if... if you had responded a little differently to Peter, if you'd been a little more astute in reading the signs he was sending you, if you'd just given him and yourself a little more of a chance to make a go of it. I'm confident I can beat Peter here and now, but I don't want to have to do battle with his memory at some later date, because memories come armed with an arsenal that doesn't give a flesh-and-blood man the chance of a snowball in hell. I can tell you that from very bitter experience." The statement piqued Jenny's curiosity, but he wasn't about to elucidate. "Do you hear what I'm trying to say?" he asked her. "If I lose, I lose. It won't be the first time, even if it probably will be one of my most painful defeats. If I win, I want it to be because I was the man you really wanted. However, I could never be truly convinced of that as long as you were determined to keep your head buried in the sand concerning Peter's feelings for you."

"I think you're mistaken about Peter," Jenny said, trying to convince herself that that was what she really did think, "but I promise I'll give the matter serious thought. Satisfied?"

"That's all I ask," Abdul said with a wide smile. He slipped his robe off his broad shoulders and dropped it in the chair on the other side of the one he was using. His body was tightly muscled and was displayed to excellent advantage in a skimpy European bathing suit that would have been more at home on the Riviera. The suit was a bright orange that contrasted attractively with the natural bronze of his skin. His pectoral muscles were developed, while Peter's were less so. His navel was deeply indented, whereas Peter's was but a slight depression. There was a swath of hair across the top of his chest that funneled downward over his stomach to disappear beneath his swimsuit; Peter's torso was hairless by comparison. Abdul's skin was marred in several places by scars, whereas Peter's skin had seemed flawless when he had stripped off his shirt in that desert tent.

"Ah, I've miscalculated, haven't I?" he said, startling Jenny into thinking he was about to reverse what he had just said concerning the possibility of a relationship between Peter and her. That wasn't his intention. "I've just revealed my ace in the hole," he said, shaking his head at what he could pretend was a major faux pas. "Something I usually do only after first enticing the beautiful young lady up to my room."

"Your battle scars, you mean?" she asked in a moment of amused lucidity, at the same time realizing she hadn't been as repulsed by them as she might have thought she would be. Actually, they seemed an intricate part of his strong and handsome body.

"Bullet wound," he said, lifting his left leg so Jenny could see the small circle made on the inside of his thigh and the puckered asterisk where the bullet had exploded out the tissue on the other side. "Knife wound," he said, his fingers tracing the fine line that ran from his right side to a position on his stomach.

"Another knife?" Jenny asked, indicating the scar that stood out like a small check mark on his left hip. She had touched her finger to her own hip instead of his in order to pinpoint the location of the scar to which she was referring.

"A skiing accident in Saint-Moritz," he said. His fingers ran downward to a spot almost invisible in the hair at the top of his waistband. "A car accident at Le Mans."

"Why do I get the impression you're accident-prone?" she asked, flashing a wide smile after he had pointed out several other past wounds so healed as to be virtually unnoticeable. "Could it be because of all the evidence?"

"Actually, I merely push everything I do to the limit," Abdul said. "There's an exhilaration I experience whenever I push myself as far as I can possibly go, or push an automobile or an animal I'm riding to their fullest potential. Unfortunately I've been known to misjudge on occasion." His smile was attractive, his teeth exceptionally white in the sunlight, startling against the blackness of his mustache and neatly trimmed beard. Jenny noticed another scar, crescent-shaped, on his lower neck. She was going to ask about it when a slight torquing of his muscled body drew her attention elsewhere. "I picked this up in Maracaibo," he said, his fingers gently outlining a burn scar across the top of his left shoulder. She hadn't spotted the mark until he turned it toward her. "We were fighting an oil-well fire—three of them, as a matter of fact, all set off by one freak arc of lightning."

"You were fighting well fires in Maracaibo?" Jenny asked, wondering if she had really heard correctly. "Venezuela?"

"None other," Abdul verified. "I spent some time with Darrel Crane, best hell fighter in the business."

"Hell fighter?" Jenny echoed, although the word in context really made no further explanation necessary.

"Putting out a well fire is pretty hairy business," Abdul said, rubbing the burn scar as if he could still feel the intense blast of heat that had seared his flesh. "As involved as I've been in the oil business, I was naturally drawn to that aspect of it. Darrel agreed to take me on for some on-the-job observation. He was called in for the Maracaibo holocaust, and I flew in with him." His dark eyes took on a slightly dreamy quality, and Jenny knew he was suddenly thousands of miles—a continent—away. "I remember we came in at night," he said, licking his lips as a protection against the heat of the sun. "You could see the conflagration for miles, lighting up the sky like all hell had been turned loose on earth. On the spot it was brighter than noontime. I couldn't believe there was a holy chance of extinguishing it, but Darrel moved right in as if there were no bigger challenge there than some he'd had previously. And I guess there wasn't. He snuffed the fires out one at a time using nitroglycerin blasts to smother the flames." Although Abdul seemed to see Jenny, it was doubtful whether he did. He was so deep into his recollections that he seemed to be looking right through her. "Each time the nitro went off, there was this sudden spray of fire three hundred feet high and two hundred feet wide that suddenly dissolved into a black gushing of sticky crude."

"And the scar?" Jenny asked, knowing that everything couldn't have run smoothly if Abdul came away with what had obviously been a bad burn.

"After the last one was blown, I moved in too

close without an asbestos suit," Abdul continued, his wry grin saying, as much as anything, that he should have known better. "Someone suddenly yelled that it was going to torch again, and I barely got turned around before it did just that. I didn't feel a damned thing, although I found out later that the force of the reignition had sent me through the air like Superman and knocked me unconscious against the side of a shed nine feet away. The burn was less bother than the cracked ribs turned out to be."

"I'm a little confused as to why it was reignited after it had been put out once," Jenny said. "Lightning again?"

Abdul shrugged. "It could have been anything—a spark caused by someone dropping a wrench, even the static electricity of someone running his hand through his hair. All I do know is that it did torch, and when I got out of the hospital, Darrel wasn't too anxious to take me back. I had become a little too important to too many people for him to want to be the one who had to write home about my going up in a ball of flame."

"I can't say I blame him," Jenny said. "You didn't actually want to go back, did you?"

"Sure I did," Abdul replied, looking at her as if she couldn't possibly have thought he had wanted to do otherwise. "You can't really believe the excitement inherent in one of those operations. There's a beauty to it that you're not going to find anywhere else on Earth—all that billowing smoke and red orange flame. The noise is like a hundred cannons going off simultaneously.''

"I would think cracked ribs and a nasty burn would be just a little too high a price to pay for the show," Jenny said, amazed at his nostalgia.

"When I heard somebody yelling that the baby was going to go, I felt closer to death yet more alive than I had ever felt previously. Not when I was knifed, not when I was shot, not when I totaled the race car in France, did I feel like that. It was an experience I really can't even begin to explain.''

"Obviously," Jenny said. He could talk until he was blue in the face, and she still wouldn't understand what impulse could drive a man into seeking the hypnotic macabre beauty of the horrible catastrophe he'd just described.

"Anyway," he said, having learned from earlier experience that he wasn't likely to make any converts but hardly upset because of it, "you can now say you've had the guided tour of the battlefield, with only one big surprise left." He chuckled at that bit of suggestiveness and, shutting his eyes, settled back in his chair to enjoy a heat that would be far more kind for a moment's exposure than an exploding oil well had ever been.

Jenny opened her magazine and tried to read, with no more success than she'd had since Abdul had first joined her. She closed the magazine silently and turned her attention back to the man beside her. She had thought him one of the most handsome men she had ever seen when he'd had his clothes on, and her opinion hadn't been changed by the removal of his robe. There was an aesthetic beauty to his lines that had been made somehow more masculine by the imperfections of his scars. She couldn't help comparing what she saw here with what she had seen that moment Peter had peeled off his shirt in the tent outside Saqqâra. Abdul's body had a classic masculine beauty, but Peter's physique was somehow more exciting. She was disturbed at the prospect of forever finding herself comparing every man she met with Peter Donas. Without meaning to, she found herself wondering whether Peter's body was as smoothly perfect everywhere as it was in the areas she had already seen.

She must have dozed, because the next thing she remembered was hearing the discordant clang of something hard being struck against metal. She opened her eyes, immediately having to shield them from the sun with her hand. Abdul was awake and looking at her with a degree of tenderness that made her almost wish she wasn't always forced to compare him to Peter.

"I think the racket you are presently hearing means lunch is being served," he said. "It's the equivalent of the pleasant chimes you would have heard had this been one of your larger oceangoing liners. Hungry?"

"A little," she admitted, reaching for her robe and letting him help her on with it. She had eaten hardly at all the night before and had had only a roll and coffee for breakfast. "You?"

"Famished," he said, giving her a mock-lecherous glare and smacking his lips. She couldn't help laughing. "I hope you don't mind my having already arranged for the two of us to share the same table," he said, his voice apologetically asking her please to forgive him if he had somehow once again overstepped certain acceptable boundaries.

"I don't mind at all," she said, getting to her feet. She suddenly felt much better about everything. Perhaps Abdul's words had sunk in. He had been right about the wisdom of clearing the air between them. He had been right about a lot of things, not the least of which had been the fact that she was fighting off the feelings she had for Peter by refusing to accept even the possibility that he felt something for her in return. Maybe there was such a thing as love at first sight. Abdul had convinced her it would be better to rush in, even to take big chances, rather than to sit back and let the world pass her by. She felt a bit guilty about her feelings toward Peter in the face of Abdul's rather fearless—and certainly selfless—honesty, but she knew Abdul would understand. He played his games fairly, and she intuitively knew he wouldn't be a bad loser, either. That he had lost, Jenny knew already. "I can think of nothing I'd rather do than have lunch with you," she said. It was a harmless white lie, far better than the needlessly cruel truth that she would have far preferred having lunch with Peter.

"I'll meet you in the dining room in about ten minutes."

She hurried back to her cabin. Taking off her robe and swimsuit, she was pausing when her gaze was helplessly drawn to that one small splash of orange floral color amid the surrounding whiteness of the other flowers. She went over to the rosebud and drew it slowly from its vase, feeling the coolness of clinging water on her fingertips as moisture drained downward, forming a small drop at the base of the thornless stem. She brought the flower to her nose and smelled deeply of its surprisingly heady perfume. Its fragrance brought back reminders of how Peter had looked standing there in her doorway, so handsome, humbly offering her the rose in apology. She forgave him his rude exit. She forgave him everything, most of all his being Frederic Donas's grandson.

She held the rose gently, letting its delicate petals rest against her heated cheek. "Peter," she voiced softly, just wanting the pleasure of forming his name on her lips and hearing it spoken. She guided the rose down her chin and along the arc of her throat. "Peter," she repeated, shutting her eyes as the caressing flower progressed down along the smooth curve of her breast and, held in shaking fingers, settled over her heart.

CHAPTER SEVEN

LUXOR, KARNAK, THEBES: a closely grouped triad of Upper Egyptian archaeological sites whose combined total area included the ruins of the most mammoth monuments and greatest accomplishments of the Thirteenth to the Thirtieth Dynasties. It wasn't, however, the magnificent Temple of Luxor, whose mighty obelisk now graced Paris's Place de la Concorde, that made the locale so special to Jenny. Nor was it the Temple of Karnak, whose hypostyle hall boasted one hundred and thirty-four massive columns, any one of which might have held one hundred standing men on a capital mushroomed sixty-nine feet above the ground. In fact, as Jenny stood at the guardrail of the *Osiris* sun deck, it was the opposite side of the Nile that held her attention. She looked toward Thebes and a landscape that would have appeared of no particular archaeological significance to a novice. There was immediately visible only the glare of sun on the Nile; the greenness of gardens and plantations; the stateliness of date palms—never coconut palms, which required a substantial rainfall; and, beyond all that, a desert not so much loose sand as a series of rocky buttresses ascending to impressively rugged cliffs. Viewed through the undulating heat of midday, the desert was a fluctuating distortion of whites, yellows, ochers and browns, all without shadow.

"You know this is really madness, don't you?" Abdul said, coming up behind her and touching the coolness of a glass of freshly squeezed orange juice to the back of her arm. She turned toward him and smiled, taking the offered refreshment and letting a couple sips momentarily relieve the dryness of her mouth and throat. "The bus just got back, and the whole sweaty group looks as if it's about to expire en masse," he said, gazing off across the river. "It's like a blast furnace over there at this time of day, especially this time of year."

"I'll survive," she said confidently, knowing she had always found her metabolism more adaptable to extreme warmth than extreme cold.

"Sure you wouldn't like company, just in case you keel over from heat exhaustion?" he asked, more than willing to join her scheduled afternoon of sight-seeing.

She had welcomed his company when the ship had docked at Tell al-Amarna, the capital of the heretic pharaoh Ikhnaton, who had married Nefertiti—"The Beautiful One Is Come"—and been succeeded to the throne by the boy-king Tutankhamen after an unsuccessful attempt at a religious reformation designed to replace permanently the Egyptian pantheon of gods with only one god, Aton, in the manifestation of the sun disk. She had stood with Abdul watching as the ship had leisurely cruised by Antinoöpolis, a city so obliterated by time that few on board had even realized the modern sugar refinery pinpointed the locale of a once major metropolis erected by the Roman emperor Hadrian in memory of his handsome young lover Antinoüs— he of melancholy expression, large eyes and beautiful mouth who drowned at that spot on the Nile, or more likely committed suicide. Jenny and Abdul had strolled through the ruins of Abydos, where the head of the god Osiris, whose brother Seth murdered him, was supposedly buried. At Dendera they had admired the unencumbered symmetry and undeniable beauty of the Temple of Hathor. This afternoon, however, the cruise almost ended, Jenny wanted to be alone in Thebes, having chosen the hottest part of the day because she knew the intensity of the heat would drive most tourists to cool ship lounges or into equally air-conditioned hotel lobbies. "No, thank you," she said, tempering her rejection with a smile. "Some things are best done alone, without the company of even a friend."

She had been using the word *friend* a lot lately in regard to their relationship, hoping to prepare him for what might occur as soon as she was reunited with Peter a little farther up the river. There was something to the old adage about absence making the heart grow fonder. Jenny, despite the companionship and admitted good times Abdul had offered, found herself more and more often thinking of Peter. She had even kept the fallen petals of his rose, gathered them up for preservation, while having allowed the steward to dispose of all the finally wilted gladioli. She found herself experiencing so much anticipation regarding her proposed meeting with Peter at Hierakonpolis that it actually overshadowed the afternoon's pilgrimage to which she had looked forward for so long. "I guess I really should be going," she said, finishing off the welcome orange juice and placing the empty glass on a nearby table.

"A kiss in parting?" he asked, and she gave him one. There were kisses between friends and kisses between lovers, and she felt confident Abdul, as self-admittedly expert as he was in the nuances of romance, could determine the difference between this one and the other.

She left him on the sun deck and descended to the gangway after passing through air-conditioned rooms that reinforced the intensity of the outdoor heat when she stepped back into it. She turned to see him watching as she topped the stairway that brought her from the river's edge to the main street of the town. She waved, and he waved back. She was slow in being accosted by the drivers of horse-drawn carriages, who were obviously surprised to see a tourist foolish enough to brave the heat. She didn't want a carriage anyway. They were fine for the shorter rides around Luxor and Karnak, but her business was across the river in Thebes. She took the ferry and found herself a taxi on the other side. The cabdriver was no less surprised than the carriage drivers had been to see her out in the midday heat, but he drove her northwest through greenery extended by the al-Fadleva Canal. Where the vegetation abruptly ended and the desert just as abruptly began, the car passed the famed Colossi of Memnon, so dubbed by the Greeks in honor of their mythical hero. The two, seated, seventy-foot-high statues were actually representations of Amenophis III, now guarding a temple complex no longer in existence. When strange sounds were reported on occasion to be emitted by one of these stone figures at the crack of dawn, less superstitious observers would be quick to explain it had nothing to do with anything more mysterious than the expansion and contraction of rock during temperature changes. Farther on the road made a sharp right, and ruins became visible: the Temple of Minepaht; the Temple of Thutmosis IV; and finally the Ramasseum, funeral temple of the megalomaniac Ramses II. A roadway to one side led to the three-tiered funerary temple of Queen Hatshepsût, complete with its distinctive rampways. It seemed fitting that the monument to this particular Egyptian queen should be found perched at the base of an escarpment that probably contained more than its share of falcon aeries. Jenny, however, refused to let her mind dwell on Abdul's falcon, merely reminding herself that Peter, when asked to pick between her and the bird Hatshepsût, had picked Jenny—even if she hadn't realized it until Abdul had pointed it out.

The car turned sharply left and was soon veering

into the Bibân al-Molûk, the "doors of the king," a winding gorge that swallowed them momentarily into a maze of stone before spitting them out into a scorched and sunbaked depression. This place might well have seemed the end of the world were it not for the conspicuous presence of a government rest house that beckoned with cool rooms and cool refreshment. She gave the driver leave to wait for her inside, and she started off along a pathway free from the swarms of tourists found there in the comparative coolness of early morning. She paused only when she finally came to the one opening among many she was looking for in all that weather-worn stone.

Tomb sixty-two in the Valley of the Kings at Thebes wasn't impressive inside or out. Its physical layout seemed particularly pitiful compared to that of tomb seventeen, those burial rooms of Sethi I found at the end of one hundred and seventeen meters of descending corridor and known for their wealth of decoration; or tomb nine, that of Ramses VI, whose long gallery had been separated by a series of doors and intermediary chambers. Yet tomb sixty-two was the most famous burial vault in Egypt—and possibly the world. Here sixteen steps leading to a small vestibule that opened into a funerary chamber measuring only six and a half by four meters, flanked by two side rooms, was the final resting place of the boy-king Tutankhamen. Crowded into a space so cramped that ceremonial chariots had to be dismantled, their axles sawed in half to allow them entrance, was the only pharaonic treasure trove known to have escaped the tomb robbers of ancient times and see the light of modern day. It had been the excavation of this site in 1922 that had brought Frederic Donas and Geraldine Fowler together. Here at Thebes they had met. Here they had loved. Here Geraldine had died of a broken heart.

Jenny hesitated before entering, hearing the sounds of someone else inside. Having not come this far to have company, she stayed put, enduring the incessant heat in its climb to even higher temperatures. She was beginning to perspire in the long-sleeved blouse and short skirt she had worn for coolness and protection. Her cheeks and forehead were noticeably damp. She waited patiently until finally the bearded young man and the skinny young girl emerged with their Arab guide. Only then did she go inside.

She noticed a slight drop in the temperature as she moved deeper. Reaching the vestibule, she turned toward the balustrade separating her from the stone sarcophagus, now glass-topped and set in a recessed chamber that allowed viewing of the inside golden coffin containing the mummy come home to rest. Deprived of the bulk of his treasures, including his gold death mask and the two most valuable of the coffins that had cocooned him like the pieces of a Chinese puzzle, Tut had still managed to come out better than any of the other pharaohs buried in the surrounding necropolis.

"Jenny?"

She turned to the sound of Peter's voice, amazed that she had no more heard his approach here than she had in the Egyptian Museum. In a telescoping of those sixty years between the opening of the tomb and the present, she felt many of the same feelings Geraldine Fowler must have felt when rendezvousing with her young lover. Like Geraldine Fowler, Jenny glided across the rough-hewn floor. Like Frederic Donas, he took her securely in his arms, gazed momentarily into her eyes as if all the treasures of Egypt weren't comparable to the beauty he found there and kissed her. How wonderful was the touch of him, the taste of him, the smell of him! She gave herself freely to those sensations in which he seemed determined to immerse her, wishing only that the moment might stretch on into infinity. Never had she known such ecstatic bliss from just one erotically lingering kiss.

"I knew you'd come!" she said once his lips had released hers for the speaking. She heard her exclamation as something Geraldine Fowler might have voiced after a trip, even through death, to find Frederic Donas awaiting her at the scene of her greatest joy and her greatest heartbreak.

"Jenny, Jenny, Jenny," he chanted, his voice a pagan litany to conjure up the fires inside her. She tilted her head back, giving his hot kisses free access to the smooth arching of her throat. He gripped her hips tightly in his amazingly strong fingers, pulling her in so closely to him that she lost awareness of all else besides the compelling virility of his body.

"I love you," she said, her fingers suddenly in his hair, entwining the silky black strands and taking hold. If that, too, was a statement Frederic Donas's heated kisses might well have brought from Geraldine Fowler's yearning lips, it was also the end result of emotions that had been building inside of Jenny Mowry for as long as she could remember. She had once denied those feelings, arguing that her love for Peter was nothing more than the result of runaway childhood fantasies, but she would admit to the strength—the reality—of those feelings now. She would drop the barriers, take the chance, dare to go near the flaming inferno that, while it might consume her, might also release in her a capacity for love she never dreamed she had. Abdul had convinced her that life wasn't lived to its fullest without taking some chances. She wasn't prepared to carry nitroglycerin to the edge of a burning oil well, but she *was* prepared to be more daring than she might once have been. For she had a chance to make fantasies reality, and there could be no denying that Peter's coming to her at Thebes suggested a love controlled by destiny. Somehow he had been miraculously drawn by the same forces that had intuitively told Jenny to come there alone.

She tightened her fingers in his hair, fearing her tremendous desire to have him with her at that moment had merely conjured up an illusion. Simultaneously she knew he was real. No phantom could feel as he felt: hard muscle vibrant beneath her exploring fingers, demanding lips raining kisses on her face, neck and on that portion of her creamy breasts exposed by the open vee of her neckline.

Reaching once again for the tangled blackness of his hair, she gently tipped back his head, staying his eager lips. She wanted to see his face, to hold his handsome visage in her eyes, although it was obvious he was anxious to return more hungry kisses to her flushed cheeks and neck. "Could you love me?" she asked, remembering it was Abdul who had told her something about there being nothing more apt to get a direct answer than a direct question. "I have to know, Peter," she said, aware she was on the verge of making a commitment she might find impossible to carry through on if it proved to be too one-sided. "Could you love me?" she repeated.

"You mean, you don't know the answer to that already?" he answered. "Haven't I made it only too obvious?"

That wasn't enough! "I have to hear you say it," she said, her fingers entwining more tightly in his hair as she became fearful that another of his passionate kisses would deprive her of the ability to speak, to ask what she wanted to know. "Please, Peter, it's so very important that I hear you say it."

"I can love you, Jenny Mowry," he said. "In fact, I *do* love you, incredible as it may seem. I've never been so taken so quickly before. And these past few days without you have been torture for me. I had to see you."

She felt his words causing shivering pleasure deep into her being, making her weak in the knees, taking her breath away. "I told you once already that I loved you and you didn't believe me. Remember?" She nodded, because she remembered each and every conversation they'd ever had. She remembered each and every moment they'd been together. "So I'll tell you again, hoping you can tell a lie from reality," he went on, his eyes golden suns that filled her with a warmth more powerful than the flash of heat that had burned Abdul's shoulder, more intense than the blazing Egyptian sun that baked the valley landscape outside. "I love you, I love you, I love you. And had I thought there'd been a chance before now that you might love me in return, I wouldn't have let you get away from me for these past few days so easily."

"I thought you knew how I felt about you," Jenny said, hardly believing she hadn't made her feelings clear until now. But then it had only been during the past few days that she'd been able to sort out her emotions. Prior to now, prior to this moment, in this place, she hadn't been willing to trust herself for fear she would end up hurt like her grandmother.

"I thought you wanted Abdul Jerada," he said, desiring to kiss the pulse spot on her neck and being allowed to do so. He burrowed his face in closer, his tongue moving sensuously against her skin. "Oh, but I didn't really think I had a chance!" he moaned, as if memories of that past misconception could deeply mar the beauty of the present moment.

"Abdul is a friend," Jenny said, her fingers combing through the thick luxurious strands of his hair. The nearness of him, the thin cloth that separated their eager bodies, the feel of his skin beneath her palms as she took his face again in her hands—everything filled her with new excitement. "That's all he ever could be while I love you."

"Oh, Jenny," he said, embracing her as though he had waited forever to have her in his arms. "Jenny, Jenny, Jenny," he sighed, as if all other words had temporarily failed him.

She was glad he had come, glad he had had the perceptiveness to know that this moment was the right moment for defining and cementing their relationship. Before now it had really been too early. After Thebes, though, it might well have turned out to be too late. They were so radically opposed in their opinions of the significance of Hierankonpolis as a potential burial site for the Scorpion King that *that* friction, combined with all of the misunderstanding that had come previously, could easily have spoiled everything for the both of them.

"You know what you make me feel like, don't you?" he asked, his smile revealing amusing reminiscence. "You make me feel like a young kid whose recent sexual awareness has him quite ready to make love on sandy beaches, in sleeping bags, on kitchen tables, or even in King Tutankhamen's tomb."

As if on cue, they heard the sound and came apart in a nervous embarrassment when confronted by one of the tourist police. In a country whose major monuments had seen past defacement by early

Christians thinking to annihilate pagan gods by simply chiseling away their likeness and by tourists who thought that they, too, might achieve immortality by leaving their names scratched beside those of the pharaohs, there were now more security measures taken in the Valley of the Kings than there had been when every tomb had been stacked from floor to ceiling with unbelievable treasures.

"Come on," Peter said, taking her hand and giving a gentle tug toward the tomb entrance. The policeman immediately began scanning for any damage they might have done.

"He looked as if we were preparing to march off with Tut, stone sarcophagus and all, didn't he?" Jenny said after she'd recovered from the blast of scorched desert air that greeted their return to the outside. Actually, no visitor had access to the mummy, and any attempts to progress beyond the protective balustrade would have set off alarms to bring someone far faster than it had taken one policeman to stir himself from his lothargy in a spot of rare shade.

"You know, between you and the sun, I'm hot enough to be downright uncomfortable," Peter said, his hand still holding hers. He gently squeezed her fingers. "Let's find some place cool, quiet and private."

"The rest house?" she suggested. It was the only place within walking distance that seemed capable of offering adequate shelter from sunstroke.

"I was thinking more of my hotel," Peter said

sheepishly. He stopped and turned to her in the bright Egyptian sunlight, his eyes so beautifully golden, his face a deep bronze. "I've taken a room at the Etap," he said uneasily. Jenny knew the hotel. Its opening had been a great boon to Luxor and had vastly improved available tourist accommodations. It was located almost directly across the street from the *Osiris* docking area. "Let's find my driver to take us there, shall we?" he said, making it a question that was desperately in need of an affirmative answer.

"All right," she said, flashing him a smile that portrayed happiness as well as nervousness. She'd taken one more step toward commitment, and she couldn't help wishing that the journey to the hotel were less lengthy. It would have been easier to let things run their natural course there in the tomb, for there was no longer any chance she was going to be able to rationalize whatever happened now by blaming it on passions that had flared out of control on the spur of the moment and had swept her away. Granted there was more than a good deal of passion involved here, but she was being given enough time to maneuver a safe withdrawal—if that was what she really wanted.

"How did you know I'd come to Thebes?" she asked when he'd dismissed her driver and she was seated with Peter in the back of the taxi that had brought him to the valley after her.

"Abdul told me," he said. His arm was around her, and he gave her a loving hug. Jenny felt a pang of guilt about Abdul, hoping they had treated him as fairly as he had treated them. She was sure she would be grateful to the attractive Arab for the rest of her life. Without his help and his sane rational judgment, she would never now have been en route to Peter's hotel. "He also informed me that you wanted to be alone, but I told him my seeing you wouldn't wait," Peter added.

"I'm glad it wouldn't wait," she said, her right hand resting on his left thigh. She felt the hardness of his leg beneath his faded jeans, and she could tell just by the way he held her body so close beside his own that he wanted her with a desire no less powerful now than it had been atop the pyramid or in King Tutankhamen's tomb.

"I do love you," he said, his voice a caressing whisper, his mouth very near her right ear. "You believe that, don't you?"

"Yes," she said, and the knowledge filled her with joy.

"I wouldn't ever willingly do anything to hurt you, Jenny," he breathed.

"I know you wouldn't hurt me," she answered. "I trust you." Her fingers nervously kneaded the muscle of his thigh. "Really I do."

"I hope so," he said, kissing her cheek. "Damn, but I do hope so."

Perhaps Peter had not been concentrating on the scenery when their cab sped by the Deir al-Bahari of Queen Hatshepsût. In any case, Jenny was glad he didn't mention the delicate brown terraces so exquisitely constructed. She wanted nothing to spoil the moment, not even a vague reference to a dead Egyptian queen who had a peregrine falcon named after her. It made no difference that Jenny felt ridiculous about her continued jealousy of the bird, especially when Peter, put to the test, had chosen her over it. She had seen the attraction the hawk held for him and suspected that attraction still existed.

She laid her head against his shoulder, the archaeologist in her giving way completely to the woman as she ignored funerary temples put to ruin by centuries of decay and earthquakes. On the ferry, sitting beside Peter in much the same position as in the cab, she was little bothered by the clouds of blue black diesel smoke continually erupting from the laboring engine to engulf them in greasy foul-smelling fog.

The Etap Hotel, across the main street from the Nile, had a basically unimpressive exterior but surprised one with its spacious interior public rooms attractively done in rich woods and expensive marbles. Jenny and Peter took large wicker chairs just off the main lobby and ordered drinks. She had a cold *carcadet*—a red tea brewed from dried flower petals. He ordered a gin and tonic.

"Damn, I can't believe this!" he said, actually looking ill at ease. Jenny found it an attractive change from the confident, arrogant and sometimes cold face he had shown her in the course of their brief relationship.

"Believe what?" she asked, deciding not to tell him he looked exceedingly attractive with all of his defenses down.

"That I'm as nervous as hell, feeling like a schoolboy on his first date and not knowing how to proceed."

"Have you thought of merely asking a direct question?" Jenny suggested, smiling coquettishly and experiencing the exhilaration of assuming a role that was basically unfamiliar. "A good friend once told me such questions saved a lot of beating around the bush."

"Very well, then," he said, turning his golden eyes on her with smoldering intensity. "Would you come up to my room with me?"

"Yes," she answered, her voice a whisper, not so much because she had consciously tried to make it such, but because that was just the way it came out.

"Good," he said softly, running one lazy finger along the inner side of her arm in a gesture at once both innocent and provocative. His eyes focused on hers, a sensuous languor weighing down his lids. He smiled lovingly and reached for her hand. He took a deep breath that came out sounding very much like a sigh. "I was afraid you might say no," he said finally.

"Really?" Jenny replied with an affectionate smile. "I thought I'd made my answer perfectly clear back at Thebes."

"Oh, Jenny," he said, "do you know how happy I am at this very moment?"

"I only know how happy I am," she said, leaning across to briefly touch her lips to his seductive mouth. And hand in hand they rose and left the table, forgetting even to drink what they had ordered.

Entering his room a few minutes later, Jenny walked immediately to the open window. She gazed out on the contrasting landscape of the steely-gray Nile, the brilliant green foliage along its banks and the burned earth shades beyond. She was glad they had returned to Luxor for this moment. Not only had it given her the opportunity to decide this was really what she wanted to do, but it was more fitting that they consecrate their love on the east bank of the Nile—the side that had for centuries been devoted to the living—rather than on the west bank, which had long been dedicated to the dead. There was nothing dead or dying about the feelings Jenny had for Peter. Those feelings were alive and thriving.

"I love you very much, Jenny Mowry," he said, coming to stand behind her, making her tremble with the way she could feel him before he even touched her. His left hand moved her hair to one side as he gently kissed her ear, sliding his lips down toward the back of her neck and shoulder. His kiss sent a tingling through her that danced across her every nerve fiber and back again. He slid his powerful arms around her waist, locking them in place, while his mouth moved back to her ear, never losing contact with her skin.

She was unable to prevent the low groan that escaped as his teeth closed gently on the lobe of her ear, his breath a steady beating that was maddening in the way it affected her. She helped him unfasten the buttons of her blouse when his fingers suddenly seemed too charmingly clumsy to manage the task on their own. If she appeared outwardly calm and sure of herself, it was only because she was trying to slow the tumultuous eagerness of her own response.

Softly he lifted the blouse from her shoulders and gazed at her exposed loveliness. "You're beautiful," he whispered, his voice a heated stimulant against her ear. His calloused hands, sensuously rough, cupped her breasts without hurry, the slowness of his actions intensifying the impact of his hard skin against the softness of her own. Her nipples went taut against his palms, and passion rose in her like a captive bird begging for release.

He turned her in his arms, holding her tightly so that her surrendered breasts were now pressed hard against his chest. His kisses became more intense, his motions quickened with gentle impatience. "Oh, Jenny, Jenny." His lips formed her name before he lowered his manly head and took her nipple in his mouth.

"Peter!" she moaned, her hands first on the back of his neck and then buried in his startlingly black hair. She spoke his name again, just to hear the way it rolled off her tongue, the way it sounded, the way it somehow even seemed to taste as she shivered with the exquisite pleasure of his touch.

Easing his hands along the length of her back, he dropped slowly to his knees, his kisses like fluttering butterfly wings against the flat smoothness of her stomach. He angled his fingertips into the elastic waistband of her skirt, hooking skirt and underclothes with his thumbs and peeling them all down along her lower body, leaving her naked and enticingly vulnerable.

He kissed the inside of her right thigh, sending a bolt of electricity through her that made her automatically clamp her fingers onto his shoulders for support and balance. His hands cleared her feet of the pile of clothing that had been dropped around them so he could free her of her shoes. Then he gently pulled her down so that they were kneeling face to face.

He loved her with his hands, his lips and his tongue until she thought she would collapse. Then he came to his feet and swept her into his arms, her trembling hands clasped behind his strong neck. He carried her to the bed and lowered her easily onto it. He kissed her once on her lips before proceeding in a line of gentle touches down the length of her body.

When he pulled away, it was only to remove his boots and socks. His eyes never left her, his fingers unfastening the buttons on his shirt and baring his muscled chest. When the material came off, revealing all the perfection beneath, Jenny felt a warmth rushing through her that added to the heat already caused by his intimate caresses. Her breath caught in her throat as his large fingers unfastened his belt and unsnapped the top fastener of his trousers.

He wore tight-fitting jockey shorts, and when he peeled them away, she turned her head, surprised at her sudden shyness. But he noticed the gesture and bent toward her, gently turning her face toward him. His physique was more powerful than she had imagined, so much the epitome of masculine perfection and virility that it held her stunned. He lay down beside her, and the feel of him against her, the rock-hard muscle beneath his amazingly smooth skin, was a pleasure in itself, even before he moved to wrap her in his strong arms, just holding her for the longest time before his fingers finally renewed their sensuous tracing of her body.

There was nothing hurried or greedy about the way he made love with her, not even when he discovered for the first time that she had come to him completely innocent of such pleasures. Jenny had looked forward to this moment with a strange combination of anticipation and dread—anticipation of giving to this man the precious gift she could give but once in her lifetime, dread that he might be resentful that what should have been pure bliss for the both of them would now contain certain elements of discomfort, even pain. But he paused briefly, uttered her name and kissed her deeply in response to his pleasurable surprise. She felt only a momentary vague discomfort before all resistance was suddenly gone, a closeness achieved with Peter that she had never known with any other man. If there was pain—and due to his gentleness and control of his own needs there had been surprisingly little—it had been a small enough price for her to pay for the wondrous joy of discovering the new world of loving sensations that he had suddenly opened for her.

She willingly joined him in a dance whose age surpassed even that of crumbling monuments along the Nile. Theirs was a shared sensuousness that echoed times past when man had no conception of city or civilization. And in their shared ecstasy, Jenny knew Peter was giving to her the same gift she was giving to him. Joined in a final cataclysmic shudder, they clung desperately to each other. "Oh, Jenny, Jenny!" he groaned, burying his face against the soft pillowing offered by the curve of her neck at her shoulder.

"Peter," she answered. And his name was the most important word in the world.

He embraced her, kissed her, rocked her and told her over and over again that he loved her. He lay beside her and supported himself on one arm. He cast his golden gaze down on the beauty of her flushed face and inquired why she hadn't told him he was her first lover. "Would you have believed me?" she asked. Her voice was made light and teasing by the new intimacy she felt with him, but her question was a serious one.

"Probably not," he admitted. "You're too beautiful a woman to have stayed a virgin for so long."

"I was merely waiting for the right man," Jenny

said, deliriously happy. "He was a long time in coming."

"You haven't seen anything yet," he told her, smiling like a little boy about to be accused of bragging but confident in his boast. Then slowly, gently and ever so patiently he took her back one more time to that wondrous world of flaming sensation that the two of them had so recently discovered. She willingly joined him in the fire.

CHAPTER EIGHT

ABDUL CAME QUICKLY to his feet and almost tipped over the table in the process. It was obvious he was surprised to see her. He was wearing a very expensive European-cut white suit with a cream-colored tie. He looked extremely handsome, extremely vulnerable, and Jenny wished there could have been some way to avoid hurting him. But life, unfortunately, wasn't a fairy tale in which everyone came through unscathed to live happily ever after. She felt that Abdul was certainly man enough to understand that their relationship had never had a future. Besides, it had only been a matter of days since they had first met. She got a sudden uneasy feeling when she realized she and Peter hadn't known each much longer. Yet somehow it seemed that she and Peter had ties that went far beyond those formed during their short period of social contact. There was a sense of destiny to their love, something that had drawn them both to Thebes to set right the tragedy of sixty years earlier.

"Whom, I wonder, were you expecting?" she asked with a smile, sitting in the chair the waiter pulled out for her. "This is my assigned table, isn't it?"

"I thought..." he began, but didn't finish. She knew what he thought, and tearing herself away from Peter to make the sailing had been the hardest thing she had ever done in her life. However, she owed Abdul a lot more than to simply disappear without any explanation.

"How's the chicken?" she asked, noticing that the food on his plate was virtually untouched. He shrugged, indicating it was no better or worse than usual, so she ordered it. The meal selections on board were satisfactory for Jenny's palate, but Abdul, who retained several personal chefs, must have found the food far less enticing than what he was used to. There was a big buffet of over fifty different dishes representative of Egyptian culture scheduled for the last day of the cruise. However, Jenny would not be there to enjoy it. Although she had been forced to book as far as Aswân, there being no official intermediary stops for disembarkation, she was really going to get off at Idfu.

"Did Peter find you?" Abdul asked, the excessive care with which he was suddenly trying to cut dark meat from a chicken bone pretty much portraying what little interest he really had in what he was doing.

"Yes, he did," Jenny said. "And thank you for telling him where I was."

"I also told him you wanted to be alone," Abdul said, hoping that her comment had been a small rebuke but fearing it wasn't. "Which meant I was quite delighted when he insisted he had to see you anyway. I understood, I guess, that his barging in wasn't going to annoy you. I was right, yes?"

Jenny's chicken arrived, and she no more cared about it than Abdul cared about his. "He loves me, Abdul," she said, trying to keep the sheer joy of that statement down to an acceptable minimum. She didn't want to appear too much happier than she had when Abdul had confessed his own love for her.

"So what else is new?" he asked with just an edge of bitterness. "I told you that all along, didn't I?"

"Yes," she admitted, "you did. You were also right about my feelings for him."

"I see," he said. Whatever he was feeling, he was putting up a good show of being a civilized loser.

"Yes, I think you do see," Jenny replied, glad there would be no nasty accusations, no scenes. "I think you've seen all along and were intelligent enough to realize it would have been a big mistake for us to fool ourselves into believing that my feelings for Peter and his for me wouldn't have eventually intruded between you and me."

"Yes, of course," he said. A solicitous waiter approached, and Abdul had to take a brief minute to explain that the chicken was just fine but that they weren't hungry.

Jenny would have felt guiltier about Abdul if she hadn't thought she'd always made it a point not to give him hope where there had been none. "You're a wonderful man," she said. "You're handsome, charming, witty, fun to be with, and you've got loads of money." That got a smile out of him.

"You're everything a girl could possibly want in a man. I'm just not that girl."

"I seem to have rotten luck chosing the women I really like," Abdul said with a note of sincere regret. "Oh, there seem to be plenty of the others available, mind you."

"There's nothing that says we can't be good friends, is there?" Jenny asked, knowing it was difficult for some people to make a permanent transition that depended upon altering their hopes drastically. She really did like Abdul, and she would have hated for him to suddenly exit from her life forever, but she knew he might feel that total separation was necessary for his own well-being. She was better able to adjust, because she had always known down deep that there could never be anything serious between them.

"I really don't want you just as my friend," he said, looking down at his plate of chicken, fried eggplant and French-fried potatoes, all of which were quite cold by now. He looked up and tried his best to give her a smile. "But if it's all I can hope for, I suppose it will have to do, won't it?"

"I'm glad you feel that way," Jenny answered with an inward sigh of relief.

"We're all civilized people, are we not?" Abdul said. "That we have momentarily been thrown into this silly triangle doesn't mean we can't come through with a little reshuffling of emotional perspectives, does it?"

"Oh, Abdul, I'm so happy," Jenny said, wanting

to reach across the table to touch him so that he could feel the sheer joy flowing from her to him. She didn't, however, make any attempt to do so.

"Yes, I see that you are," he acknowledged. "And believe it or not, I'm truly happy for you. There's nothing more wonderful than the utter bliss of loving and knowing someone loves you in return." He gave her a wistful smile. "Anyway, that's what I hear. I've only managed to be on the delivering end of the deal, although I shall continue to hold out hope of one day entering into a relationship not so overbalanced." His smile widened, and he locked Jenny's eyes with his own. "I really didn't want that to come out sounding like sour grapes, you know. I'm the first to realize that certain things click between certain people, and it's no personal insult to anyone involved if he's not one of those certain people. I'll be more than happy to be your friend, Jenny, just as I would have been delighted to be your husband or lover. Is Peter going to be confident enough of his position to accept my being in the wings, or should I quietly disappear into the backdrop to give you both some breathing space?"

"I think Peter isn't going to want you out of our lives any more than I do," she said. "You do, after all, have a great many things in common." At that moment she was feeling magnanimous enough even to forgive them their mutual infatuation with falconry.

"Yes, I'd say you were right there," Abdul replied, delivering an accompanying sigh of fortified resolve. "And I rather like him. I told you that once already. I should have possibly liked him less. I would have far preferred his being an obnoxious bastard upon whom I could have relished wreaking an evil revenge."

Jenny laughed at the exaggerated drama of his statement. "I can't imagine your playing dirty with anyone," she said, knowing Abdul had come through all of this too much a gentleman to seek revenge.

"Someone very dear to me once told me love wasn't a game to be won or lost," Abdul said. "I think I shall believe her." He pushed his chair back from the table. "I'm really not hungry. What about you?"

Jenny hadn't touched her food. "No, as a matter of fact, I'm not," she confirmed.

"Then maybe you wouldn't mind coming down to my cabin for a minute. Unless, of course—" and he smiled "—you fear I may be preparing to do all sorts of horrible things to you in retaliation for allowing Peter to steal you away from me."

"Are you planning to do all sorts of horrible things?" Jenny asked, coming to her feet with him. Her question was offered as a joke, but she was curious as to why he would want to see her in his cabin.

"I have something I'd like to give you," he said. "I'd rather hand it over in private, but I can very well do so in the public lounge of the ship if you would so prefer."

"Friends don't spend their lives arranging to meet *only* in public places," Jenny said. "Do they?"

"No," he admitted.

"I think it would hardly be smart to begin planning our lives that way, do you?" They had left the dining room and had paused in the space adjoining the small souvenir shop and boutique. "Although I don't think you should be giving me gifts, either," she added.

"Don't friends give gifts?" Abdul asked in challenge. He didn't give her a chance to answer. "It's a little something I knew from the very beginning I might be giving to you as one friend to another. As I consider it to be something special, something suited to you alone, it would hurt me deeply if you were to be so ungracious as not to accept it."

She took his hand in both of hers and held it. "You're a very, very dear person to me, Abdul," she said with all sincerity. "I don't know if you can appreciate just how dear. Without you I'd be a far less happy woman than I am today. And if you presently find yourself tempted to begrudge me my happiness because it has deprived you of happiness you had hoped for for yourself, I can tell you only that the gift you've so willingly given is more precious to me than anything else you could possibly offer."

"I don't begrudge you anything, Jenny," he said, his eyes velvety pools of darkness. "I don't now, I never have, and I never will. Truly! And you must believe that. You want me as a friend, then I shall always be there as the friend you want. A friend to you *and* to Peter. And if ever—*ever*, Jenny—you find need of the comfort or the counsel of a friend you know you can trust, you must promise to get in touch with me wherever I am. Because I promise to be there for you—always.''

She felt like crying. For someone to have gone twenty-nine years without finding one man she really cared for, except her father, she couldn't believe how lucky she was to have suddenly had two enter her world at the same time. One was friend, and one was lover, but that fact didn't dilute the intense feelings she had wrapped up in each of them. She probably *would* have cried if an elderly woman hadn't exited from the dining room at that moment to look slightly embarrassed at finding Jenny so tenderly holding Abdul's hand in the vestibule. The old lady's expression made Abdul laugh, and Jenny joined in, laughing harder when the woman found the outbreak of mirth even more disconcerting. "Come on," Jenny said, keeping hold of his hand. "I love surprises."

She was, however, little prepared for this one. "I couldn't possibly accept it!" she said when she had finally found the words to speak. Before that she'd had to sit down, as if the mere weight of the jewelry case in her hand had been too much to bear. She tore her eyes from the exquisite necklace laid out on plush black velvet and, shaking her head, locked in on Abdul's dark eyes, which were watching her.

"Oh, Abdul, accepting it is quite out of the question!" she stated emphatically.

"Why?" he asked, as if he couldn't begin to fathom any possible reason for her rejection. "You don't like it?"

"Who could not like it?" she asked, knowing it was ridiculous to believe any woman wouldn't have adored what was in that case lying open on her lap. It was a necklace of lapis lazuli scarabs linked together by a delicately filigreed gold chain from the midpoint of which hung, by its two lapis lazuli antennae, a larger scarab carved from one, deep, blue black sapphire that caught even the poor lighting in the cabin to flash back a brilliant asterisk. From the main setting, outlined in the same gold that held the sapphire secure, were upward curving wings in delicate inlay of alternating blue and black faience, matching by a balancing faience tail between golden bird-shaped legs whose terminal talons gripped matching star sapphires. "It must have cost you a fortune," she said, still a little agog at the sight.

"A fortune compared to the resources of whom?" Abdul asked. "Of the kid from the Cairo slums, who's lucky enough if he can buy food, or of me, for whom the cost of this trinket is no more than a drop in the proverbial bucket?"

"It's still too expensive for me to take," she said, yet unable to make the mental leap between this and the small token gift she had expected. "Certainly as a gift between friends."

"Don't look upon it, then, as merely a friendship gift," he said. "Look upon it as a wedding gift for you and Peter." Which had Jenny realizing, for perhaps the very first time, that there had yet to be any mention of marriage. All there had been was her and Abdul's assumption that marriage was what resulted from two people being madly in love with each other. "Or look upon it as your dowry," he suggested as an alternative. Jenny flinched as she remembered that Frederic Donas had jilted Geraldine Fowler to marry a woman for her dowry. "It is certainly customary for all Egyptian women to have one," he added.

"I'm not an Egyptian woman!" Jenny shot back, realizing immediately that her being upset by visions conjured up by the word *dowry* had made that come out sounding as if she somehow considered it an insult to have it implied she was Egyptian. "I mean, I'm American, Abdul," she explained, trying to temper her impolite remark, "and dowries for us went out of fashion a long time ago, except for those with far more money than my family ever had." Fortunes were certainly still known to be merged by marriages among families with money. The Donas family might certainly have been considered wealthy enough for such things. Maybe there was a rich woman somewhere already lined up to be Mrs. Peter Donas. Love and family fortune seemed to have been inextricably connected in the oh-so-practical Donases' scheme of things.

"Jenny?" Abdul asked, obviously aware that she had momentarily left him behind in her thoughts.

"No matter how good you are at giving me a rationale, I can't possibly," she said, lowering the lid to conceal all temptation. "Although I'll be forever flattered to think that you considered me worthy of such a gift." She laid the case on his bed and came to her feet.

"You can leave it here or wherever else you please," Abdul said stubbornly, "but it's yours from this moment on."

"No, Abdul," Jenny replied, shaking her head, wondering if she could make him understand. Maybe it was par for the course for rich men to give expensive gifts that had no strings attached to them. She'd heard of sheikhs giving out thousand-dollar tips to bellboys in hotel lobbies, of others renting whole fleets of 747s for parties on the other side of the world. She was, however, aware of one thing: Peter would wonder how she had warranted such a parting present from a man she had known so briefly.

Abdul called out to her when she crossed to the door to leave. She thought he was prepared to be even more insistent that she take the necklace with her. She turned back to him, just as prepared to keep her resolve to refuse it. "I want to thank you for being gracious enough to come back to the ship and break the news about you and Peter to me personally," he said instead. "Dear John letters are so infinitely lacking in class."

"You're welcome," she said, remembering once again how tempting it had been to stay with Peter in

Luxor, to drive to Hierakonpolis from there. It would have given them an extra day together. Abdul, though, had deserved far more than a hurriedly scribbled note. Besides, what was one day without Peter when they would have the rest of their lives together? If Peter really planned on them having the rest of their lives together, that is. "I really wish I could love you," she told Abdul, and he smiled— the sad smile of an experienced man who could be suave even in defeat.

She stepped into the hallway and pulled the door gently closed between them. Her flush of happiness had been somewhat tempered by the niggling realization that she and Peter hadn't discussed marriage. She had gone to bed with a man after knowing him only a few short days because she loved him, because she believed he loved her, too. Even her grandmother had probably held out longer than that before succumbing to Frederic Donas's advances. Once again Jenny feared she had been too caught up in a dream of romance that had whispered to her of Egypt and tragedy and love reborn sixty years after the fact. If her happiness now turned out to be an illusion, she had no one to blame but herself. She had begun engineering this situation ever since she had stood by that portrait of her grandmother and had been told she so strikingly resembled the dead woman. She had immersed herself in the tragedy, devoting endless hours to reading about Egypt, Tutankhamen and the Donas family. She had become an archaeologist knowing that Peter Donas had decided to be one, plotting possible parallels in their lives even then. She had jumped at the chance to come to Hierakonpolis because Peter was going to be there. The question suddenly seemed to be: who had seduced whom? As much as she hated to admit it, it could be argued she had been scheming to get him into her arms for years. But she had never even subconsciously thought to seduce him and then leave him high and dry as his grandfather had left her grandmother. She had walked into her own trap and slammed the door shut behind her. She loved him, damn it, she loved him!

Her anxiety wasn't relieved by a night of restless sleep. She was one of the few up when the ship reached the locks at Isna in the pale light of morning. She watched men use brute strength to open and shut gates that would have been operated by electrical or diesel power in more industrialized countries. Here labor was cheaper even than converting to energy made abundantly available by the High Dam at Aswân.

The ship docked shortly after clearing the locks. Jenny went to breakfast, not because she was hungry, but because she thought Abdul might be concerned if she didn't show up. She was persuaded to go ashore only when it became apparent that Abdul would have stayed on board with her if she hadn't gone. Her tour of the Temple of Khnum at Isna, which had been constructed in Ptolemaic times on the ruins of another temple built by Thutmose III, was an unsuccessful distraction. During the sleepless night she had spent, her thoughts had returned again and again to Peter. But instead of the tender reminiscences she should have enjoyed when she thought of the previous hours they had shared, only wracking doubt had come to her. Not once had he mentioned the future.

The boat didn't stay long at Isna. The Temple, of which only the hypostyle hall remained, presented some interesting columns with stylized foliage and complicated geometric designs, but for Jenny it was rather anticlimactic after the more extreme grandeur of Luxor, Karnak and Thebes. Besides, the ship was scheduled for Idfu that afternoon, and that site offered the Temple of Horus, the greatest temple in Egypt outside of the one at Karnak. When the ship sailed, Jenny used the excuse that she needed to pack and went straight to her room. She stayed in her cabin far beyond the few minutes it took her to put her things, a small box of dried rose petals included, into her suitcase. "Is anything wrong, Jenny?" Abdul asked when he came checking to see what had happened to her.

"I didn't sleep all that well last night," she admitted. "I guess all the excitement finally just got to me."

"Ah, true love!" he said. If there was sarcasm in his voice she couldn't find it.

"That and the fact that I'm always a little apprehensive before a new dig," Jenny said, anxious to make all the excuses she possibly could for her preoccupied attitude. She didn't want any third-degree treatment that might make her confess that she was beginning to have second thoughts about the time she had spent in Peter Donas's bedroom. "There are invariably new people to meet, personality differences to sort out, details to attend to. And everything has to be done in quick order for maximum use of the surprisingly little time we have available to us at a site as extensive as Hierakonpolis."

"Why not just stay longer?" Abdul asked. They had gone to the lounge and had found empty seats by one window.

"Government red tape," she said, glancing toward shoreline vegetation that was funneling to narrower and narrower borders as the ship pushed farther south. At Aswân the river's green edges would peter out almost to nonexistence, fertile soil giving way to bedrock. "There's an unimaginable amount of paperwork that has to be done months, sometimes years, in advance for one of these undertakings. There are security checks on every member of the group so that there's little chance of any of us walking off with a valuable artifact if we find one, and there are just the pure mechanics of getting eight to twelve people together at one spot at one time, due to conflicting schedules and a work force of college kids who can get away only during summer vacations." They continued with the small talk, but by the time they went to lunch, Jenny's inner turmoil had not abated, and she feared that her dreams were liable to be shattered as soon as the ship reached Idfu.

Nor was she reassured by Peter's greeting upon docking, either. He kissed her and accepted Abdul's congratulations with obvious good humor, but there was a certain reserve about the way he acted, a certain aloofness that remained even after he was alone with Jenny in the Land Rover and they had left Abdul and the *Osiris* behind them in a cloud of dust.

The road north to Hierakonpolis was not a good one. Its rutted unpaved surface made the highway running along the east side of the Nile seem like a freeway in comparison. The Land Rover tipped precariously one way and then the other as one wheel after another disappeared into deep pockets of dust. Vehicles passed from the other direction, looking like filthy monsters emerging suddenly from a miasmic haze.

"We could have made better time, but there's a little trouble with the transmission on this baby," Peter said, the road momentarily smoothing into a washboard surface that sent Jenny's teeth chattering. "Actually, the shocks aren't all that good, either," he added, his voice coming out garbled.

Jenny knew the ride wouldn't have been quite as uncomfortable if she hadn't been so tense. Her nervous state didn't allow her to roll with the jarring motion of the car. Her back and head were beginning to ache; her nose and mouth were desperately dry, and she felt as though she had eaten grit.

"Our group lucked out in renting a house close to the dig," Peter said after successfully weaving the

Land Rover through a maze of two oncoming cars and a camel cart overloaded with sugarcane. "It saves everyone from having to make this drive every morning for the next two months."

That was welcome news, but it really wasn't what Jenny wanted to hear. She wanted something said to put her doubts to rest. Why was Peter acting so professional, so cool? Why was his conversation confined to comments about the dig, rather than about his happiness at seeing her again?

"Abdul seems to have taken it all very well," Peter said, breaking into Jenny's thoughts. For a brief moment the Nile came into view on their right, visible through banana trees and sugarcane. Just as quickly it disappeared amid that thin stretch of vegetation still possible between desert and river.

"Taken what well?" she asked, aware of the answer as much as he was but hoping he would take the hint and begin to talk about their relationship. She didn't want to believe that what they had shared had merely been one brief interlude motivated by little more than desire.

"You know," Peter said with a small laugh that offered Jenny no reassurance, "I wonder if I would have been able to manage it with the same finesse."

"I wonder, too," Jenny answered. It was doubtful he noticed the edge to her voice since he was suddenly involved in passing a donkey cart piled high with used tires.

"I'm glad he didn't challenge me to the Egyptian equivalent of an old-fashioned duel," Peter said.

He was making an attempt at humor, but Jenny couldn't bring herself to laugh because it occurred to her, despite herself, that a challenge might well have proven how committed Peter really was. A man involved in a casual affair wasn't likely to put his life on the line. "I would have hated dropping him low," he added. "I mean, I genuinely liked the guy before it became so obvious he was out to get you." He flashed Jenny a smile that seemed a little strained.

"And do you like him now?" Jenny asked, wondering if it really were possible for a man to like his chief rival in love.

"What's not to like about a gracious loser?" Peter asked. "Damned civilized of the man—the way he's handled himself—if you ask me."

Jenny could have wished Abdul a little less civilized in refusing to offer challenge to Peter's too easy conquest. But it was true that Abdul had unarguably done more than his share to try to convince her he had more to give than Peter. He'd told her he loved her before Peter had ever decided it was necessary to go that far. He'd said he would have welcomed being her husband, whereas Peter hadn't yet thought it obligatory to bring that subject up. He'd been a gentleman, whereas Peter had been making sexual overtures from their very first date. Finally, he had given her a hint of what her life could have been when he'd offered her a necklace worth a small fortune. She could have expected no more effort put forth by any man.

"It's nice and convenient, isn't it—your both managing to come through this as friends?" Jenny commented. He turned to give her a look that said he didn't quite follow her reasoning. "He's had his hawks shipped to Aswân ahead of him," she explained. "Aswân isn't all that far upstream, is it? I'm sure you'll be able to get away from the dig a few times to see Hatshepsût put through her paces. Right?"

"I never thought about that," Peter said, and she didn't appreciate his insinuation that it might have completely slipped his mind if she hadn't brought it up. "You're sure you wouldn't care?" he asked, finally sounding as if he were getting hints of her unease and was putting himself on guard. She had to admit that her present behavior was not what one would expect of a woman recently reunited with the man she loved. But neither was he especially solicitous, and Jenny was still preoccupied with the fear that what had been a beautiful experience for her was for him simply a way of avoiding months of celibacy on an archaeological excavation.

"Why should I care what you do or don't do?" she inquired bitterly, and he stopped the car. They were momentarily engulfed in a cloud of dust that slowly drifted off to one side, leaving them in a position that blocked traffic from either direction.

"Okay, what the hell is going on here?" he asked. It wasn't so much a question, though, as a command for her to explain her unfriendly attitude—and an opportunity for her to tell him what was bothering her. But she held back, because even feeling as she did she was wise enough to know he could justifiably charge that her love left a little to be desired if she was beginning to doubt him already. Besides, there was a pickup truck barreling down on them.

"Peter, please!" Jenny cried, sure that the oncoming vehicle couldn't stop short of a collision. Peter waited until the very last minute before starting up the Land Rover and moving it out of the way. He immediately turned onto a side road that cut through that last bit of vegetation separating them from the desert. He didn't drive on through, though, but stopped the vehicle again. He leaned forward to put his forehead to the top of the steering wheel as if he were tired. Then, with a loud sigh, he lifted his head and shifted in the seat to face her.

"What you're really trying to tell me is that you know, don't you?" he said. And the question shattered Jenny like a wrecking ball suddenly swung through a delicate crystal palace. She nodded, unable to find the words she knew she'd quickly have to find in order to bring her through this with some shred of dignity intact. "So what can I say?" he asked. "Make apologies for something over which I had no control?"

Jenny couldn't believe he was about to offer her the classic excuse for two people to make love without love. So he had lost control. She wondered what further well-worn lines he was about to come up with. She didn't want to hear another word. What she did want was to cry. But she pulled herself together and faced him squarely, her cool voice hiding her seething emotions.

"No need to apologize," she told him, figuring two people could play this little game. "If I've somehow given you the impression I expected apologies for what happened between us, I'm sorry for giving that false impression. Actually, it was no big deal...something neither of us could help at the time. Casual couplings happen between men and women every day of the year."

"What?" he asked, looking genuinely shocked. She was glad she had shocked him. He probably thought she was going to come apart at the seams when she found out how much the grandson of Frederic Donas he really was. Well, if she was stupid enough to be coming apart, she wasn't about to give him the satisfaction of knowing it was happening. She had given him far too much satisfaction already.

"We'll simply chalk it up as a good time had by all, and leave it at that, shall we?" she said, wondering if he noticed just how strained her voice was. It took all of her willpower not to tell him just what she did think of him. She succeeded in restraining herself only because there was no way she wanted him to know how he had got to her in just a few short days. "If the right circumstances come up again, well, then, maybe we can once more jump on the pleasure wagon. If not...." She shrugged. She had no intention whatsoever of ever letting this man get that close to her again.

"Well, that's just great!" he said, and she was surprised at the anger in his voice. "You damned little liar! After all that garbage you were spoon-feeding me about love!" Jenny would have told him that was rather like the pot calling the kettle black, but he didn't give her the chance. "What happened, huh?" he asked loudly. "Did you simply decide you were tired of lugging around your virginity and grab the first available man you thought might oblige in removing that inconvenience for you?"

"You have no right..." she began, but wasn't allowed to finish. He reached across the seat, took hold of her and glared into her eyes.

"Don't you dare talk to me about rights!" he commanded, releasing her so suddenly that she fell back against the car door. "I'm the one who was gullible enough to believe your line to the point of calling home to tell everyone about the great woman I was bringing back to marry."

Jenny could not believe her ears. "You never once mentioned marriage," she stuttered, confused by his words.

"I don't know what two people in love do where you come from," he said, his face red and twisted into a grimace of genuine rage, "but they certainly marry in all civilized parts of the world."

He opened the car door and got out, slamming the door behind him with a bang that rocked the Land Rover and sent dust flying.

"You're the one who's lying," Jenny accused weakly, watching him disappear into a growth of sugarcane at the side of the road. She told herself she was not going to cry. She told herself she had not just ruined the best thing that had ever happened to her. "You're the damned liar!" she screamed after him, tears of heartbreak and confusion already flooding down her cheeks.

CHAPTER NINE

JENNY GOT HOLD of her emotions as soon as she realized that the more distraught she was, the more she would look like a fool. What she should have done was run after him, take him joyously in her arms and beg him to forgive her for her doubts. And then she would have been a fool indeed—just like Geraldine. She just couldn't believe all this talk about Peter's having planned to marry her. There seemed a strong chance it was nothing more than his last-ditch effort to come out of this smelling like a rose. Thinking of roses, she had better get rid of those wilted rose petals in her suitcase. They no longer could represent to Jenny anything other than one more tool of a man who would have used her as his grandfather had once used her grandmother. She would have dug into her suitcase at that very moment, except that she was distracted by a glance at her reflection in the rearview mirror that told her she looked like death warmed over. She was covered from head to foot in fine, powdery, brown dust that was absent only where her tears had washed gullies down her cheeks. She repaired as much of the damage as she could with the tip of a handkerchief and a little saliva, but it wasn't nearly enough. What she needed was a bath, and she became immediately determined to find one. There was nothing better for getting her thoughts back into proper order than the soothing flush of steamy water over her physically and emotionally drained body.

She got out of the Land Rover to take better stock of her present situation. Cars were still raising clouds of dust on the main road. She had to decide whether to go back to that road and continue north or stay headed in her present direction. She was pretty sure the dig couldn't be too far distant, not only because of the distance they had already traveled, but because Peter had so readily gone stomping off. He wouldn't have concluded his bit of theatrics the way he had if there'd been any real chance of his being stranded in the middle of that sugarcane. She was quite certain he was far more clever than that. It wasn't as if he had taken the keys to the Land Rover with him, since they were still in the ignition. While Jenny knew very little about mechanics, previous experience would certainly give her sufficient expertise to turn a key, put a Land Rover in gear and get on her not-so-merry way.

Her problems regarding where she was and where she had to go from there were quickly solved by the arrival of Barbara Temple. "Hi, there," Barbara said, suddenly appearing out of the sugarcane as easily as Peter had disappeared into it. She then proceeded to introduce herself as an eighteen-year-old student from Northwestern University, majoring in archaeology, minoring in anthropology and having signed on for the Hierakonpolis dig through connections had by her fiancé's father. She managed to get all this out in one breath, punctuated by a small gasp at the end. She then added that her fiancé was Timothy Journer, who was assigned to the dig, too. Jenny hoped Timothy's and Barbara's romance was destined for a happier ending than hers and Peter's seemed to be at the moment. Barbara followed by blurting out that she was so nervous because Jenny just happened to be her idol. She had read everything there was to read about J. Mowry and thought that what Jenny had done to open up the field of archaeology to women could only be compared to what Margaret Mead had done in anthropology.

Jenny had to laugh, not only because the young girl's admiration was so evident, her compliments so effusive, but because Jenny could just imagine what kind of an apparition Barbara's idol now presented there on that dusty Egyptian roadway. Jenny's memory of the reflection she had seen in her mirror was still fresh. She certainly wasn't at her best, especially in comparison to the younger woman, who looked as if she were out for a Sunday stroll in a primitive country and had dressed for the part. Barbara's shirt, the kind with button-down epaulets, looked as if it had just been cleaned and pressed for someone in the French Foreign Legion.

Her pants, just as fresh, were the convenient kind
with pockets up and down both legs. Her shoes
were less new, giving the impression of having been
sensibly broken in before being brought to a locale
that would have turned newer ones into painful blis-
ter makers. Her hair was cut short in a swingy
casual style. Below the brown hair was a freshly
scrubbed face, quite attractive, with large brown
eyes, pert nose, nice mouth, all looking quite perfect—as most young people's features could—with
only little makeup. Jenny immediately pegged Barbara as one of those lucky ones whose appearance
was in good order even after a hot and sticky workday on a dig. Jenny presently seemed and felt as if
she had been put through the proverbial wringer.
Which she had. "If I'm not looking my best," Jenny apologized, "you can well imagine why." Actually there was no way Barbara could imagine any
such thing, unless she'd been hiding in the sugarcane all the while—which hardly seemed likely. The
only logical reason for anyone being found there
was the fact that they were going to, or coming
from, somewhere else. "The ride in from Idfu was a
little dusty, besides which I managed to get something in my eye," Jenny said, explaining the redness
caused by her tears.

"You want me to see if I can get it out for you?"
Barbara volunteered.

"I think I finally managed that a few seconds
ago," Jenny answered. "What I'd like you to do,
though, is point me toward the nearest shower."

"That your only piece of luggage?" Barbara inquired, having bent slightly to check the back seat of the Land Rover. Jenny nodded. "Then we might as well take it with us," Barbara said. "It's really only a short walk."

"I imagine it's a shorter drive," Jenny replied, hardly able to conceive of why they should walk any distance lugging her suitcase between them, when she certainly had no plans of making any sacrifices just to leave Peter transportation. "Why don't we just take the Land Rover?"

"Is it running?" Barbara asked. Jenny could see immediately how the younger woman might have jumped to the conclusion that it wasn't working. It hardly seemed logical that Jenny would be standing in the middle of a dusty road, the Land Rover stopped dead, if the vehicle were operational. The scenery didn't seem to warrant any stops for a closer look. "I assumed," Barbara continued, not wanting Jenny to think she was really silly enough to prefer walking to riding, "that when Professor Donas—" she paused and snapped her fingers as if she'd once again forgotten something often forgotten, and Jenny had visions of how Peter might have turned on the charm at some time in the past, telling Barbara to call him by his first name "—Peter," she continued, "arrived at the house and told me I'd better come out and see that you made it in safely, it was because the transmission had gone out."

"It just stopped suddenly," Jenny said, motioning toward the Land Rover and deeming it wise to come up with something besides the complete truth. She didn't think it smart to start washing her dirty linen in public before the young woman she had just met. Barbara might be the nice sweet thing she appeared. Then again she might be one of those bored persons on digs who delighted in hearing and spreading gossip. There was no sense in having it get around immediately that Jenny and Peter were on the outs because of their emotional involvement. "However, I tried it a few minutes ago, and it started up again," Jenny added, indicating that life was still full of surprises.

A Land Rover having suddenly returned to working order certainly didn't do much to explain why it was still stopped, or why Jenny was still standing in the middle of the dusty road beside it. Thankfully Barbara was naive enough—or diplomatic enough—not to press for a more complete explanation. "This one has been giving them all kinds of problems lately," she said, slipping into the driver's seat and turning the key. Defying even a suggestion of having been out of order, the engine turned over with embarrassing ease.

Jenny climbed in as Barbara put the car in gear. In a few minutes the Land Rover managed a dilapidated bridge over stale and slimy green water to exit in sight of a small village built at the exact spot where the vegetation ended and the desert began. Farther in the distance, perched upon an apron of sand and rocky ground that stretched to bone-dry hills, was the only visible evidence that this spot might be slightly more special than any other area of desert wilderness. Even then, that solitary ruin, called Khasekhemui's fort, after a Second Dynasty pharaoh, wasn't much to look at, especially considering to what Egyptian grandeur Jenny had been exposed during her few days in Cairo and along the Nile. It was a crumbling rectangular structure that had deteriorated far more than was suggested by the pictures taken of it in the 1930s, which Jenny had seen before leaving Seattle. Its startling degree of further decay was due mainly to the climatic changes caused by the backing up of Lake Nasser into previously barren regions behind the High Dam at Aswân. While the water evaporation from the lake's surface was hardly enough to bring precipitation to an area that hadn't seen rain in fifteen years, there was no denying that whatever the increased atmospheric moisture content, it boded ill for something constructed entirely of mud brick. Efforts were in progress in certain quarters to bring in an architectural team to bolster and preserve what was still there, but red tape seemed destined to convert this fort, possibly the oldest standing structure in Egypt, into nothing more than a pile of windblown dirt. In a country hard pressed to preserve even its major monuments of the past, this paltry unimpressive heap of disintegrating rubble, which didn't hold much attraction to tourists quickly jaded on the more majestic fare of Giza, Karnak, Luxor and Idfu, wasn't given a very high priority.

"Home!" Barbara exclaimed after steering the Land Rover through the small village that little hinted of the past importance of this site—first called Nekhen, city of the falcon-headed god Horus, by the ancient Egyptians and later called Hierakonpolis, city of the hawk, by the Greeks. Jenny didn't miss the irony of having come to a place named after the bird of prey that had already caused her so much heartache.

"Home," as Barbara termed it, was a fairly large house at one edge of the village. It had been rented for the group from a wealthy Arab whose dealings in the area's sugar crop allowed him and his family the luxury of spending their summers in the more pleasant temperatures afforded by the sea breezes at Alexandria. Despite the wealth of the owner, the place could be considered, by American standards, as luxurious only in size. Composed entirely of mud brick made in very much the same way brick had been made in the time of Moses' exodus from Egypt, the house had been no more impervious to decay than those more ancient buildings once erected on the spot before it. That the house was standing at all was only because the weathering process hadn't had quite as much time to work on it as on the fort visible from the balcony of Jenny's second-floor window. Great hunks of the house's construction material plus the stucco that covered it had simply dropped off, both inside and out. Additional damage to walls and foundations had been sustained from bomb blasts during attacks on the strategic bridge crossing the Nile at Idfu. A great crack—accompanied by so many smaller ones that the total effect was that of a topography map depicting some intricate river system—took up the whole wall behind the twin beds.

"I hope you don't mind having me as your roommate," Barbara said, setting down Jenny's suitcase after having insisted she be allowed to carry it up the stairs. "As big as this place looks, we still had to double up, and I, quite frankly, gave battle for the privilege of being put in with you."

Jenny felt a little better than she had, although she knew she was bound to feel even better as soon as she got a chance to wash up. There was no denying the ego-boosting pleasure of having someone present who appreciated her contribution to her profession. "I remember once being crowded with three other women and a few scorpions into a tent about half as big as one of these beds," she said.

"This is my first dig," Barbara admitted, seeming genuinely sorry she didn't have any anecdotes about her past experiences in the field. "Actually, I came expecting to do a bit more by way of roughing it."

"Take what comfort you can get, when you can get it," Jenny said, the voice of experience. "You'll wish you had all this back the minute you suddenly find yourself assigned to a tent, believe me. Now if you'd like to tell me which of these

gloriously comfortable beds is mine and then point
me toward the nearest spigot of running water, I'll
try to prove that Jenny Mowry is in this dustbin
somewhere.''

"I think you look just great!" Barbara offered,
and Jenny thanked her for the lie with a laugh of
genuine appreciation. There was, however, no
chance on God's green earth that the way she presently looked and felt could be called even remotely
acceptable—let alone great!

"My bed?" Jenny tried again.

"Whichever one you want, Miss Mowry," Barbara replied obligingly.

"First, it's Jenny, okay?" Jenny said. Barbara
nodded vigorously, as if the privilege of being on a
first-name basis with Jenny was more than she
could have hoped for. Jenny shook her head, not
really believing she could be the object of such admiration from a young woman who might have
been expected to be too caught up in football heroes
and homecoming games even to know who Jenny
Mowry was. "Second," Jenny continued, "and this
is probably the most important thing of all, you
mustn't make the mistake of lionizing me, or I will
certainly find myself taking advantage of it.
Right?" Her smile let Barbara know that she was
really more appreciative than she was letting on.
"Now, since I was so poky in getting here and
you've obviously had time to settle in...." She
waited as Barbara pointed to the bed on the left and
mentioned that she had slept there for the past few

nights. "Right!" Jenny said, hoisting her suitcase to the other bed and watching the bedspread puff dust as she did so. "And the bathroom?" she asked.

"It's down the hall," Barbara said. "We have to share it, too—all the women anyway. The men have use of the one downstairs. Tim says it's a little archaic the way we've been segregated one sex to each floor, but I told him there was no way I would be rooming with him, even if it were allowed. Not that I'm a prude, mind you," she added, as if she certainly hadn't wanted it to come across that she was. "But we're here to work, and that comes first."

"Right you are there!" Jenny said, thinking of how much better off she would have been if she had held a similar philosophy in dealings with Peter. "You stick to that and you'll find yourself coming out a lot better in the end." Then, afraid she would start taking advantage of an obviously willing ear to start bemoaning her shabby treatment by Peter, she headed for the bathroom and the welcome shower she found there. As much as she would have liked to talk to someone, knowing from her college days that there was nothing more cathartic than good old-fashioned girl talk, she didn't want to be the one to let the cat out of the bag. Also, things told to Barbara offered the decided possible disadvantage of eventual routing, intentional or not, to Timothy Journer. Jenny didn't want her private life bantered around the male locker room any sooner than Peter would probably see that it got there.

She was right about the shower. It did do wonders in reviving her spirits—so much so that she was able to clean up the resulting mess on the floor without having it seem like one more of a long line of catastrophes specifically designed to get her down. Egyptian showers were famous for drains that somehow always managed to be located at the highest spot on the bathroom floor, allowing the whole room to fill to at least the depth of an inch before any water whatsoever could even begin to escape.

She went back to her room to finish dressing. Barbara was standing at the entrance to the balcony. "You'd never know that there was once a teeming metropolis of thousands right out there," the young woman said, while Jenny laid out slacks and a silk blouse. "I mean," Barbara continued, "when you look, there doesn't seem to be anything out there but one pitiful heap of rubble and endless nothing. Yet a few thousand years ago it actually rained out there. There were pockets of water all over; trees and grasslands; gazelles and larger antelope; people hunting, putting up shelters, marrying and having babies."

Jenny certainly didn't want to hear about marriages and babies. "I suppose I should be checking in with Professor Kenny," she began, sitting on the edge of the bed to put on her own well-worn but comfortable hiking boots. "He's probably wondering why I haven't had the professional courtesy to report to him earlier than now." She knew something was wrong the minute she looked up from tying laces to see the expression on Barbara's face.

"Professor Kenny went back to Chicago three days ago," Barbara said.

"Went back to Chicago?" Jenny asked in shocked surprise. "Why did he go back to Chicago?"

"We expect he had a small stroke," Barbara said. "I thought you knew."

"How could I have known?" Jenny asked. "I just got here."

"I guess I just assumed Peter told you," Barbara said. And if that brought to mind possibilities that Jenny didn't even want to think about, Barbara wasn't going to leave it just at that. "Strange he didn't mention it," the young woman said reflectively. "That's what everyone assumed he went to Thebes to do. He and Professor Kenny had some kind of a big argument about who should take over as director after Professor Kenny left. Peter thought you should. Professor Kenny, though, wouldn't hear of it; he insisted it should be Peter. I felt the professor's attitude reeked of male chauvinism myself, but I wasn't invited to give my opinion."

"Peter thought I should succeed Professor Kenny?" Jenny asked, still not wanting to think through all the implications of that. If Peter had gone to her in Thebes not because of some mysterious pull of destiny but because of a more practical need to explain about the professor's return to Chicago, then hadn't told her because of circumstances that had probably made him leery about revealing his replacing the professor instead of her, it seemed logical to assume he might have been attempting to tell her just that when he stopped the Land Rover en route to Hierakonpolis.

"Sure Peter thought you should replace the professor," Barbara verified. "He was so insistent, as a matter of fact, that some of the guys finally had to get him off to one side and tell him he was liable to send the poor professor into another stroke if he didn't give in to him."

"Oh, no!" Jenny moaned, feeling sick to her stomach. Whatever rejuvenation had been accomplished in the shower was now completely undone. She felt literally drained knowing she had spoiled everything by reading all the wrong things into what Peter had started to tell her. No wonder he had been so angry when she had insinuated that their affair in Thebes had been nothing more than a casual coupling. "No, oh, no," she cried, wrapping her arms across her body and rocking slowly from side to side on the bed.

"Yeah, I know how you must feel," Barbara commiserated, trying to comfort her. Jenny, however, was aware that no one could possibly even suspect the torment she was experiencing at that moment. "But Tim told me the Arabs hired to assist on the dig wouldn't have stood for a lady boss," Barbara continued. "Not that Tim himself would have minded—I wouldn't be engaged to a man who was hung up on his own macho image! But these countries, I guess, are years behind the times as far as giving women equal rights goes. I even heard that up until a few years ago a man could divorce his wife by merely standing on a street corner and saying, 'I divorce thee,' three times. But then I guess you've dealt with this sort of thing. Right?"

"Where's Peter now?" Jenny asked, knowing she had to find him, knowing she was somehow going to have to explain. Although she could hardly blame him for not wanting to listen. How he must hate her! She had come across sounding hard and unfeeling, a woman who had only been out to use him, when in reality she had only been out to protect herself from the pain of his using her. "Where is he, Barbara?" Jenny repeated. "It's important I talk with him."

"He really *did* try to persuade Professor Kenny," Barbara said, continuing to think Jenny's state was the result of bruised professional pride. There was no denying Jenny was angry that the job of director had gone to Peter instead of to her, but that momentarily took a back seat to something she found far more important in her life. "Since he promised the professor he'd take over for him, I don't think there's much chance of his going back on his word," Barbara said.

"I just think it might be smart to sit down and clear the air between us," Jenny said, remembering how Abdul's words to that effect had helped her previously. "It's not Peter's fault Professor Kenny chose him over me, is it?"

"Right!" Barbara agreed, pleased Jenny was prepared to adjust to the power shift. "I still can't figure out why he didn't tell you all this earlier. He certainly seemed to think it important that you find out at the time."

"Yes, well, I'm certain he had his reasons," Jenny replied. She wasn't blind to those reasons, either, although she was hardly prepared to go into them with Barbara. Peter's reluctance to tell her the bad news had been the direct result of the spontaneous way they had come together at Thebes. It had been such a wonderful moment between them that he hadn't wanted to spoil it with something he knew Jenny was likely to take as a professional affront.

Peter might even have been aware of the incident between her and Professor Klenick Maxwell at a dig in Avaris. "You understand, Jenny," Professor Maxwell had told her at the time, "that this really had absolutely nothing to do with your qualifications versus those of Roger." Roger Daugan had been the man in question. He had arrived fresh out of graduate school, while Jenny had come qualified with two years of fieldwork. "It's merely the reality of a native work force," Professor Maxwell had continued, "that isn't going to take orders from a woman unless there's a man in a position of authority to back her up. Understand?" Jenny hadn't

understood. She had packed up immediately and
left Avaris as a matter of principle. "Most unfor-
tunate," Professor Maxwell had said, but he hadn't
rescinded his adjustment of dig hierarchy that had
put Roger Daugan above Jenny in the chain of command. It had been no secret in the scientific community after that that Jenny and Professor Maxwell
were anything but warm friends. If Peter had been
aware of the incident, he could have expected a
similar reaction to a slight made greater by Professor Kenny's having known that Jenny, not Peter,
was more sympathetic to his beliefs on the importance of Hierakonpolis as the burial location for the
Scorpion King. In fact, Jenny was well aware she
might indeed have packed up and gone home as a
result of this incident if the blow to her professional
ego hadn't been so thoroughly overshadowed by
her personal hurt in having so cruelly misjudged
Peter's love. He had merely been trying to protect
her sensibilities. His feelings for her had been genuine, and she had thrown his feelings back in his
face, pretending they couldn't possibly mean as
much to her as they really did.

What she feared was that her actions had been
spurred by forces over which she had had no conscious control, forces that had her bent on destroy-
ing Peter Donas as Geraldine Fowler had been
destroyed by Peter's grandfather. It made Jenny
genuinely ill to suspect she had known his sincerity
but had acted from some inner sense of revenge
even then. No, she was her own person! If she had

botched all this, there was no way she could rationalize her blame by pinning responsibility on a man and a woman dead for years. She was the one accountable, and it was going to be up to her to rectify her horrible mistake. There was no denying she loved Peter. She loved him so deeply that the pain she had caused him threatened to become a constant ache inside her.

"Your best bet would be to catch him when he comes back," Barbara said, checking her wristwatch. "He's taken the other Land Rover to check the exploratory trenches."

"Trenches?" Jenny asked, her professional curiosity triggered even through her emotional pain. "I thought they'd been taken care of three years ago." Professor Kenny had been working the dig officially for that long—longer if one considered the two additional summers of general surveying he had done before actually bringing in a work team. Test trenching was a process for determining the initial archaeological potential of a site too large for immediate total excavation. It usually consisted of digging a trench two feet or so wide and then examining what turned up at various ground levels. Several trenches might pinpoint the most archaeologically rich strata, as well as those spots likely to yield artifacts.

"Peter has decided to abandon present excavation on the upper wadi and concentrate on a couple of prehistoric graves sites farther down the slopes," Barbara explained, once again finding it strange that Jenny seemed so uninformed. Peter supposedly had spent a day with her in Thebes and had certainly had plenty of time to fill her in on the drive from Idfu.

"He's abandoning the Scorpion King grave site?" Jenny asked. While it didn't diminish the love she felt for him, there was no denying her chagrin at his having taken it upon himself as new director to abandon an area originally scheduled for excavation by this work team. Not that she had any trouble defining his motivations for having done so. It was logical that a man who had been adamant that the Scorpion King wasn't even buried at Hierakonpolis would be prepared to discontinue work in an area that would have proved him wrong if evidence showed up that was contrary to his theory.

"I think he might be heading back now," Barbara said, pointing to a small swirl of dust on the horizon.

"I have to see him," Jenny stated, coming to her feet, the hurt she had caused him once again becoming her main concern.

Peter, though, and expectedly so, seemed less than pleased to see her. His rather rude, "I'm really tremendously busy at the moment, Miss Mowry!" brought quick glances between several members of the group who had come back to the house with him.

"I'm afraid it's really quite important," Jenny replied, "or I assure you, I wouldn't have made the request in the first place." She thought he was still going to refuse her—which would have made her remaining in Hierakonpolis impossible. If he was unprepared even to listen to what she might have to say, there was little hope left for them. It would have been better for her to go somewhere far away to suffer in private.

"Let's go into the library," Peter said, leading the way into the house. He opened the first door on the left, entering a room whose vast majority of books had been shipped in for reference by Professor Kenny and various other members of the group. Peter went immediately to a table that was being used as a desk. With an air of authority he sat down behind the table, motioning toward the several other chairs in the room from which Jenny could pick. What she really wanted to do was throw herself into his arms and beg his forgiveness. What stopped her was her fear that he would have tossed her to one side before she could have even started explaining.

She glanced nervously around the room, trying to muster up the courage to tell him the things she so desperately wanted him to know. "Well, if you seem a little reluctant to begin after insisting this little meeting is so important, let me guess why you're here," Peter said, leaning back so his shoulders touched the cracked wall behind him. Jenny felt a rush of resentment that he didn't seem able to sense how difficult this was for her. "First, you found out from Barbara that I'm now your boss," he said. "Second, you found out I've stopped the excavation at the supposed tomb of the Scorpion King. Right?'' He didn't wait for affirmation. ''Well, about the first I can say only that I was Professor Kenny's choice as his successor. As for the second, I did so not because I feared further digging would somehow prove that hole to be the once final resting place of some long-ago pharaoh and thus knock my theories all to hell. Nor did I do it to aggravate you, knowing you and Professor Kenny are of like mind regarding its importance. While it's really not your place to question my decisions, since I have been selected to direct this dig, I will make an exception this one time by telling you why I decided to move excavation elsewhere.'' Jenny didn't interrupt. She wanted to hear what kind of excuse he could come up with, and she welcomed the additional time it gave her to gather strength for the more important confrontation ahead. ''I did it because I reckoned that if, by some extremely rare chance, it turned out that the tomb revealed evidence to support the professor's claims, it should be he who brings that fact to light and not you or me.''

''But the man had a stroke!'' Jenny reminded him, her automatic response making it seem she had come specifically to discuss this particular subject.

''We don't know that for a fact,'' Peter insisted. ''Nor will we have positive proof until he undergoes tests back in the States. But even if he did have a stroke, that doesn't mean he won't be back next year if he follows a prescribed regimen of diet, rest and exercise. A stroke nowadays doesn't mean a man is permanently out of commission.''

"I wasn't insinuating that it did!'' Jenny replied indignantly, insulted by his suggestions that her ambition made her underestimate Professor Kenny's power of recovery. It soon became obvious that Peter might not have been alone in this thinking on the subject.

"Had the professor really wanted the Scorpion King excavation to continue without him, he would have had no qualms whatsoever about putting you in charge,'' Peter stated. "Despite what Barbara might have told you to the contrary, his decision wasn't based on male-chauvinist motivations but on fear of a certain someone moving in prematurely to snap up laurels she hadn't yet worked to get.''

"I don't believe that for one minute!'' she said, angered at his absurd suggestion.

"Why did he choose me, then?'' he challenged.

"Because he knew the Arab work force wouldn't take to a woman giving the commands,'' Jenny replied smugly, aware she was letting him lead her further and further from the real subject she had come to discuss.

"Oh, there is *certainly* that argument,'' Peter admitted with a wry smile. "However, I'd have thought by your reaction to similar circumstances at the Avaris dig that you wouldn't have put so much stock in that reason.'' He did know about her and Professor Maxwell, then! "I would suggest, though," he continued, "that Professor Kenny's decision was based more on his knowledge that leaving me in charge would result in the excavations being shifted to those areas I personally find more apt to turn up something of interest." He raised his hand to stop the outburst he was expecting. "Now, Miss Mowry, you're still a young woman, and you can assuredly spare another year of your life before finding what really lurks at the bottom of that probably empty hole. I'm frankly a little disappointed in your curiosity—or whatever would cause you to want to reap rewards, if there are any, deserved more by the man who has worked far harder to get them. Where were you, after all, when the professor was spending his summers wandering through blistering desert heat to uncover clues, misleading or not, that finally led him here? If it does turn out that Professor Kenny is unable to return next year for health reasons, I feel quite sure you'll be more than rewarded for having been restrained from rushing into the breach now. The man, after all, could really do worse than look to someone to carry on his work who is so similarly inclined in her misconceptions."

"I think you've said quite enough on that subject," Jenny said, fighting to keep down her anger at his innuendos regarding her professional motives for objecting to the change in excavation site. "Not that I won't have plenty to say later. But it wasn't *any* of this that made me ask to talk to you this afternoon."

"I'm afraid that's all we do have to talk about," he said, pushing his chair away from the wall and coming to his feet. He knew what subject she was heading toward, and he found it too painful to allow himself further exposure to it. "So if you will excuse me, Miss Mowry, I'm an extremely busy man."

"Are you afraid, damn it?" she cried to him in a voice that could very well have penetrated the closed door and registered on listening ears elsewhere in the house. Frankly, she didn't care who heard. "Are you afraid to listen to my explanations because they might be valid enough to put you once again in the position of having to reaffirm a love you were never committed to in the first place?"

"Don't you dare try to dump responsibility for any of this in my lap!" he warned, turning on her like a cornered animal, his anger contorting his usually handsome features. "I entered a relationship in the very best of faith and was rewarded by a knife in the gut. If I'm a little reluctant to listen to your so-called explanations now, it's only because I can see that you're not merely content to have the knife inserted but are anxious to give the buried blade a few hearty twists for good measure."

"I love you, Peter!" she said. For a moment he was speechless.

"You've got that a little wrong, don't you, Jenny?" he managed finally. "As I recall the scenario, it was I who loved you. It was you who looked upon me as a candidate for a casual coupling." His voice got even louder. "What we did was nothing more than what thousands of promiscuous people do every day of the year, right?"

"I never meant any of those horrible things I said to you," Jenny nearly shouted. "It was all a horrible mistake!"

"A mistake?" he asked, as if he must have misheard. "A mistake, did you say? Damned right it was a mistake! It was my mistake ever to be taken in by you in the first place!" He looked so hurt, so beaten, so painfully vulnerable, that Jenny's heart went out to him. She could hardly control her need to go to him. She wanted only to hold him, soothe him, explain to him that this misunderstanding between them was all her fault and make right the horrible hurt in both of their aching hearts. Peter, however, wasn't about to let her take any easy way out. "Don't take one step closer!" he told her, seeing what she had in mind and having no intention of having his barriers suddenly tumbled by being fool enough to allow himself the exquisite pleasure of once again feeling her in his arms. "If you do, so help me, I'll leave this room, leave Hicrakonpolis, leave Egypt and forget you even suggested there were explanations to right what you've so completely destroyed between us."

"There *are* explanations," Jenny assured him, so badly wanting him to believe her. "There really are. Why don't you want to believe it?"

"Why don't I want to believe it?" he echoed incredulously. "It's my damned desperate need to believe that has me standing here like a bloody fool, when I should have been through that door like a bat out of hell. It's my wanting to believe that has me trembling at the futile hope there might be some kind of rationale spilling out of your mouth that will somehow make all the hurt go away."

So she told him about his grandfather and Geraldine Fowler, and he in turn confirmed what she had for so long suspected—that he'd never heard the story. There was simply no way his professed ignorance of those past happenings could have been so well faked. The tragedy that had played so much a part in the forming of Jenny's character, bringing her to this moment in the first place, meant absolutely nothing whatsoever to Peter—until now.

"You mean, you set out to punish me for something my grandfather did sixty years ago?" Peter asked, frankly amazed. "Well, you damned well succeeded, didn't you?" he added, and Jenny realized he had completely missed the point of the story.

"Don't you see?" she pleaded anxiously. It was obvious that he had taken what she'd told him merely as more proof that she had used him. It left her heartbroken. "I thought *you* were out to use *me*," she said, trying to make him understand. "I thought it was all happening again the way it had happened sixty years ago. You, me. Frederic, Geraldine. Tutankhamen, Thebes."

"How could you have possibly been so ridiculous?" he asked in such a way as to give her hope he might somehow be beginning to understand.

"When you stopped the Land Rover, I thought for sure it was to tell me you really didn't love me," Jenny explained, wishing he would take her in his strong arms and tell her he forgave her. "I was hurt, and I didn't want you to know how successful you had been in making me love you. I acted the way I did to save myself a bit of the dignity I thought you'd completely taken from me."

"You little fool!" he said, shaking his head, giving her additional hope that he understood. "You silly, silly, silly little fool!"

There should have been a storybook ending. She should have rushed to him, her eyes brimming with joy. He should have opened his arms for her, enfolding her against his strong chest while he whispered loving words of forgiveness. The only thing that opened was the door, after a knock that startled them both with its jarring untimeliness.

"Sorry to disturb you," Barbara said, the very atmosphere in the room telling her no one was sorrier than they were, "but I've got a rather insistent man out here who wants to see Jenny."

Jenny thought it must be Abdul—although a moment's reflection would have made her question what he was doing there. But though the visitor was not the sheikh, his appearance was disruptive. The man, whom she had never met or seen before, had arrived with a jewelry case that he immediately held out toward her once she'd been identified. "I'm to tell you this is yours,'' he said. She didn't take it immediately, probably making matters worse because of her hesitation. She could have surely come up with something to bluff her way through instead of merely standing there in startled immobility. All she could think of at that moment, though, was how everything she had worked so hard to mend over the past few minutes was going to be destroyed by this unexpected intrusion. ''Sheikh Jerada told me I wasn't to leave until I had personally delivered this into your keeping,'' the messenger continued. Later she would not be able to remember what he looked like, forever finding it ironic that someone who had played such a part in her life should have entered and exited as nameless and faceless as a diaphanous apparition.

''I don't want it,'' she said, her voice coming out a low frustrated moan.

Everyone was staring, frozen momentarily, as Jenny could have wished them frozen for eternity. But there was no stopping the ticking of the clock. Knowing that, she reached for the case and took it. If, however, she thought that that would be the end of it, she should have known better. The envoy stood there waiting. Barbara stood there waiting. Peter stood there waiting. ''He wants you to make sure the contents are intact,'' Peter finally told her.

Like a somnambulist functioning without conscious awareness, she opened the case. ''My goodness, that's beautiful!'' Barbara gasped in admiring surprise. Jenny, though, did not feel very appreciative of the necklace's beauty just then.

"You obviously have a way of making your spurned lovers come running back to you, don't you, Jenny?" Peter said sarcastically. "I suppose I should be complimented to find you thought me worth the effort." He did a quick about-face and exited into the light of a day that, beyond the doorway, was fading fast.

CHAPTER TEN

"A WHAT?" Abdul asked.

"A scorpion," Jenny repeated.

"A scorpion?" Abdul said, looking more than a little dubious.

"Sure it is," Jenny insisted, reaching up to trace her forefinger along a single petroglyph among several old and faded ones that had been painted on the rock overhang thousands of years ago. "See the way its body curls up this way into its tail?"

"A bit stylized, isn't it?" Abdul asked. "Those primitives were into abstract art, were they?"

The truth was, the figure might well have been something other than a scorpion. There were professionals in the field who argued it was definitely something else, who said seeing it as a scorpion was just wishful thinking. Jenny, though, disagreed with them, as did Professor Kenny and a few others who had a hunch about such things. And hunches were often what archaeology was all about. It had been a hunch that had convinced Carter that Tutankhamen's tomb was somewhere in the Valley of the Kings, while the experts had laughed.

If Abdul was little impressed with the ancient artwork, he was even less impressed with the Scorpion King grave site. "This is what the fuss is all about, huh?" he said, shaking his head as if he really found it a little hard to believe. The rectangular hole was still partially filled with debris that had tumbled in when, thousands of years earlier, grave robbers or the elements had collapsed the roof and ravaged whatever was inside. But it was important even if it had been robbed of its contents, even if it hadn't once housed the body of the Scorpion King, because it showed a hole chiseled into solid bedrock at a time in Egyptian history when most burials consisted of shallow diggings in dirt. The fact that greater care had been taken in the construction of this grave suggested that a very important personage had been laid to rest here. And if the Step Pyramid at Saqqâra was a link between mastabas and the perfection of the later pyramids at Giza, here was indication of an earlier transition from common earth grave to burial vault in stone.

"I don't know why, but I always pictured archaeologists as being forever poised on the brink of some pharaoh's tomb, chipping away at a large seal bearing the inscription: Death will slay with his wings whoever disturbs the peace of the pharaoh," Abdul said. "And what do I find instead? A group of people thoroughly caught up in the simple sifting of sand, totally delighted by a few kernels of grain, some animal bones and, perish the thought, treasured pieces of dried feces." Jenny had spent the morning taking Abdul on a tour of the dig, ending up at the vacated Scorpion King grave site. She thought that his misconceptions were no more distorted than those of the majority of laymen, who really know very little about archaeology aside from what they saw in the movies.

"Well, this is what an archaeologist is ninety-nine times out of a hundred," Jenny said, leaning against one of the large slabs of sandstone that composed the surrounding outcroppings. "There are few discoveries of pharaohs' tombs anymore—certainly not of the kind Carter came up with at Thebes. Nor is that altogether bad, if you must know the truth. Not that Carter handled his find badly, because he was as methodical as they come. But prospects of great treasure often get searchers too concerned with materialistic values to remember the intrinsic and historical value to be had from a single kernel of grain. Grain tells us about a primitive people's agriculture; bones show hints of its animal husbandry, and, believe it or not, those coprolites you were wrinkling your nose at can give us vital clues to its diet. The mad rush once on for Egyptian valuables often did far more harm than good," Jenny continued, although she couldn't really be sure Abdul was all that interested. Actually, she was talking, had been talking most of the morning, merely to keep from using "poor" Abdul as her father confessor regarding the state of her present unsatisfactory relationship with Peter. "Someone sees a glittering piece of gold," she proceeded, realizing her mind had been drifting, "and the human reaction is to grab it up immediately without any real concern for where that piece has rested in relation to its surroundings, to accompanying less valuable artifacts, or to soil layers. Many archaeologists, being only human, have ended up spiriting off obviously valuable pieces, only later to find they can't actually date them because they removed them too quickly from their vital context. Follow?"

"Mmmmmmm," Abdul replied—which could have meant anything.

"Take the case of the Narmer palette," Jenny said, determined to keep up the illusion that everything was right in her world. "I mention it because it was found right here at Hierakonpolis. Although not of gold but of carefully carved dark green slate, its value as a historical artifact was quickly recognized. Not only that, but it was found by an archaeologist. Yet because the man who found it didn't keep accurate records, so delighted was he with the mere materialistic importance of his find, we don't know whether the piece originated within this area as part of a cache from an Old Kingdom storehouse or whether it was brought in and deposited at a far later date as part of a nearby cache of 'antiques.' Not even the archaeologist could remember, since he had been so anxious to simply get this prize and others off for display before his admiring peers."

"Mmmmmmm," Abdul responded once again, making Jenny think she really was boring him. "Actually, I'm probably more interested in what's gone wrong in your world," he told her, sending her into an overreaction of denials that wouldn't even have convinced someone far less astute than Abdul. "Come on, Jenny!" Abdul chided when she had finished. "Did a snake somehow manage to crawl into your Eden?"

So, since she had really wanted to tell him all along, not having taken the risk of dumping her troubles on Barbara, she let it all come spilling out—even the part about the untimely arrival of the necklace. The latter brought immediate apologies from Abdul. "Oh, it isn't really the necklace that's to blame for anything," Jenny assured him, not wanting him to think she was blaming anyone or anything but herself. "If I hadn't made such a fool of myself in the Land Rover, Peter would have trusted any explanation about the necklace. The way it was, he didn't even bother sticking around to ask for one."

"So you've had one lovers' quarrel," Abdul said philosophically. "Surely the two of you can get past that, can't you?"

"Maybe not," Jenny had to admit, although it pained her to do so.

"Don't be a fool once again, Jenny!" Abdul warned, leaning against the rock beside her. They were in one of the few pockets of shade left to them. The sun was climbing higher, and most of the team was probably already back at the house after a day that had started for them before sunrise so they could take advantage of cooler working conditions.

"It's obvious you still love him. And I certainly saw no signs that Peter had stopped loving you."

"Do you really think he still loves me?" Jenny asked, not missing the irony of seeking reaffirmation of one man's love from another.

"Take my word for it," Abdul said. "He loves you." He laughed and shook his head at Jenny's need to hear that. "I'm the one who told you he loved you in the first place, right?" he added, his wide grin making his attractive face even more handsome. "Are you now going to accuse me of being mistaken? Besides, has he come right out and told you he no longer loves you?" Jenny shook her head. "His problem," Abdul said, "is no different now than what it has always been. He has a tendency to drag his you-know-what. He is also overly confident that he can take his own sweet time and still come out on top of things. Makes me jealous as all hell, by the way, that he's probably right, too. You would go running if he just opened those strong arms of his in forgiveness, wouldn't you?" Jenny didn't answer, but she didn't have to. "So you see!" Abdul said, successfully hiding whatever jealous hurt he did feel. "I know it, you know it, and he certainly knows it. He's probably out to make you suffer a little while longer before once again deigning to share himself with you. You put far too much stock in the parallel between you, Peter and your grandparents." While Jenny might have reached the point of not blaming her problem directly on Frederic Donas and Geraldine Fowler, she knew she would have acted far differently if she hadn't been preprogrammed by that tragedy of sixty years earlier. "Anyway, I'm somehow inclined to be more sympathetic to Jenny Mowry than to Peter Donas," Abdul said. "Why do you suppose that is?"

"I don't know," Jenny replied, knowing very well. She slipped her arm around his waist to give him a hug. "But, oh, am I glad you're here!" Then, actually finding herself glancing around for signs of Peter, who might have misinterpreted her show of friendly affection, she pulled her arm away with an obviousness that made Abdul laugh.

"Jenny, Jenny, Jenny," he said, his voice full of amusement. The chant had Jenny immediately remembering how Peter had kept repeating her name while he made love to her. As usual, memories of that past time did very little to dispel the despair of thinking there would be no repetition of those wondrous moments between them. "What you should have done just now," Abdul confided in a conspiratorial whisper, "having expected as you so obviously did that Peter was waiting to leap out at us with accusations, was to have carried right on through with the hug and added something even more demonstrative like a big wet kiss."

Jenny was embarrassed that her paranoia had been so easily recognized. "I'm in enough hot water the way it is," she replied apologetically.

"But you want your man back, don't you?" Abdul asked, finding it thoroughly charming that he'd found a woman so innocent she didn't seem to have the foggiest notion of how to play the game. Then, remembering she had more than once been adamant that love was serious business...no game, he determined not to make any such references.

"Of course I want him back," Jenny answered, taking the pause offered by Abdul's inner reflection as indication that he had expected her to answer his comment.

"Then let me be the first to assure you that you're already well on your way to a reconciliation," Abdul said, rather enjoying his ability to make Jenny happy, if by no other means than by playing matchmaker. "I could see that the minute I noted the expression on Peter's face when you told him you were going to take the morning to show me around the site. Did you or did you not recognize his sudden relapse into the same monosyllabic way of speaking he used that time he discovered us kissing in the Scrapeum?"

"Do you really think he's jealous?" Jenny asked, hoping she didn't sound desperate but knowing she did so want to believe that Peter cared.

"Damn right he is!" Abdul confirmed. "And he should be. I mean, just take a look at this charming, debonair, handsome chap who has suddenly shown up on the scene! Peter has probably spent the whole morning stewing over how he might just have waited a bit too long before coming up with his magnanimous show of forgiveness. I mean, it was one thing when he had the monopoly on masculine good looks in the area, the poor damsel in question being isolated in her desert kingdom, but he's got to whistle another tune now that the Sheikh of Araby has come riding back on the scene. Look at how quickly he came rushing to you at Thebes when he'd stewed long enough about my having you all to myself on that cruise ship.''

"He came to Thebes because he wanted to break the news about his getting Professor Kenny's job instead of me," Jenny reminded him, wanting to hear Abdul give her all the right arguments to the contrary—which he willingly proceeded to do.

"Ah, that might well have been his rationale!" Abdul proclaimed like a wizard revealing the mysteries of the world to an attending neophyte. "But did he tell you anything in Thebes other than that he loved you?" Jenny, knowing Abdul must have intuitively sensed the extent of what had happened between her and Peter in Thebes, felt a little guilty that she was still unable to repay his kindness with anything besides friendship. How much easier it would have been if she could have loved him instead of Peter. "Of course he didn't tell you about his getting the professor's job," Abdul stated. "Why? One, he had never really come to Thebes to tell you that. Two, he knew if he did, you might hightail it out of Egypt before the two of you had had enough time to tie the knot. He figured he'd be safer revealing the news after he got you to Hierakonpolis, knowing no one in her right mind was going to be any too anxious to risk her life by making the return trip over that thing called a road between here and Idfu. I know I'm not looking forward to it!''

Jenny laughed, unable to help herself. She felt good. She felt better than she had in a long time, and she knew the reason why. Abdul made her feel good. He always made her feel good, whereas with Peter it was a constant roller coaster of depressing lows and exhilarating highs. She tried to tell herself she preferred the even emotional keel offered by Abdul, only to remember the soaring heights of pleasure to which Peter had once taken her. "I'm glad you came!" Jenny said, kissing him on the cheek, not caring if Peter came out of the rocks to accuse her of taking up with Abdul once again. She'd known from the expression on Peter's face when the necklace had arrived on her doorstep that he held such suspicions anyway. Well, she had suffered and apologized enough for her mistakes. From here on out it was going to be another ball game. "I really am glad you came," she repeated for emphasis.

"I'm glad you're glad," he said, meaning it. "Now do you want to head back for lunch with you-know-who, or cause some gossip by joining me and my bodyguards for another of my famous desert lunches?" Jenny couldn't help shivering slightly at her memory of the climactic ending to their last desert lunch on the outskirts of Saqqâra. He sensed her thoughts. "I can't guarantee such exciting entertainment as last time, however," he told her.

"In that case, what girl in her right mind could turn down such an invitation from a handsome desert sheikh?" she asked, echoing what she had answered that other fateful time at Giza. "Besides which I'm starving. What's being offered in the sheikh's picnic basket this time around?"

"Cold white wine, cold chicken and turkey, cold asparagus in aspic, cheese and juicy tangerines," he enticed, taking her arm as the two maneuvered through the rocks toward his Land Rover, which was waiting. There was still no electricity from his touch, like there had been from Peter's fingers when they touched her arm, but Jenny didn't care. Abdul had compensations that were unbeatable at that particular moment.

If Jenny hadn't been expecting the three Arabs with submachine guns who emerged from the rocks at the Land Rover before she and Abdul did, having had them in attendance all morning, she would have undoubtedly been frightened by the sight. As it was, she merely hoped to God they would somehow be able to prevent any recurrence of the frightening events at Saqqâra. She got in the front seat with Abdul, and the three men all crowded in the back. Jenny touched her hand gently to Abdul's forehead, something she had been going to do all morning but which had been prevented by her suspicions that Peter would see her and misinterpret her gesture. "Looks as if it's healing nicely," she said, speaking of the scar from the bullet wound.

"Nothing spectacular like some of the others,"

he said, starting the Land Rover and putting it in gear.

"Nothing at all like a few of the others," Jenny agreed, remembering how those scars had looked on Abdul's near-naked body, remembering the unscarred perfection of Peter's body as he had walked toward her in that hotel room across the Nile River from Thebes.

They drove deeper into the desert, finally stopping in a spot that would have seemed no different from any other, except that Abdul seemed to recognize it. "We have arrived!" he said, flashing her a smile before opening the door to get out. She came out into the hot sunshine with him, the gunmen in quick attendance. "Let's let them make the site a little more comfortable for our lunch while we take a walk, shall we?" Abdul suggested. "I've got something I want to show you."

As they set out, Jenny noticed Abdul kept one of the three bodyguards with them, even if he remained at a discreet distance that afforded them their privacy.

"Who could guess there had once been so much water in this desolation?" Abdul said, leading the way along a gentle rise of sandstone dusted with loose sand.

"The substantial rainfall made this area very special in Egypt," Jenny said, taking her cue. "Usually along the Nile, settlements grew up close to and paralleling the course of the river. Here, though, they also extended virtually miles perpendicular."

"You mean, it once rained enough out here to support life?" Abdul asked, making Jenny a little confused. His previous statement about rainfall had led her to suspect he had already known the answer to his last question. He must have read the confusion on her face. "Oh, I see!" he said suddenly. "You thought I had meant rain when I talked of all the water. Actually, I was talking about an ocean. We just got our references mixed by a few million years, right?"

"Like maybe you confused an archaeologist with a geologist?" Jenny suggested in a good humor.

"Actually, I'm not confused at all," he bantered. "You're the archaeologist. I'm the geologist."

"You are?" Jenny replied, wondering why that came out sounding as if she were so surprised. Except possibly she was surprised.

"As much as a degree in geology is apt to make me," Abdul answered. "Although I'd be the first to admit that there are those in the field far more up on their facts than I am. I've diversified to the point where I seldom trust myself in geological matters without seeking a second or even a third opinion. Quite frankly, it was an associate who spotted the potential of the area around here."

"Its potential?" Jenny asked, again confused. Then she connected what he was saying with the business she knew he was in. "Ah, for oil, you mean?"

"Yes, oil," Abdul admitted. "That gooey black stuff that has the capability of thrusting poor nations into richness overnight. And people in the know feel that we're standing atop a great reservoir of the stuff right here.''

"Here?" Jenny asked, aware that Abdul would have far more information about that than she would. Her knowledge of what existed below the ground—her interest in what lay there, as a matter of fact—was limited to the small veneer that had once experienced the tramp of human feet.

"Sometime between ten and five hundred million years ago, right here, I'm told, there was an ocean teeming with countless tiny sea creatures," Abdul began, "creatures that, when they died, sifted down to the bottom of that sealike dust that now settles here. There the decaying sea life mingled with decaying vegetable matter and the fine silts washed in by rivers, and eventually all of that squeezed together to give us oil."

They reached the top of a rise, and he pointed toward the derrick erected in the depression immediately below them. Jenny was astonished. The last thing she had expected to find here, even with all of his talk about oil, was this sign of twentieth-century civilization, its sounds suddenly audible to her when earlier they had been contained by the natural cupping of the land. "I've been sent down to check on several exploratory wells between Luxor and Aswân," Abdul said. "Imagine my surprise in finding one right here, almost on top of your dig."

There was something about what she heard and what she saw that assaulted Jenny's sensibilities.

Her disconcerting feeling was only increased by a small stone that caught her attention at this moment. She bent to pick it up from its position at her feet, turning it over in her fingers. It was a pre-dynastic animal figurine of chipped flint shaped liked a bird—possibly a falcon. Her experienced eye knew immediately that it had been crudely fashioned a few thousand years earlier by human hands. That once discarded or misplaced piece of rock seemed more at home in the desolate landscape than the oil derrick ever possibly could.

"Something from the past?" Abdul asked, reaching for the small chip and taking it from her, examining it in the flat of his palm. He returned the flint falcon to her after a few seconds. "Dealing with the past is a luxury you can afford that Egypt no longer can," he said. "A country ceases to be much concerned with men who lived and died five thousand years ago when there are thousands in Cairo today who might soon die if there isn't some way to show them a better life tomorrow. And oil can do that for them, Jenny. Oil *will* do that for them. You see this derrick as an intrusion," he told her. "Ah, don't deny it! I see it on your face. You're holding on to that little flint bird and you're asking yourself how many of these same little animal figurines, how many shards of predynastic pottery, how many pieces of prehistoric bone and dried lumps of feces all of this has destroyed already. In addition, you're wondering how much more will be destroyed the minute oil is found, and more people come hurrying in to sink more wells, using more bulldozers and more earthmovers to build more pipelines and more refineries.''

"Yes, I guess you're right," Jenny admitted. "That is how I see it."

"Of course you do," Abdul said, not really having needed verification. "You see it that way first, because you're an archaeologist who has chosen to devote your life to the past and naturally you're disturbed by an intrusion of the twentieth century into what you consider your own private preserve. Second, you're a citizen of a country whose wealth can assure you your present and future well-being, and this affords you the sheer luxury of dabbling in other countries' pasts. But of what practical use to the present-day Egyptian is all that gold from King Tut's tomb that your grandmother and grandfather, that Peter's grandfather, helped bring to light?" His question left Jenny slightly aghast in that she couldn't believe he was even asking it seriously. "I mean, the total meltdown value of the gold is nothing compared to the money that could be brought in from a single oil well," Abdul argued. "And think how much more that oil money can benefit modern Egypt than all of King Tut's gold.''

"I think you're confusing worth with dollars and cents," Jenny accused him.

"There is no practical worth *but* dollars and cents to a modern Egyptian faced with starvation," Abdul stated.

"But any country's past is its chief heritage," Jenny insisted.

"You can't eat a pharaoh's gold," Abdul reminded her. Which Jenny found not only cynical but disturbing, coming as it did from a member of Egypt's monied and educated class. Had he been one of those starving multitude about whom he was talking, his attitude wouldn't have been so shocking. The poor were no different today than they had been when they'd been creeping nightly into the Valley of the Kings to loot the tombs. Tomb robbers had become so prevalent by the late Twentieth Dynasty that Ramses III had been taken from three resting places by faithful priests intent upon preserving his sacred mummy. No less than thirteen royal mummies had been moved into the tomb of Queen Inhapi for safekeeping, still others to the tomb of Amenophis II and more of them unceremoniously dumped for their own protection into a hole not far from the funerary temple of Queen Hatshepsût. If hungry men could so easily despoil the bodies and fortunes of kings considered gods in their own time, what could be expected from those hungry men of twentieth-century Egypt? However, she had expected much more understanding from Abdul.

"You can't eat crude oil, either," she reminded him.

"Yes, but you're more apt to be able to convert it to a foodstuff."

"You're actually trying to tell me that this," Jenny said, motioning toward the exploratory drilling operation in progress below her, "is being done more to feed Egypt's many poor than to line the pockets of its few rich?"

"Like my pockets, you mean?" Abdul asked, unable to keep the smile off his face.

"Well, if the shoe fits, wear it!" Jenny said, telling herself she really wasn't angry but aware she was. The very idea that a man who should have known better had insinuated that King Tut's gold would have been of more benefit if it had been melted down into coins and distributed to the poor was ludicrous. Too few people could have benefited that way, because only too quickly the gold would have been gone. In a museum such treasures could be enjoyed by millions for far longer than all of the oil in the ground was ever going to last. Besides, treasures like those of Tut's weren't Egypt's alone. They belonged to the world community, to all nations, and it was exceedingly shortsighted of Abdul not to admit that he recognized that fact.

"Granted I hope to see a substantial profit out of all of this," Abdul admitted, "as do my associates. But benefits are bound to filter down. In fact, it would behoove us to make sure they do if we want to preserve what wealth we've managed to accumulate. Millions of today's poor aren't liable to have any more respect for those of us living in great wealth than their grave-robber ancestors had for dead pharaohs with too much money."

Jenny would have said more, but she was distracted by the sudden emergence of a jeep from behind one of the buildings clustered about the derrick below. She turned to find Abdul checking his watch.

"Their security is not what it should be," he said almost to himself. "How long would you say we've been standing here?" The question was rhetorical, because he didn't wait for her answer. "And it's only now that they've decided to come to investigate. In the interim I could have done extensive damage with a hand-held rocket launcher." He seemed suddenly to realize he might be scaring Jenny needlessly with his hints of sabotage. "Although it's highly unlikely the enemy is going to waste valuable time and energy on every exploratory well we've set up, isn't it? Far easier for them to wait and see whether anything comes in."

The bodyguard with them made himself readily visible to the approaching jeep, his submachine gun aimed downward to indicate that he was offering no challenge to the heavily armed men in the vehicle. "Galal Baseeli," Abdul said, introducing one of the three to Jenny. "He's in charge of site security." If Abdul saw Galal's handling of his duty as less than satisfactory, he was prepared to discuss it in less public circumstances. "I'm merely showing Miss Mowry the sights," he explained. "She's attached to a party of archaeologists working in the area." Galal inclined his head slightly in Jenny's direction. He was dressed in quasi-military uniform without insignia, his face disfigured by a nasty scar that puckered the entire length of his right cheek from eye to jawline. His eyes were about the coldest two pinpoints of black ice Jenny had ever seen.

The jeep and its occupants didn't linger, and Abdul was soon turning Jenny back toward their own vehicle. "I'm hungry," he said. "How about you?" She could have jumped back on the bandwagon regarding the merits of pharaonic gold as opposed to modern crude oil, but she didn't. The day had gone well so far, and she didn't want to spoil it. Besides, Abdul seemed just as desirous of steering clear of that bone of contention as she did. He proceeded to describe, in glowing terms, his villa at Aswân.

They lunched under an awning stretched between four poles. It offered suitable shade for Jenny and Abdul, as well as for the three guards. The latter ate in one-man shifts from a far less grand menu than that of their employer and Jenny. "You will come visit me soon?" Abdul persisted while the leftovers were being packed up, the awning hauled down and folded for storage in the Land Rover. "I'll invite Peter, too, giving you both the chance to get into surroundings a little more romantic than those of a house full of earth sifters."

"I doubt he'd come," Jenny said, wondering if a change of scenery would do her and Peter any good. It might. His comments upon seeing the necklace and his dramatic exit must certainly have caused talk about there possibly being a bit more between them than a purely professional relationship, although

Barbara had shown remarkable restraint in not trying to probe Jenny for any additional information.
Peter's continued cool attitude might have been
merely an effort to keep down any further gossip.

"Oh, he'll come if you do," Abdul guaranteed,
starting the motor while his men finished storing the
last of the equipment.

The drive back was shorter than Jenny had imagined, bringing home to her just how close the twentieth century was in its intrusion upon the echoes of
those earlier centuries laid witness to by these barren wastes. The whole group, Peter included, was
on the veranda outside when the Land Rover pulled
up.

"Try not to look too much as if we're on the
point of confronting your irate parents after staying
out until dawn, will you?" Abdul said with a wide
grin once they were out of the Land Rover and
heading toward all the curious faces. "It's okay to
make Peter a little jealous, but I'm not out to get a
busted jaw for a perfect effort."

"Shhhhhh!" Jenny hissed, afraid that someone
would overhear. But the only thing overheard was
her hiss—which had everyone immediately, curious
about what Abdul had said to warrant it.

"Hey, you two, do you want me to see if there's
anything left over from lunch to feed you?" Barbara asked, deciding someone was going to have to
start the conversation.

"We had a little something already," Jenny replied curious as to why she couldn't master that

simple statement without feeling and sounding so horribly flustered.

"Drove into the nearest desert McDonald's, did you?" Peter asked with obvious sarcasm. Jenny didn't look at him, afraid she wouldn't see the signs of jealousy she wanted to see there.

"I really must be going, anyway," Abdul said.

"Already?" Jenny asked, blushing when she realized how that must have sounded. It was just that she felt so much better when Abdul was there. She didn't want to lose the little support she had so quickly.

"You should be thankful Sheikh Jerada was able to take even a few minutes out of his busy schedule to stop by," Peter said. If Jenny glanced at him, it was only for a second—too short a time for her to put any real meaning to the expression she saw on his face. "Things keeping you pretty busy, are they, sheikh?" Peter added.

"You know the old bit about all work and no play," Abdul replied good-naturedly.

"Right!" Peter answered, as much as saying he knew very well to what kind of "play" Abdul had been referring.

"Speaking of all work," Abdul said, in far more control than either Jenny or Peter, "I was thinking maybe you and Jenny might like to take the opportunity to join me for a little rest and relaxation at my villa in Aswân."

"Well, that is terribly decent of you to extend the invitation," Peter said, although he made it sound as if he really didn't find it that decent at all. "However we've got only a total of two months to do a frightful lot of work around here. Not that Jenny probably won't be able to find some spare time. But what with my being director—" he paused to give the gibe emphasis "—I'm left rather strapped when it comes to getting away myself."

"Surely you get half a day now and again," Abdul persisted.

"Yes, but that's usually spent recouping my strength," Peter answered, "not bumping over the rutty road between here and Idfu, let alone braving the road between Idfu and Aswân."

"I'll send my helicopter for you," Abdul replied magnanimously—which brought an echoing "helicopter?" from Barbara, who was obviously far more impressed than Peter.

"That's very kind of you," Peter said, the pause between Barbara's exclamation and his thanks being the only indication that he wasn't as blasé as he might have wanted to appear and was aware of Abdul's generosity and was considering the offer.

"Just think about it," Abdul said. "I've got a few falcons with me at Aswân that my trainers are dying to show off to someone besides me."

"I'll see what I can arrange," Peter said begrudgingly. He didn't want to sound too much like the jealous lover, especially since Abdul seemed so determined to come across as an all-around Mr. Nice Guy.

"Good!" Abdul replied, pleased with his hard-won concessions. "I'll get back to you, then, and see what the three of us can arrange. Right now I've really got to be going." He nodded to the others present and extended his hand for Jenny. "Walk me to my car?" he asked her, smiling as if things were working out perfectly. She really didn't want to take his hand, but she couldn't see any way of getting out of it, receiving very little comfort from his reassuring squeeze of her fingers. "See," he said softly after they were out of earshot. "The two of you will find Aswân more private than here."

"If he goes to Aswân, it will only be because of those damned hawks you once again held out in enticement," Jenny stated, more than a little jealous of those birds.

"Ah!" Abdul replied. "That may be the rationale he gives himself, but we know better, don't we?"

"Do we?" Jenny asked, questioning how Abdul could be so positive when she remained so full of heart-rending doubts.

"Trust me!" Abdul said, all confidence. He opened the door of the Land Rover and climbed in, turning toward her through the open window. "You do trust me, don't you? Hey, didn't we go through this routine once before?"

"So I trust you," Jenny said, unable to keep from smiling at his good humor. She wondered, though, if he knew just how badly she did want to trust him, how badly she did want to believe his promises regarding Peter.

"Good!" Abdul said. "So bend down here and give me a quick goodbye kiss."

"Abdul, I..." she stammered, feeling all of those eyeballs zooming in on their leave-taking.

Abdul pleaded with a winning grin. "One that could *possibly* be a kiss between friends but then again might be something a little more." She bent down and gave him a very quick peck that left him laughing. "Don't ever go before cameras, will you, Jenny?" he said between chuckles. "You can't take direction worth a damn!"

He gave a parting wave, and Jenny watched until the Land Rover disappeared. She steeled herself to face Peter, disappointed when she turned to find he had already left the rest of the group and had gone into the house.

CHAPTER ELEVEN

LUCK AND ACCIDENT: at Thebes in 1922 when, after much hesitation and several revisions of plans, Howard Carter decided to spend that one last winter of excavation in the Valley of the Kings and located Tutankhamen's tomb in the late fall; at Thebes when, after eight weeks of futile work, one of the workers of H.E. Winbock's excavation of Meket-Re's long-looted tomb noticed stone chips trickling into a crevice and discovered twenty-four brightly painted models depicting life in ancient Egypt; at Hierakonpolis in 1897 when, after just settling in at the site, James Quibell directed one of his men to begin digging and uncovered a copper statue of the Sixth Dynasty king, Pepy I; at Hierakonpolis when, without really looking, Jenny Mowry glanced down at a section of dirt and saw the piece of white limestone fragmentized from a First Dynasty ceremonial macehead.

She didn't believe it, even glancing away twice and looking back again just to make sure it was actually there, thinking maybe the light reflected off of the nearby oil derrick was playing tricks with the tan-colored soil. The white object remained, however, and she knelt beside it. She knew she was being watched. The security team had picked her out quickly, making her think Abdul must have had his little talk with Galal Baseeli, the officer in charge. Galal, having recognized her as the woman who had been there with Abdul, had still eyed her suspiciously with cold black eyes when she told him she'd come to look for artifacts possibly turned up by the bulldozer that had leveled the area. She hadn't expected to find anything. In fact, she really wasn't sure why she had come—unless it had been the promise held out by that small falcon of chipped flint she had picked up on the overlooking bluff, or unless it had something to do with the strange attraction, like windmills to Don Quixote, that the derrick held for her. The filigreed tower continued to be an intrusion upon her world. It had no place in the territory she had staked out. This place belonged more to past centuries during which oil had not been drilled from the ground but had been ladled from surface seepage, a time in which oil hadn't been used for combustion engines but to waterproof the cradle in which the baby Moses had floated down the Nile.

Her fingers actually trembled as she pulled the chunk of limestone free and brushed clinging brown dirt from it. This was but a fragment broken from a whole piece, but her trained eye knew what the whole had once looked like, because the engraving on this fragment duplicated the engraving on the famous Scorpion macehead found by Quibell at

Hierakonpolis in 1898. That latter ceremonial macehead, used more as an insignia of pomp and circumstance than an actual weapon, showed the protodynastic Scorpion King wearing the white crown of Egypt and ritually breaking ground for a canal, his courtiers looking on while a bearer squatted before him with a large basket for the resulting dirt. The piece Jenny now held in her hand contained only one small fraction of that total picture—nothing more than a portion of the pharaoh's legs, a portion of the offering basket and a portion of the digging tool. The scorpion insignia, found on the complete macehead, was lost here. Jenny desperately surveyed the ground around her, hoping against hope to find even one more fragment but having no success. The way the bulldozer had raked the immediate area the rest of the splintered macehead could have been anywhere. She pinpointed the spot of her present discovery for future reference by wrapping her handkerchief around a nearby stone, wondering what the watching security people were making of her actions. Then she pocketed the segment of limestone, got to her feet and, trying to look as inconspicuous as possible, walked back to the Land Rover and drove away.

She maneuvered the vehicle over the gentler swells of the desert wadi, knowing just exactly where she was going. Peter had been dropped off earlier that morning in a section of sandstone farther south, having wanted to make an initial survey for possible tomb sites. Jenny had been scheduled

to pick him up later that day to drive them both
back to the house for a noon rendezvous with the
helicopter being sent to fly them to Abdul's villa in
Aswân. Arriving at the pickup point early, she
honked the horn and kept on honking until Peter
finally appeared and descended from a high embankment on a slideway of fractured sandstone. He
looked displeased, even making an obvious point of
checking his wristwatch to indicate he was nowhere
as anxious to get to Abdul's as she apparently was.
She managed to wipe that expression off his face
fast enough. "Good heavens, where did you pick
this up?" he asked, reaching for the segment of
white stone and examining it more closely. "This
isn't what I think it is, is it?"

"What do you think it is?" Jenny asked. She'd
been afraid of being just as overly anxious to at-
tribute importance to this artifact as she was to the
scorpion petroglyph.

"Looks like a chunk of macehead, doesn't it?"
Peter asked. "Very similar to the scorpion macehead, if I'm not mistaken." He glanced up, locking
eyes with her. "This is pretty damned wonderful,
you know?"

"You really think so?" Jenny asked, knowing
that this segment, plus that other macehead plus the
scorpion petroglyph did not add up to proof positive that the protodynastic king of Egypt had lived
and been buried here. But it was circumstantial
evidence that pointed toward that possibility—in
contradiction to Peter's theories that the early

pharaoh belonged farther north. Thus Jenny was actually surprised that Peter could seem so pleased to have one more clue that the Scorpion King had been no stranger to the area.

"How did you think I was going to react?" Peter asked, his voice offering a dangerous challenge that Jenny realized was potential for another quarrel between them.

"Let's not bicker, shall we?" she pleaded. "The way I wanted you to react is just the way you are reacting. Must you try to read something more into everything I say and do?"

"Are you certain you didn't simply rush this over here so you could gloat?" Peter asked, his golden eyes flashing fire. "So you could squeal, 'Look here, buster, one more shred of evidence has turned up to prove your theories about the Scorpion King are pure poppycock!'"

"I brought this to you because you happen to be the director of the dig," Jenny answered, hoping she had come to share the find with him, rather than, as he suggested, to boast of professional superiority. "To whom else should I have brought it, I wonder?"

"I'm sorry," he replied, managing it with just the right degree of appealing humility. "I would hate to have you or anyone else think that I wasn't flexible enough to amend my own theories if enough proof to the contrary turned up."

"I accept your apology," Jenny said, feeling a little guilty that she had always assumed him far less flexible than he apparently was. She seemed to be forever misjudging him, and she worried that all of her preconceptions might continue to taint her image of the real man.

"So let's go see where you picked this up, shall we?" Peter said, getting into the Land Rover beside her.

"The area was disturbed beyond the point of being able to date the find where it lay," Jenny said, not wanting him to think that she, like many archaeologists before her, had gone running off with her treasure without a thorough analysis of the location in which it had been found.

"I've never questioned your professional competence," Peter said. "If I've criticized at all in the past, it's merely been because I've always found criticism healthy. It makes us all stand back and take another look at things, makes us all attempt reevaluations, work harder to plug loopholes we've lazily managed to camouflage only with defective putty." Jenny knew he was referring to his past comments about her Crete-Atlantis theories. She felt a little embarrassed that she had ever taken what he'd said as a personal affront rather than merely constructive criticism offered by one professional who merely wished another to look more closely for proof to support conjecture. Seeing now how willingly he seemed to accept new proof regarding the Scorpion King, she wondered if she would have been as receptive if this latest evidence had supported his claims instead of her own.

If Peter was anxious to see the discovery location, and Jenny was anxious to show it to him, they were both frustrated. The security jeep from the drilling operation intercepted them on the rise, and Galal Baseeli refused them permission to proceed closer, apparently having regretted giving Jenny previous access without Sheikh Jerada in attendance. Galal certainly wasn't prepared to let Jenny get any closer with a complete stranger in tow, and no amount of persuasion seemed capable of changing his mind. Whatever arguments they tried using to impress upon him the importance of the protodynastic pharaoh, whose life was a possible link between un- recorded and recorded history, their words fell on deaf ears. Their job was archaeology, his security, and he scooted them off none too gently.

"I suppose he was just doing his job," Jenny said as the Land Rover bumped over rough ground on the way back to the house. "And there really wasn't much to see that would have proved anything with- out extensive digging. The bulldozer has raised havoc with once-existing surface strata. The frag- ment could have been scooped up from anywhere within the depression."

"That find is damned important!" Peter said, his anger this time, thank God, not directed at her. "You'd think the man might have understood. This is his country's history we're talking about, isn't it?" he continued. Jenny didn't bother going into Abdul's theories regarding Egypt's past versus its present. The security man's prerogatives placed oil at the top of his list, and Jenny could see where he might have been loathe to let some dusty rock perhaps jeopardize his meal ticket. "Maybe we'll have more success getting Abdul to help us!" Peter suggested. However, considering Jenny's remembrances of her past discussion with Abdul on the subject, she really doubted they would get help from that quarter. Her suspicions were pretty much verified when they tried to explain it all to Abdul later in the day.

"Let me get this right," Abdul said, holding the piece of limestone as if Jenny had just handed him a coprolite and told him it was gold and not dried manure. "This is somehow—although it certainly escapes me how—very important?" He handed back the stone, preferring the iced *carcadet* a servant brought him. They were seated on the veranda outside his villa. The Nile, Elephantine Island and the modern city of Aswân were all laid out before them beyond a low balustrade that heralded a steep descent to the river. The setting was exquisitely beautiful, even in the intensity of an afternoon sun that had sucked the landscape dry of all shadow.

"It's very important!" Jenny emphasized. "It moves us one small step closer to proving Hierakonpolis was one of the very first capitals, if not *the* first capital city, Egypt ever had. The Scorpion King was believed to be an immediate predecessor of the early pharaoh, Menes-Narmer, or even one and the same. Think what it would mean to be able to say once and for all that it was at Hierakonpolis that the First Dynasty really began."

"What *would* it mean?" Abdul asked, eyeing Jenny over the lip of his glass. Jenny, who had been expecting some such reply, could tell that Peter hadn't. "What could it possibly mean that could warrant the interruption of a drilling operation?" Abdul added.

"How would a couple of people scrounging around in a dirt pile interfere with the drilling?" Jenny asked, unable to follow his logic. "We don't even have to go close to the machinery. We can do what we have to do on the periphery."

"And if you don't find anything on the periphery, what then?" Abdul asked. "An end to it? Or would you then want to move in and check under the storage sheds?" Howard Carter's last-ditch effort at Thebes had seen him tearing down his workmen's huts in order to get to the ground that suddenly surrendered secrets of King Tutankhamen's tomb.

"Look," Peter said, obviously trying his hardest to make Abdul see reason. He hadn't quite recovered from the frustration of trying to talk sense to the security guard, who hadn't a notion in hell of what a piece of rock had to do with him, so it was even more disturbing to find himself dealing with an educated man who should have seen the connection immediately. "Somewhere in the past, possibly right there at Hierakonpolis, history emerged from prehistory and a series of events took place that triggered much of the civilization we know today. Doesn't it make you wonder just what this first pharaoh was like—a man who was able to take scattered groups of simple fishermen, farmers and stone-wielding hunters and unite them into an empire that erected the pyramids at Giza a mere three dynasties later?''

"You're right, of course," Abdul agreed, though Jenny heard his response as that of a man merely tired of the conversation. "Why don't you let me look into it and see what I can come up with?"

"We'd appreciate whatever you could manage," Peter said, seeing far more progress in this than Jenny did.

"Don't expect miracles, however," Abdul warned, then tempered his comments with a winning smile. "Not right away, anyhow. There's been a good deal of paranoia around since several of the wells started showing signs of nearing pay dirt. Also, a cache of weapons believed smuggled into the country by hostile factions was only recently uncovered not two miles from one well site near Luxor. Possibly no connection between the two events, but—" A servant interrupted with an announcement that dinner was ready, and Abdul brought Jenny and Peter to their feet. "I shall certainly keep you posted on any progress I make regarding your request," Abdul said, the finality of his tone insinuating that he hoped for an end to a conversation that was apparently of very little real interest to him. Jenny put the fragment into her bag.

The dining room, banked by large picture windows at two ends, gave access to contrasting views of equal beauty. Standing to face across the Nile, Jenny was treated to a world of rose-colored hills

that descended to a busy city nestled at the river's
edge. The Nile was in its first cataract, narrowed to
a low boil as it moved around great boulders. The
channel seemed especially complex because of several islands, the largest called Elephantine. This
island had once boasted not only a nilometer, which
measured the rise and fall of flood waters, but also
a well that had been used by Erastosthenes in 1230
B.C. to calculate the diameter of the Earth. Turning
away from the river and toward the rear of the
house, Jenny saw only desert gone earth-brown, its
dunes ascending on the left to the mausoleum of the
Aga Khan and on the right to an escarpment once
used for the tombs of Nubian nobles.

Inside the room the dining table was oak, long and
centered by a low arrangement of red, white and
pink gladioli that ran its entire length. *Shorbât*—a
red lentil soup—was served in a silver tureen. There
were gigantic prawns called *bamia*, with accompanying fresh sea urchins. There was *sefrito*—fried shin
of veal—and *belehat*—sausages of minced beef.
There were stuffed green cabbage leaves, sliced
orange carrots, diced creamy marrow, fluffed saf-
fron rice, with side dishes of red radishes, scarlet
beetroot, pale green cucumber and snow-white
onions.

It had been neither the magnificent view nor the
attractive table and floral arrangement that had
caught Jenny's immediate attention when she
entered the room. Rather, it had been the black mar-
ble fireplace that connected the dining room to the

sunken living room. It was ablaze with leaping orange red flames. "My wife got me hooked on log fires and fireplaces during our Princeton days," Abdul said. "It gets mighty cold in New Jersey in the wintertime." Considering the hot temperatures of Egypt at that period of the year, the holocaust was saved from complete incongruity by an air-conditioning system that successfully voided all but the fire's visual and audio effectiveness. After a while Jenny actually came to enjoy the atmosphere created by wood crackling and sparks spiraling up the chimney.

"I didn't know you were married," Jenny said when they were seated, it having taken all of her willpower to wait that long to make the comment. She didn't miss the wry smile Peter was giving her.

"Divorced," Abdul corrected, which wiped the grin from Peter's face fast enough. It was apparently a subject Abdul was sorry he had brought up, because he shifted the conversation to the latest hawk he had acquired from one of the aeries right there near Aswân. When it became obvious that that subject would entertain Peter indefinitely but not Jenny, he diplomatically moved on to other things, culminating with comments on the bowls of large juicy strawberries served with a light sprinkling of powdered sugar that suddenly appeared for dessert. Jenny did find it a little strange that his divorce hadn't been mentioned previously, although a man out to court a lady was hardly likely to start bringing up his ex-wife to score points, particularly if the

marriage had left a little to be desired—which, if
Jenny could remember certain things Abdul had
hinted in the past, had possibly been the case.

"And now a dessert especially for Jenny!" Abdul
proclaimed theatrically when Jenny, feeling deliciously decadent, had popped the last of the strawberries into her mouth. As if on cue, a servant
appeared with a large silver chafing dish from
which Abdul, moving around the table to do so, removed the lid with a flourish.

"Please don't tell me that's what I think it is,"
Jenny pleaded with a low groan.

"You're going to deplete even your large fortune
if you keep buying Jenny jewelry," Peter said face-
tiously, recognizing the similarity between the un-
veiled case and the one that had arrived with the
necklace.

"Actually, it's the same piece," Abdul admitted.
"Do you know how many times the young lady in
question has refused it as of now? Twice. And I can
tell just by looking that she is on the verge of turning it down again, aren't you Jenny?"

"It's too expensive," Jenny confirmed. She had
made no effort whatsoever to remove the case from
the tray, and the servant looked a little at a loss as
to what he was expected to do.

"Maybe you could prevail upon her to take it off
my hands, Peter," Abdul said, turning toward him
for assistance. "I bought the thing especially for
her, and it certainly isn't doing me any good. I look
silly in lapis lazuli and sapphires."

"Why don't you take it, Jenny?" Peter asked, sounding as if he really would like to hear her answer. Jenny could tell that he was a bit confused by the jewelry's reappearance. Apparently he hadn't the faintest notion that she'd shipped the necklace back to Abdul the day after its last untimely arrival.

"I already told you both," she said. "It's too expensive."

"I've decided the only way I'm ever going to get her to take it is to leave it to her in my will," Abdul said. "I figure she'd feel obligated if I upped and dropped dead." Without waiting for comments on that, he returned the lid to the chafing dish and sent the servant off to the kitchen. Jenny wanted, at that moment, to give the handsome Arab a big kiss, because she had finally understood what he'd been trying to do. He'd been subtly clueing Peter to the fact that any fuss over the necklace's arrival at the other house had been an overreaction. "Now if the two of you think you might be able to amuse yourselves for a couple of hours, I'm afraid I've got a bit of unfinished business that I hoped to have managed by now but didn't. Peter, if you like, I can either arrange for the hawks to be flown this afternoon, or we could wait until it's cooler in the morning."

Jenny could have shot him. She had been so grateful that he had primed Peter for an apology— and arranged to leave them alone long enough for her to accept it. But now he had reversed his favor.

The last thing she wanted was Abdul off on business, Peter off with those damned birds and herself cuddled up and sweating by the raging fire.

"Let's make it morning," Peter said, and Jenny heaved a sigh of relief that was so nearly audible she was instantly embarrassed to think that the men might have heard it.

Abdul flashed her a see-you-had-nothing-to-worry-about smile and told them just to call Sadid if they needed anything. Sadid, the servant who had returned to the room to clean off the table, nodded his willingness to comply.

"Maybe a couple of cold drinks out on the veranda?" Peter suggested.

"I'll have Sadid bring out some chilled champagne," Abdul said, raising a hand to head off any protest. "You'd both be doing me a tremendous favor by drinking the stuff. It's very French, very good and too much of a temptation for someone who, like me, has given up alcohol."

"Well, since you put it that way," Peter said, graciously accepting for the both of them.

"Now if it were only as easy to give away necklaces," Abdul said with a laugh. He gave Sadid instructions about the wine, delivered a slight bow to his guests in parting and left the room, taking the outside stairs to his speedboat.

Jenny and Peter went out on the veranda, not saying anything even when Sadid arrived with champagne and glasses that smoked in the heat. The champagne felt refreshingly cool going down.

Jenny moved to the balustrade, looking out over the Nile to Aswân and the rose-tinted hills in the background. Abdul's boat had already reached the opposite shore, but Jenny was far more interested in the man behind her than in the view. She waited for him to speak.

"Why didn't you tell me you sent back the necklace?" Peter asked. Jenny could tell by the sound of his voice just how far away he was. She wanted him closer, so close his lips might blow his sensuous breath against her ear when he spoke.

"Would you have believed me?" she asked. A cruise ship was docking at the quay across from Elephantine Island. Not the *Osiris* or its sister ship the *Isis*, but one of the boxier Sheraton fleet.

"Probably not," Peter admitted.

"Case closed," Jenny said. Feluccas plied the water, skimming like waterbugs, their triangular sails reflecting on a surface gone slate in the midday heat.

"Still, I would have been comforted, even if I'd have thought it a lie," Peter said. "And God, Jenny, but I could have used a bit of comforting. I'm jealous of Abdul, you know? Always have been, probably always will be."

She turned from the panorama before her to the sight she preferred over it. There was nothing she enjoyed looking at more than Peter Donas. He was especially appealing now, standing there in a white shirt open to show a swath of bronzed chest, his brown breeches hugging his muscular lower body.

"You needn't be jealous of Abdul," she told him, desperately wanting him to come closer, to discard the champagne glass in his hand and enfold her in his arms. "He's merely a friend."

"Truly?" Peter asked, wanting to believe but having trouble doing so.

"I never lie to you, Peter," she said. "Not when I tell you Abdul is just a friend. Not when I tell you I love you."

He did come to her then, assaulting her senses with the perfection of his rugged handsomeness, the smell of his lime cologne, the touch of his hand, the taste of his lips, the sound of his voice against her ear. "And I never lie to you, either, Jenny," he whispered, his face nestling against the soft curve of her neck at her shoulder. By turning her head slightly to one side, she could feel the soft caress of his silky hair against her cheek.

"You did actually call home to tell them about me?" she queried, not daring to ask him of marriage for fear that she might have imagined that part of the statement to which she now referred.

"I called," he verified, gently kissing her throat, working his body maddeningly against her.

"And what was said to your revelation?" she asked, knowing his family now consisted of only one uncle, since his parents, like her own, had died.

"Uncle George is ill," Peter said, pulling back only far enough to run his hand along the side of her face, opening his fingers so that his thumb could trace the gentle fullness of her lips. "He has been for some time. His illness has made him a little cranky and hardly romantic.''

"He wasn't pleased by the idea of you bringing me home, then?'' Jenny asked. The thought bothered her.

"My uncle and I have never been close,'' he said, telling her not to worry needlessly. "My call was made merely as a courtesy to an old man who is beyond loving anyone the way I love you. I certainly didn't call for his approval or blessing. I need no approval from anyone to marry the woman I love.''

"Marry?'' Jenny echoed, the word slipping out accidentally, so anxious had she been to hear it spoken.

"You will marry me, won't you, Jenny?'' Peter asked, his body as tight against hers as any two stones on the Pyramid of Cheops.

"Yes,'' she said, her voice catching in her throat so that it came out a small gasping of pleasure. She wrapped her arms around his neck, knowing she wanted this man more than she had ever wanted anything or anybody in her whole life. "Yes, oh, yes, oh, yes!''

He kissed her deeply and lastingly, moving his mouth and tongue to draw the essence from her with an ecstasy that made her dizzy. When they came apart, it was only because of an unspoken agreement between them. Jenny owed Abdul the courtesy of not going as far as she would have liked with Peter in Abdul's house. The sheikh, obviously still in love with her, had always considered her happiness paramount to his own, and Jenny didn't wish to flaunt her joy before a man who was unhappy himself. When Abdul hadn't joined them by ten that night, Sadid showed them to their separate rooms.

It didn't take Jenny long to realize she was too excited to sleep. Hearing Abdul's speedboat shortly after two in the morning, but not hearing any sounds of him on the stairs by three, she slipped on her robe, determined to thank the man whose sacrifices had so assured her happiness.

The rooms downstairs seemed deserted at first glance, so much so that Jenny began having doubts that she had heard his speedboat at all. Then she began getting strange chills that had nothing whatsoever to do with the shivers she had experienced while in Peter's strong arms. These sensations were not pleasurable, and they recalled images of a Land Rover barreling down at her across burning desert sands, bullets whipping past her face, Abdul wounded and dropping in front of the tent. She refused to believe, however, that assassins would have access to Abdul's home. He would surely have taken sufficient precautions to....

She turned swiftly toward the sudden sound behind her, her taut nerves responding with a breathless gasp that would have quickly progressed to a high-volume scream if Abdul hadn't immediately appeared behind the strange old man in the doorway.

"Jenny?" Abdul asked, surprised to see her.

Jenny's attention was back on the old man, who was pinning her to the wall with a look of sheer malevolence. His gaze crossed the space between them, seemed to say that he wanted to wrap his bony hands around her lovely neck and squeeze her breath away.

"There!" the old man accused loudly, pointing at her in emphasis. His head was a wrinkled ball—like one of those dried apples used in making dolls. It seemed too small to keep aloft the massive blue turban perched precariously atop it. His forearms and hands—all that appeared from the long sleeves of his *galabia*—were thin, his fingernails long and cracked. "There!" he repeated, "is one possible cause of your holocaust!" He then moved with such swiftness that Jenny thought he was coming for her. She found herself rooted to the spot, despite the alarm signals going off inside her, warning her to run. Although it had to be obvious that she was certainly a match for the old man's strength physically, she felt helpless to put up any defense, feeling great relief when he merely rushed on by and out of the door behind her.

"My God!" Jenny said, caught up momentarily in a shuddering shiver of delayed panic that gave her goose bumps.

"Don't mind Rashid," Abdul said, coming to offer comfort. "He tends to be overly theatrical at times. It's a common trait of those in his trade."

"What trade could that possibly be?" Jenny asked, offering no objection when Abdul helped her to a chair and then moved to pour her a bit of cognac in a large snifter. "Scaring old women and children?"

"I shall tell you; you shall laugh, then possibly lecture, and our pleasant night chat will have disintegrated into something far less enjoyable than it might have been," Abdul prophesied, sitting across from her. "However, I suppose that after that you do deserve some kind of explanation, so here goes. Rashid al-Hidda is my astrologer, found this evening waiting on my doorstep to whisper to me of stars recently conjuncted within the vastness of the universe foretelling certain unpleasant consequences for me if—I repeat, if—I'm not especially careful." He tried to make it sound rather amusing, but Jenny was aware enough of the Arab world's belief in the occult to know that he probably took what Rashid al-Hidda said far more seriously than he was willing to let on. Granted that his education and exposure to Western culture might have tempered his belief in such things as astrology, but erase them? Jenny thought not.

"And he thinks I'm going to be somehow responsible?" Jenny asked, recalling the old man's hateful stare and pointing accusation. She took a swallow of cognac from the bubble of baccarat crystal.

"Oh, you mean his little song and dance about you being one possible cause of my holocaust?" Abdul asked with such genuine good nature that Jenny was comforted. "Actually, all of that was purely extemporaneous, I'm sure, undoubtedly called up at the last second not because he dislikes you personally, but because he dislikes all Occidental women. He considers them disturbing influences on the Arab world. I suspect that for a moment there he might even have thought you were Regina returned. There is, I've always realized, a decided similarity." He laughed nervously. "At least as far as your exceptional good looks are concerned," he added.

"Regina was your wife?" Jenny asked, knowing that the question—as well as the immediate answer—was superfluous.

"Yes," he said. "She was. And quite a beautiful creature, too. Quite took my breath away. I was madly in love with her from the very first moment I set eyes on her in the Princeton library, and I simply had to have her. It made little difference to me that she was engaged to a young man struggling through law school at the time. I was cocky, young and certainly far less wise than I am today." He got up, crossed to the windows opening onto the veranda. He peered out at Aswân, seeing a city mainly dark except for the street bordering the Nile. He turned back to her and smiled sadly. "But I'm probably boring you."

"Of course you're not boring me!" Jenny replied, and Abdul had to have known that all along. It was logical that a woman so susceptible to the romantic tragedy of Frederic Donas and Geraldine Fowler at Thebes would have been drawn to facts concerning another tale of unrequited love.

"I was exotic, handsome and very wealthy," Abdul said with a smile that asked her please to forgive that comment if it came out like boasting. "Her fiancé was someone she had known since first grade, as American as baseball, with only average looks and as poor as the proverbial church mouse." He came back to his chair and sat down. He pyramided his fingers and touched them to his full lips. "And I can be quite persuasive when I really turn on the old charm."

"Yes, I know," Jenny said, smiling back at him.

"Oh, but you've seen only the tip of the flame," Abdul said. "Had I found you before I had been tempered by past mistakes, you would have hardly held out hope of keeping me from you. Then again," he said, eyeing her over his fingertips, "I might be mistaken there. You, after all, wouldn't take one simple necklace, where as Regina took a small fortune in jewelry before we even got around to tying the knot. Not that I blame her. She, like her fiancé, was going to school on a scholarship, and her family was really hardly better off than his. Don't think that I'm trying to pass her off as a gold digger, either," Abdul said, as if he thought it suddenly important that he not paint a picture that was unfair. "In the end she left everything I'd given her, exiting with only the clothes on her back. She always did have a sense of fairness, having found no harm in accepting gifts from the man she was going to marry but returning them all when she decided she couldn't be bought after all."

"I'm sorry," Jenny said. "Really, I am."

"It's harder than you might know being an Arab in the twentieth century," Abdul said. "Especially when you're an Arab who's been able to see a bit of the world beyond Egypt. For such exposure comes with its own built-in cultural shocks, placing those of us who experience it in an interim void where we're really not part of one world or the other. We're westernized, but the country of which we're an intricate part and which we love isn't. Maybe that's one of the reasons I'm so anxious to find more oil and catapult *all* Egypt into the twentieth century. At the moment I feel as if I'm flying too far ahead, with no chance of my countrymen ever catching up. I tire of the attitudes of men like Rashid al-Hidda, who are too set in their ways, men who can't begin to fathom the challenge and joy of having a wife as a partner and companion instead of as chattel. It wasn't easy for Regina when she married me and came back here to live, despite all of the luxury offered by this villa built especially to cocoon and protect her. It isn't easy for any Western woman to make the transition from modern times to distant past. And it was wrong of me to suppose I would be setting up Regina as some kind of role model for Egyptian women to emulate—just as it was probably wrong for me to wish to subject you to the same prejudices that Regina found too overpowering. However, it's very difficult for me sometimes to be guided by my head instead of my heart, even though I do try my damnedest."

"You do very well," Jenny said quietly.

"I hope I don't do it to a fault, though," Abdul countered, his expression thoughtful. "I would hate to think I was fool enough to have let a woman go who might have surmounted all of the obstacles, whereas Regina buckled under the pressure."

"You haven't acted wrongly, Abdul, believe me," Jenny said, knowing it would have been just as difficult for her, if not more so, than it had ever been for Regina. Twice in her life already Jenny had balked at having been given less than her professional due because of the archaic position of Arab men regarding women's rights: once at the dig at Avaris, when Roger Daugan had been promoted over her; once at Hierakonpolis, when Dr. Kenny had Peter succeed him.

"So all that remains now is the ending to the story of Regina and me, right?" Abdul ventured. "Which I tell merely to tie up the pieces into a neat little package, because it's certainly not the kind of happily-ever-after ending that one prefers hearing. She went back to find the man she had really loved all along, discovering that he had married a woman on the rebound and had one child already and another on the way. She and he carried on an adulterous affair for more than a year that ended in his divorce from his wife and a very nasty fight for custody of the children. He didn't get the children, but he did marry Regina. The two divorced within the year. Since then she has so successfully dropped out of sight that not even my money has enabled me to track her down."

"I'm sorry, Abdul," Jenny said.

"Just be happy, Jenny," Abdul replied, coming to his feet, embarrassed that he might be on the verge of displaying too much emotion. Even he could be affected by certain stereotyped role images. "You be happy for the both of us, and maybe that will be enough."

She went back to her room but was still unable to sleep. She was awake hours later when a maid knocked at the door to see if she was going to join the men then preparing to fly the falcons. Jenny said no, finding it ironic that she had been deprived of one of the few times in ages that she could have slept in since beginning work at the dig. She got up for breakfast and spent the morning on the veranda, thumbing through magazines Abdul had shipped in monthly from America and Europe. Shortly before noon she glanced up to see Abdul, disappointed that Peter wasn't with him.

"He's out in the mews," Abdul said, referring to a building that had been specifically constructed to house hawks and falconry equipment. "I told him I'd come see if you wanted to take a look at his newest acquisition."

"His what?" Jenny asked, not certain she was getting the gist of the conversation. She was piqued that Peter was once again so entranced by the birds that he had, just as at Saqqâra, decided to outdo Abdul in spending time with them.

"I've given him a haggard for his very own," Abdul said. "You do remember my mentioning her, don't you? She's the bird caught right here at Aswân."

Oh, Jenny knew what Abdul had done, all right. She just wondered why he had done it. Surely he must realize that Jenny wanted to spend some of this rare free time with Peter. And she still saw Peter's interest in the cruel sport as a character flaw. "How could you?" she asked him, feeling betrayed and put very near the brink of tears. "How could you possibly have done this to me after being so kind?"

"Jenny, Jenny," Abdul chided gently, "I am not in the least being unkind. You're an intelligent woman, but you have a few things to learn when it comes to patience and trust. A man such as Peter has many interests in life. You're chief among them—of that I am sure. But you mustn't begrudge him his other endeavors. You can't be upset each time he leaves you to pursue one of his interests."

"Are you insinuating I'm jealous of a damned bird?" Jenny asked guiltily, her laugh implying that the notion was ludicrous.

"Are you coming?" Abdul asked, hardly persuaded.

"No," she said, unable to bear the thought of Peter's face gone radiant with personal possession of something other than herself. "I'm not coming!"

"This problem of trust would not have been

solved by merely keeping Peter away from the birds, Jenny,'' Abdul insisted. ''It would have cropped up eventually and perhaps the reality of your uncertainty would have been far more difficult for you to accept than it is now.'' He turned and left her.

I am being silly, she admitted to herself. And yet she felt that she wanted Peter's presence so continually, so much, that she even envied the desert wind that ruffled his black hair. It should have been her fingers that tousled the fine strands.

CHAPTER TWELVE

SOMEONE—JENNY FORGOT JUST WHO, knowing only it had been neither Abdul nor Peter—had told her that no falconer who had ever enjoyed a good flight with a haggard would ever really be satisfied in flying even the best eyas. An eyas was a hawk taken from its nest while still without feathers, but the haggard was a bird caught after it had gained adult plumage in the wild. The difference most often was in the degree of skill wild hawks acquired by experience. Hawks raised and trained by man did not acquire such skills quickly. The disadvantage was that the haggard, having had a taste of freedom, was less inclined to "take to the fist." It fought with obstinacy to retain its wildness and independence.

Several days previously, upon first setting eyes on the haggard that Abdul, the trainers and Peter seemed so intent upon breaking to their will, Jenny had found it hard to hate any bird that, through no fault of its own, had captured Peter's attention. It also helped that the bird didn't look like a mere twin of Hatshepsût. Oh, the same basic characteristics were present, but the two birds were definitely not cast from the same mold, physically or otherwise. Hatshepsût had been taken as an eyas from her aerie long before she could have known what freedom was all about. Phoenix, for so Peter had dubbed the haggard in memory of his and Jenny's first discussion of the *bennu* hieroglyph in the Egyptian Museum, had known the ecstasy of freedom and had a look about her that definitely said she preferred the wild to captivity.

Jenny empathized with the captured bird. Unlike the falcon, Jenny wasn't bound to any perch by a leash, or held to any fist by a jess, or restrained by any fifty-yard creance to keep her from flying too far afield, but she *was* secured by love. Empathizing, however, did not make her less jealous. Yes, she wanted to be able to allow Peter the joy of something he so obviously considered a pleasurable pastime; she wanted to understand what a grown man could get out of making something into less than God had intended. But all she had come to understand was that she, like that falcon, had once been completely free, had once enjoyed the miracle of her independence, but had somehow been caught against her will. She found she was made extremely uneasy by the way the falcon seemed so determined to regain its freedom. The hawk resisted and continued to resist, whereas Jenny had long since been conquered to the point of willingly welcoming any small attention Peter gave her. Watching the extra pains Peter took in his efforts to win the bird over, with less attention paid Jenny in the process, she began to remember all the things she had ever heard about men being interested only in the chase, their fun and games ending when the pursuit was finally over. She saw Peter as having moved off to a more difficult challenge. It was of small consolation that he continued to tell her he loved her, that he still, now and again, delivered a kiss, that he even announced to the other members of their group that he and she would be married. The bitter fact remained that despite all those things he seemed to prefer the company of the bird to her company.

"Perhaps you will be kind enough to explain something to me," Jenny said, knowing she wasn't speaking from any motivation except jealousy. She had chosen one of the few precious moments Peter had deigned to accord her, and she should have been enjoying it rather than being on the verge of shattering even that little pleasure. Still, she had held her peace for longer than she would have thought possible.

"If I can," he said, turning toward her on the veranda where they were sitting. The sun had already set in all its glory, giving way to the blackness before moonrise. Stars were brilliant in the inky dome above, Khasekhemui's fort a shadow within the darker shadows in the distance.

"Why were you so upset by the prospect of my accepting a necklace from Abdul when you turned right around and accepted a bird from him?" she asked.

"It's hardly the same thing, Jenny," Peter answered.

"Why isn't it?" she pressed. "Although you can't wear the bird around your neck, you have it on your fist often enough. Besides," she continued, "it seems to me that Abdul has given you a few other things in the bargain, like that shed he so conveniently had whipped up so you wouldn't have to share your bedroom with the bird—although I imagine you probably would have far preferred the hawk right there in bed with you."

"Very funny!" Peter retorted, beginning to show signs of impatience.

"Like the trainer Abdul so graciously supplied to baby-sit with the bird whenever your archaeological duties interfere with her training," Jenny added.

"Shed, trainer, *and* hawk, as I see it," Peter said, "have all merely been lent to me."

"Lent?" Jenny asked, not willing to accept that. "The day he gave you the bird, Abdul didn't come in and tell me he had just lent you anything. He asked if I wanted to go take a look at your latest acquisition. The word *acquisition* does denote possession, does it not?"

"Please don't argue semantics with me!" Peter said gruffly. "The simple fact is, everybody knows it would be impossible for me to take the bird back to England."

"Well, here's one person who doesn't know any such thing," Jenny contradicted. "Do you want to tell me how everybody but me has come to that particular deduction?''

''If you knew as much about falconry as you profess, you would have figured it out,'' Peter replied, his tone insinuating that she couldn't tell the difference between a hack bell—heavy bells used to hinder falcons from hunting for themselves during certain periods of training—and a bewit bell—smaller bells attached for tonal identification. In truth, Jenny knew not only that but a lot more. ''You would be aware that a peregrine like Phoenix requires access to vast acres of open farmland reasonably populated with game.''

''You have a big house with lots of acreage in England, don't you?'' Jenny countered. So far he hadn't succeeded in convincing her of anything. She had visions of his excusing himself on their wedding night because his hawk had come down with a bad case of mites. ''As for game, all you have to do is buy enough pigeons to shake free of their cages, as Abdul does to keep his birds from having to fly too far afield for dinner.''

''Actually, it's less a case of acreage and game than it is a simple case of time,'' Peter amended. ''Peregrines have to be flown every day and more than once a day if they're to be kept in first-class condition.''

''So hire a trainer in England,'' Jenny said, wondering why she was so intent upon pointing out his options. The last thing she wanted him to do was to pack up the bird and take it home with him.

"She'll be far better off here," Peter argued, having thought the thing through. "Here there is plenty of land, with less chance of the bird being shot by farmers anxious to protect their chickens. Abdul has the best facilities for her care and training."

"Thinking only of the bird all along, are you?" Jenny challenged, knowing what he was going to answer and knowing she was going to shoot him down. He wasn't thinking of the bird, certainly not of Jenny, but only of Peter Donas.

"The hawk deserves the best," Peter said, coming right in on cue. "She shouldn't be owned by someone who can only do a half-baked job by her."

"What are you doing now but a half-baked job by her *and* a half-baked job as director of this dig, because you don't really have enough time to do either job the way it should be done?" Jenny asked. That left him momentarily speechless—and rightly so. She had seen him spend whole workdays that should have been devoted to the excavation and whole nights that should have been devoted to her, walking around, just trying to keep the hawk on his gloved fist. The bird, obviously nervous, had kept trying to fly away but was pulled up sharply each time by her jesses. Phoenix had looked pathetic, head hanging down, wings flapping, until Peter would get her hoisted back up on his fist again. The procedure, technically called "watching," taught the bird to perch on the fist of her master. Later the bird would trust its master enough to fall asleep while on his fist. That was something Phoenix wasn't about to do until she had learned to trust Peter and to feel confident of her safety.

"Are you accusing me of being derelict in my duties as director on this dig?" Peter managed finally. Jenny had to admit that the dig was proceeding exactly according to schedule, but the archaeological work was not her primary concern at the moment.

"Let's forget about the dig for a minute, shall we?" Jenny said. "Let's talk about us."

"I think it might be smarter if we broke off this discussion completely, before we both end up once again saying things that would have been better left unsaid," Peter suggested, his voice angry.

"Hit a raw nerve, have I?" Jenny asked, plowing right ahead. Any communication between them, even the disturbing sort, could only be an improvement as far as she was concerned. Because if Peter hadn't had ample time for his job or for the bird, he certainly hadn't had enough time for her. "Well, let me tell you that what I see here is a simple case of unadulterated self-indulgence."

"Stop it, Jenny!" Peter commanded, coming to his feet. "Just stop it!"

"Sure, hurry off without listening," Jenny heckled. "That's just what I thought you'd do anyway. You still don't realize your selfishness is cheating that bird of the time and devotion she has every right to expect from the man who's forced her to surrender her freedom." She didn't know what was holding Peter to the spot, since it was obvious he was anxious to bolt, but she was going to take full advantage of his immobility to spit out all of the bile she'd been accumulating these past few days. "What good is it for you to work so hard at forming any kind of relationship of love and trust with a bird that you've already admitted you're going to desert at the end of a month's time? Granted it's going to give you the satisfaction of knowing you once lived out a childhood dream of playing falconer, but playing is all it is, Peter. You don't take on anything, falcon or woman, make her love you and then simply move on to something else. Not, that is, unless love is nothing but a game to you. You wouldn't get involved if you really cared about those left suddenly in limbo, having neither you nor the freedom they had before you."

"I didn't take the bird's freedom," Peter rationalized. "She lost that before I ever came into the picture."

"All I see is that you stand between her and her freedom now," Jenny said, pushing home her point. She wasn't talking about *just* the bird, either. She was talking about Peter and herself. "And I don't know about you, but I see freedom as far more preferable to temporary love."

"You know what you're doing, don't you?" Peter asked.

"You bet I know what I'm doing!" Jenny answered with all the assurance of a zealot among disbelievers. "I'm pointing out a few facts of life that should have been pointed out a long time ago."

"No!" Peter contradicted. "You aren't doing that at all. You're coming right back to the old rut of looking at the whole world in terms of Frederic Donas and Geraldine Fowler—*that*'s what you're doing."

"You're crazy!" Jenny replied, coming quickly to her own defense but afraid that his accusation might be close to the truth.

"Yes, you are," Peter said. "You're so involved in something that happened sixty years ago that you can't see anything but a series of repeats. You question my love because you see me running off and leaving you, despite all of my reassurances to the contrary. You see me playing Frederic Donas to a bird you've assigned the role of poor Geraldine. Love her and leave her, isn't that what you've just described here? Well, maybe I did take on Phoenix knowing I was merely fulfilling a fantasy, but I was at least prepared to surrender that fantasy at the end of my time with her and get back to the reality at hand. You're so immersed in this thing that happened between our grandparents at Thebes that I don't think you're ever going to come up for air."

"That's not true!" Jenny insisted, her denial sounding weak because Peter had only put into words what she'd been thinking and fearing all along. "That simply is not true!"

"Well, you just think about it, Jenny!" Peter insisted. "Because I'm suddenly beginning to wonder if you wouldn't be happiest if I did just run off and leave you standing at the altar.'' Jenny's gasp was audible. ''Then at least you would have the satisfaction of moving one step closer to *being* Geraldine Fowler—which is what I think you've really wanted all along,'' he added to shock her even further.

''That's sick!'' Jenny accused, her heart pounding so hard and loud it was like a timpani sounding drumrolls inside her head.

''Damned right it is!'' Peter said in ready agreement. ''And the sooner you realize it's sick, the better it's going to be for you, for me and for anyone else caught up in your morbid fascination with something in the past that would have been better left forgotten in the first place.''

She didn't wait for him to make another of his exits, making one herself. She got up and headed for the house without a backward glance or another word. Barbara saw her coming and diplomatically removed herself from a collision path by slipping into the library, but Jenny hardly even noticed. She had kept her problems from Barbara up until now, and she saw no sense in suddenly dumping them on the younger woman. Which left her pretty much without a shoulder to cry on. She certainly didn't have Abdul's obliging ear this time around, not because he wouldn't have been willing to volunteer, but because Jenny saw him as the sole cause of her present predicament. If Peter hadn't been given— or lent—that bird, depending upon whose definition one accepted, none of this would have happened. If Abdul had any plans of benefiting from this catastrophe he was sadly mistaken. She felt she'd been better off before she'd met either of the men who seemed so set on complicating her life.

She went to her room and lay on her bed for a long time with her eyes shut, trying to still her rampaging heartbeats. When she opened her eyes, it was to see the cracks in the ceiling and know the whole house was slowly disintegrating around her. Everything in Egypt seemed in one state of decay or another, and it was probably the wrong place to have thought a romance could have endured without decaying, too.

She felt miserable, not remembering when she had felt worse. Peter had actually accused her of wanting to be Geraldine Fowler. That simply wasn't true. Jenny wanted to be Jenny, not some woman dead for sixty years. She wanted Peter, not his grandfather. "Oh, Peter, Peter," she said, her voice a low moan of utter despair. She got up and walked over to the window, wishing there had never been a woman named Geraldine Fowler or a man named Frederic Donas. She wished she could have found Peter on her own somewhere besides Egypt, loved him, married him, had his children, all without constant reminder of two haunted souls from another time.

She could see the small shed that had been erected between the house and the desert. It wasn't very solidly constructed, and light leaked out from its thatch of palm fronds. She was heartsick to know Peter was in there now, stroking the speckled breast feathers of a falcon, cooing words of endearment to the hawk. "What's happening to us, Peter?" she asked, her voice catching in her throat.

She leaned on a nearby table for support. The table, none too stable, tipped precariously with her weight, endangering them both with a fall. Two books and a hairbrush landed with a thud on the floor. She quickly became concerned that the falling objects might bring someone to see what had happened. She listened for footsteps on the stairs, thanking God she didn't hear any. Probably it would have taken more to bring anyone. The members of the group had apparently decided among themselves that it was better not to become involved in Jenny's and Peter's personal problems. Jenny suspected they would all have sided with Peter if forced into making a choice.

Jenny picked up the books and the hairbrush, putting them back on the table, rearranging them several different ways without getting them to look right. She suspected her mundane fussiness was a diversion to keep her from thinking of Peter. Suddenly, though, she knew it was more than just simple puttering. The grouping didn't look right because something was gone. She looked for the missing piece, searching the floor between the window and the bed. In falling, the limestone fragment would have made a sound different from that of either the books or the hairbrush—and it would have left a dusty splotch where it landed.

The piece of the Scorpion macehead discovered

by Jenny at the site of the oil derrick was gone. Her immediate reaction was confusion, but she quickly decided it couldn't have been on the table as she thought it had been. Peter must have picked it up and laid it somewhere else. He could tell her where it was, and Jenny welcomed the excuse to go back to him, hoping she had the strength to use this perfect opportunity to confess to him her jealousy of the falcon. Peter had been brave enough to confess his jealousy of Abdul, and Jenny had reassured him. Now she wanted some reassurances of her own.

She stepped out on the veranda, descended the steps and walked around the house, assured that differences with Peter would be cleared if she just made the additional effort. She was pulled up by the human sounds of affectionate clucking and cooing coming from the shed. They were the sounds of a man trying to soothe and calm a bird. It was Jenny who needed loving reassurances at the moment.

She opened the shed door so loudly that she sent the falcon off her perch. Jenny had known what would result: the sudden cessation of flight, the plunging earthward—the leash preventing actual contact with the ground—the frantic flapping of wings as the bird became more and more disoriented by being upside down. The precarious dangle really did Phoenix no harm; the poor falcon had been in that position often enough during Peter's attempts to get her to sit obediently on his gloved fist. Jenny felt a moment's guilt, though, in know-

ing she was responsible for the bird's present discomfort. Then her guilt turned to surprise as she
realized that the startled man before her was not
Peter, but the bird's trainer.

Jenny didn't need to be told that those fingers
suddenly squeezing her right shoulder, turning her
around in an about-face that was almost a complete
circle, were those of the man she had thought to
find inside. Even when Peter touched her in anger,
he delivered an electric shock that made her weak in
the knees. "What in hell are you doing here?" he
asked loudly, his fingers tightening. He didn't give
her time to answer, apparently more concerned with
the scenario behind her. "Khalil, take care of the
bird!" he instructed the trainer, who remained as
disoriented as the struggling falcon.

Peter pulled Jenny out of the shed and banged
the door closed behind them with a force that sent
the hawk into further spasms of panic. "Don't ever
do anything as stupid as that again!" he commanded Jenny, his face livid in the dim light supplied by a
slice of moon on the horizon. "Do you hear me?
Ever!"

Jenny's resulting anger came not because she was
being reprimanded. She guiltily realized she had
carelessly frightened a helpless bird who couldn't
possibly have known what the fuss was all about.
The bird would undoubtedly have preferred being
out of Peter's clutches and free in the sky again.
Jenny should have considered Phoenix as a kindred
spirit, not an enemy. What infuriated Jenny was the

way Peter was telling her off. He should have had the intuitive sense to know she acted the way she had only because she loved him. If she didn't care so much, she wouldn't be here now, grasping at whatever straw had given her the excuse to seek him out again that evening. "What did you do with the fragment from the Scorpion macehead?" she managed finally, interrupting some further comment he was making about how stupid she had been.

"What do you mean, what did *I* do with it?" he asked, letting go of her shoulder as if he had been holding on to an eel that had just released a powerful electrical charge.

"Just what I said," Jenny answered, knowing this wasn't going at all the way she had planned it. "What did you do with it? It's gone."

"Gone where?" Peter asked. "From your room? From the house? Gone from Egypt? Launched from the Earth and floating around somewhere in outer space?"

"It's gone from my room," she replied, infuriated at his sarcasm.

"And you naturally assumed I stole it?" he challenged.

"I didn't say anything about it being stolen," Jenny countered, trying to be calm and cool but actually furious that he was trying to put words into her mouth. "I'd merely like to know what's happened to it."

By the recurring sounds of flapping wings from inside the shed, it was obvious that Jenny and Peter were still disturbing a bird whose nerves had been put on edge. Peter removed himself farther and waited for Jenny to join him. His continued concern for the falcon didn't alleviate Jenny's inner rage and jealousy. She felt like staying where she was and screaming whatever she had to say across the distance separating them. She didn't because she never had been one to air her dirty linen in public. If she and Peter were at it again, there was no sense in the whole village knowing—if everyone didn't know already.

"Now," Peter said when she had joined him. She wanted him to touch her, but he gave all indication that any touches he felt like delivering were best kept under control. "Did you happen to ask Betty if she picked up the fragment to get some better sketches of it for the files?" he asked. Betty Anuke was the group's resident artist and cameraperson. A rather plain-looking but competent young lady, she'd got the position through someone her father knew at the University of Chicago, the university footing a good portion of the excavation bills.

"I'm sorry," Jenny apologized, glad she could now move on to more important things. "I didn't know Betty had it."

"I don't know Betty has it, either," Peter said, not yet finished. "But that certainly is one viable explanation, isn't it, one you probably didn't consider, though Betty was more readily available to you inside the house than I was out here." She wanted desperately to tell him she hadn't wanted to be with Betty but with him. He didn't give her the chance. "How's this for another alternative?" he asked, the same maddening edge of sarcasm in his voice. There was also a trace of hurt. "What do you say to its having been one of the other members of the group who wanted to take a closer look? Did you stop to ask any of them if they knew where it was? No you came right out here, positive I was the guilty culprit. Did you really think I'd be low enough to spirit off a piece of evidence that pointed to the Scorpion King being buried where you thought he was? Do you think I'm more concerned about appearing to be right than I am about being honest?"

"I never insinuated any such thing!" Jenny protested, refusing to let him accuse her of such thoughts. "Don't you dare try to say that I did!"

"You might not have had the courage to make that accusation to my face, but your actions speak louder than any words, lady," he replied, once again not giving her an opportunity to get a word in edgewise. "But before you do go running off at the mouth to anyone who'll listen about how I'm so inflexible about my theories that I'm prepared to cover up evidence to the contrary, you'd better stop to consider that if the fragment does turn up missing, it might well be none other than Sheikh Abdul Jerada who had it lifted."

"Abdul?" Jenny responded automatically, unable to believe Peter was resorting to such a cheap shot. Abdul hadn't given the piece more than a passing glance.

"Didn't give him a thought, huh?" Peter asked triumphantly. "Don't bother answering. I can tell just by looking that you didn't. Whom do you think had a better motive for theft: me, who sees that fragment as a threat to one theory among many theories that are being proved wrong every day, or Abdul Jerada, who just might have seen that fragment as a threat to his oil-drilling operation at Hierakonpolis?"

"How could it possibly be a threat to his oil operation?" Jenny asked, afraid to hear the answer if for no other reason than that she didn't want to consider Abdul a suspect.

"You and I both told him it was important, didn't we?" Peter pointed out. "Had he any reason to think we weren't telling him the truth? He didn't put any value on the piece himself, but surely he realized there was a chance that the Bureau of Antiquities in Cairo might be very interested. They just might be convinced that important artifacts should take precedence over a hole presently turning up nothing."

"I can't believe that!" Jenny said.

"Of course you can't," Peter said, hardly surprised. "That's because you would rather believe I'm guilty."

"I never thought you were guilty of anything except possibly moving the fragment from one room of the house to another," Jenny replied, wondering how everything she did and said seemed to get misinterpreted.

"And I, Miss Mowry, can't believe that! No matter that I would very, very much like to oblige you by doing so." He turned from her in hurt and anger. It seemed one was always turning from the other in hurt and anger. It was as if unseen forces were controlling their lives, refusing them happiness. Maybe they *were* victims of the past, or maybe there was something to the supposed curse that surrounded the opening of King Tutankhamen's tomb, something that had been passed on from generation to generation to plague even the innocent grandchildren of those who had violated the grave site. Jenny had read somewhere that twenty-two people either directly or indirectly involved in the exploration had died prematurely under peculiar circumstances within the seven years following the opening of the tomb. She remembered the number specifically because the article had listed Geraldine Fowler as one of those victims.

"I didn't believe you stole it," Jenny said softly. "Really, Peter, I didn't. I love you, I love you."

Too late, a voice came whispering to her from the past, blown to her on a breath of cool night air that had touched the oil derrick and the fort of Khasekhemui before reaching her. It *was* too late—at least for the moment. Peter, swallowed by the darkness, was no longer within hearing.

CHAPTER THIRTEEN

HER DREAMS WERE NIGHTMARES, so horrible they woke her, so illusive they were forgotten as soon as she had escaped them. She got up and was reading as Barbara's alarm went off. The younger woman stirred as reluctantly as always. It was amusing to watch her roll to the opposite side of her bed, cover her head with blankets and burrow deeper, issue small grunts and groans when faced with the undeniable realization that it was time to get up. Her hand managed to disengage the buzzer just seconds before it would have spent itself.

"Don't you ever sleep?" Barbara asked wearily, coming up in a movement that had her reaching for her robe as her legs dropped to give her feet access to her slippers. It was the same question she always asked when she awoke to find Jenny already dressed. The question was rhetorical, however, since Barbara was hardly up to any rational listening before her morning coffee.

Jenny never went to breakfast, never having managed to get used to eating that early in the morning no matter how many times she'd been given the opportunity. She was surprised when Barbara returned to their room before joining the others downstairs. It seemed especially curious that Barbara's expression questioned not only Jenny's right to be where she was, but also her right to be doing what she was doing. "Did Peter say anything about where he was going?" the young woman asked.

"Going?" Jenny echoed, startled by the question. She put her book to one side, not having the faintest notion what she was supposedly reading anyway. Her mind had been more occupied in wondering how and why the fragment of Scorpion macehead had disappeared. She had made the rounds of the other members of the dig, none of whom knew what had happened to it. That Peter might be missing, too, was even more disturbing.

"He's not here," Barbara said. "One of the Land Rovers is gone, and Tim said he thought he heard it pulling out earlier this morning."

"Which means I had better get up and get going, yes?" Jenny said, taking the not-so-subtle hint. The excavation team had been divided into two groups, each working a different predynastic cemetery. Peter usually left the house early with the first group because they had farther to go. Jenny followed shortly with the second. However, if Peter had driven off with one of the vehicles, Jenny was going to have to provide shuttle service for both groups—a chore that was going to set everyone's workday behind schedule, especially if afternoon pickups were to be arranged using just the one vehicle. "Tell the others I'll be right down," Jenny said. "Peter obviously decided to check some site deeper in the wadi and forgot to mention it to me." She was making excuses, while everyone knew it wasn't like Peter to forget something like that. Everybody was probably blaming Jenny's poor memory, but she didn't care. She was suddenly too worried that Peter might have pulled out for England, leaving without a word. Frederic Donas had left Geraldine Fowler in Egypt, never coming back. Jenny reached for a sweater needed at the moment but destined for a quick rejection once the sun came up. She told herself Peter wouldn't just leave for England without warning. He would have delegated the position of director to someone. While it probably wouldn't have been to Jenny since she was a woman, albeit the most qualified of the group, it would have gone to someone. As of that moment, everyone seemed just as much in the dark as to Peter's whereabouts as she was.

She left the second group at breakfast, loading the first into the remaining Land Rover. Since Peter had taken the vehicle with the bad transmission, Jenny saw another horrible possibility. He might have decided, after their fight, to get some air by driving into the desert. The car might have conked out. He might be stranded in the middle of nowhere, too far away to walk back in a heat capable of exhausting him before nightfall. There were, of course, emergency provisions in the Land Rover, and Peter certainly knew enough about desert survival not to attempt making any great distance on foot after sunrise.

While Jenny was chauffeuring the second group, Barbara spotted the missing vehicle. Timothy then saw Peter on the spine of a sandstone ridge outlined by the predawn light of morning. Peter was walking with his falcon perched on his fist. Jenny swerved back to her original course, knowing he didn't need rescuing. Her relief in finding him safe was countered by anger that the only thing that had kept him from his duties as director—and had needlessly worried her silly—was his eagerness to put his falcon through her paces in the coolness of an early-morning dawn. By the time Jenny reached the second dig site and made sure everyone was busy at his assigned ten-by-ten-meter plot, she had cooled down to where she figured there was no time like the present to get things straightened out between her and the man she loved. She was losing him, and that was the last thing she wanted.

She was delayed in her resolve by the arrival of the government inspector who had been assigned to their dig mainly to make sure everything found was properly recorded. Had the dig been expected to uncover something of great value, Mamud Said would have been on the site on a more regular basis. Hierakonpolis showed little evidence of turning up any big surprises, its chief points of interest being settlements and cemeteries predating the times when great caches of gold were buried with mummies, so the inspector made only infrequent checks. Jenny

had seen him just twice, merely for a few minutes
on each occasion. She begrudged the time she had
to spend with him now, finding ridiculous his suspicions regarding Peter's absence from both sites.
"He's not off plundering some newly discovered
tomb of a pharaoh, I assure you," Jenny said when
the man's query sounded as if it had been insinuating the like. "He's taken the day off to fly one of
Sheikh Jerada's falcons." If Peter considered the
bird on loan from the sheikh, Jenny had decided to
do so, also.

"Fly it where?" Mamud asked politely. It was
obvious he wasn't going to let the subject drop. He
was a small man—probably no more than five foot
five; thin, but not unpleasantly so, dressed in a
Western-cut business suit that looked out of place
in the wilderness setting. His eyes were large and
black, part of a total expression that asked Jenny
please not to try to put anything over on him. It was
natural for him to be concerned, since Egypt's
treasures had been sacked by the Greeks, Romans,
Turks, French and English before an independent
government finally got around to clamping a lid on
the outflow. It was lucky anything of value had remained in the country. Hierakonpolis seemed barren, but there was always the rare chance something
might turn up, and Mamud knew he should have
been keeping closer tabs on the operation. He
hadn't even seen the fragment of Scorpion macehead—which Jenny figured was just as well, considering it was now missing. But even if he had seen it,

it was doubtful he would have been as excited as the group. The only things that really would have got his juices flowing would have been hints of some major find, the chances of which were very slim at Hicrakonpolis. The suspected pharaohs of the area, Menes-Narmer, Scorpion and Aha, had lived previous to the time when a ruler's mummy was laid to rest in anything more complicated than a simple two-compartment burial vault, and their treasures were usually no more elaborate than earthenware jars filled with wine, grain, meat and dates. Had there been any gold, as had been found in the First Dynasty tomb of Zer at Abydos, it would have been nothing compared to the truckloads unearthed by Carter at Thebes, and it would probably have been long gone as a result of those generations of looters who had ransacked the area extensively.

"If you'd like to follow me, I can show you where he's flying it," Jenny said, wondering how she would have explained not having had the faintest notion where Peter was. Mamud would have undoubtedly found that suspicious. "Unless you'd like to stay here a little longer and examine our considerable collection of pottery shards." Mamud had had quite enough of what little was turning up, and he was anxious to go. The workmen were raising dust that settled a tan powder over his fine suit. His own vehicle followed Jenny in the Land Rover.

Peter was on his spiny ridge of sandstone. He was sitting now, but the falcon was still on his fist. Jenny waved, but Peter didn't wave back. "Coming up with me?'' she asked Mamud, his company being the last thing she wanted. She couldn't imagine him or his clothes making the steep climb. ''I promised Peter a verbal report as soon as I got the group settled.''

''Wish him good flying,'' Mamud said, a decidedly envious look in his dark eyes. Jenny would have never pictured him a falconry aficionado. The bug obviously bit all kinds!

Jenny watched Mamud leave before she turned and headed up an embankment that proved the Sahara wasn't all sand. The ground underfoot was packed hard beneath a covering of soil as powdery and dry as sifted flour. As Jenny climbed higher, wondering what pathway Peter could possibly have taken to assure the safe ride of the falcon on his fist, the dust gave way to earthworn rock that crumbled beneath her feet and hands whenever they sought support from it.

The summit was a narrow ridge that paralleled the distant Nile before disintegrating on all sides. Peter sat at the far end. He didn't turn to greet her, and he had made no effort to assist her when she slipped twice before managing the final foothold at the top. She could hardly have expected him to be too concerned when to help might have disturbed the bird. She took a deep breath, reminding herself that such thoughts would not help her in her determination to reach Peter—in both senses of the word. She had come to do everything in her power to repair the breach between them, even if she had to end up sharing him with a bird. She sat down beside him ever so slowly so as not to disturb the falcon, whose hood was complete with a plume of brilliant, green, cock's hackle feathers. She was glad such hoods had superseded the older method of obscuring the sight by sewing threads through the bird's eyelids, although the latter technique was still widely practiced in India.

"Come with greetings from our government inspector?" Peter asked. His left hand, the one supporting the bird, was sheathed in a buckskin glove, the leather doubled over on the thumb, first two fingers and upper part of the wrist. An even heavier glove would have been necessary for a goshawk—a shorter winged hawk whose sharp talons and vise-like grip were much more dangerous than the more delicate hold of the peregrine. The goshawk's talons would have penetrated the heaviest leather if the bird were *yarak*—a Turkish term for "in top flying form."

"Mr. Said was only curious to know why you weren't at the dig," Jenny said, watching Peter's right hand stroke the breast of the hawk, wishing it were stroking hers instead. "I told him you'd been working hard lately and had taken the day off."

"Did you tell him my working so hard was caused by my having tried to take on two full-time jobs at the same time?"

"I don't want to fight, Peter," Jenny said, hoping he wasn't going to make this more difficult for her than it was.

"What is it you do want, then, Jenny?" he asked, still not looking at her, concentrating on the way his right forefinger moved along speckled black feathers.

"I want *you*," she said, wondering why she hadn't managed that simple statement in anything more than a hoarse whisper. She knew she had to say even more, and none of it would get any easier. "I want you, and I'm desperately afraid I'm going to lose you," she hurried on, the bird's head movements showing an awareness of Jenny's voice and presence. "I came to apologize if it came across, even for a moment last night, that I thought you responsible for the missing fragment of macehead."

"Then it's still missing?" Peter asked, sounding interested, even if he didn't look at her.

"I figure Abdul took it," Jenny said. "Or more probably, he had it taken."

"He confessed that to you, did he?" Peter asked, finally focusing his sunny eyes on her and making her melt inside.

"I haven't seen Abdul today," Jenny said. "I, like you, just can't come up with anybody else who had a motive."

"What happened to *my* motive?" Peter asked, that well-recognized edge of sarcasm in his voice.

"I never suspected you," Jenny said. "You just anticipated, remember? I thought you'd probably moved it. I wouldn't even have bothered coming to ask, except I was desperate for the excuse to talk to you again—and I was jealous."

"You were jealous? Of what? The falcon?" Peter inquired, hardly able to believe what Jenny had just confessed. He laughed—which made Phoenix open her wings nervously, as if she were about to attempt flight.

Jenny waited until the hawk had dropped her wings and settled down, noting how much more cautious the bird had become after having spent so much time hanging upside down. "Yes, it is rather funny, isn't it?" Jenny said, not thinking it was funny at all.

"Funny only because I can't imagine why you'd be jealous of a bird," Peter said, seeming truly at a loss. "A bird, Jenny! A bird?"

"You spent time with the falcon that I wanted you to spend with me," Jenny said, bringing her knees up and wrapping her arms around her legs. She looked out over a vista of rocky hills descending to sand, sand flowing to vegetation, vegetation dipping to gray river, more vegetation ascending the opposite bank to more sand and more rocky hills. It was a mirror image in which she expected to see two people and a hawk facing her from some distant ridge across the river.

"I knew this bird was somehow coming between us, but I thought that was only because you were using her as an excuse to criticize the job I was doing as director," Peter confessed, shaking his head, unable to believe the mix-up. "I thought you were brooding childishly because you didn't get the job and I did."

"I still think it should have been mine," Jenny said, wishing to make that perfectly clear. "However, the fact that Dr. Kenny wanted you and not me to take over for him has never clouded my true feelings for you."

"You'll still marry me, then?" Peter asked.

"Oh, Peter, you fool. Of course I'll still marry you!" Jenny said, eager to fall into his strong arms but aware that her doing so would only upset the falcon and send the poor bird into another nose dive. "Marrying you is what I've dreamed about ever since I first realized I loved you."

"Stealing my line, aren't you?" Peter asked with a wide smile. A slight breeze caught his hair and tousled it attractively. Jenny would have liked to run her fingers through it but controlled that temptation.

"Well, then," she said, bursting with happiness and feeling it was time to make her exit before anything spoiled this moment of accomplishment. "I shall leave you two and get back to whatever new pieces of pottery and bone have been discovered in my absence." She got up.

"Don't go, Jenny!" Peter said. "Please." He came to his feet beside her, the falcon fluttering her wings to maintain her balance during the sudden move. "Share this moment with me, will you?" She knew he was preparing to fly the hawk because he carefully unfastened the hood and pulled it free. The bird blinked her large eyes to adjust to the light, eyeing Jenny and Peter before turning to a panorama remembered from times past when those distances had been covered without the constriction of creance, leash or jess. "I want our whole life to be a mutual sharing of things," Peter said, "starting now." He raised his left arm suddenly, then dropped it forcing the hawk loose. The bird became airborne, flapping her wings as she entered the sky, probably wondering why she hadn't yet been pulled up short, probably still expecting the sudden end of her flight. Peter peeled off the gauntlet and let it and the hood fall at his feet. He moved closer to Jenny, wrapping an arm around her waist, holding her tightly against his side, as they watched Phoenix spiral upward on air currents produced by the sun's heating the rugged stones. "She belongs there, doesn't she?" Peter said, speaking into Jenny's hair. "Just as you belong in my arms." He gave her a harder squeeze as the falcon soared higher, ever higher.

Jenny listened for the dissonant tones of bewit bells but heard none. She realized for the first time that the bird wasn't wearing bells—or dangling jesses. It hadn't been flown to be called back to the fist. It had been flown to its freedom. Peter had given it back to the sky, to the wind, to the sun. He'd done it for her, surrendered his fantasy because he had seen that it interfered with what he wanted with Jenny. The fact that the jesses had already been off when Jenny had reached the top of the ridge meant he'd been preparing to make the sacrifice even when he'd considered Jenny's dislike of the bird nothing more than a cover-up for her anger at having been passed over for the job of dig director.

"Peter, I . . ." she said, turning in his arms. He stopped her with a kiss that lingered as he moved both his arms around her, drawing her closer against his hard and muscled body.

"You were right, Jenny," he whispered. "I shouldn't have taken the falcon! Shhhhhh!" he insisted, sensing she was about to protest when protestations were no longer necessary. "I should never have taken her because she deserved my time and my love, and I could give her neither. My time I had already committed to my profession, my love I had already committed to you."

"Peter, Peter," she said, kissing his warm chest at his open shirt collar. Above them Phoenix soared, nothing more than a diminishing speck in the clear blue sky.

"I've willingly turned the falcon free," Peter said, his embrace taking Jenny's breath away, "but I'll never let you go, Jenny Mowry. Never!"

"Never!" she agreed readily.

"The bird may need freedom," he told her, nibbling along her neck to her ear, "but I need you."

"And I need you, darling!" Jenny admitted, having never known joy like this before she'd been captured by his love for her and hers for him. "Oh, Peter, how I love you!" She held to him, fearful he would disappear as suddenly as the falcon that had faded to nothingness in the heights above them. "I love you, love you, love you. So very, very very much!''

He slowly opened her blouse, exposing her firm breasts to a sun whose warmth provided but a portion of the heat building to consume her. He gently bit her nipples, her neck, her chin and finally her lips. His mouth claimed hers in a mutual exchange—tongues as well as lips meeting.

Her hard nipples chafed against the front of his shirt, growing tauter in their eagerness to touch the naked hardness of his muscled chest. She tore at his shirt buttons, it having suddenly become too time-consuming to master their unfastening any other way. His skin became an exposed warmth against her as his kisses continued to rain down on her eager mouth, her cheeks and her throat.

''I want you, Jenny,'' he whispered, his breath a maddening caress within her ear. She wanted him, too, and she would never stop wanting him.

They used their quickly shed clothes to make themselves a soft place on which to lie. The hardness of ancient stone beneath that thin covering of cloth went unnoticed in a swirl of need that would have converted a bed of thorns into one of roses.

His magnificent body was the sun, warm and golden. She delighted in the feel of it against her, in the taste and smell of it. It was hardness overlaid with velvety softness. It was salt and lime cologne. He gave her free access to his nakedness, just as she gave him free access to her own. They were each other's for the taking, and she delighted in the exploration of her fingers and lips along the rippled ridges of his fine hard shoulders. She touched him everywhere, made bold in her passion. Her fingers dallied in the damp hair at the nape of his neck, traced downward along his chest and came to rest— for the briefest of moments—over his pounding heart. It seemed as though the very life of him beat there beneath her eager hand, but she did not stay its movement. Instead, she continued, downward over his sleek thighs and forward to where the touch of her on his most sensitive flesh elicited from him a passionate moan. He slid his hands and mouth over her, covering her in touches that burned the very core of her being, making her insides melt to warm dew. He kissed her in places only he had known before. She kissed his jaw, the soft joining of his shoulder and his neck, his bronze chest made salty by the desert heat and the heat of his desire. Wonderingly she noticed again the taste of him—the exotic, fiery flavor of his skin. Each kiss, each wanton uncontrolled touch, added fuel to the flame raging inside her.

"Love me, Peter," she begged beneath a ceiling of blue Egyptian sky, her bed snow-colored sandstone. "Love me, love me, love me!"

"I do love you," he swore in eternal allegiance, bringing his hard and muscled body more fully over her soft and yielding flesh, her thighs opening to him. The weight of him was a gentle yet urgent pressure. Jenny wrapped one trembling arm around his strong neck, the fingers of that hand clenched in an-

ticipation, while the fingers of her other hand were
spread open beside her as though she could commu-
nicate her ecstasy to the rock beneath them—to
nature itself. At the very moment that Peter was
about to complete their joy, her trembling stopped
as though she waited, as though her body were ut-
tering a still, silent yes. And he, sensing the specialness of the pause, held there, allowing them both to
savor the anticipation of renewal. When he did
move to make them one, it was no more sudden or
violent than it had been the first glorious time, even
though his vivid memories of pleasure once had,
and now to be regained, made him more anxious
than ever. He was gentle, and his manly tenderness
was a new excitement to the woman who received
his passionate gifts. He recognized his inner commands to hurry as being holdovers from prehistoric
times when such unions often had little to do with
the kind of love he felt for Jenny and she felt for
him. He was able to conquer his impatience because
he wasn't just an animal drawn to this woman solely by physical need. He was giving a special token of
love he had given to no other woman before her.
The mechanics were no different from what millions of uncaring men and women did each day.
The result, though, was destined to be unique, because love always unlocked degrees of pleasure
never experienced when the physical act was performed without the accompanying tenderness of
genuine affection.

   "Peter," she whispered, her fingers clinging in

his hair as he uttered a low moan against the throbbing pulse spot on her neck. "I love you," she said. He lifted his head, and she luxuriated in the sight of black hair tumbled over his forehead, of eyes golden and dilated even in the brightness of the Egyptian sun, of lips slightly parted, of his powerful neck tensed with striated muscle.

"Jenny," he uttered in a hushed voice that said in one word the thousand and one things she had always wanted to hear from him. Her lips once again sampled the pleasure offered by his own. His whole body kissed hers, his hands sliding along her back, lifting her from the hardness of the stone. His cupping fingers offered her hips a supporting cushion as he held her close to his powerful body.

She gasped in wonder as his movements led her off into those worlds only he could show her. He guided her one step at a time, never running lest they miss those subtler satisfactions hidden along the way. He took her to the top of small hills, let her descend into gentle valleys before coaxing her ever onward to hills higher than the ones before, to valleys never quite as deep as the last, until ahead loomed just the final ascent—a mountain whose lofty summit would be gained only by his having so expertly prepared her for the challenge of its climb.

If he paused on occasion along the way, battling inner demands that were out to push him forward at a pace that would have left her far behind him, those moments of pause were precious ones for Jenny. She took enjoyment from the taut silence punctuated solely by their breathing. She took pleasure from their being one—his body her body, her body his. She delighted in having found his demanding hardness so perfectly matched to her own yielding softness. It was as though they had been one in some far distant time, had been separated, were now whole again.

"Jenny, Jenny!" he whispered, beginning up that final mountain. His fingers kneaded her pliant flesh, his kisses lingering on sweet lips on which mingled her groans of passion and his own.

She ran her hands down his back, feeling his muscles working beneath damp flesh as her fingers glided along solid curves that would dimple and then go hard again. She opened more fully to him— a rose whose petals had spread for sweet summer sunshine. She was engulfed in flames on a dizzying mountainside, wanting only to go higher and feel hotter fires burning. Peter obliged her wishes by making her tremble with shudder after shudder of pure pleasure. No man could have done so much for a woman as Peter had done, as Peter wanted to do, for Jenny.

"My love!" he moaned, his mouth against her ear, his voice triggering more sparks. "My sweet love!" he said, lifting so he could look at her, his face made more handsome than she had ever seen it, made that way by the near peaking of passions inside him. His hair was tousled, his face flushed even through his heavy tan, his lips sensuously pouted, his eyes hot burning suns.

"Peter!" she cried out, knowing he had brought her to the top of the mountain with him and not left her behind. There was nowhere for either of them to go but into the final glory of the awaiting abyss. So he kissed her, and she kissed him, and the two soared together into the void, held aloft by waves of pleasure that buffeted and buoyed them far longer than either could have possibly thought imaginable, although not nearly as long as the airstreams far above would allow the soaring of the falcon that was the only witness to their passion.

CHAPTER FOURTEEN

PANIC. That was what Jenny was feeling. Pure unadulterated, one hundred percent panic. It did no
good whatsoever pretending it wasn't. Peter saw it
and knew what she was thinking.

"It won't be the same, Jenny," he assured her.
She'd heard enough of his side of the phone conversation to know he might have to go to England, just
as Frederic Donas had gone back for a "family
crisis." "Jenny!" he said loudly. When that didn't
work, he came to her and took her in his arms.
Which only made it worse, bringing home as it did
all she would be missing once he was gone from her
life forever. "Tell me that you know it won't be the
same," he pleaded, smoothing her hair with his
strong fingers, holding her close.

"It won't be the same," she said, wondering if he
really believed that any more than she did. No matter what he said, history was repeating itself. There
was no escaping it. She was going to lose him, and
there was nothing she could do about it. She had
been a fool to think their lives were their own to
live.

"Besides, it's not as if it's definite that I have to

go, is it?'' Peter said encouragingly. ''Uncle George has gone to the hospital many times with his pains, and he's always come back.''

Peter would go. She knew he would. Just as Frederic Donas had gone before him. If he was giving her a brief respite, it was only a tease before the inevitable.

''Look at me, Jenny,'' he said, holding her at arm's length. He used his cupped right hand to elevate her chin when she refused to do it on her own. ''Would it help if I swore to you that I'm not leaving you for good, even if I do have to go back to England before you go? I'm certainly not running off to some rich woman waving her moneybags from the wings. If I go—*if*, Jenny—it will only be to sit at a dying man's bedside. Although my uncle and I have never been very close, I do owe him that much.''

''Yes, of course, you do,'' she agreed, still wishing it wasn't going to happen. When she had made love with him on that sandstone ridge, she had thought she might actually cast Geraldine and Frederic out of her mind completely. What a foolish thought for her to have had! She couldn't wish away interlocked destinies merely because she wanted to do so.

''What do you say to our taking the day off and going someplace?'' Peter suggested. ''How about to Aswân to see Abdul? Since the fragment of macehead has disappeared, he's managed to make himself rather scarce, hasn't he? It might be fun to drop in and see how his oil wells are doing, don't you think? He'd probably like to check my story about the falcon with the one the trainer brought back to him.''

"What if the hospital calls?" Jenny asked, wishing she could keep quiet. He was offering them a few final moments together, and she was warning that time spent with her might take him out of reach when the bad news came.

"They won't be calling until they've taken all sorts of tests," Peter said. "It will do neither me nor Uncle George any good for me to spend the day hanging around the telephone, waiting for bad news that may never come. I'll tell them here where we're going, and if a call does come through, they'll know where to reach me. What do you say?''

"They need the Land Rover," Jenny said, afraid to stay because a call might come, afraid to go because his uncle might start fading fast and Peter might not get to him because she had been selfish enough to want a little more time.

"They can make do with the one," Peter insisted. "You know they can. You made out well enough yesterday morning with one, didn't you?''

"I supose Betty wouldn't mind sticking around the house," Jenny replied, giving in because she did want the day with him. "She can catch up on her sketching and do whatever she's been wanting to do with the photo file. We could stop in Kom Ombo and check back by phone, then check back again from Aswân.''

"It's settled, then," Peter said with authoritative finality. "The bosses are going to take another day off. One of the advantages of being boss is being able to set your own hours, right?"

"Right," she admitted, telling herself that the bottom had not dropped out of her world. It wasn't as if this were some suspicious excuse that Peter had dumped on her out of the blue. He had told her previously that his uncle was ill. She even remembered reading about it somewhere before coming to Egypt. She wrapped her arms securely around Peter's neck and held him tightly, afraid the phone was going to ring before they could leave. "I love you so very much!" she told him.

"No more than I love you, I assure you," he whispered, delivering an affectionate kiss to the tip of her nose. "Now let's go tell everyone the latest change in today's plans, shall we?"

It was still early when Jenny and Peter set out for Aswân in the Land Rover with the faulty transmission. Jenny wasn't unaware that the car could break down anywhere, leaving them stranded while doctors in England tried desperately to reach Peter to verify that his uncle was on death's doorstep. That fear, no matter how strong, was overridden by another that told her she should be gathering up whatever memories she could stockpile. They were liable to have to last her for a very long time.

They slowly maneuvered the dusty creviced road between Hierakonpolis and Idfu, feeling the vehicle shudder around them as if it were giving up the ghost. Their final emergence onto the smoother road at Idfu had them breaking into simultaneous cheers, followed by laughter. "What if Abdul isn't at the villa?" Jenny asked, finally able to talk without the washboard road making her sound as if she were gargling water. "What if he's off at some drilling site—maybe even the one at Hierakonpolis?"

"We usually hear his chopper go over, right?" Peter reminded her. "Besides, if he's not home, we can wait for him. I'm ready for a soothing drink and a bit of relaxation in comfortable surroundings." They crossed the Nile at Idfu and turned south on the highway that ran along the east side of the river from Cairo to Aswân. If the roadway seemed in good condition, that was only because they were comparing it to what they had gone through to reach it. "And if he's gone for several days, I will at least have had the opportunity of getting away from the dig for a little while with you," he added. "Being in the same house with you but sleeping in different beds has led me to question severely the wisdom of maintaining our professional reputations!"

"That's sweet," Jenny said, scooting closer to give him a quick peck on the cheek. "But seeing as how we're the senior members of this party, supposedly the ones being looked up to as examples to be followed, I can hardly see us pulling off any other arrangement. If we did, Tim would want to move in with Barbara, and she wouldn't resist that temptation for long, no matter what she might say now, believe me. And if I'm not mistaken, Gary and Pam seem to be hitting it off quite nicely, too. There would be a lot of mothers and fathers a little upset at a harmless archaeological dig in Hierakonpolis suddenly having metamorphosed into a free-love commune."

"Point well taken," Peter said in good humor. "However, I'll be glad when this dig is over so you and I can tie the knot and start sleeping in the same bedroom without causing some kind of minor scandal."

"That would be nice, wouldn't it?" Jenny had to agree, wondering what the chances were of it ever happening if he went back to England without her.

The low hills to their left blocked most of the early-morning light, keeping the road and car in chilly shadow. They passed several fires, bundles of humanity gathered around them, by the roadside. There was an early bus due, and those waiting had sought protection from a cold morning as best they could.

About forty-five minutes later they slowed for the first of the roadblocks between Idfu and Aswân. Oil barrels had been set up to funnel all traffic into one lane, and soldiers inspected license plates and occupants as the cars drove by. There was seldom a request for anyone to come to a complete stop. A wave onward was what Jenny and Peter received from a military man who looked a little weary after his night watch. His fellow soldiers, all with automatic weapons, looked no less tired than he did.

The sun, finally out from hiding, was a large orange disk seen through a dense haze of blown dust and sand that masked its full burning potential. Stars could still be seen at the far western curve of the sky, resting there amid the last blackness to dissolve.

"Shall we come right out and ask Abdul if he had anything to do with the missing macehead fragment?" Jenny asked. She spotted several hawks circling in the distance and wondered if one was Phoenix.

"Well, I myself don't see that he'll ever admit to anything, even if he's confronted," Peter commented. "Why should he? There's nothing but conjecture linking him to the theft. He's not going to be too anxious to put himself in the role of villain in front of the woman he loves."

If Abdul had nothing to do with the missing fragment, Jenny would have hated endangering their friendship by insinuating that he had. There was certainly no denying Abdul was a good friend and had been one from the beginning. Even his giving the falcon to Peter had turned out to be a blessing in disguise. She should have gone to Abdul to thank him, not to accuse him of having had something to do with the theft of an artifact he had never seemed to find of any real interest.

"We don't have to say anything about the missing fragment," Peter proposed, attuned to Jenny's thoughts. "We can say we stopped by to see him for the day and leave it at that. Maybe the piece will show up somewhere around the house." Both of them doubted that, since the whole group had been over the residence with a fine-toothed comb.

"Let's play it by ear," Jenny suggested. She wished the fragment would turn up, though. It might never lead to headlines, but it would be worth a few paragraphs in one of the archaeology journals. While she had enough witnesses to swear that the piece was more than a figment of her imagination, there was no proof such as having the real thing in hand. All the sworn testimony in the world, all the verifying sketches, didn't alter that.

They stopped at Kom Ombo, with its impressive temple on an acropolislike jutting of rocky cliff overlooking the right bank of the Nile. The temple was unique in that it had been dedicated not to one god but two: Sebek, the crocodile god, and Horus, the hawk-headed master of the sun. A colonnaded court, hypostyle hall and antechamber led to two doors, beyond which were two precincts and two *naos*, or inner sanctums. One of the outer buildings housed a pile of mummified crocodiles stacked like cordwood. The relative newness of the buildings, dating only from Ptolemaic and Roman times, made them less interesting to Jenny and Peter than ruins of an earlier date. However, the stop allowed a stretch of legs, a few stolen kisses and a phone call back to the house at Hierakonpolis. Peter placed the call from a small restaurant, while Jenny waited in the Land Rover. She prayed there would be no news, no news being good news, but she had the undeniable feeling that she could pray on bended knees until those knees were black and blue, and it wouldn't make any difference. Peter was going to leave her in Egypt as Frederic had left Geraldine. She knew that with a chilling certainty, and she was not reassured when he reappeared smiling. "All's quiet on the northern front," he said, getting into the Land Rover. Jenny, though, knew in the depth of her worry-ridden heart that this was merely another brief respite. She read the writing on the wall as surely as Daniel had read it for Belshazzar.

Half an hour and two roadblocks later they were in Aswân, the river on their right, the town climbing up the pink hills on their left. They drove the korneish to the Cataract Hotel, which, for half a century, had been a favorite spa of wintering European nobility. It sat on a hill that gave a fantastic view of the Nile, its porch open to the breeze and offering an Old World elegance that sharply contrasted with the high-rise modernness of the New Cataract Hotel that adjoined it.

Feluccas, shallow-bottomed boats little changed since the time of Christ, with large triangular sails already unfurled for a day of skimming the water, lined the shore. Downstream the launch from the Oberoi Hotel was making its journey from Elephantine Island to the mainland. The motorized craft for the island's hotel patrons was designed to resemble one of Cleopatra's famous Nile barges.

Peter bargained with several of the feluccca owners, feeling lucky he spoke Arabic and had a rough idea of reasonable fees. Even with spending three times what would have been necessary just two years earlier, he was still getting off easy. Some unwary tourists paid more to use these simple conveyances than they would pay to ride in the gondolas of Venice. "I told him to sail around the islands before docking," Peter said, pointing out their boat and helping her aboard. Within seconds they were off, sliding across water that always flowed north into a wind that always blew south. If Jenny couldn't help thinking about the telephone call that might be waiting at Abdul's villa, she still enjoyed these extra minutes with Peter. It was pleasant on the water, and she was lost in that special serenity of being under sail. It was enjoyable turning to the wind and having her hair whipped around her face, Peter snuggled close to fight off any chill. Their course paralleled Elephantine, the biggest of the islands, taking them by the Isle of Amûm, with its strands of sturdy date palms, and then Kitchener Island, named after the British lord who had achieved his glory farther south at Khartoum. Kitchener Island was now a botanical garden where agronomists tested plants for possible extensive cultivation on the banks of Lake Nasser. On it, visible from the boat but forever fruitless for want of a substantial rainfall, were some of the few coconut palms to be seen in all Egypt.

Neither the massive 3600-meter High Dam, nor

the smaller old dam could be seen as the felucca made its final glide toward the sheikh's villa. Jenny shivered with new thoughts of gloomy news awaiting her in that gleaming rectangle of whiteness. Peter, thinking she was chilled from the early-morning breeze, pulled her more tightly to him as the boat tipped precariously in a move designed to bring it more smoothly to the waiting dock. Water splashed over the side, and Peter laughed at Jenny's frantic efforts to scoot forward to avoid getting wet. He had a wondrous laugh and looked so exceptionally handsome that Jenny's heart constricted painfully at the idea of living a life without that smile and that tender countenance. She held him closer, her arm hugging his firm body to hers, telling herself to enjoy and not to worry about a destiny neither of them could control.

The welcoming committee on the private dock was even more extensively armed than Jenny remembered. Abdul, who'd been watching their approach from the veranda, having been informed that a felucca was maneuvering for docking, was quick to join them. "What a pleasant surprise!" he said, reaching for Jenny's hand and helping her from the boat. "I was just thinking about the two of you this morning." He shook Peter's hand and immediately directed them up the stairs that led to the villa above.

"We decided to take the day off and stopped by on the chance you'd be home," Jenny said, wondering if she wouldn't have preferred Abdul's not being there. There were plenty of hotel rooms in Aswân, surely one of which might have been available for.... She consciously thrust such thoughts from her mind. Going to bed with Peter one more time wasn't going to solve anything, wasn't going to hold him to her any longer; it would probably have only made things worse by driving home how empty her life was going to be without him. She should have been trying to figure how to live without him, instead of fantasizing on how to hold him longer than the fates would allow.

"I'm so pleased you came," Abdul said as they topped the stairs. He waved them toward chairs in sunshine not as uncomfortable as it would soon be. "I've wanted to get back to see you, but things have become more hectic than usual around here as of late."

"We see your helicopter fly over Hierakonpolis every so often, and we wave," Peter said, grateful Abdul didn't drop from the sky more often. While the sheikh always seemed to keep Jenny's best interests at heart, certainly never having been anything but fair in his dealings with Peter, there was no denying he cared more for Jenny than any mere friend would. If Jenny could have been so ridiculously jealous over a bird, Peter felt a definite right to entertain a certain uneasy feeling about a man who wasn't the run-of-the-mill kind of competition he might have expected in a romantic rival.

"I've ordered hot *carcadet*," Abdul said. "But there's always tea or coffee, if you prefer. Even fruit juice, for that matter.'' They told him the *carcadet* was fine, and he asked them if they had come across any more monumental finds like their last one. He voiced the question with such seeming innocence that Jenny didn't take the perfect opportunity to mention that her "monumental" find was missing. Peter followed her lead and let the subject be, both aided by the sudden arrival of the warm red drink that resembled grenadine but had a flavor all its own. The servant poured.

"I suppose you've heard I freed the falcon," Peter said, deciding it was best to get that out of the way. Abdul, of course, had heard, the trainer having told him. "I hope you don't find that terribly ungrateful," Peter added.

"Of course not," Abdul replied, his smile full of understanding. "I knew you would free it all along. It was Jenny who insisted upon playing doubting Thomas." His smile widened, telling her he certainly understood what had led to her misconceptions, but he was genuinely pleased she could see he had been right from the beginning. "Actually, the bird seemed little disposed to captivity. That is always a problem with haggards. All of which reminds me," he said, putting his cup and saucer on the glass-topped table between them, "that I have something to give you before I forget."

"Please tell me you haven't hidden that necklace in the *carcadet*!" Jenny said with a roll of her eyes that sent both men into laughter.

"You'll have to wait until they read my will to get

the necklace now," Abdul answered, his laughter making his dark eyes more velvety in the increasing morning sunlight. Peter's were made more golden. "This is something I shan't have to convince you to take, believe me." He left them, Jenny looking curiously at Peter, who delivered a let's-wait-and-see shrug. Abdul returned shortly and handed Jenny the fragment of Scorpion macehead. "I'm afraid my borrowing this did absolutely no good for you whatsoever with my contacts in Cairo," Abdul said. If he was aware of their surprise, he pretended not to be. "Those bureaucrats seem to think there's little value in anything that doesn't sparkle like gold and dent when you bite it. That doesn't mean you still might not rustle up some support for your project. As a matter of fact, I rather think you'd be more apt to have people listen to you than they listened to me, since you're the professionals. I merely stumbled around when asked questions such as: 'Sheikh Jerada do this fragment's Middle Eastern stylistic motifs offer, further proof regarding predynastic invasions of the Nile Valley?' Do either of you have the foggiest notion what that means?"

"A question possibly more relevant to the Narmer palette than the Scorpion macehead," Jenny replied, hoping to get her thoughts in order while reciting facts and figures that came automatically. Having Abdul so nonchalantly produce the missing fragment was the last thing she had expected. "The Narmer palette was found by the same expedition that located the Scorpion macehead now at Oxford,'' she went on. ''The macehead and palette were found at basically the same time, were possibly even part of the same cache. The preponderance of fantasy animals of the type used in the art styles of Sumeria and Elam and carved upon the palette and on several items found there at the same time, has some authorities theorizing that Egypt's early spurt in development may have been spurred by invaders from the more urban societies of the Iranian plateau and Mesopotamia.''

''Well, you see there!'' Abdul replied, as if Jenny had somehow solved a riddle that had been puzzling him for the longest time. ''I hadn't a clue. Therefore I suggest you run this fragment up to the National Archaeological Treasures Bureau in Cairo and ask to speak with a Dr. Ramin Abuseer. If you can convince him of the artifact's genuine importance, he'll put all the necessary machinery in motion to have the site you desire isolated for further excavation.''

''Actually, we're rather pleased to see that,'' Peter said. If he'd been going to hold off, he saw little point in doing so now, since Abdul had brought up the subject. ''We, believe it or not, thought it had been stolen.''

''Stolen?'' Abdul responded, as if on cue, possibly engaging in a bit of overacting. ''How did you come to think it had been stolen? Didn't my man Karoon explain?''

''None of us saw your man Karoon,'' Peter said, willing to hear Abdul's story, even if he suddenly had his own ideas regarding the fragment's abrupt reappearance.

"You mean, he just walked in and took it without your permission?" Abdul asked, looking duly shocked.

"Apparently so," Jenny admitted. She still wasn't sure what she should think about all this.

"Well, that is really most unforgivable!" Abdul said. "I had assumed...well, it's obvious what I had assumed, isn't it? I'd call him in right now to explain if I hadn't sent him to Cairo on business. You may rest assured, however, that I will take him to task for what was obviously a breakdown in communication."

"Undoubtedly a breakdown in communication," Peter said, wondering whether to voice his alternate explanation.

"But the important thing is that you have your fragment back, isn't it?" Abdul said, preparing to pour them each more *carcadet*.

"What I really think the sheikh is trying to tell us, Jenny," Peter began, figuring nothing ventured, nothing gained, "is that the drilling operation at Hierakonpolis has struck oil and we could take the fragment to any authority, offer conclusive arguments for the importance of it and similar fragments and still not get access to the area."

Abdul handled himself like a pro, not faltering as he filled each cup. He picked up his own cup and saucer and balanced them on his knee. He took a swallow of the liquid, looked at each of his guests in turn and smiled. "Security prevents my confirming or denying any recent drilling successes," he said. He appeared on the verge of saying more—Peter certainly had more to say—but they were interrupted. Jenny recognized the hate-filled stare immediately. Its coldness had pulled her attention to the newcomer before either Peter or Abdul had realized his presence. "Ah, it seems this is a morning for unexpected visitors!" Abdul proclaimed, Jenny's shift of attention having drawn his gaze to Rashid al-Hidda. Rashid was still the same malevolent gnome Jenny remembered from her run-in with him in the villa at three o'clock in the morning. "If you'll excuse me for a few moments," Abdul said apologetically, coming to his feet, "my astrologer calls with undoubtedly more bad news of the catastrophes I can expect on my horizon." He shrugged as if his momentary departure was designed merely to humor the withered old man. He disappeared into the villa, Rashid al-Hidda drawn in his wake.

"If looks could kill!" Peter said mainly to himself, it having been obvious that Rashid hadn't been too fond of someone on the veranda.

"Isn't that the truth!" Jenny admitted, feeling another chill reminiscent of those she'd experienced after her first meeting with the old man. "He can't stand Western women," she said, trying on a sunny smile for size and finding it just didn't quite fit. "He sees them in general—Abdul's first wife and myself in particular—as being bad influences on Arab men in general—Abdul in particular."

"Well, I'm glad those nasty stares weren't meant for me," Peter replied with a laugh. "And I wouldn't allow myself to be caught in a dark alley with Mr. Rashid al-Hidda if I were you," he added in a conspiratorial whisper that couldn't help but make Jenny smile.

She took another swallow of her *carcadet*, deciding she'd had enough of Rashid al-Hidda. Actually, she'd had more than enough of him the first time it had been her misfortune to meet him. "Do you really think they've struck oil at Hierakonpolis?" she asked, directing the conversation back to a subject she found of more interest.

"Of course they have," Peter answered, more convinced than ever. "Which means that if we ever had a chance of getting excavation rights to the area around that well, we certainly don't have the chance of a snowball in hell of doing it now. Even if we had a piece of solid gold to wave around, it's highly unlikely anyone would want us prowling around a producing oil well. Abdul has acted in a logical— but very opportunistic—manner. It made sense for him to withdraw from the scene just at the time we might have most expected him to respect our privacy. But obviously politeness was not the only motive for his actions."

"That wouldn't be your jealous nature talking again, would it?" Jenny asked, her smile dissolving the sarcasm that seemed to tinge Peter's words. "Please say that it is," she added, teasing him.

"Yes, I guess I still am jealous," he admitted.

"But that doesn't mean I'm not reading Abdul loud and clear at the moment. Hell, had his man actually walked in and taken that fragment without a by-your-leave, Abdul would have come down on top of him like a falcon swooping for prey. And it wouldn't make a feather's difference if the man were in Cairo at the moment or not."

Jenny sat back, balancing her cup and saucer. "You know, it's funny, but none of this really comes out making me like him any less," she said. "*Like*, as in friend," she clarified further, certainly not wanting to be misunderstood on that point. "Even though it probably should." She was remembering how desperately Abdul wanted Egypt to step out of the past and join him in the twentieth century.

"My problem is, it doesn't make me like him any less, either," Peter confessed. "And I think I would really enjoy being able to muster a bit more dislike for the handsome bastard."

Jenny laughed. She couldn't help it. "Those were almost his exact words concerning you," she said. It was a very good indication of her radical shift in priorities that she now put her friendship for Abdul over her disappointment in having been deprived of the excavation site. It was true that she would have reached a high point in her career if it had turned out that the evidence there proved that the Scorpion King had been in the area. As it was, her career was suddenly running third to her friendship for one man and her love for another. She was not the same

Jenny Mowry who had turned to find the handsome Peter Donas standing next to her in that dimly lighted alcove of the Egyptian Museum.

Abdul wasn't gone long, and when he returned he looked strained, even though he tried to cover with a smile. "Now where were we?" he asked, pouring himself fresh *carcadet* from the new pot the servant had brought in his absence. There was a deliberate preciseness to his movements that told of efforts being made to portray more calmness than was really there.

"What is it, Rashid al-Hidda and his warnings of fire again?" Jenny asked, glad the astrologer had not returned.

"Yes, Rashid and his warnings of fire," Abdul admitted with a small smile. "Always the fire as of late." He realized Peter was probably in the dark about the whole subject, Jenny knowing only because she had been present at another of Rashid's surprise visits. "My astrologer keeps predicting danger by fire," Abdul explained. "All very vague, mind you, much like ancient oracles that could be interpreted in a million different ways. I ask him, 'What kind of fire are we talking about here? Gunfire, Rashid? The fire of burning sun in the desert? The fire of fever in sickness? The kind that could burn this villa down around me?' He just says, 'I would tell you more if I could. The stars are not clear.' Imagine, the stars holding out information, as if they were all members of some universal cabal! A ludicrous notion, wouldn't you agree? Stars are not minds plotting evil or good. They are merely balls of gaseous matter, with no influence whatsoever on the way we run our daily lives."

"Exactly!" Jenny agreed too quickly. Egypt was a country steeped in superstitions held over from the past. The same incantations, charms and potions were available in modern bazaars as had been sold in the times of the pharaohs—incantations to cure the sick, charms to bring good luck, potions to calm fevers, men to look skyward for the answers to all questions.

"When I was eight years old," Abdul said reflectively, "Rashid al-Hidda told me to beware of cobras. Cobras, would you believe? The only cobras seen in Egypt in this day and age are the fangless serpents used by fakirs and dancers in the marketplace. Once, however, they were so prevalent that they were made the symbol of Lower Egypt and put with the vulture of Upper Egypt on the pharaoh's crown. But they had long been driven out by the constant tramp of tourists' feet, even when I was a child. Two nights after Rashid's warning the servant he sent to my bedchamber to check my sleep killed a cobra but inches from where I slept." His eyes met Jenny's.

"Couldn't the man who killed it have been the same who put it there?" she asked.

"Not only could he have done so, but I'm quite sure that's what he did do," Abdul answered with an uneasy laugh that was supposed to take the sudden chill off the conversation but that didn't succeed. "I, of course, didn't disbelieve at the time. After all, I was only eight. Later, though, when I became intelligent enough to reason out such things as motivation, I saw how Rashid had probably done it for the reward my father predictably gave him for 'saving' the sheikhdom's sole heir." Which didn't explain what the supposed charlatan was still doing delivering up further prophecies to a man who professed disbelief. Aware of the incongruity but not wanting to deal with those traces of ancient superstition still present within his supposedly rational twentieth-century mind, Abdul changed the subject, asking when he could expect his invitation to their wedding. A servant interrupted their answer. "Not now, Sadid!" Abdul commanded with a frown, attempting to wave the man off. "Whatever or whoever, it can surely wait until I've spent a few minutes visiting with friends."

"It's a call for Mr. Donas," Sadid explained apologetically. Jenny felt the veranda move around her. If she hadn't been sitting, she would have lost her balance and fallen. Her hands gripped the arm of the chair tightly, her knuckles turning white. She hadn't even heard the telephone ring.

"Well, then, if it's for Mr. Donas, I can hardly put it off," Abdul said with a nod in Peter's direction. "Sadid will show you to the telephone, my friend."

Peter was looking at Jenny. He covered her hand with his own, finding her fingers stiff and cold. He tried to pry them loose from the arm of the chair, but they wouldn't budge. "Don't be an astrologer who sees the end of the world when it's not there!" he warned her, getting up to follow Sadid into the villa and leaving Abdul infinitely curious as to why both his guests had reacted so strangely to a phone call.

"Jenny?" Abdul asked, wondering if he had any hope of being enlightened.

"It's happening again," Jenny said, turning toward him, her skin raised in tiny goose bumps.

"What is?" Abdul asked, no better informed now than he had been. So she told him, furious when all he did was laugh at her fears. "I'm sorry to seem so callous about what you obviously look upon as catastrophic," Abdul apologized immediately, although a smile lingered on his lips. "It just seems so ironic that the beautiful, educated, intelligent woman who but moments earlier was questioning the validity of an Egyptian astrologer should still be suggesting that spirits from the past are somehow controlling her life. What chance have I to extricate myself from superstition when you, from a culture further removed from them than my own, persist in claiming their power?"

"He's leaving me, Abdul!" Jenny insisted, not having to be told she had been a hypocrite to belittle Rashid al-Hidda's warnings when she could accept a curse spanning sixty years.

"Go with him to England," Abdul suggested simply.

"He hasn't asked me to go to England with

him!'' Jenny replied loudly, feeling words torn from her heart that she had tried to keep concealed from Abdul—and from herself. "He hasn't asked me,'' she repeated in a barely audible whisper.

"And why should he? What man in his right mind would invite his fiancée to a funeral prior to their wedding?'' Abdul asked, wondering as usual why he didn't simply move into this latest breach and take advantage of Jenny's paranoia to his own advantage. He should have loved her less, been more inclined to think of his own happiness instead of hers.

"I couldn't go with him, even if he did ask me,'' Jenny confessed, albeit reluctantly. "The dig has already lost one man in charge and is now scheduled to lose its second. Granted I'm only a woman on a dig in an Arab country, but I am the remaining senior member. No matter what college kid Peter decides should have the titular head as director, that young man is not going to keep the dig running without the help of someone with a bit more expertise than his own.''

"Then what's all of the fuss about, Jenny?'' Abdul asked. "Peter probably knows as well as you do that your professional ethics won't allow you to desert a project that would collapse without you.''

"It's not that he knows I couldn't leave that's important,'' Jenny said. "It's that he hasn't even bothered offering me the choice.'' Abdul shook his head, not understanding, but it was all very clear to Jenny. She desperately wanted some sign that Peter would have taken her with him if that had been possible.

"Listen to me, Jenny," Abdul said, leaning nearer across the table. "A time must come in any relationship when trust is either there or it isn't—it's as simple as that. If trust isn't there, your friends can talk until they're blue in the face giving you all the reassurance you think you need and it won't make one bit of difference in the long run. I think that time has now come for you. Therefore, I'm not going to waste my energy or yours once again listing Peter's merits, telling you how you've continually underestimated his love from the beginning. Not that I no longer think Peter worth the effort, but I'm no longer sure that you yourself are capable of making it work between you."

"I love him!" she said defiantly, shocked that he was taking her fear and grief and twisting it into something less than the result of her love.

"Then maybe love isn't enough," he answered with a conviction that only added to her shock. "Maybe it's just a part of what's necessary, like friendship, understanding, passion. If love isn't enough here, Jenny, then realize it's not enough and let him go! Because whether this works between you and Peter has less to do with what happened between his grandfather and your grandmother at Thebes sixty years ago than it has to do with Jenny Mowry and Peter Donas in the here and now. You make a wrong decision and you're liable to ruin your life and Peter's life—not to mention mine."

"My uncle is asking for me, Jenny," Peter said, coming out onto the veranda and voicing the worst of her fears.

"Then of course you must go," she said, marveling at how, when faced with a fait accompli, one simply adjusted.

"You can have the use of my helicopter to fly you as far as Cairo," Abdul said, knowing the tragic look Jenny gave him was condemnation for his having cut away more precious moments she could have had with Peter on the drive to the Aswân airport. Yet she would thank him one day—if and when she saw the light. Not that Abdul really condemned her morbid fascination for something that had happened in the past. He knew that it had been just such curiosity and interest on her part that had probably made her so good an archaeologist. Besides, he, too, believed there were such things as destiny and fate, maybe written in the stars, maybe written elsewhere. "I'll leave you two for the moment," he said diplomatically, "and tell the pilot to get the chopper ready."

Jenny got to her feet, turning to face Peter, telling herself this wasn't really goodbye forever. He would go to England and later come back for her. "Oh, Peter!" she said softly, tears welling up in her eyes.

He came to her, took her in his arms and held her close, kissing away her tears, telling her everything was going to be all right. It would be hell for him, too, being separated from her for even a few days, but a few days weren't forever. "Look," he said suddenly, "why don't you just come with me?" She cried harder, hearing the request she had so wanted to hear. He held her more tightly. "Of course, why not?" he insisted. "We'll call them at the dig and tell them we've had a major catastrophe in the family. My family is yours now, too, isn't it? Anyway, it soon will be."

"Thank you for asking," she said, willing herself back to some semblance of control. She sniffed and reached into her pocket for a tissue with which to wipe up her remaining tears. "But you and I both know we can't leave the team completely rudderless. Someone has to be there to see that things get done. Good money was paid to send us here by backers who deserve scientific professionalism for their investment." He didn't say anything. Both knew her decision was right, and the only one she could have made. He wouldn't have respected her for making any other. "Whom do you plan to leave in charge?" she asked. "Tim seems to get along well with everybody."

"I'm leaving you in charge," he said, as if that must have been obvious. "You should've been director when Professor Kenny left anyway."

"The Arab workmen won't like it," Jenny reminded him, appreciating what he was doing but prepared to admit certain facts she had once refused to recognize out of professional egotism.

"I'm leaving the dig in your hands because you're the person most qualified to handle it,"

Peter said. "If problems arise, you'll know how to handle them in a manner most beneficial to the dig. as a whole. Why anticipate problems that can only be pure conjecture until they've been found to be fact?" He wasn't referring just to the problems she might have with the workers. He was talking about her worries over his departure. The helicopter suddenly came to life on its pad off to one side of the villa. "I do love you, Jenny Mowry," he said, kissing her. "And I will be back. Believe that!"

"I'll be waiting," she told him, holding to him tightly, kissing him one more time before Abdul came to tell them everything was ready.

Jenny stayed on the veranda, not wanting to prolong the painful goodbyes any longer. When the helicopter lifted, finally making itself visible from the veranda, Jenny didn't look at it but kept her eyes focused instead on the Nile, on Aswân, on the pink hills ascending beyond. To have looked toward the disappearing aircraft would have meant looking north toward Thebes, and Jenny didn't want to think of Thebes or of what had once happened to Geraldine Fowler and Frederic Donas when they had met and loved there sixty years earlier.

CHAPTER FIFTEEN

IT SOUNDED OMINOUS, like thunder.

Jenny put down the small brush and the surgical scalpel she was using to uncover the skeleton she had discovered by accident the previous day. A few ragged bones had been exposed by wind erosion, and Jenny had decided to excavate them on her own, not wanting to pull anyone from either Group One or Two to help her since work on their sites was proceeding so nicely. She hadn't completely isolated herself from her comrades, having often glanced down the wadi to see them working. She wasn't looking at them now, though. She and they were gazing westward in an effort to put some meaning to the continuing sounds. A frisson of fear shot through her, but she shrugged it off. No doubt there was a logical explanation for the noise.

She wiped the back of her hand across her forehead, bringing away a combination of perspiration and dirt. She had been working hard lately, throwing herself into her job as director with a determination designed to counter the heartache and despair experienced upon and since Peter's leaving. She saw her work as a panacea, receiving more comfort from the exhaustion following a hard day's work than from the two telephone calls Peter had made—one to tell her his uncle was tenaciously holding on, the other to inform her that his uncle had died. She had momentarily taken heart at the second message but had immediately felt ashamed to think she had almost rejoiced at hearing of someone's death. Still, she had thought it meant that Peter would be free to return to her. She'd thought wrong. His uncle's death had actually resulted in his extending his stay in England. "He's left his estate in a frightful mess, darling," Peter had tried to explain over a phone crackling with infuriating static. "I'm afraid I've got to remain here long enough to straighten things out." How long he didn't know. "The sooner, the better," was all he could assure her.

In the face of her continuing fears that he was gone from her forever, and despite his reassurances to the contrary, Jenny had devoted herself more and more to her work. She had been forced to make certain compromises as a result of the native labor force having predictably walked off the dig the day after her being named the new director, but she had adjusted. Abdul, when asked, had been more than willing to act as the needed male authority figure, and he had personally berated the workers, convincing them to go back to their jobs. Since Abdul wasn't an archaeologist and had little real conception of or interest in what was needed on the dig, Jenny was left with the same carte blanche she would have had if she hadn't needed him as a figurehead. It wasn't the way she might have liked it, but it had certainly been one way of circumventing work stoppage while leaving a woman in charge.

Abdul came by frequently, saying he wanted to check on the workmen, but really he just wanted to see Jenny. The continual sifting for bones and artifacts had never really managed to catch his fancy as much as the oil being pumped from the well farther up the wadi. If he never came right out and said oil had been discovered, Jenny was sure that it had been, just as Peter had been sure. The sheikh was devoting too much time to the well at Hierakonpolis for it to have turned out to be just another dry hole. That morning his helicopter had dropped out of the sky before proceeding one more time to the drilling site. "Maybe you'll invite me to supper this evening?" he had asked before takeoff. So she had extended the invitation, always welcoming the diversion he offered plus the encouragement he would continue to give between lectures on how reassurances were of little real value if she didn't have the trust to back them up. Jenny wanted to trust Peter to come back to her, but too many days were passing without her seeing his promise fulfilled.

Thunder again! In a cloudless sky. In a spot that hadn't known rainfall in more than fifteen years.

"Oh, my God!" she exclaimed, dropping her brush and scalpel as she ran to the Land Rover. Recognition that had lain dormant within her from the first had finally sparked in her conscious. Not thunder, but explosions and gunfire! She whipped the Land Rover around several sandstone outcroppings, almost rolling the vehicle twice. Each time she was tempted to ease up on the gas, she heard more of those death-dealing noises. Sudden pauses in the sounds began to make her somehow more anxious. She hadn't the slightest notion what she was going to do once she got to the well. She knew only that Abdul was in danger and there was no possible way she could have stood by and done nothing. The feelings she had for Abdul might not have been the same as the love she felt for Peter, but that didn't make them any less precious to her.

She saw the smoke—a great billowing column that recalled visions of the children of Israel being led out of Egypt. "And the Lord went before them, by day a column of smoke to lead the way, by night a pillar of fire to give them direction." The analogy was reinforced as Jenny topped the ridge and stopped to view the plume of flame accompanying all that smoke. In retrospect she would come to view the scene as more like one out of Revelations than out of Exodus. Not only was the oil itself aflame, but the thatched roofs of all the surrounding brick buildings and sheds were burning, too. The helicopter was afire—a metal phoenix being consumed with no possible chance of resurrection this time. Dead and wounded men littered the sand, human cries drowned beneath the constant whooshing roar of fire.

Jenny hadn't seen them coming from behind her,

having been too totally absorbed by what was below her. They didn't keep their presence secret for long, though. The door of the Land Rover was jerked open, and Jenny was grabbed and forcibly pulled out of the vehicle, then shoved painfully to the ground. Looking upward she could see nothing but male silhouettes against a blinding sun. She did, however, intuitively know the hot metal suddenly branding the base of her throat was a gun barrel. The undeniable realization that she was but seconds from death, perhaps wouldn't survive for Peter's return, made her desperate for survival.

"Take me to Sheikh Jerada!" she commanded in Arabic, knowing that if these men were the enemy, she could expect no quarter by declaring acquaintance with Abdul. "I'm his friend," she hurried on. "I heard the explosion." The machine gun barrel, no longer burning against her neck, was still within inches of her face. She could feel its radiating heat. "Get Galal Baseeli, then!" she offered as a hopeful alternative, blessedly remembering the man in charge of site security. "For God's sake, get Baseeli!"

"Stand up!" she was commanded as she was roughly assisted by the viselike grip of a hand on her upper arm. She wasn't encouraged by being unfamiliar with all three men now that she could see them better. They could have been anybody dressed in nondescript *galabias*: friends or foes. One had a head wound that was bleeding, turning one corner of his white headband to scarlet. "Get in!" the man still holding on to her arm insisted, jerking her toward the Land Rover and unceremoniously shoving her into the back seat. He crawled in beside her, smelling of sweat, blood and fear—not fear of Jenny but of those other forces that had suddenly exploded so unexpectedly around him on that hot summer day.

The other men climbed into the front. The ensuing descent down the ridge was performed at full speed, straight on—a nauseating ride like that of a roller coaster out of control—that brought them out on flat terrain. She took consolation in being brought to the site because it might mean that the enemy had hit and run and not decided to stay and occupy. She surveyed this hell at closer range, her fingers automatically straying to the circular burn that had been made on her neck by the hot gun barrel.

"Galal Baseeli!" she screamed in relief, pinpointing the security chief amid men at whom he was obviously shouting orders. She would have recognized his scarred face anywhere.

"Stay put!" the man beside her insisted, one of his companions exiting from the vehicle at a run and reaching Galal, who glanced quickly in their direction. The man came back with instructions to drive off to the rocks on one side. There were renewed cracks of gunfire, telling Jenny the battle wasn't over.

They yanked her out of the parked vehicle and pushed her into a shallow depression among the rocks. One man stayed to guard her, the other two fanning in opposite directions to help locate and stop an enemy still capable of splattering the area with gunfire. Jenny's attention was helplessly drawn to the helicopter, whose rotors were being spun in slow motion by an updraft caused by the very flame consuming it. She shuddered at the thought of Abdul's having been anywhere near the aircraft when it had burst into flames as her mind echoed the words of Rashid al-Hidda: "Beware of fire!" There was enough fire here to glut even Lucifer. She felt chilled despite the oppressive heat, and she wished Peter were there to hold her and make the horror less frightening.

The gunfire finally stopped, but not the flames. The thatched roofs had been completely consumed and the helicopter emerged as a black skeleton from behind the smoke, but the spurting oil would burn for days... continue its roar as occasional gusts of desert breeze shifted thick smoke to give fleeting glimpses of a fragmented derrick gone luminescent orange within the holocaust.

Well after dark, her body cramped and aching, she was pulled to her feet by an unspeaking Galal Baseeli, who led her through a landscape made macabre by shadows and light cast by dancing flame. She stumbled twice, unsteady on legs that had fallen asleep more than once during her long vigil. Galal helped her, preventing her from sprawling facedown on the ground, but he immediately let her go when she had regained her balance. His touch was entirely different from Abdul's touch, a million times different from the loving way Peter would have helped her had he been there.

They stopped by one of the smaller buildings, its roof long since burned away. Its walls were discolored by smoke, great hunks of its mud brick gouged by the same forces that had ignited the flames and pockmarked the area. "He's inside!" Galal said, motioning toward a blanket that now replaced the original door. The entrance was flanked by two armed men who seemed little inclined to allow Jenny through. "She's his...friend," Galal informed them, obviously having struggled for the suitable designation, and having somehow managed to come up with the right one, whether he realized it or not. The two men moved imperceptibly in their only recognition of her right to pass between them. Before Jenny could do so, however, Galal stopped her with a hand on her shoulder. When she turned toward him, he didn't have to say anything. The look in his eyes, far removed from the coldness she had always seen there previously, told her more than she wanted to know. She pushed back the blanket and went inside.

The plume of flame so dominant in the outside landscape managed to illuminate only the upper sections of roofless interior, not penetrating to the lower limits of the mud-brick enclosure. There were, however, three strategically placed candles that supplied enough light to show Abdul lying on a makeshift cot in one corner, a man kneeling beside him. The man stood, pulling a blanket up to Abdul's chin as he did so. He nodded to Jenny on his way out. "Abdul?" she asked, dropping by the cot, seeing that his handsome face was badly burned. For a brief moment she thought he was dead. But when she said, "It's Jenny, Abdul," her voice catching in her throat, his eyelids flickered and came open to show her the very same velvety eyes she so well remembered.

"Jenny?" he asked, sounding as if he were seeing an illusion.

"Yes, Abdul," she assured him, watching as he struggled to bring his arms and hands out from beneath the blanket. "I'm here."

"I do love you, Jenny," he said, taking her hands in his and giving a gentle squeeze. "You do know that, don't you?"

"I know," she said, feeling a lump growing bigger in her throat, trying to swallow it away. She knew her cue had been given . . . saw the rightness of looking down on this man who loved her and telling him she loved him, too. "Abdul, I . . .," She paused, and he, still holding her hands, put his right index finger to his blistered lips in a sign for her to be silent.

"You've never lied to me, Jenny," he said, dropping his hands and hers down to his chest. "It would do neither of us good to do so now. And even if—" and he smiled "—it were true that you loved me, think what needless heartache that knowledge would give me—my knowing that I had finally attained the one thing in life I wanted most, only to be forced into surrendering it so quickly."

"You're going to be fine," she told him. "You're going to be fine."

"I shall forgive you that one lie," he told her, trying a smile that wasn't too successful. "But you must remember that I have lived life fully, tested it to its limits. If I've played with fire once too often, think of those who have never dared go near the flame. What dull, dull lives they must lead."

She started to cry, feeling the warm tears overflowing her eyes, draining along her cheek to stain the blanket pulled over him.

"We did have something very precious together, Jenny," he said, "for we shared if not a love of each other, then a love of things—of cold desert nights; hot blue, blue days; the flow of the eternal Nile; shifting sand meeting the silent palm sentinels standing watch on the edge of the wilderness. We shared a love of Egypt. And we have been friends. In the end your friendship has been more precious to me, Jenny, than you can ever possibly know. For I die having had many, many lovers but very few true friends."

He raised her fingers back to his lips and kissed them.

"'I am come that the inquisition might be made of Rightfulness and the Balance be set upon its fulcrum within the bower of amaranth,'" she said. It was a quote from the Egyptian *Book of the Dead*, and it was fitting. For Sheikh Abdul Jerada, her friend, had just died.

CHAPTER SIXTEEN

Who was Dylana Carter?

"I'm sorry, Miss Mowry," the English-accented voice had said at the distant end of the connection. "Mr. Donas is at Dylana Carter's. Would you like the number?" She hadn't wanted the number. On top of everything else she didn't need the sound of Dylana Carter calling Peter from his shower to the telephone. Nor did she leave a message. "Tell him Sheikh Abdul Jerada has been killed," wasn't something he should have got thirdhand. She'd call him later from Cairo or from the States. Not from London, because she wasn't going there. Geraldine Fowler had run to London after Frederic Donas, and look what had happened to her.

She surrendered the phone to Barbara, who was still trying to reach her parents after the sudden change of plans that had resulted from the sabotage of the nearby well and the death of Abdul Jerada. The excavation had been brought to a close by government troops arriving to cordon off the area. Jenny thought it was rather like closing the barn door after the horse was gone, but she didn't say anything, so busy was she in trying to keep her world from completely falling apart around her now that the two special men in her life were no longer there.

She tried to put some final order to the wrap-up of dig operations, which hadn't been scheduled to conclude for at least two more weeks. Trying to do everything needed in so short a time was impossible, and she had tried to convince the colonel in charge to let her stay on a few more days to do a proper job of it. He had only smiled condescendingly and told her that that was impossible, arrangements having already been made to put everyone on the evening train for Cairo. The dig at Hierakonpolis was officially closed, sacrificed in the same flames that had ignited an oil well and taken Abdul Jerada's life.

At least those hectic last hours occupied her mind with something other than Abdul's death and Peter's being in the arms of some other woman. But when everything was done that could be done in the time allowed and the group stood waiting at the Idfu station for a train making a special stop to pick them up, Jenny's mind returned helplessly to all the painful memories. "Jenny, are you sure you're all right?" Barbara asked, obviously concerned.

"Not really," Jenny admitted with a weak smile, "but I'm a survivor. Come around and ask me that same question a month from now and I'll undoubtedly have a more optimistic reply." Barbara also wanted to know if Jenny had reached Peter. "He was out," Jenny said, the pain welling in her heart. She didn't tell Barbara her fears that Peter was out with another woman.

"Jenny is over there," she heard Tim saying. Turning, she saw an Arab in a tan *galabia* heading toward her.

"Miss Jennifer Mowry?" the man questioned, not sure which of the two women he should be addressing. "My name is Banir Ranshar."

"What can I do for you, Mr. Ranshar?" Jenny asked, hoping there had been a change that would allow her to stay in Hierakonpolis. Despite the opportunity all this presented for her to join Peter in London, she kept resisting that further paralleling of her life to that of Geraldine Fowler's. Both women had come to Egypt on archaeological digs, had met and loved a Donas man. Geraldine had gone to London to learn of her betrayal, and Jenny couldn't help fearing a similar fate.

"I have something here that is yours," he said, putting his briefcase on a nearby pile of luggage and rolling small dials to a correct combination that gave him access to the jewelry case inside. Jenny took the case and opened it, not because she didn't know what was inside, but because Mr. Ranshar would want her to verify the contents. She felt tears immediately building in her eyes, and she closed the case as soon as she saw the necklace was there. Someday she would be able to see it without crying, but not today. Abdul had been right, though, in that she wouldn't refuse it this time. She took it and the paperwork required to get it through Egyptian and American customs and unlocked her bag on the railway platform, securing the case inside. Mr. Ranshar, his signed receipt for delivery in hand, disappeared into the terminal. Barbara diplomatically drifted over to Tim in order to give Jenny some privacy.

The train was the new *Wagons-lits Egypte*, whose regular run from Aswân to Luxor to Cairo and back again normally saw it speeding right through intermediate stations like Idfu. So little time was wasted getting the group on board. The streamliner was soon heading north toward Cairo—north toward Thebes. Barbara, assigned a compartment with Jenny, spent most of her time next door with her fiancé and Tom Banker. Jenny sat alone, watching Egypt and her dreams speed by outside, remembering how Geraldine had taken a train to Cairo, a ship from Cairo to England. Had Jenny been going to follow a similar itinerary, she would have gone by plane. But no matter what the mode of transportation, the similarity was too undeniable for mere coincidence.

When the train stopped at Luxor, she surprised everyone by asking Tim if he would please hand her bag out the window of her compartment to one of the baggage men on the platform who would take it from there. "I still have a few things left to do in Egypt," Jenny said, explaining her sudden desertion. She was getting off to say an official goodbye to Thebes across the river, suddenly doubting she would ever be back, unlike Geraldine, who had returned from London to die of a broken heart.

She took a cab to the Etap Hotel, tempted to go

elsewhere but deciding it was best to face all of her past memories, good ones and bad, head-on. By facing them, she hoped to make them less painful, even in this place that so reminded her of Geraldine, of Frederic, of tragic love, of Abdul on the *Osiris*, of Peter now in London with Dylana Carter.

"Peter, Peter," she said, telling herself the pleasure she had once derived from merely muttering his name was no longer possible. However, that was a lie. She loved him, still wanted him. One part of her said not to tempt fate by following him to London, as Geraldine had followed Frederic. Rashid al-Hidda had foretold Abdul's death, hinting of forces turned loose in the universe that could control human destiny and might well exalt in the repeat of a sixty-year-old tragedy. Another part of her told her to go and find happiness.

She closed the curtains in her room, sealing herself off from the view. She had faced enough today, and tomorrow would be soon enough to face Thebes across the river. Except that it wasn't until two days later that she felt up to leaving her hotel in a heat far in excess of what she had experienced the last time she had started off on this particular journey. She crossed the Nile on the ferry and took the road by the Colossi of Memnon, then proceeded on to the Valley of the Kings. She sent her driver to the rest pavilion, and she walked through the oppressive heat that shrouded the tombs. She took the sixteen steps to Tutankhamen, looking down on the golden sarcophagus that contained his mummy. She waited, hoping to hear Peter call her name like last time, hoping to turn and find him standing there. She grew damp and sticky while waiting, bathing in heat able to penetrate thick stone. A tourist policeman appeared to indicate that any further lingering would be considered suspect. So Jenny left, since Peter wasn't there and wasn't coming. He was in London with somebody else.

The cabdriver thought she was crazy when she told him to make the turn into the funerary temple of Queen Hatshepsût, there being no rest house nearby in which either of them could retreat from the sun. She predicted a large tip for his efforts, and he did as he was asked.

She could admit to having always derived a certain sense of strength from this impressive edifice carved into an escarpment of gold-colored stone, its ascending sequences of colonnaded courtyards pointing the way toward a rock-hewn inner sanctum—a sense of strength that had nothing whatsoever to do with the pain she derived from the unavoidable association she was forced to make between its builder and Abdul's falcon of the same name. Here was a structure erected at the order of a queen who had triumphed in a male-dominated society, a woman who stood remembered while many of her male counterparts had long since been forgotten. Anything was possible if a woman could rule in Egypt as its pharaoh. It was even possible that Jenny could somehow survive the death of a friend and the desertion of a lover.

She turned toward the east, having walked up the two ramps to the temple's second level. She bid farewell to Egypt, to Thebes, Tutankhamen, Geraldine Fowler, Frederic Donas, childhood fantasies and the friendship and companionship of Abdul Jerada. She was not, however, yet ready to say farewell to Peter Donas.

Queen Hatshepsût wouldn't have got very far if she hadn't met adversity head-on and fought tooth and nail to get all that she had wanted. But here was Jenny, no less a woman, actually on the verge of surrendering Peter because of her fear that history would repeat itself. Jenny was independent, with no obligations tying her down; Geraldine had had a husband and two children. It had been impossible for Frederic and Geraldine to marry. However, it wasn't impossible for Peter and Jenny—quite the contrary!

Abdul had warned about continually underestimating Peter's love. Business actually might have been fully responsible for keeping him in London. Dylana Carter might be a lawyer or someone else connected with his uncle's estate. Jenny was always jumping to conclusions. Not even Geraldine had done that. She'd given up hope only when she had thoroughly investigated her alternatives. What Jenny had to do was decide whether she was merely out to savor being the victim of a romantic tragedy or whether she really wanted to accept the possibility of a happily-ever-after ending. The choice was no choice at all.

"Goodbye, Thebes; hello, London!" she said, taking one final look at the landscape laid out before her. For the first time, she didn't feel threatened by this stretch of ruins, hot sand, cool vegetation and distant gray ribbon of Nile.

Suddenly there was a cloud of dust on the roadway leading to the funerary temple. Someone else as insane as Jenny was risking sunstroke in order to experience the grandeur of Deir al-Bahari sans scampering hordes of tourists. The car came to a stop beside hers, and a startlingly handsome man got out to look in her direction. He began walking toward her. Jenny's heart leaped into her throat. Her head swam, her eyes blurring in fear that it was overexposure to the sun that made her see this mirage.

"Jenny! Jenny!" he called to her, coming ever closer, up the lower ramp and then up the second, the muscles of his body moving sensuously beneath a shirt open at its collar to reveal a vee of tanned chest, his trousers molded sexily to his lower body. "Jenny? Jenny?"

"Peter?" she whispered, taking two steps toward him and knowing she would have fallen if he hadn't been there to catch her in his strong arms. "You came. . . you actually came," she said in wonder. She had decided that they weren't really locked into a repeat of their grandparents' tragedy, and now she was overjoyed to know she'd been right. Frederic Donas had never returned to Thebes for Geraldine Fowler.

"I think it must have had something to do with Mohammed going to the mountain, since Tim and Barbara called from Cairo to tell me that it didn't seem it was going to be the other way around."

"I *was* coming to London," Jenny insisted, wanting him to know her decision had been made even prior to his wonderful appearance on the scene. "Really, I was."

"Well, I obviously couldn't wait," Peter said, his large fingers tenderly stroking her silky hair. "I'd been forced to wait too long the way it was. Besides," he added, stepping back just a bit to draw the small box from his pants pocket, "I felt it would be fitting to give you this at Thebes, although I thought I'd missed you when you weren't at Tutankhamen's tomb after I got there. I just took the lucky chance on my way back to your hotel in Luxor that the cab parked here was yours. Who else, I figured, would be braving the midday sun but Jenny Mowry?"

"The view is better from here," Jenny said, not looking at the landscape but at the small box Peter was holding out to her.

"Go on," he said, "take it. It's yours."

She took it, tracing the elaborate initials engraved in gold on the top. "D...C," she said. "Dylana Carter?"

"You know it, then?" Peter asked, genuinely surprised.

"It?" Jenny responded, confused by the pronoun.

Peter eyed her curiously, an amused glint sparkling in his golden eyes. "You wouldn't have thought it was a 'she' now would you?" he asked mischievously. "Another woman, perhaps?"

Jenny blushed with embarrassment. "Actually, I'd convinced myself she was an ugly old bat who had something to do with your uncle's estate."

"Actually, 'she' is two old bats; Teddy Dylana and John Carter. They just happen to run a jewelry store called Dylana Carter, after their last names," Peter said. "When I needed something cleaned and reappraised that had been in the musty old vault for a few years, I went to them."

"I feel a little silly," Jenny admitted, although she was also deliriously happy.

"Well, I didn't come here to make you feel silly, Jenny Mowry," he told her, folding his arms across his powerful chest and smiling that wonderful smile that could make her melt inside. "I came to make you feel bloody wonderful! Now open your little gift and tell me I wasn't a fool for having come all the way back to Egypt to prove to a silly goose that the two of us really have nothing whatsoever to do with the tragedy that happened here in Thebes prior to our even being born."

She opened the box, the diamond solitaire immediately catching the light and almost blinding her with the rainbow fires set to burning within it. "It was my mother's," he told her, "and her mother's before her. It would have been Geraldine Fowler's had things worked out differently between her and my grandfather."

"Oh, Peter, it's lovely!" Jenny said, the only thing able to pull her eyes from it being the drawing warmth of Peter's hypnotic golden eyes.

He took the ring out of its box and slipped it on her finger. "It's not anywhere as lovely as my wife-to-be," he said. "It doesn't even come close." He opened his arms and once again drew her to him, kissing her deeply, all of Egypt spread out at their feet. They were oblivious to the heat that had sweaty cabdrivers marveling at the madness of two tourists who would risk sunstroke to kiss on the terrace of Queen Hatshepsût's Deir al-Bahari in the midday heat. "I love you, Jenny Mowry," Peter said, his lips so close to hers that they sensuously brushed her mouth when he spoke.

"I love you, Peter Donas," she responded, once again letting herself become part of that special world only he could create for her.

Far above a lone falcon soared on updrafts caused by summer heat baking rugged desert stone. The bird luxuriated in a freedom that neither Jenny nor Peter would have taken in exchange for the wondrous captivity offered by the chains of love that bound them so securely to each other.

What readers say
about SUPERROMANCE